a magpie's

Eugene
Meese

a magpie's smile

Library and Archives Canada Cataloguing in Publication

Meese, Eugene, 1947–

A magpie's smile / Eugene Meese.

ISBN 978-1-897126-42-4

I. Title.

PS8626.E36M36 2009 C813'.6 C2008-907030-5

Editor for the Board: Douglas Barbour
Cover and interior design: Natalie Olsen
Cover photo: Natalie Olsen
Author photo: Donna Meese

NeWest Press acknowledges the support of the Canada Council for the Arts, the Alberta Foundation for the Arts, and the Edmonton Arts Council for our publishing program. We also acknowledge the financial support of the Government of Canada through the Book Publishing Industry Development Program (BPIDP).

201.8540.109 Street
Edmonton, Alberta T6G 1E6
780.432.9427
newestpress.com

No bison were harmed in the making of this book.
We are committed to protecting the environment and to the responsible use of natural resources. This book was printed on 100% post-consumer recycled paper.

1 2 3 4 5 12 11 10 09

printed and bound in Canada

With thanks to Donna, for her love and her belief …
and her sharp critical eye.

may 2, 1977 7:45 AM

The job was taking too long. He had been at it for close to two hours. He should have been finished by now. He was supposed to be. He had been told to get the house on the ground and get out before any protesters could arrive. Yet here he still was, and there the house still was.

Again and again, like a giant, one-pawed mechanical bear clawing at the flanks of a cornered deer, his bulldozer had lunged, growling, at the boarded-up two-storey house in the Beltline district on the fringe of downtown. With each advance, the wide cutting edge of its heavy blade smashed through fading green clapboards and splintered studs and beams. The narrow house had creaked and groaned and let out gasps of dust. But it would not fall.

The structure was only the husk of a house now, stripped clean of anything of value. Gone, the leaded-glass panels on either side of the front door and the arched blue, green, and gold stained-glass window above the upstairs landing; gone, everything inside, from the hammered-tin ceiling to the polished spruce floors—all pried loose, pulled up, and carted away. But if this was a skeleton, the bones were sturdy. The house was not so old, built at the end of the last century to last until the end of this, and the skill and strong timber of its construction were stubbornly resisting, as if the house itself were protesting its demolition.

But Clarence "Chip" Holloway was not given to such figurative thinking.

"Goddamn you!" he cursed from the plexiglass-enclosed cab as he yanked the machine back for still another assault. "Damn you to hell anyway!"

He had two other buildings—an abandoned service station a couple of blocks east and another derelict house in Eau Claire—to knock down before knocking off. And all he was thinking was that he was in for another long, dry day to go with the month of long, dry days that had just passed.

He backed the bulldozer nearly to the front edge of the property, where a gate to the front walk dangled from one hinge off of what remained of a once-painted-white picket fence. He raised the blade. Taking aim at what had been the far corner of the front porch, he gunned the engine and jammed the gears forward. The machine lurched ahead, a spume of white exploding from its exhaust pipe, its wide track chewing up the once-tidy, tiny front lawn. The cutting edge drove deep into the corner of the house.

It was a killing blow.

Holloway ground the bulldozer into reverse and, with some difficulty, backed away, withdrawing the blade, taking the guts of the house with it. The machine paused, still growling. For a few moments, the house remained standing. Then it groaned again, a deeper, more visceral sound, a death rattle. And, like a dying animal going slowly to its knees, it sagged to its side, almost, but not quite, collapsing.

"Got you now, you son of a bitch," Holloway whispered to himself, gloating, sensing that one more strategic push would bring the structure down and get him back on schedule. "Got you now."

He climbed down from the cab, took off his gloves and pulled a cigarette from the chest pocket of his red and black plaid shirt-jacket. He struck a match on the floor of the cab, cupped it in his palms at the end of his cigarette, tossed the match away, drew deeply, held the smoke in his lungs for a long moment, then exhaled audibly. He stretched, leaned against the track, tilted his head back, and closed his eyes. His arms and shoulders ached, as if he had brought the house down with his bare hands. He was sweating, even though the early spring air still had a late-winter bite.

He missed spring, real spring, Ontario spring—true thaw by March, greening by April, lilacs in May, promise of summer. He hated this yellow, cold season, and this year so dry.

It hardly rained in April. The radio this morning said towns around the city—Olds and others—were already running out of water and holding crisis meetings. Down south there had been early dirt storms. It seemed nothing would ever green. The buds on the trees remained closed. The brown grass of his own lawn, new last summer, crunched underfoot. If the rains did not come soon the grass would die, and he would have to re-sod; and if the rains still did not come, the new sods would die too, because the reservoir would be too low by summer to allow for the watering of lawns. Funny, for him to think about lawns, to worry about watering, about chickweed and crabgrass and fairy rings. He had always hated yardwork, and got out of it any way and as often as he could, usually dumping the job on his mother. Now—

A single drop of rain hit him in the middle of the forehead. He opened his eyes. He looked around. Another few pitiful drops fell, exploding in the dust like miniature bombs. Then nothing. He looked up, into the grey but brightening sky. He cursed again, quietly.

"You stingy old mother.... That the best you can do?"

Holloway shrugged, flicked his cigarette butt into the mangled yard, and climbed back into the cab. He put on his gloves, revved the engine again, and prepared to finish the job.

Slowly, almost stealthily, he maneuvred the bulldozer to the other, still-standing side of the house, stalking it. He raised the blade again, as high as it would reach, about forty-five degrees, the hydraulic cylinder straightening like a knee unbending. His gloved hand eased the gear forward. The machine moved forward, slowly. Then, when the machine was about ten yards from the house, he jammed the gear down hard and the bulldozer made one final lunge, the extended blade smashing into the building just below the window to what had been an upstairs bedroom, half-pushing, half-kicking the house to the ground.

As the house collapsed, the sheet of plywood covering the arched window where the stained glass had been popped out like an eye from its socket. Through the cloud of dust and debris, Holloway thought he saw something tumble out of the uncovered window: shimmer of bright green, sheen of pale bluish-white, glint of gold, ugly gleam of reddish-black.

"What the f—?"

Holloway jumped down from the cab, leaving the low-growling engine still idling. He went round the back of the machine and moved toward the splintered window, tip-toeing over broken boards, loose shingles, and bricks from the tumbled-down chimney. He knelt down.

There was something hanging over the window ledge, something green, blue-white, gold, and reddish-black, something, not stained glass the salvagers had missed, something cold and stiff and staring, something … dead.

Holloway cringed, shivered reflexively, jerked upright, and turned to run, gagging. He tripped over the fallen boards, smashing his knee on a piece of shattered brick, driving a rusty square-headed nail through his thick leather glove into the palm of his right hand as he reached out to break his fall. He screamed, scrambling, half-stumbling out of the ruins. He reached the bulldozer, collapsing hard on his extended arms against the side of the rumbling machine, knocking the yellow hard hat from his head, driving the nail all the way through his hand. He screamed again, and threw up violently on the wide, dusty track.

8:50 AM

Fry's first apartment after he and Carol separated was a hastily renovated one-bedroom basement suite in a recently fire-damaged forties stucco bungalow here in the Beltline, in a seedy going-to-the-developers neighbourhood. He had rented it from McKnight, a patrol sergeant in the morality squad and part-time real estate speculator who had picked up the property cheap, fixed it up on the cheap, and offered the basement to Fry for a "cheap" three hundred dollars a month.

"Rent controls? Why, whatever do you mean, rent controls?" McKnight had asked him with mock innocence, winking. "Look it, I could get three-fifty for the place easy, maybe four, maybe more. But I don't want to hold you up. I just need a body in the basement to help me carry the place until I can flip it. I, ah, heard you were looking. You interested or what?"

Fry was tempted to say "what." In fact, he was not interested—not in the apartment, at the time not in anything. But he moved in anyway, without even inspecting the premises, which turned out to be dark, damp, with low ceilings and loud upstairs neighbours. Not that it mattered. He was almost never there. Mostly he worked. And when he was not working, he walked.

Not that Calgary was a good walking city.

The downtown was a forest of wind-tunnelling, sun-blocking towers, a jungle of construction, with cranes perched high overhead and heavy equipment running in packs on the ground. It was a kind of factory, spewing out the paper that fuelled the business engines that drove the city: oil and finance, development, government. The high-rises were like the smokestacks of white-collar industry. The suburbs were a lesser Los Angeles to downtown's mini-Manhattan, sprawling as tangled and dense as buffalo grass for miles north and south.

Traffic was the worst in the country. One car for every two people. Roads (too clogged now to be called streets) were too narrow, torn up, barricaded, one-lane, one-way or otherwise, and often, impassable. Built to accommodate traffic in a city of one hundred thousand, they simply could not handle the four hundred thousand of the city's now half-million population who lived in the suburbs. And when the commuters from the A streets in Acadia and the B streets in Bowness and the C streets in Canyon Meadows and all the other winding, generic streets in all the other winding, generic developments in the mad planners' alphabet did manage to make their way near the city centre, they had to squeeze under the railroads, which sliced the city in half and cut access into its centre to a trickle.

It was like threading a needle with a rope.

The planners' solution was roads, more roads, wider roads, "trails" named for Indians and old Mounties, trails having nothing more in common with their namesakes than the names. And they planned a new railroad, a "light" railroad running north-south to coax, they hoped, motorists out of their cars and help ease the congestion.

Walkers did not figure into the planners' calculations, any more than did the old, once-stable communities that happened to be in the way of their solutions. They became, in planning parlance, "transitional" neighbourhoods—neighbourhoods, that is, in the process of ceasing to be neighbourhoods.

Fry walked in these neighbourhoods, in the shadow of the cranes, in the bulldozers' path—in the Beltline and Eau Claire, the Hillhurst, Sunnyside, Victoria, Sunalta, and the Mission—where once-formidable nineteen-twenties three-storey walkups sat dwarfed and threatened by eight, ten, twelve storeys of concrete and reflecting glass newly moved in next door; where renovated late-teens townhomes sat at one end of an inner-city block, and boarded-up stucco bungalows sat at the other.

In the beginning he did not think about the neighbourhoods as he walked through them. He hardly saw them. He tried not to think at all. It was better not to think. It was better to be numb.

Fry had looked for numbness in the twenty-five-ounce bottle he refilled at first once a week, then twice, then three times. And he found it. But on the week he came to the fourth refill, he stopped, finding in the empty bottle a deeper emptiness, an ending he was not ready to accept. He kept the empty bottle. He still had it.

He started walking instead. He numbed himself on the street, walking, hour after hour, the sound of his scuffed, old pointy-toed boots on the sidewalk the only sound he allowed himself to hear, a kind of metronome marking time, step after step after step. He did not see. He did not think. He walked. Hands stuffed in the pockets of his well-worn sheepskin coat, the collar turned up, his head bent down, he walked, and walked, and walked.

He had walked past the old woman every day for a month before he saw her, and then only by chance, when he happened to raise his eyes as he passed her while she worked around her fading-green house with the striking blue, green, and gold stained-glass window upstairs. And he truly paid attention to her only later, in hindsight. For the next five months he made a point of seeing her almost every day, a little bird of a woman with snow-white hair under a bright floral-patterned scarf and thick half-glasses slipping to the end of her nose, a heavy black-cloth jacket over a filmy faded print dress, old-fashioned dark stockings, and worn blue sneakers.

She lived on a street that looked like a set of bad teeth. High-rises—drab grey snags of concrete, already rust-stained—rose the width of a football field on either side of her street, about fifty yards apart. On both sides of one of them were black asphalt gaps where the bulldozers had razed houses to make way for parking lots. On one side of the other stood a decaying three-storey stucco walk-up; on the other a tiny, discoloured bungalow with paint chipping from its clapboards in layers of tan, green, and white.

The old woman had lived in one of those terminal "transitional" neighbourhoods. But she had not appeared to be resigned. She coaxed green out of the grudging spring, raking and weeding, watering and feeding, reverently tending her lawn and her flowers. She made summer seem possible. She reminded Fry of the sheer, stubborn persistence of life. And she helped him to see again.

She had become a kind of constant to him, a constant in a city constantly changing, being changed. He liked to think of her emerging purposefully from her house, scarf on her head, rake in her hands, refusing to see the obvious, refusing to bow to the inevitable. Sometimes he even fantasized about taking over for her when she was gone, buying the house, taking up her rake, her battle. He knew it was a fantasy, even as it occurred to him. He knew the house would not long survive the old woman. The house could not afford the land on which it sat. In the planners' minds, and probably on their maps, it was already gone. The old woman would be the last person to live in it.

Now Fry lived in a little house he rented in Eau Claire, just south of the Bow River. He still walked, though he had found better places to do it. Sometimes he retreated to the old, serene, virtually untouched neighbourhoods near the water, the lush quiet and the Victorian gingerbread and fine wide porches speaking of a Calgary of another time. Usually he walked along the meandering river pathways, where, among the stately cottonwoods and fragile wildflowers and under the impossibly big, impossibly blue vault of sky, he could almost forget the steel, concrete, and glass that were literally just around the corner.

The eastern papers said that the best view of Calgary was from the air at night, coming upon it suddenly out of the black, a filigree of light at the end of the prairie. They were wrong. Fry preferred the city on the ground, at the centre, where the rivers curled together, defying the neatly gridded street plans of the last century's planners, creating natural curves and slopes and open spaces that this century's planners had not yet managed to destroy.

Sometimes he still walked through the Beltline neighbourhood that they *were* managing to destroy, to see the old woman defiantly at work on the tiny lawn outside the doomed narrow house. But not lately. In fact, he had not been by since the fall.

It was not the weather. The winter had not been too cold. There had been hardly any snow.

He had simply been busy.

The twenty-five hundred people a month the boom brought into the city brought with them whatever problems they had had wherever they came from; and their coming created problems for both them and the city that neither had ever dreamed of—Fry's kinds of problems.

He wished he had not been so busy. He knew now that the old woman had not made it through the mild, dry winter, and he could see that her house had not survived the even drier spring. As he stooped under the yellow and black police cordon where the white picket fence had been, Fry—John Jacob "Jake" Fry—a detective in the homicide unit of the Calgary Police Service, had a dull aching feeling that summer would never come.

8:55 AM

Fry walked toward the rubble that had been the old woman's home, hands in the pockets of his open black overcoat, dust quickly coating his highly polished black shoes.

His eyes studied the scene, as if trying to memorize it, to photograph and file it away. He had already made a mental sketch of the scene behind him:

Multi-coloured lights flashing in the street—yellow from the ambulance backed onto the sidewalk, red and blue from the two blue and white cruisers parked at the curb, red from the single police motorcycle at the edge of the mutilated lawn. Faces peering down from apartment balconies and around the corner of a crumbling stucco porch. Faces of children crowded around a finger-smeared window in the basement daycare centre across the street. Faces of curious passersby craning their necks for a glimpse. Faces of three women in faded jeans and expensive leather jackets huddled beyond the yellow cordon, Bristol-board protest placards held limply in their hands, the felt-penned messages upside down: Cottage yes/condos no, Save the cottage, Cottage industry kills history.

On his left as Fry approached the ruins, a paramedic was leaning over an ashen-faced man wearing a red and black plaid work shirt and sitting slumped forward on the track of a silent bulldozer, his right arm strapped to his chest, a huge white bandage wrapped around his right hand, a small circle of blood soaking through. On Fry's right, two officers in blue uniforms knelt like archeologists at a dig before what remained of a window frame, examining, but not moving and hardly touching, the debris around them. A few paces behind them, another uniform with three stripes on his jacket shoulders stood, feet spread well apart, scribbling in a small black notebook. Two other uniforms, one in high black motorcycle boots and a white helmet, stood on opposite corners of the property just beyond the cordon, keeping the rubber-necking passersby passing by.

"What've you got, Strahan?" Fry asked the uniform with the shoulder stripes and the notebook, who looked up under the bill of his cap and said, "Oh, you're the one got the call, did you, Ghost? That's funny."

"Ghost" was Fry's nickname, from "the Grey Ghost," which came from his prematurely gun-metal-greying hair and the dark circles around his deep-set, penetrating eyes the grey-green colour of a cold mountain lake. It used to get a rise out of him. No longer. The only officers who dared use it to his face were those who had been on the force as long as he—nearly twenty years now—and most of them had stopped because he had stopped letting them know that it bothered him. Patrol Sergeant Paul Strahan, homicide, however, did not easily let things go, which frequently made him an asset as a police officer, but—Fry caught himself thinking again what he had thought more than once before—all too often an asshole as a human being.

"Yeah, I got it. Your sense of the obvious is as acute as ever. Why funny?"

"You'll see."

"Show me."

"Follow me, as Custer shouted to his troops." Strahan tried to snicker, but managed only an odd, sharp bark. "You guys all clear here?" he called to the two kneeling constables.

"Clear? How the Christ do I know?" one of the constables answered, looking back at Fry and Strahan. "Come on ahead. But be prepared. This ain't no crime scene, it's a friggin' bomb scene. Wha'say, Jake?"

"Adams—MacElroy," Fry nodded, squatting between the two uniforms.

They were matching bookends of current police-recruitment policy: tall, heavy-set, bright-eyed, with neatly trimmed moustaches on their scrubbed-looking fresh faces, slightly fleshy around their tight collars, like ageing college football stars—which Adams actually had been, at the University of Calgary, later becoming a third-round draft choice of the Edmonton Eskimos. But he had turned down a chance at the pros to become a cop, studying what Mount Royal College liked to call "police science." MacElroy had been a military policeman stationed, among other places, in Shearwater, Cold Lake, and Cyprus. He left the forces for the force so he could stop travelling and start making babies and some money.

"Not much," Fry continued. "I like the sound of Strahan's voice so well. What about you boys? What've you got to say?"

Adams only looked at Fry and whistled noiselessly, shaking his head, something like disbelief haunting the back of his blue eyes. He gestured with his head toward MacElroy, whose right hand held the corner of the police blanket spread below the ruined window.

"Pull it," he said.

MacElroy, who had the same look in his eyes—and it was not simply disbelief, Fry could see, but something closer to horror—obeyed, slowly, almost delicately, lifting the blanket.

Her satiny green dress was tight fitting and low-cut, with a ruffled hem just above the knees and three-quarter-length ruffled sleeves. A wide silver belt was cinched tight at her waist. The top of her left nipple had popped out of the dress. On her right breast just inside the line of the garment, at the end of a fine silver chain, lay a jade-coloured stone carved in the shape of a cat. On her right wrist was a silver bracelet, on her left a silver watch, five minutes fast. She wore silver and jade-coloured rings on three fingers of her right hand and on the index and pinky fingers of her left. The third finger of her left hand looked as if it might have once worn a ring, but there was no ring now. Her legs were splayed, her arms stretched over her head. The right leg of her patterned panty hose was torn at the calf. She had no shoes. Her skin was the blue-white colour of snow in the moonlight, heavily rouge-darkened at her cheeks. Her long, fake nails were painted nearly the same poppy-red as her mouth. Her lips were slightly parted, her hazel eyes wide open, one long, false lash askew. Her ash-blonde hair reached from just below her shoulders almost to the top of her head, where it stopped abruptly in a crude circle of blood, blackening, shiny and hard.

She had been scalped.

Fry choked down the bile rising in his throat and tightened his stomach. He glanced at Adams, then at MacElroy with, despite his effort at self-control, he was sure, the same disbelieving horror that was in their eyes. He looked up at Strahan, who was standing over his shoulder, his glasses hiding his eyes.

"Ought'a see the look on your face, Ghost," Strahan said, in a half-hearted attempt at a joke. "You're livin' up to your nickname."

Fry stiffened but let the remark pass.

"MacElroy," he snapped, "cover her up. And I still don't see what's so funny, Strahan."

"Funny?"

"Yeah. Remember, you thought it was a real hoot that I got the call."

"Well, you saw her—how she was done."

"Yeah, I did. So?"

"Ah, your new job and all, the Indian liaison committee, you know...."

"Oh, I see. You've already got a theory about this, do you?"

"Could be, say, a hooker who wouldn't put out for a—"

"Wow! You not only know what happened but why," Fry broke in. "In that case, why don't you just give me the perp's name and I'll run along and pick him up? No point in wasting any more time here." Strahan ground his back teeth, flexing the muscles in his jaw, but did not open his mouth. "You giving up police work for shamanism or something?" Fry continued. "Sure sounds like a Ghost Dance to me."

"I'd think that'd be more up your alley, wouldn't you, Ghost?"

"Oh, give it a fucking rest, Paul, will you for Chris' sake," Fry said coldly, annoyance at the old nickname welling up, spilling over, along with anger at some of the new nicknames—Chief Fry and Grey Howl and Buck—he had been hearing in the halls. "We can play our little games of Bleeding Hearts and Name That Bigot another time."

Strahan looked away, sniffed, and cleared his throat. He said nothing. Fry sighed, silently cursing himself for insulting the sergeant, who was as sensitive about himself as he was insensitive toward others. Fry knew it. He should have known better. He put his hands on his knees and pushed himself to his feet. He took a deep breath and blew it out audibly. He stepped back a few paces from the ruined window, nearly tripping on a fallen brick. He regained his balance, took a look at the debris, and suddenly laughed out loud.

"What's funny now?" Strahan asked defensively.

"Me."

"You?"

"Yeah. Me."

"How?"

"I almost asked if there were any signs of forced entry."

Strahan smiled in spite of himself. The tension eased. Clumsiness does have its virtues, Fry thought.

"Let's catch us a bad guy, Strahan," he said. "And whoever did this is a *bad* guy."

The sergeant gestured with his head toward the man in the plaid shirt sitting on the track of the bulldozer.

"Fella there found her. Thought he was just knockin' down an old house. Got himself a surprise."

"He notice anything else?" Fry asked, studying the man from the distance.

"Don't think. He's pretty shaken. Put a nail through his hand runnin' to get away from her."

"He all right?"

"Yeah, I think. Lost his breakfast, but not much blood. Paramedic gave him something for pain. Can't take the nail out here, though. He's got a damned board nailed right to his hand. Almost fainted twice."

"No point in talking to him here, I don't imagine. Tell the medic to get him to emergency. I don't want the bugger to die of shock—in case he did see anything useful. Send Fellows there with them," Fry said, nodding toward the motorcycle uniform directing pedestrian traffic beyond cordon. "He can get a statement, for what it's likely to be worth. And what's with the demonstrators there? Thought the sixties were history. They witnesses?"

"Only to the one thing they didn't want to see."

"Which was?"

"Oh, not what happened to her. To the house. Don't you read the newspapers, Ghost?"

"Not if I don't have to."

"Well, this here building, excuse me, what used to be this building here is, was, a real cause celebrity."

"Oh?"

"Yep. Real heritage stuff. Built before the turn of the century. Only one of its kind left downtown, or was. Heritage groups, historical society had a big fight with city hall and the developer."

"And we know who won."

"Yep."

"And you know what we're going to have to do with these sticks of heritage," he said.

"Yep," Strahan said, resignedly. "Try to put them back together, and see how the lady got inside."

"You got it, Strahan. And you, MacElroy, you got enough pictures?"

"Yeah, Jake, enough—too many."

"Yeah. Don't let it get to you. I know, easy to say. Keep her wrapped up. I don't want anyone to see her. No-body. Call in another ambulance. Get it backed up close to the, ah, house as you can. Get her out of here. And keep the press the hell away, whatever you do. I know I didn't need to say it, but I did anyway. And something else I don't need to say but will: nobody makes a statement unless his name is Fry. Are we clear?"

Half an hour later, Fry stuffed his notebook into his inside jacket pocket. The man in plaid had been taken to the hospital, the woman in green to the morgue. Three additional uniforms had been summoned to help comb through the wreckage of the house. So far, they had found a fake silver-fox fur jacket with its lining soaked in blood and one high-heeled silver shoe. They were still looking when Fry turned to leave.

On his way across the torn-up front yard, he stepped over a sign knocked down and tracked over by the bulldozer, a City of Calgary Notice to the effect that an outfit called Cottage Industries had made application to the city to build a twelve-storey, one-hundred-twenty-unit condominium tower on the site, and anyone who wished to comment on the application was advised to apply in writing to the city clerk's office.

"Too late now," Fry mumbled to himself. "Too bloody late now."

The media were waiting for him on the other side of the cordon, a tangle of cameras and microphones thrust at him, a babble of questions shouted at him. Before he went over to officially say nothing to them, he stopped at the front walk, leaned down and righted the gate against its post, then carefully swung it closed behind him.

10:00 AM

"Jesusfuckingchrist ... Whaddayawha'time...? Whatthe fuckwhy...? Comeon ... Cutitoutcutitthefuckout...! Comeon...!"

Lesley Connor stammered half out of sleep, his eyes fluttering open painfully to the bright light shining through the uncurtained French doors to the dormer porch outside the second-floor bedroom of the rambling condemned mansion at the foot of Mount Royal. He closed his eyes, cursing again. Lying nude on his stomach on a soiled mattress in the middle of the uncarpeted and otherwise unfurnished room, he groped blindly for the old steel alarm clock on the floor beside the bed. On the third swipe, he found it, knocking it over just as it began to clang. He grabbed for it, missed, grabbed again, clutched it, yanked it into the bed and tried to turn it off with both hands, but failed. Finally he smothered it under his single pillow until the ringing slowed, then stopped. He peeked under the pillow and groaned.

"Tenfuckingo'clock! Whothechristsetitfortenfuckingo'clockinthemorning? It'sthefuckingmiddleofthe night!"

He slid the clock across the floor on its face, pulled a rumpled sheet over his body, except for his feet, and collapsed onto the mattress.

"I fucking set it, Lee Boy," said the girl kneeling on the floor beside the mattress, poking him again with her right hand, then, when he did not respond, with her right fist. "Come on! You gotta get up! They'll be here any minute. Come on. Come on!"

"Behere? Who'llbehere? Whaddaya...?"

The sleep-befuddled youth—twenty years old, maybe—raised his upper body from the mattress on his two wiry arms, shaking his head, his long, luxuriously black hair cascading over his shoulders and down into his eyes.

"You know. The reporter from the *Bulletin*. And the photographer. Remember? They're coming to do a story on us, on what we do, in the house, you know, how we live."

"If I don't get some zees I won't live and neither," he swung the pillow weakly at her, and missed, "will you. Come on, just fuck off. I'm not gettin' up."

"Lee Boy—"

"No, godfuckingdammit, no. Ah ... just give 'em one of my T-shirts and my glossy, my pretty picture. You talk to 'em, you and Benny and Gina and John. You don't need me—unless they got a music deal for me—ha, ha ..."

He pulled the pillow tight over his head with his two hands and held on, refusing to budge, refusing to react even when she tried tickling the bottoms of his feet.

"Oh, Lee Boy, you ... you prick," she said, getting up from her knees, seeing the clock, grabbing it and throwing it at him, hitting him in the back.

"Ouchfff," he said with his face in the mattress. He did not move.

"You're such a shit, Lee Boy, just a shit, a shit, shit, shit!" she yelled at him as she slammed the door so hard it sprung back open.

The girl—actually a woman in her late twenties, with lines of laughter and sun already around her heavily shadowed blue eyes—skipped quickly down the winding stairs to the ground floor, her large braless breasts and long, straight ponytail bouncing with every step. As she descended, she passed stair walls decorated with felt-markered mountains with happy faces, obscene graffiti, and holes the size of a fist. The wall on the ground-floor landing featured a black silhouette of a fleeing cartoon figure. Her full figure jiggled to a stop in front of it.

A scrawny, scruffily bearded man in his mid to late twenties in frequently patched faded jeans and a clumsily hand-lettered "Calgary Stoopede" T-shirt lay on the tattered sofa in the parlour directly across from the landing, absentmindedly picking at the strings of the guitar in his lap, his bare, dirty feet dangling over the back of the sofa.

She said to him, pouting: "Lee Boy won't play."

"Told ya so."

"Told ya so," she mocked him, making a face and sticking out her tongue.

"Now, now, don't be bitchy. He didn't get in 'til after three, as usual. And you know he wouldn't recognize a morning if it reached out and hit him."

"Yeah, right, Benny. You tell him that when he

finally does wake up and gets all pissed off because he missed out on the publicity and he'll reach out and hit you."

"Oh, I'll survive. And so will you. And maybe even Lee Boy."

"Where's John and Gina?" she asked.

"Where do you think?"

"Oh, Christ. Like a couple of rabbits."

The scrawny young man wiggled his nose at her.

"Fuck you," she snapped.

"Now you've got the idea."

She was just cocking her tongue for a reply when the doorbell chimed, a deep, rich, melodious sound that now seemed out of place here, a strange, ghostly echo of another, better time.

"Oh, shit! They're here!" the young woman said, raising her arms in exasperation and stomping her feet on the landing. "Get the door, will you, Benny. I'll go upstairs and try to unscrew those two."

"Good luck, little mother."

"Oh, don't you take anything seriously?"

"Sure I do," he said, picking one string of the guitar, "pluckin'... and fuckin'."

She looked at him, at first sarcastically, then almost wistfully, with a momentary twinge of regret, then turned and bounced back up the stairs, shouting.

"John! Gina! Come on you guys! It's Cinderella's sistyugler. The balling's over."

10:15 AM

The second chiming of the bell was still echoing when Benny reached the heavy oak door with the intricately patterned leaded-glass window. He turned the solid-brass knob and pulled.

"Say, man," he said to the tall, gangly, boyish-looking man with Clark Kent glasses, dishevelled dark-brown hair, and drooping moustache who was standing on the wide veranda. Then, noticing the big, moon-faced man behind the camera at the foot of the veranda steps, he corrected himself. "Mans."

"Grant Melton," said Clark Kent, extending a right hand with a misshapen thumb and only three fingers. "The *Bulletin*. We arranged to do a story on you folks, sort of the other side of the boom."

"Right," Benny said, accepting the reporter's hand comfortably, without a flinch, or a look. "The *flip* side of the boom. Come on under, er, in, that is."

"Well ..." The reporter's face indicated that he was not sure how to reply, but it quickly regained its confident mask, and he his cocksure composure. "Come on, Donnie, let's go," Melton yelled back at the photographer, who snapped another shot of the front of the house, lowered the camera from his face, clicked the high heels of his shiny, pointy-toed new boots, saluted with his left hand, and clambered up the steps, camera bag flapping at his side. His new denim jeans, rolled up once at the bottom, rustled stiffly and the fringe of his new leather jacket fluttered as he ran.

"This is Donnie Miloche—" Melton began to introduce him.

"G. Donald," the photographer interrupted him, grabbing Benny's hand, shaking it hard. "G. Donald Miloche—and you are?"

"Benny—Benny Sunshines."

"Benny Sunshines?" Melton asked, reaching for the notebook in the inside pocket of his grey tweed sports coat.

"Yeah, Sunshines," Benny said. "Well, Chambers,

Benny Chambers, Benjamin Charles Chambers on my birth certificate. But everybody calls me Benny Sunshines. It's the group I'm in, you know, The Sunshines. Last names don't mean much to us. First names and group names are what we usually go by. Good enough. Better, really, for sayin' who we are. Come in and meet the rest of the Sunshines family."

Grant Melton followed Benny inside, with Donnie "G. Donald" Miloche close behind him. The journalists had scarcely taken two steps into the wide, oak-wainscotted entryway when they stopped, or were stopped by, the smell of human excrement.

"Holy shit!" Miloche exclaimed without thinking. Then, embarrassed, he added, "Sorry, but I mean ..."

"Holy shit's what you mean," Benny said. "At least shit. Shit's what it is. How holy it is I can't say. But it is shit. Sewer pipes are busted all to hell in the basement. When you live with it you forget about it—ten minutes inside and you won't notice anymore."

"Whoa!" Miloche said, waving his right hand in front of his nose. "Why don't you complain to the landlord?"

"Whoa! yourself," Benny said. "You think the landlord doesn't know? How do you think folks like us get to live in a Taj Mahal like this? If the place wasn't condemned we sure as hell wouldn't be here, and if there wasn't shit floating in the basement it probably wouldn't be condemned. So in a way we owe the shit a debt of gratitude."

"What, you get it rent-free, just to keep an eye on the premises?" Melton asked.

"No."

"No? What's it cost you?"

"Three-fifty a month."

The reporter rolled his eyes but said nothing, merely jotted in his notebook. The big photographer Miloche had continued down the hall, admiring the wood floors and panelling and the delicate cut-glass chandelier.

"They condemned this place?" he asked, to no one in particular, incredulous.

"Yeah, it's a bitch, isn't it," Benny said. "Guess the land's worth more without it. We'll just crash here until ..." The rumbling on the steps behind him stopped him in mid-sentence. "And here they are, well, all but one, the Sunshines family. This here is Bonnie Irwin," introducing the big-figured mother figure, who was wearing a blue sweatshirt over black tights. "And these sleepy sheepish-looking people behind her are John Mackenzie and Gina Stoltz." The two looked at the journalists, at each other, and then giggled like children. "Our missing fifth mouseketeer is Lesley Connor.... He hates 'Lesley,' thinks it's sissified. Lee Boy. But then, he's from Texas," as if that were explanation enough. With a feigned stiff British accent, Benny then said: "Shall we all adjourn to the breakfast room?"

The breakfast room was actually a house-wide, glassed-in sunroom filled with new healthy plants and well-worn, once-white-painted wicker furniture that looked to be original to the house. Melton sank into the soft cushions of a deep, wide-armed wicker club chair. He crossed his long legs and rested his notebook on the arm of the chair. Miloche prowled the room unobtrusively yet intently, with a kind of stealth, punctuating the reporter's open-ended questions with the pointed click of his shutter.

For the next three-quarters of an hour, Benny and Bonnie, John and Gina—the Sunshines—filled Melton's notebook with impressions of the underside of the boom, of what it was like to be the frail vanguard of alternative music in a city where the only musical alternatives for most were top-forty, soft country, or some no-edges, middle-of-the-road version of both:

Gigs in wino bars where business was so bad the owners were glad to have a band, any band, even *their* band playing anything, even *their* thing. Running a gauntlet of rednecks from some mop closet-cum-dressing room to a postage stamp of a stage. Sharing the spotlight with local drunks so drunk they would climb up and shove pencils up their noses or straightened clothes hangers down their throats, and usually get hoots of encouragement and louder applause. Knifings in the johns. The night John's nose was broken and the Sunshines' van's windows smashed by a gang with baseball caps and tire irons. One-night stands in rooms rented under false pretenses (the only way they *could* rent them), where fan damage to the hall usually took most of the haul from the performance. "Posers—" rich kids from the suburbs who dressed the part and came to the clubs for a weekend evening on the wild side. Kraft dinners and Ramen noodles at five boxes for a buck, salad from a Safeway dumpster. Clothes from Sally Ann, customized at home with scissors, thread, and magic markers. Drugs? Sure, Lee Boy ... never mind that, scratch that ... but nothing heavy, just hash, a little mushroom, beanies and black beauties—the trucker's wake-up call.

"Wait a minute, you guys! Wait!" Bonnie Irwin called from the hallway as the two journalists were leaving. "Lee Boy, Lesley, he wanted you to have a T-shirt and his glossy."

"His glossy?" Melton asked.

"Yeah," she said, handing the reporter a photo with creases and turned-down corners and two Calgary

Stoopede T-shirts—white undershirts with a smirking bull riding a bewildered-looking cowboy, done in felt pen and fabric paint. "Well, not so glossy now, I guess. Only one I could find. He had a modelling gig. He *is* pretty."

"Well, I ah, thanks for the shirts. But I don't know about the pic." Melton handed the photograph to Miloche, who took it and glanced at the beautiful boy with the sleek black hair and the fold across his forehead. "Donnie, G. Donald, here is pretty particular about using only *his* shots."

Miloche shrugged and smiled and handed the photo back to Bonnie, who shrugged. "Well, whatever, I tried. If he doesn't get in, it's his own damned fault for not getting up."

"Oh, well, he'll be up in time for the demo party," Benny chimed in. "You'll have to come back then."

"Demo party?" Melton asked.

"Yeah. Demolition. I don't figure it'll be long now. Bring a sledge and a six-pack and get hammered while you hammer. Lee Boy's real good with a hammer."

"You mean you trash the place?" Miloche asked, with a trace of indignation.

"Well," Benny said matter-of-factly, "we trash what they're gonna trash anyway, walls, ceilings. What they can salvage and sell—we know what it is—we leave it, usually. Doesn't get out of hand. Cops hassle us enough as it is. It's a party, that's all."

"And then what?" Melton asked, scribbling in his notebook again.

"Oh, another place. They're around, if you know where to look, eh, Bonnie?" She nodded her head. "And that's good for six, eight months, and then … well … probably another party. See ya there."

"Yeah, maybe." Melton lied. "Anyway, thanks for the talk, and the shirts. But there's one thing I gotta tell you," he added, taking a deep breath of outside air.

"What's that?"

"You were wrong about the shit."

1:15 PM

Fry had never seen anybody who was dead look anything but dead. And he had tried.

He remembered the night his grandfather died. Fry was eleven. It was nearly midnight when the telephone rang. He did not hear it. He was asleep in the bed he shared with his younger brother. His first memory of the night was his father's rough hand shaking them awake and his rough voice shaking as he told them they had to get up, that they had to go, that Grandpa was gone. Gone where? Fry remembered asking, and remembered his father not answering, but standing silently at the bedside, tears welling in his eyes, glistening in the light from the hall. His father bundled the two boys and their mother into the old Buick. They drove all night, the car's two headlights and the round, bright moon the only lights on the prairie.

He recalled his grandmother swooping down on them when they opened the door and hugging them, squeezing them tightly, even though that was not her way.

He could not remember the service, nothing the minister had said. But he could not forget standing in line to say a final goodbye at the open coffin and hearing the old people say they had not seen his grandfather look so good in years, so alive, such a good job. Try as he would, he could not see what they saw. And he wanted to tell them they were wrong, that his grandfather did not look good, did not look alive, that the hard and stone-cold—he had touched it and he knew—*thing* lying there looked only dead. But he did not tell them. He said nothing. He only cried.

Fry was not crying now. But he was trying to see the living in the dead, to see a life in a death. And again, try as he would, he could not. He was studying a photograph in an open manila folder on the fake-walnut top of his old desk in the recently renovated, but already crowded, stone and glass police headquarters building on Seventh Avenue SE.

It was the face of the youngish woman whose body had tumbled out of what used to be the stained-glass window of the old woman's ruined Beltline cottage. She had been cleaned up, scrubbed plain. Her eyes had been closed, her hair combed. The photographer had tilted her head back slightly and zoomed his lens in tightly to hide her wound. And he had succeeded. She looked only dead.

No. Like all the corpses in all the clinical photographs Fry had ever seen, she looked somehow never alive, unreal, a flat, pallid, grey creature no imagination could envision in the flesh. "Or identify," Fry said to himself, closing the folder, slumping back in his swivel chair, rubbing his eyes, sighing. "Or identify."

Fry knew now what had killed her, at least how she had died: one crushing blow to the top of her head with a blunt instrument that had fractured her skull, probably killing her instantly. He knew roughly how long she had been dead: since sometime late Saturday night or early Sunday morning. Soon, he would know almost exactly when she had died, the shape and possibly even the nature of the weapon that had killed her, and the one that had scalped her. And he would know everything else an autopsy could tell him: her blood type; her age, give or take a year or two; whether her hair colour was true; if she had eaten, what she had eaten, when; whether she had been drinking; whether she had used drugs; whether she had had sex recently.

What the autopsy report would not tell him, what the medical examiner's photograph would not help anyone else tell him, what the uniforms at the scene, despite their painstaking and risky search around, through, and under the timbers of the briefly resurrected house, had been unable to tell him, was who she was. They had found her other silver shoe and a silver-sequinned evening bag. Inside the bag, they found a poppy-red lipstick, dark red blush, an unopened pack of gum, half a pack of menthol cigarettes, tissue, and one house key—but no wallet, no driver's licence, no credit cards, nothing to identify her, nothing to tell him who she was. He needed to know who she was before he could begin to know why she had died, before he could begin to find who had made her die.

Fry went to Alf Mathews for help. He had seen him shuffle into Identification earlier, a coffee in one hand—probably a double-double—his scarred-leather saddlebag of a briefcase dangling from the other. He found him in a cubicle at the side of the building, at a desk under one of the high, narrow windows. Artists pencils were spread out before him like arrows spilled from their quiver. His big, balding head, its few stringy hairs parted just above his right ear and slicked over to the left, was bent over a sheet of white paper. The pink tip of his tongue stuck out of the corner of his mouth. A pencil buried in his big right hand was moving across the paper. Fry walked over to the desk, softly flapping a copy of the photograph of the dead woman in the palm of his right hand.

"What ya doin', Alf?"

"What the hell's it look like I'm doin'? Tryin' to colour inside the lines."

"The rapist again?"

"How'd you know?" Mathews raised his head and squinted at Fry through thick glasses perched halfway down a broad, aquiline nose.

"You always act like a prick when you've got to work on it."

"One, it's not an act. And two, it's 'cause I never have enough to go on. And I always end up with a picture that sorta looks like him that sorta looks like everybody that sorta looks like nobody at all."

"You make yourself sound like one of those—what do you call 'em?—identi-kits."

"Not much better sometimes, 'm afraid."

"Yeah, you are—until people come in kits, like Mr. Potato-Head."

"You come all the way over here to make a crack about my head?"

"Nope."

"Whaddaya want then?"

"To give you a break."

"You're gonna give me a break?"

"Well, at least an easier one."

"Easier what?"

"Picture to colour."

"If it's so easy, whyn't you do it yourself?"

"I would, but I hate it when I get that little knob on my middle finger—you know, from pressing too hard on the pencil."

"*You* would have other uses for your middle finger. Let's see."

Fry tossed a copy of the photograph onto the desk over

the beginnings of a sketch of what the press had taken to calling "the southwest rapist," and had taken to wondering why the police could not seem to catch him.

"Looks to me like you already got a picture," Mathews said, glancing at the autopsy photo.

"Yeah, I do—look like anybody you know? Look like anybody *anybody'd* know?"

"Nope, guess not. What you want me to do with it—with her?"

"Put the life back. Give me a sketch somebody can identify. Give me a person."

"And you want it when?"

"Five minutes ago."

"Now who's a prick?"

"Sorry. And Alf?"

"Yeah?"

"Tart her up a bit—lips, cheeks, eyes. It's what she wanted, I think."

2:05 PM

Fry sat fidgeting at his desk for nearly an hour, waiting for the police artist to finish, rifling through the evidence box of the dead woman's few belongings, opening and closing the folder on her photograph, opening and closing his eyes, trying to form some mental image of the flesh-and-blood woman she had been, managing only to see the puffy grey thing she had become.

He was startled from his reverie by a hard slap on the back and a too hearty, "Hey, J.J., how's the boy?"

It was Grantham.

Inspector Phil Grantham was a sleek bespectacled senior officer in the organizationally unnamed dog's breakfast of a division that included everything from Internal Affairs to Public Affairs. He was an able man—

even, in his bureaucratic way, an able cop: tough, smart, focused, ambitious. Too ambitious, as far as Fry was concerned. Too narrowly focused. Too smart for his own good, or for anybody else's.

He smiled too much. He talked too much. He exercised too much. He was around too much. He knew too much, and too little.

All Fry could see in Grantham was a careerist, a politician in a uniform with one eye always on the main chance, the other usually on his image—in the mirror, in a car window, in a glass door, any reflecting surface would do. Fry had never liked him. He had never trusted him. But that had never deterred Grantham. It might even have encouraged him. Like the cat that instinctively heads for the one person in a room who cannot stand it and rubs against him, purring, Grantham always headed for Fry, purring, calling him by the two-letter little-boy nickname that annoyed Fry even more than "Ghost," rubbing him the wrong way.

"Looks like you could do with some gym-time downstairs, J.J." Grantham said, grinning, pointing toward the tiny spare tire beginning to inflate over Fry's belt, smacking his own hard, slim middle. "Hear you caught a nasty one."

"Bad news travels fast."

"Big ears, I guess," Grantham grinned again. Fry said nothing. "I was in dispatch when the call came in. And I was talking to Strahan a little while ago." *Another one who talks too much,* Fry thought. "And he seems to figure—"

"That it was an Indian, right?"

"Well, yes."

"He's right, too. Damned renegade that bolted the reserve and went on the warpath."

"Come on, J.J., don't go off half-cocked. Remember that temper of yours, what trouble it can get you in."

If you had your *way, asshole*, Fry thought. "Strahan's been staying up too late, reading too many western novels," he said.

"Could be, J.J. But she *was* scalped, Indian-style, and there *was* that Wolf Child business last year and—"

"There was the chief's kid."

"Yes."

"As I remember Inspector, he was all by himself when he hanged himself. Himself. And not because he was full of anger, just a quart low on hope. That's how it usually happens. And that's what they usually do, kill themselves, or each other, when they actually do get mad enough to kill anybody at all."

"I know, J.J., but you can't be sure—"

"Listen, when was the last time one of ... *them* took after one of ... *us*? I discussed Strahan's 'theory,' if you want to call it that, with him earlier. A bit premature, at least, I told him. Now I just think it's fuckin' nuts."

"Oh, I'm not suggesting that you—"

"Throw up road blocks around Victoria Park and do a house-to-house?"

"Of course not. But we think—"

"We?"

"We think it's," Grantham pressed ahead, ignoring Fry's question, to which Fry knew the answer anyway, "well, unfortunate, the timing."

"The timing?"

"Yes. You know, Stampede only a couple of months away. And this year the salute to Indians ... to Native peoples. It's unfortunate ... damned unfortunate."

"I'm sure the lady agrees," Fry said coldly, flipping open the folder and revealing the photo.

Grantham looked at it, unfazed.

"What? You're going to shock the pencil pusher with a picture? Don't get holier-than-though on me. I've seen my share of bodies, J.J. I am a cop, too, you know. You're not the only one here."

Fry lowered his eyes. "All I'm saying—"

"There ya go, Jake," Alf Mathews' hoarse voice croaked as he dropped the drawing onto the desktop beside the photograph. "Whaddya think?"

Fry studied the two pictures. They were of the same woman, there was no doubt. And both were in black-and-white, with shadings of grey. Yet the difference between them was between night and day, between dead and alive. In the photograph, she was a flat, expressionless thing that seemed devoid even of the memory of living. In Alf Mathews' pencil rendering, she was alive and vibrant.

Maybe too vibrant, Fry thought at first glance. But then, looking more closely, he thought, *No.* This was the woman. It was as if the artist's pencil had resuscitated her. This was how she had looked at the beginning of the night she had been murdered, Fry was sure. This was the life somebody had brutally crushed and defiled.

"I think, Alf," Fry said, smiling up at the artist, "that if you can do this from a photocopy, you could make a fortune at the malls, making little old ladies look ten years younger."

"Oh, but I already do, Jake," Mathews chuckled. "I already do. But it's twenty years, not ten. Well, to coin a phrase, back to the drawing board."

"Thanks, Alf."

"Oh, don't mention it. I'll get even."

"I know you will. And you, Inspector, you were

saying?" Fry looked up at Grantham, who was looking at Mathews, then at the drawing.

"What?"

"You were saying. The unfortunate timing and all?"

"Oh, yes. All I was saying was that, well, what I was saying must not have been very clear. I'll try again. I'm not Strahan, J.J. He has biases. I don't. Can't afford them. We—*we* are not looking, are not asking you to look, for a scapegoat. We're not asking you to look for anybody in particular, nobody but the bad guy. We are asking you to catch him, quickly. If it is an Indian, let's get him and get him behind us. And if it is, well, you do have a certain ... feeling for the people, a rapport. I can tell you it's why you were assigned. And if it's not an Indian, hey, so much the better. The important thing isn't the who, but how fast we get to him. It's important that this thing not get out of hand. You agree?"

Fry sat back in his chair and put his elbows on the arm rests. He pressed his hands together and brought them to his mouth, blowing on his fingertips as he tapped his lower lip. He looked up at Grantham. He nodded, once.

"Good. What's with the composite?" Grantham gestured toward the artist's drawing. "You've got a photo."

"That's exactly what Alf said to me. Well, which one you think anybody'd recognize?"

"Hmmm. Maybe you've got a point. Hope so, J.J." Grantham aimed his index finger at Fry, cocked his thumb, and clicked his tongue loudly as he fired. "It really would do you some good to put one in the W column."

He grinned broadly, everywhere but in his cold eyes,

and walked briskly away, whistling a tune from one of John Ford's boots-and-saddle John Wayne westerns, *She Wore a Yellow Ribbon.*

4:30 PM

Somehow the leaded-glass window had not shattered when Lesley Connor slammed the heavy front door and stormed down the veranda steps, cursing. The intricate panel had quivered as the door rattled in its frame, but it had stayed in place, intact except for the half-dozen pieces that shook loose and fell, scattering down the hallway. Bonnie Irwin/Sunshines had quickly found and replaced five of them. For the last ten minutes, she had been scrambling frantically on hands and knees, looking for the sixth.

"Lighten up, babe," Benny mumbled from the far end of the hall, where he was leaning outside the entrance to the kitchen, holding a dampened washcloth wrapped around ice cubes to his upper lip. "What's it matter? No one's gonna notice. Window's still in the door. It's only one little piece."

"It *does* matter," Bonnie said sharply, pausing briefly in her search, looking back down the hall on all fours. "*I'll* notice."

"For Chris' sake, Bonnie, you forgettin' they're just gonna trash this place anyway? Another few weeks. Shit, for all we know tomorrow. Whatever, it's history."

"No, Benny, I'm not forgetting. I'm just tired of living in a place—in places—we can treat like trash. And, speaking of shit, I'm tired of the shit, Benny. That reporter was right. You *were* wrong about the shit. I've never stopped smelling the shit."

"And now I suppose you want to start smellin' the roses?"

"Benny!"

"Sorry. I am. Must be the spirit of a top-forty jock tryin' to possess m'body—I'm sorry, babe. What? What's wrong?" He came toward her down the hallway, lightly dabbing the washcloth to his lip as he walked. "I mean, what's *really* wrong? It's for sure not just a fuckin' piece of glass."

Bonnie sat in the middle of the panelled hall, crossing her legs in front of her, putting her elbows on her knees, propping her face in the V of her hands, studying Benny with her steady blue eyes. She sighed deeply.

"Oh, I don't know, Benny. I guess I'm just tired of trying to keep it all together, to hold it together, covering it over with magic marker when it doesn't work, pretending none of it matters. *Some* of it matters, doesn't it?" Benny did not answer. "I want," she continued, "something solid for a change, something, I don't know—something permanent."

"Permanent? Whoa!" He took the washcloth from his face and held it at his side. "Not much of that around here. Christ, even people got the money to buy into it aren't buying into it forever, just for now."

"Well, for however long it is, it doesn't have to be here, does it? I mean, we don't have to be here. We could go."

"Go where, babe? Oops." Benny almost dropped the washcloth, which dangled from the index fingertip of his right hand. The remains of the ice cubes skittered across the parquet floor, under a cold steam radiator. "Dammit."

"Vancouver maybe. The island. You know, all the fantasy stuff—a little house by the ocean, a farm, just a garden maybe. Remember the house plans I cut out of the Saturday paper? The ones you can send for?" She could see from his face that he did not. "Oh, you ... A place is what I want, Benny. A real place."

"And this place," Benny sniffed, "isn't real enough for you?"

"Oh, yeah, it's real enough that way—*too* fucking real." She crinkled her nose, almost smiled. "But that's the only way. I mean, Jesus," raising her arms, "just look at it—"

"Aha! And look at this," Benny said, tossing the soggy washcloth onto the radiator, kneeling down, reaching under the cold pipes.

"Look at what?"

"The last piece of the jigsaw, m'dear, the last piece of the jigsaw."

He walked over to her, bent down with a flourish, took her right hand, opened it, and dropped the diamond-shaped piece of window glass into her palm. Bonnie looked at the glass for a long moment. Then a single tear ran down her cheek.

"Hey, no, babe, no, don't," Benny said softly, genuinely moved, and at the same time uncomfortable. "What? What is it?"

She bit her lip and shook her head, looking up at him. She said nothing. He bent down and lifted her gently to her feet. He held her. She held tightly to him, tears coming freely now, streaks of blue-black running down her cheeks. For several minutes they held each other, slowly swaying in the hallway, not speaking. Finally, her arms still encircling his neck, she pulled her head back and examined his face.

"How's your lip?" she asked.

"Ith okay," he said. "Tho long as you don't try to kith me—ouch."

"Funny. Serves you right. Swelling's down, though."

She stood on tiptoes and softly kissed his lower lip. “Good thing you don’t play the trumpet. The little bugger.”

“Hey, it’s cool, babe. I don’t play the trumpet. And he didn’t mean it.”

“Lee Boy never means it. He never *means* to do anything. But he still does it. He always does it—this time he’s really done it.”

“Come on, Bonnie, don’t come down so hard on him. He doesn’t—”

“Come on nothing!” She pushed herself away and began pacing up and down the hallway. “Hard on *him*? You should see your lip—actually you probably shouldn’t, it’s really gross-looking. Who was hard on who? I told you he’d be pissed off. I knew he would be when he realized he’d slept through the interview, *his* big chance. His. Him. That’s all he ever thinks about. I never thought he really would take a swing at you, though.”

“Well, come on, he didn’t *really*—not *at* me. That was an accident. You know how he is when he goes into one of his tantrums, all wild and flailing, like some berserk child.”

“You got that right.”

“I just got in the middle. Teach me to practise child psychology without a licence.”

“You needed a net.”

“He didn’t mean it, Bonnie. You know he didn’t.”

“Yeah? Do I? Fine. We’ll tell that to his boss when he doesn’t show up for work tomorrow. No offence, Papa Sunshines, but we can’t afford to lose the money he brings in.”

“You don’t know he won’t show up.”

“Oh, the hell I don’t. I know Lee Boy. I know

what he does when he gets like this. All pissed off. He'll storm around, fume around for a while, then come down. *Come* down, not calm down. And then he'll try to score some dope. If he doesn't get himself busted, he'll get himself stoned. And he'll come stumbling back here wanging on the door in the middle of the night—doesn't remember his key when he's normal, might as well say he doesn't *ever* remember his key—probably knock the window right out this time before we let him in, then knock himself out on the sofa, dead to the world. Dammit! He's dead from the neck up now! I'm tired. I'm tired of feeling like his mother, like everybody's goddamned mother! Especially now." She stopped pacing, turned, and faced Benny. "Now … when I'm … I think I'm gonna be somebody's *real* mother, Benny."

What she had just said surprised Bonnie almost as much as it surprised Benny. The two stood at opposite ends of the hallway, silently, expectantly, unsure what to say next, uncertain what came next, what should come next, what could come next. What did come next was Benny looking down at the pattern in the floor, shuffling his feet, jamming his hands into his jeans pockets, mumbling.

"Hey—hey, come on now, babe, let's ... why don't we drop all the Lee Boy talk now."

"Yeah. Yeah, Benny, let's drop it. Let's drop everything," Bonnie sighed, quietly, resignedly. Then she laughed, a rueful, hollow laugh. "I'd like to drop Lee Boy—right on his head from his porch up there."

"All right, all right, that's enough of that, old girl." Benny motioned her toward him with his right hand and gestured over his shoulder toward the leaded glass. "Come on, let's finish your puzzle."

9:15 PM

Fry's workbench was a once slightly warped solid oak door planed smooth and mounted on the sturdy legs of a junked grand piano—garbage-day finds from his days in uniform patrolling the neighbourhoods along the Elbow. He had had to dismantle the bench to get it out of the basement of what was now his ex-wife's sprawling rancher in Canyon Meadows. To get it into the low cellar of his tiny rented house in Eau Claire, he had to saw two inches off the top of the legs, which meant he now had to stoop while working at the bench and could only work for an hour or so before it got him in the back. He had to stoop slightly to walk around in the cellar anyway, and had learned, after a couple of painful lessons, to duck under the low load-carrying beam that bisected the room. He worked in the shadow-throwing light of two utility lanterns swung over the beam and plugged into an outlet he had screwed into the base of the light at the foot of the stairs.

His power tools—the drill press and table saw, the jigsaw, the tabletop lathe and the router—were under the bench, still packed in cardboard boxes. He had tried using his electric drill once in the cellar, and had immediately blown a fuse. If he wanted to work down here, he had to work by hand.

He liked working by hand. He liked the pace, the feeling of control. Not power. He was not interested in power. He knew he could not force his way into the wood. He had to understand it, to work with it, to find a way into it. He knew he could, by hand and by eye, with time. He could.

He was working with a chisel now, cleaning out the hand-cut dado joints in the side of a bookcase he was building from scrap. The sides were solid wood, possibly a cheap grade of pine, although he was not sure. The workmen renovating the Seventh Avenue headquarters had left them behind. On his way home from a long walk along the Bow, Fry had found enough birch for one shelf, a back piece for the top, and a bottom support, discarded at the construction site just across the street. The other four yardstick-wide shelves—plywood with beech veneer—came from another renovation project, at a junior high school in the northwest. Constable Andy Stimwych's son Rick, who had a summer job at the school cleaning classrooms and repairing textbooks, brought them home, telling his father they were only going to throw them away.

"Taxpayers' fuckin' dollars, too," Stimwych had cursed, carrying the shelves into Homicide under his arm, leaning them against Fry's desk. "Maybe you can do something with 'em."

Fry could afford to go to the lumber yard and pick out any wood he wanted, matching the grain, selecting good, even exotic, stock for his projects. But he preferred working with scrap. He liked taking useless pieces and turning them into something useful.

The bookcase taking shape under his hands now would go to Stimwych's kid, who was headed for the University of Alberta in the fall to study veterinary medicine. When Fry was finished with it—even after he had sanded and sanded and sanded the piece, after he had brushed on and wiped off the hand-mixed stain to match up the mismatched woods, after he had applied coat after coat of hand-rubbed varnish—the bookcase would still look a handmade thing. But it would also be strong; it would last; and it would have a kind of primitive beauty.

As he moved the chisel carefully through the joint, a thin shaving curling cleanly over the edge of the blade, Fry thought again about the semi-beauty who had not been strong, who had not endured, who had been discarded as so much trash. To what purpose? He thought of the crude blade that had cut her, not cleanly, not carefully, not caringly. To what end?

Fry was not like Strahan. He did not have a theory. He did not believe in theories. He did not trust them. Maybe his job would have been easier if he did. It certainly would have been simpler. And maybe Strahan's theory was right, and she was the hooker she was dressed up to be, and it was an angry pimp or a trick gone bad. Or maybe it was the first skirmish in the war on the east-end prostitutes' row that "unnamed sources" in Morality had been darkly hinting at in the media for months. Fry had thought they were simply jockeying for a bigger chunk of the budget pie, but maybe he was wrong. Boom towns were good places for hookers to make their livings, even better places for the creeps who made their livings off the hookers. New pimps had already moved in—blacks from Seattle, a gang of bikers from Vancouver, a couple of brothers on the fringes of the local Lebanese community. Maybe the rumours of war were no longer rumours. Maybe she got caught in a crossfire in a battle over turf. Maybe the new black gangs, or maybe the bikers, were trying to move in on the Indian pimps off of Macleod Trail and this was the Natives' way of marking their territory. Maybe the Indians were trying to cut themselves in—he hated the pun the instant it crossed his mind. Or maybe, and he hated this thought even more, Strahan was right.

Maybe, maybe, maybe.

Fry could not deal in maybes. He could not build

on maybes. He had to know. He had to have facts. He could build on facts, even scraps of facts, but only on facts. And before he could begin to reconstruct the facts of her death, he needed to know the facts of her life. He needed to know who she was. He needed a name to go with her face. He still did not have it.

Every uniform and all the plainclothes on the force had her face by now, copies of Alf Mathews' sketch from death. The picture and story (without the scalping angle) had been on the six o'clock news—headlined sensationally on CFAC, sandwiched between the water shortage and the general strike in Northern Ireland on CFCN, at the tail end of the CBC local newscast just before the weather, but always with the drawing on the screen for a good thirty seconds. It would be in the *Bulletin* tomorrow morning, and in the afternoon *Herald*.

Fry could only wait now, and hope that somebody who saw the picture had seen her, had known her, and could tell him what he needed to know, could tell him who the shattered lady in the splintered window had been.

Fry felt the twinge and pulled up sharply, reaching for his back, which was telling him it was time to stop.

"Uh huh, I hear you."

He had learned not to disobey.

He leaned forward once more, blew away the shavings, and eyeballed the clean, sharp edges of the joint. He hung the chisel on the pegboard above the workbench. He left the bookcase side clamped to the bench. He still had work to do; the edges were still not quite true. He headed for the stairs. He pulled on the chain at the base of the overhead outlet and the two lanterns faded to black. He put his hands on the small of his back and stretched again, taking a deep breath and groaning. He headed for the soft, low light at the top of the cellarway.

11:30 PM

The diabolical plot had been foiled. The Palestinian terrorists and the mad American traitor were dead. The American President was safe. The Super Bowl had been saved. At the last possible second, the huge Goodyear blimp that had hovered over the Orange Bowl like a deadly cloud had been yanked away and hauled out to sea, where it burst like a punctured balloon, spewing its thousands of lethal darts harmlessly into the water. The helicopter had whisked the hero away, dangling him just over the waves. He abruptly disappeared from the screen when the white-on-black credits came up.

The credits were still running when the sparse second-show crowd emerged from *Black Sunday* into the black Monday night, briefly giving the section of the Stephen Avenue Mall in front of the theatre the look of life that twelve hours before had filled the closed-off five blocks of Eighth Avenue.

It had been warm then, the temperature pushing twenty, with a gentle, westerly breeze. The downtown shop and office workers had poured out of their anonymous towers onto the pedestrian mall lined with the distinctive low-rise-sandstone and terra-cotta architecture of an earlier Calgary boom. They sat on concrete benches and on round metal chairs at round metal tables, eating brown-bag lunches, "Alberta beef" burgers and take-out souvlaki, basking in the bright, rising spring sun reflecting off the mirrored glass rising above the mall. Most of them probably did not know, and undoubtedly would not care, that the mall was named for the first president of Canadian Pacific Railway. To them it was, simply, the Eighth Avenue Mall.

But now it was dark. The mall was deserted. Like a tide slowly receding, the workers had long ago left for home, spilling north and south on narrow asphalt tributaries into the suburbs. The west wind tunnelling between the empty towers had a bite to it now, making the ten-degree temperature seem even cooler, catching some of the movie-goers who trickled onto the street by surprise. Complaints about the weather combined with film criticism in their conversations as they hurried toward cars parked off the mall.

"Jesus-H-Christ! Somebody cancel spring or something...?"

"Went south...."

"Told you to wear your heavier jacket, Billy. But no, you'd just be too warm...."

"Told you—what'd you think, Meg? Pretty good flick, eh...?"

"I've always liked Robert Shaw...."

"The guy who flew the blimp—what's his name? Yeah, Bruce Dern. He always gives me the creeps...."

"Couldn't really happen though...."

"Oh, I don't know. With these Arabs, you never can tell...."

"What do they call *us*? Blue-eyed Arabs? Maybe we ought'a send a hot-air balloon east and scare the bejesus out of Toronto...."

Laughter fading down the street.

"Damn! It's cold! Come on, Junie, get your buns in gear, let's go."

"Oh, you know I can't run in these shoes, Jim. Dammit!"

"Dammit yourself!"

"What if these movies, you know, just give people ideas?"

"If you don't hurry, you'll give me an idea. Come *on*!"

If the last-picture-goers had been listening, they would have heard that the only sounds on the street were their shoes on the pavement, their voices and their laughter, the slurred incoherent shouts of the young wino lurching toward them, and, in the distance, an occasional wailing siren and the screeching of tires. They were alone on the street, except for the loud, skinny drunk and the heavy-set dark man with a lowered head and turned-up collar following a few paces behind him.

Lesley Connor certainly appeared to be drunk as he stumbled toward them against the tide, a lopsided, sheepish grin on his face. He was actually under the influence of a chemical cocktail, not alcohol; stoned, not drunk. Not that it made any difference.

"Wha's wrong?" he asked, it seemed, no one in particular. Then he turned and, walking unsteadily backward, asked again, of the figure trailing him, "Wha's wrong? 'm I embarrassin' you?" He laughed. "'Fraid of bein' seen with me—somebody might reco'nize you?"

The dark figure continued walking a few paces behind. He raised his head slightly and mumbled something that almost made Lesley Connor stop laughing.

"Oh, no, no, no. Sorry, man...." Lesley Connor said, assuring his pursuer. "I'll behave m'self. I'll be g … be g … be good … Goddammit watch what the fuck—"

Lesley Connor had stumbled backward into one of the fleeing film-goers, Jim, who was with June, who could not run in her half-heels and tight jeans. Lesley Connor spun to face him, reeling backward, dizzy, suddenly belligerent, spitting mad.

"Why'n't you watch where the fuck you're goin'? Wha's fuck's'matter with you, you asshole...."

"Fuck off, you little faggot creep," snapped Jim, a big man in his twenties wearing patched jeans over well-worn cowboy boots and a leather-sleeved Mount Royal College jacket. He stiff-armed Lesley Conner hard on his chest and sent him stumbling backward into his companion, who shied away, protectively shielding the big leather bag slung over his shoulder. Jim appeared about to go after Lesley Connor until June grabbed him by the sleeve and pulled him down the street like a misbehaving child.

"Come on, Jim, forget it. He's just drunk—and look, only a kid, a skinny one, too. What'd it prove, eh? Come on, let's go. It's cold, remember? I'm cold. Let's go!"

Reluctantly Jim obeyed, cursing under his breath, looking back repeatedly until he and June turned the corner onto Fourth Street.

"Who you callin' a faggot, you motherfucker? Eh? Eh!? Who?!" Lesley Connor shouted after him.

He semi-steadied himself and started after Jim until he realized that his companion had left him. He turned and looked for him. He spotted him walking quickly down the mall, away from the thinning theatre crowd, his head even lower.

"Hey, wait, man, wait a minute!" Lesley Connor called to him, running on rubber legs after him. "Come on. Wait ... sorry.... I'm sorry, man. Didn't mean—" He caught up to the big man and grabbed him by the arm, which his companion jerked away. "Come on," Lesley Connor pleaded. "Look, no harm. No harm done. We can still do it, right? I'm cool. Really, really. I'm cool. I am. See...?"

He held out his arms and made a terrific effort to keep them from shaking, almost succeeding. He closed his eyes and tried to touch his nose with the index finger of his right hand, poking himself between the eyes. He took several deep breaths, trying to clear his head.

"I'm cool. I am. Okay?" He walked beside the big dark man, his feet steadier under him. "We can still do it, right? Right?" His companion nodded. "All right! Far out! It's not far, really, jus' a coupl'a blocks, jus' off the mall—come on."

Lesley Connor looked and sounded like Chester, the pathetic little dog in the Warner Brothers cartoon, prancing around his big, Spike-like companion, trying to please him, trying not to lose him, needing him.

"You're sure you wanna do it there?" Lesley Connor pestered Spike as they walked. "You think that's the best place? It's cool for me—I mean you know your business—I can get us in, no sweat. No problem."

By now they were off the mall, on Seventh Avenue, empty too except for the genuine winos huddled in darkened stairwells and the hookers stomping their spiked heels and hugging their bare arms outside the Legion.

The boom had not detonated here in the east end. The low-rise, low-rent, low-life district of taverns and shabby hotels and second-hand, second-rate businesses could have been in a time warp. It was the only part of the city that had not changed in the past ten years, not really in the past thirty, except to become dirtier, seedier, more violent, less hopeful.

Change was coming, but it was the kind of change only planners could call renewal. Their maps already showed it: a massive five-block civic centre/arts centre/hotel/office project between Seventh and Ninth Avenues, from First Street SE to the block east of Third—a new "heart" for the downtown, transplanted in the heart of the old east end. Where the east-enders would go when the east end ended, the planners' maps did not say. Like the forlorn buildings still on the ground in the east end, the people on the ground in the east end were not yet gone, but already forgotten.

"Here it is, man," Lesley Connor said, turning again to face his companion, stopping outside a former strip club with faded beer posters still in the windows, cut-out pictures of Coke bottles pasted over the Labatt bottles in the models' hands. In big block letters on the tiny marquee above the entrance was the word: "NOIDS."

"Come on, down here." Lesley Connor darted down a narrow alley between the club and the laundromat next door, pulling a butane lighter from his jeans, flicking the flame to high, using it as a torchlight. "I know where they stash the key. I'll have us inside in a flash."

About two-thirds of the way down the alley, Lesley Connor stopped at a steel side door with a burnt-out yellow bulb in a mesh cage above it. He strained on tiptoes to reach the top of the mesh with his right hand, his left hand holding the lighter high.

"Got it," he said, pulling down a key. "And now to get us inside."

He bent toward the door, holding the lighter near the lock, fitting the key inside, about to turn it. "What?" he asked, turning his head, his right hand still at the lock, the lighter in his left.

He saw the explosion of white an instant before the explosion of red. And then he saw nothing. He heard the explosion in his ears, the sudden thunderous roaring in his ears. And then he heard nothing. He never did feel the crushing, crunching blow to the top of his skull. He felt nothing.

He did not feel the littered asphalt alleyway coming up to meet him as he crumpled toward it. He did not feel the lighter fall sputtering from his hands. He did not feel the weight on his shoulders, pushing him down, holding him down, nor the tugging on his long black hair, nor the blade as it sliced into the top of his head, describing a rapid, rude circle around the top of his head. He did not hear the frantic, shallow breathing behind him, nor the heart pounding, nor the grunting, nor the sickening sucking sound as strong hands yanked their bloody trophy away. He did not feel the hands under his armpits, his heels dragging on the pavement, his body being tossed limply, heavily into the dumpster at the back of the club. He did not hear the last low gurgle in his throat. He did not see the lighter flicker like a candle in the alleyway, flicker ... flicker ... and die.

may 3 8:55 AM

The places in the city that Fry liked best were the places that were not yet the city. Walking alone in the valleys of the Bow and the Elbow or on the banks of meandering Fish Creek. Standing alone in Edworthy Park among thick stands of straight, deep-rooted cottonwoods or on barren Nose Hill, the last stubbornly resisting expanse of prairie within the city limits. Lifting his tired eyes toward the startlingly vast and humbling sky, suddenly remembering that there *was* such a sky. He could almost forget the city then. And he could almost escape what one witty urban planner—talking about all the land disappearing under streets and parking lots, service stations, car dealerships, and body shops—called "the advance of the ICE (internal combustion engine) Age," a glacier of asphalt smothering the downtown, unlikely to recede.

Fry had never thought of leaving the city, as he knew most of those now pouring into it would eventually do. They would come, find whatever it was they were looking for, or not find it, and go. He had been here before them. He would be here after them. He would outlast them.

Maybe that was why he also liked the east end, the crowded, dirty, run-down, worn-down, worn-out east end—this place in the city that was too much the city.

Prostitutes strutted their wares outside the York and the Calgarian, thumbing their noses at the hotel owners, flashing their middle fingers at passing squad cars. Drunks staggered out of shabby watering holes with elegant names and elegant pasts—the Queens, Imperial, and Alexandra—kicked off their boots, and slept soundly in the mini-parks around the old sandstone city hall, until a passing uniform gave them a gentle kick to move them along, or simply to see if they were still alive. Sometimes, by the cold morning, they were not. Most mornings, the alleys were littered with used condoms, and with nail-punctured Lysol cans and empty bottles of vanilla extract—poor men's cocktails. After really bad nights, the neighbourhood reeked of blood and vomit and stale beer. And every day now there was the faint, unmistakable, ineradicable scent of despair.

Yet the east end *was* a neighbourhood too, a community, more of one as far as Fry was concerned than any of the "planned communities" burrowing into the prairie like gopher colonies, but even more mindlessly. The east end was Fry's first neighbourhood as a police officer, his first beat. He had liked it then; he liked it now. He smiled at its chaotic stability. He admired its pointless tenacity. It reminded him of a lone tree growing against the wind, bent low, bare of branches on the windward side, looking, even on calm, bright days as if it were weathering a storm, but, for all that, still standing.

Fry knew the east end, *this* east end, would not stand much longer. The change that had been ignoring it for thirty years was taking notice of it now. The first signs were already evident. Late in the afternoon, the dark, cold shadow of the Glenbow tower reached deep into the neighbourhood, a symbol of things to come. Even though much of the old low-rise neighbourhood that Fry had patrolled still stood, the buildings were changing. Used books still climbed floor-to-ceiling at Jaffe's and the two old men who owned the place still squabbled in Yiddish. But now they might have been arguing about how they would move them all, where they would move them all, if they could move at all. The used-furniture store where Fry used to find pieces to salvage was now an East Indian gift shop with cheap brass in the window and a heavy iron grille over it. The second-floor tailors where he had taken his blue uniforms was now an income-tax discounter's office. Other places had undergone similar temporary facelifts that revealed the neighbourhood's permanent decline.

It looked to Fry like this place was one of them.

The last time he'd been in the hole-in-the-wall club he was off duty. It was a Saturday, nearly midnight. The place was crowded and called Randy Andy's. And on the stage a skinny, young stripper was trying gamely to shake her small, big-nippled breasts to a tape of John Baldry and hoots from the up-front tables.

But he was on duty this cool early Tuesday morning. The club, NOIDS in its latest incarnation, was closed. Chairs were turned bottoms-up on empty tables. The stage was bare except for a small keyboard and an elaborate set of drums in the middle and, on each side, a four-foot-high loud speaker.

From the same stool at the bar where he had alternatively sipped a flat draft and watched the flat dancer, Fry sat sipping a black coffee from a Styrofoam cup and watching the drummer's throne, where a small, blonde, pale young man was perched, quietly, absentmindedly strumming with a cymbal brush. He had told Constable Fred Jarvis, the uniform who answered the call, that his name was T.C.—Tom Clarkson, he said, when Jarvis pressed him for more than initials. He was the manager of the club.

He had found the body of Lesley Connor.

9:05 AM

When Fry saw Lesley Connor's corpse, draped at the slender waist over the edge of the open steel dumpster, he could not help thinking of the obviously fake half-bodies hanging out of the gaping jaws of campy prehistoric monsters in bad fifties Japanese horror films. The blue-jeaned rear end pointed comically toward the sky. The long legs dangled outside the dumpster, toes of the broken-laced sneakers almost touching the asphalt. The skinny arms reached deep into the trash bin, the delicate hands and bludgeoned, bloody head disappearing among the cardboard boxes and black plastic garbage bags.

Lesley Connor's body was being removed even as Fry sat staring through the steam from his coffee toward the shaken young man on the drummer's throne. The contents of the dumpster were being bagged, boxed, and catalogued. Uniforms were poring over the cordoned-off alleyway for any physical evidence, no matter how small, seemingly unrelated, or insignificant. They had bagged the lighter. The surface of the dumpster and the steel side door with the key still in the lock were being dusted for fingerprints.

Fry's notebook was open on the bar. His right hand was tapping his ballpoint pen on the page half-filled with his almost indecipherable scrawling, keeping time with the young man's slow brushing. To get his bearings and to help the young man keep his, Fry started the questioning softly, unthreateningly, irrelevantly asking T.C. about the other initials, the ones in black block letters on the tiny marquee: NOIDS.

"Oh … that … uh," Tom Clarkson faltered, taking a deep unsteady breath.

"Take your time."

Clarkson looked at Fry with something like gratitude in his eyes. It lasted for only an instant. Then he looked as if he had suddenly remembered something, something important, something he should not have forgotten. The look in his eyes hardened. Fry had seen it happen before.

"What's this?" Clarkson asked. "Good cop/bad cop all wrapped up in one cop?"

Fry did not answer.

"You want to know about NOIDS?" Clarkson continued. "What it's got to do with anything—with this thing, I don't know. Nothing, I'd say. But I'll tell you anyway. We couldn't get a licence. Soooo, we decided not to need one. It's a non-alcoholic club. Kids. Underage. No booze. So no identification's necessary. No IDs. Voila! NOIDS."

Fry tried not to smile. "What kind of music?" he asked.

Tom Clarkson, T.C., looked down at Fry from the drummer's perch.

"Probably not your kind," he said.

"Probably not," Fry replied, returning his gaze. "You knew the victim, I understand."

"Victim? Lee Boy? Yeah, I knew him."

"Lee Boy?"

"Yeah, Lee Boy. Lesley. But nobody called him Lesley. I didn't even know he was a Lesley until the cop—the officer—told me that was what was on his driver's licence. I didn't know he was from Texas, either."

"What did you know about him?"

"What do you mean?"

"Nothing. Only what I asked. You knew him, you say. What did you know about him?"

"About his past, not much. About what he did when he wasn't here, a little. About what he did here, a lot."

"And he did what here?"

"He played here." T.C. softly touched each of the drum heads with the brush. "He played right here. He's—he was—a drummer. Plays—played—these drums for the Sunshines Family."

"The Sunshines Family—I take it that's a group. One that plays not my kind of music."

"Yeah. That's right. A group that plays not your kind of music. A couple of girls, three guys. Keyboard here, these drums, two guitars, a singer. The Sunshines Family. They're into, we're into, what the media likes to call 'alternative' music."

"Alternative to what?"

"Oh, I don't know—your kind of music maybe. Funny, though...."

"What's funny?"

"Why Lee Boy'd be here."

"Thought you said he played here."

"I did. He does—did. But that's just it."

"What's just it?"

"Well, we're not open Monday nights. He knew it. They've been playing here eight, nine months on and off now. He knew we weren't open. Unless ..."

"What?"

"Nothing. Forget it."

"Do I look like the forgetful sort?"

"I don't suppose."

"You don't suppose right. Unless what?"

"Unless ... unless he was ... well, trying to score some drugs."

Fry said nothing. He sipped his coffee. He reached for the pack of cigarettes in his outer coat pocket, deftly shook a single smoke loose, and pulled it the rest of the way from the package with his lips. He grabbed a pack of matches from the bar. He flicked a match between thumb and strike plate, put the flame to the end of the cigarette, drew deeply, and exhaled, blowing out the match just before the fire reached his fingertips. He let his steady, interrogating grey-green eyes ask the question, which had its intended unsettling effect.

"Hey! No fuckin' way, man! This place is clean!" Clarkson snapped, hitting the cymbal hard with the brush, a low reverberating hiss punctuating his anger. He tossed the brush onto the head of the snare and stepped down from the drums and started pacing around the small stage, hands thrust in the back pockets of his jeans.

He was about twenty-five, Fry would have guessed, five-eight or five-nine, a hundred forty pounds or so. He had blonde, naturally wavy hair cut just at his shoulders, a clean-shaven face with even, handsome features. Even though he was wearing faded jeans, running shoes, and a tattered white Mozart sweatshirt with

Groucho Marx features hand-drawn over the composer's face, "dapper" was the description that came to Fry's mind. The sneakers were old and worn, but clean, as if they had been washed. The neatly creased blue jeans had obviously been ironed. For all its frays and loose threads, the sweatshirt had a studied look, as if it had been custom-made for him. He wore a plain, heavy gold ring on the middle finger of his right hand and an expensive-looking gold watch on his left wrist. He was every bit as much in uniform as the blue pinstripe suits now arriving for work in the oil towers only a few blocks to the west.

Before Clarkson said anything more, Fry had already decided that he believed him.

But T.C. did say more.

"I know you cops. We didn't get a licence because of you cops, I think. I know. You probably thought we'd never open then. That was the idea, wasn't it? But we did. And you've been on our ass ever since, comin' in, hassling the groups, hassling the customers, hassling me, lookin' for dope, an under-the-table bottle, a weapon, hopin' to find something. But you haven't. 'Cause there's nothin' to find. This is a clean place. We don't allow fuck-ups in here. Not up here—" A sweep of his arms took in the stage. "And not out there." He pointed toward the empty tables. "This-place-is-clean. Course, that won't matter to you cops. You'll keep tryin'. Keep hopin' to get lucky. But, let me tell you, you won't."

"That's quite a speech, Mr. Clarkson. And I hope you're right. You *are* right about one thing for sure. It doesn't matter to me. I really don't give a shit what goes on in here. All I want to know is what went on out there." Fry nodded toward the alleyway. "You said

Lesley Connor might have been trying to obtain drugs. You got any reason to say that?"

"Do I have any reason? I told you what he did away from here, I knew a little about...?

"Yeah."

"Lee Boy was ... he was a ..."

"A fuck-up?"

"Yeah." T.C. stopped in the middle of the stage and faced Fry, his arms crossed in front of him. "Lee Boy was a fuck-up. A beautiful, talented, egotistical, exasperating, naive, irresponsible fuck-up. And I can't think of any other reason for him to be here on a Monday night, when he knew nobody else would be, except ... well, except to try to get a hit."

"You know any of his connections?"

"Nope. Didn't want to. Don't want to know anybody who could do this. Lee Boy was clean when he was in here, I know that. I made sure of that. And that's all I wanted to know."

"I assume you know the names of the other people in his group—what did you call them, the Sunshines?"

"Yep. I did. And I do—Benny and Bonnie and John and Gina—the Sunshines Family. We pay up front here, in cash, by the gig, no deductions, no payroll cheques. There—pretty dumb of me, eh, to confess like that? You'll probably want to bust me for income tax evasion or payroll perversion or something."

"Somebody might. If they heard about it," Fry said, the look in his eyes assuring T.C. that "somebody" would not hear it from him.

"I, ah, I know where they crash. I've got an address. Maybe you want that."

"May-be."

10:05 AM

The air of hostility that greeted Fry in the parlour was even thicker than the stink of excrement that assailed him from the basement. He could get past the odour. He had smelled worse. He was not sure he could get past the resentment. He had experienced worse. He had even come to expect it, to consider it as much a part of the job as the gold-plated shield he was comfortable carrying and the blue-heated-steel Smith & Wesson he was not. But he usually knew what it was about.

He was what it usually was about—his *copness*, the sudden, unwanted intrusion of authority he represented. He made other people's business his business; he made public property of private rage and frustration and despair; he made crime of them.

Maybe this was merely police business as usual. He knew he had done nothing to these people. But somebody—some other cop, he would have guessed—had. And he knew was going to have to deal with it before he could begin to deal with them.

They—the surviving members of the Sunshines Family—had been waiting for him in the condemned mansion at the foot of Mount Royal, the old CPR subdivision once nicknamed "American Hill" because of the number of rich Americans who had lived there. Fry never got a chance to hear the resonant sound of the door chime. He was reaching for the bell when the heavy oak door swung open and an ashen-faced Bonnie Irwin looked at him through unshadowed red eyes and said flatly (it was not a question):

"You the cop talked to T.C."

"I'm the cop talked to T.C."

Fry opened the black leather wallet with his detective

shield inside. Bonnie Irwin glanced at it with cold indifference. "I suppose you want to come in," he said.

"I suppose."

She did not ask him in, but turned and walked back into the house, leaving the door open, leaving him standing outside. Fry followed her through the wainscotted entry into the parlour, where the other Sunshines—Benny Chambers, Gina Stoltz, and John Mackenzie—were sitting stiffly on the derelict sofa. Fry could see that they had all been crying. He had figured that Tom Clarkson would call to tell them what had happened, and to warn them. In a way he was glad. As often as he had done it—and by now it was far too often—he had never gotten used to being a messenger of death. But, in another way, he knew it would make his job even more difficult. They had had time to get over some of their shock and to get on with some of their grieving. But they had also had time to get ready for him.

The house was cold. Fry, who could see the signs of its rotting elegance as well as smell them, wondered if there was any heat. He could tell no rich Americans lived here now. He wondered how these young people had come to live here now. He wondered how they lived *here*. He did not ask. That *was* none of his business.

The parlour seemed to become several degrees colder when he entered it. As he approached them, the three young people on the sofa eyed him warily, pressing themselves against the tufted back like animals retreating to a corner of a cage. Bonnie Irwin stationed herself at the back of the sofa, hovering over the rest of them protectively.

The room was semi-dark. The only light came from the wide, bed-sheet-curtained window behind the sofa and through the arched doorway to the window-walled sunroom on the side of the house that did not receive the sun until the afternoon.

Fry stood in the centre of the room. No one invited him to sit. He formally introduced himself. They stared at him in silence. He said he assumed they knew what had happened and why he was there. He thought he saw a slight nod of the head of the youngest looking, the slim girl with severely chopped hair, tear-stained cheeks, and heavily made-up big doe eyes sitting huddled next to the young man, the boy, on the sofa. Fry asked for her name. She looked at him as if the question were a trick, or a trap. She looked to her left, into the eyes of the boy holding her close, then to her right, toward the scruffy, youngish man in the Calgary Stoopede T-shirt, and finally behind her, searching the face of Bonnie Irwin, who nodded. The girl returned her wide-eyed gaze to Fry.

"G-Gina," she said, "Gina Stoltz."

Fry managed to get the rest of their names, their real names, into his notebook. He was not managing to get much else, although he had learned their ages. "It's just for the record," he assured them, "pro forma—cops are great ones for filling out forms." He had also found out where they worked, when they worked, those who did work. "I know—you're musicians. But I need your day jobs—the ones that pay the rent. Just in case we need to contact you. You know, the forms."

About their lifestyle, about their lives with Lesley Connor, about Lesley Connor's life, Fry had learned almost nothing.

They were tough, these young people. But they were tough in a way Fry had never seen. They were not his usual street toughs, pumped up with false bravado, filled with the promise of violence, occupying the thin edge between hopelessness and rage, as likely to tumble into the one as into the other. These youngsters were different. They were ... gentle. Yet the gentleness that others—Fry included until a few moments ago—might see as weakness, Fry could see now was anything but. Maybe, it occurred to him, it *had* to be anything but. Maybe they had to be tough to live on their edge, to be different, to be so dangerously free. Maybe their gentleness required toughness; maybe their gentleness *was* their toughness. Maybe. But at the moment their toughness irritated Fry as much as their gentleness interested him.

Finally, resorting to his best (which was not very good) calculatedly man-to-man tone of voice, he said to Benny Chambers, whom he took to be the oldest, "Look, son, this isn't getting us—"

"You're not my fuckin' father—and I'm not your fuckin' son."

"That's right," Fry said, instantly dropping the act, "I'm not. I apologize for the familiarity, *Mr.* Chambers. But, believe it or not, I'm not your enemy either, and I could use your help."

"Oh, wow! That's really a good one," Bonnie Irwin said in a quavering, half-laughing voice. "You ought'a be on stage. Maybe you could open for us—you know, the comical cop!"

"I'm sorry, but I don't see ... what *is* your problem?" Fry asked, genuinely taken aback, puzzled. He made a quick intense study of her, trying to figure the reason for her outburst, sensing that she was on the verge of hysteria, not wanting to push her the rest of the way.

"Sorry. Right. Not the enemy. Right. As if you give a shit. As if any of you ever give a shit. And you want us to help you. That's really funny. Remember the old bumper sticker, in the sixties? 'Next time you're in trouble, don't call a cop, call a hippie.' God, now the cops are calling us!" Her eyes refilled with tears. Her voice grew even more unsteady. "Shit, you don't want to do *that.* You really wanna bust me, right? Here, don't you want to bust me? Well?"

She lunged forward from behind the sofa, thrusting her right arm at him, her breasts heaving.

"Bust you? Bust you for what, ma'am?" Fry asked evenly, calmly.

"Why this, of course, asshole, this," she said, shaking a metal-studded bracelet at him, "this dangerous weapon. Aren't you going to at least confiscate it or something?"

"Why would I?"

"Why?! How the fuck do I know why you cops do anything. It's what you always do. Every time you see one, you take it. They're dangerous weapons, that's what you say. Dangerous—just like us. It's our fault...."

"Your fault?"

"Yeah. Ours. Just for being, according to you pi—you cops. Just for being. Like when John here got his nose broken by a bunch of red-neck creeps. You didn't blame them. Fuck! You didn't even look for them. You asked *us* why we were dressed so weird, like we brought it on ourselves, like it was our fault, like *we* did it. And now you're sorry. And now you're not our enemy. And now *you* want *our* help."

"And now," Fry broke in, sensing that both she and the situation were about to get completely out of hand, taking the chance that he could talk himself into control, "and now I've gotta tell you that this is the second time today I've felt like I've walked into a strange play in the middle of the third act. I don't know what you're talking about. I don't know what kind of dealings you've had with the police. Obviously not good ones. I don't know what kind of hassles you've had with the police. Obviously a few. I know *I* haven't dealt with you, though. And I know for sure *I* haven't hassled you—"

"Oh, yeah, right," Benny Chambers interrupted from the sofa, reaching back, holding Bonnie Irwin's hand over his shoulder, "as if it makes any fuckin' difference what cop you deal with."

"It makes a *fuckin'* difference, Mr. Chambers. It makes a difference. Now look, please let me finish. Somebody did a worse-than-horrible thing to your friend, and maybe not only to *your* friend. That somebody's still out there. I want to find him before he finds somebody else's friend. Now, maybe you can't help me. But maybe you can. So straighten up. Spare me the shit about bracelets and brutality. I don't have time. I've got time for one thing: some straight answers, that's all. So give me some. Can you do that? Hmmm?"

They could. They did.

They conducted a quick, glancing consultation and seemed to decide, as one, without speaking, to co-operate with him. Their antagonism toward him faded—in its place, not acceptance, certainly not trust, but a kind of stoic acquiescence to his authority, to the unavoidability of his presence, to the inescapable reality that had intruded on their lives.

They did not tell Fry everything they knew about Lesley Connor, but they told him everything they thought he needed to know.

They did not tell him that Lesley Connor was an illegal immigrant. They did not tell him that Lesley Connor's father was a three-star general in the American air force. They did not tell him that Lesley Connor's beautiful, black-haired mother died when he was ten years old, nor that he was reared afterward in a succession of military schools, until he left—"went AWOL forever," as he said—and decided to raise himself "to raise a little hellion." They did not tell him that some nights, late, they could hear Lesley Connor in his sparsely furnished bedroom at the top of the stairs, softly weeping.

They did tell him about Lesley Connor's talent and ambition. They did tell him about Lesley Connor's temper. They did tell him how Lesley Connor stormed out of the house late on the afternoon of the day he died, furious that they had let him sleep through the interview that he was sure would have been his "big break," his chance to be a star, to impress and infuriate his three-star father. They did tell him about Lesley Connor's weakness for drugs. They did tell him the names, mostly first names only, of all the dealers they knew who had sold drugs to Lesley Connor.

They showed him Lesley Connor's room, the dented, paint-chipped window ledge where he practised his drumming, the paint-spattered, wooden electrical spool where he worked on his art.

They gave him Lesley Connor's photograph, his glossy, Lee Boy's last "pretty picture."

Fry got from them the most, the best, he could. He knew it. He knew it was not everything. But he knew that most of what he needed to know that they did not tell him he could find out on his own. As he left them standing together in the rumpled bedroom and walked down the stairs past the fist holes Lesley Connor had punched in the wall and the silly cartoons and graffiti Lesley Connor had painted on the wall, Fry hoped it all would be enough.

Fry liked this "family" of tough and gentle, determinedly different young people. And he hoped they would never have to see him again. Not that it would matter now. He knew that, having seen him just this once, they would never again be so free.

1:20 PM

Fry hated the office. It was a cell with tinted-glass bars that he found as confining as criminals-in-process found the police lockup downstairs or the prisoner "dormitories" in the remand centre next door. The office was politics, petty, personal, and, to Fry, pointless. The office was a game played on an organizational chart, with pieces moving or, more accurately, being moved, up, down, sideways, sometimes nowhere at all. The game seemed to have no end. It seemed to Fry to have no good purpose. He was one of the pieces. And he resented it. He took himself off the board, out of the office, whenever he could.

He hated games. He could not play games. He had never been able to play games.

As a boy, he did not play sports. He was competitive enough, strong and quick enough. But he did not play. He did not, could not, join in. Perhaps it was all the moving. His family had never lived anywhere long enough for him to feel comfortable enough, to feel that he belonged enough to join a team. While the other boys were skating and swinging sticks on the hose-filled rink behind the Legion or in somebody's backyard, he was tramping the snow alone with his twenty-two, hunting for rabbits or birds. When the boys were batting the ball around on the Lions' Club diamond at the edge of the city or in a corner of some farmer's field, he was trying to catch frogs at the creek or seeing how close he could sneak up to a deer before it would sense him and run.

He could not play games now either, not the kind they played at the office, for power, not the kind people played at home, for fun. He did not play charades. He did not play checkers. He did not play bridge. He did have a quirky, games-playing kind of intelligence. But he did not have the patience. He could not see the point.

So while others, as the country song said, played the games people play, Fry went off on his own, doing for a living now what he had done for a lark as a boy—stalking game: following it, sneaking up on it, trying to outsmart it, seeing how close he could come to it before it would sense him and run, sometimes catching it.

The game was larger now, less predictable, potentially far more violent. And even when Fry did catch his prey, sometimes after a long and frustrating search, sometimes somebody else would quickly let it go.

He had learned, over time, not to worry about that, not to think much about the results of his work. He could see no more point in that than in keeping score, keeping a tally, worrying about who lost and won. It was his work and he was good at it and that was enough. Sometimes he hated his job, but he had always loved his work. He could see the point of it. He was made for it.

He was as good with his head as he was with his hands. He was not an intellectual, not a spinner of theories. He had high school, but no university. He was largely self-educated, with the autodidact's conscientious stubbornness—a good quality in a police officer. He also had a moralist's stubborn conscience, another good quality in a police officer. And he was gifted with a kind of simplicity, an ability to see things clearly, to distinguish between shadings, to discern a pattern, to *notice.*

He could have been a cop anywhere. He would have been a cop anywhere.

He could have followed his father into the RCMP. But he had truly hated the moving, the uprootedness of Mountie family life. He had wanted to be somewhere, to stay somewhere, to belong somewhere. He loved the expansiveness of the prairies, the jagged solidity of the mountains, the vastness of the western sky. He had assumed that this small-city police force would be less political, less bureaucratic than the federal police. He had been mistaken about that. The Calgary force was simply smaller, its politics meaner if anything, its bureaucracy even more frustrating. But he had stayed. He had given up on belonging, even stopped thinking about it. He could not see the point.

He could not see the point of listening any longer to Inspector Phil Grantham either, and was on the verge of making his already tenuous political situation even worse by telling him so when the telephone ringing on his desk stopped him short.

"Saved by the bell," he muttered to himself.

"What? What bell?" Grantham asked, still leaning against Fry's desk with his left arm, his right hand brandishing a newspaper like a club. His crisp white shirt sleeves were rolled precisely halfway up his forearms, his striped silk tie carefully loosened at his stiff, unbuttoned shirt collar.

"Oh, nothing, nothing," Fry said. "Just a cliché." He picked up the phone. "Yeah, Fry."

"You said you wanted any call about the woman.... You know, about the body they found," the switchboard operator said.

"Yeah."

"I think you better take this one."

Fry wondered why when he laid down the receiver about a minute and a half later. He did not think it likely that the small, pathetic voice he had strained to hear at the other end of the line could know anything about the woman in the window. But the voice had been insistent. Fry had nothing else to go on, and he had long since learned never to dismiss the unlikely. Besides, he thought, glancing up at Grantham, who was still leaning over his desk and looking expectantly down at him, it was a chance to get out of the office.

"A break?" Grantham asked, hopefully.

"Could be," Fry said, making it sound more promising than he thought it was.

"Well, we hope so," Grantham said, standing erect, slapping the edge of the desk with the rolled-up newspaper. "Better get on it."

Fry said nothing.

Grantham had been giving him a chance to say nothing for the past quarter of an hour or so, badgering him like a suspect from whom he wanted—no, desperately needed—a confession, yet leaving him no opening to open his mouth, even if he had wanted to. That *would* be Grantham's method of interrogation, Fry thought.

The press had the story. Grantham had the story, in the newspaper clenched in his hand, the early edition of the afternoon *Bulletin*. The headlines—black capital letters at least two inches high—told, or rather, shrieked the story: SCALP MURDERS! Fry had not actually seen the headlines for himself. Grantham had read, or rather, shrieked them at him:

"'Scalp murders!'! Jesus Christ! What kind of bullshit

reporting is this? We'll freeze that fat fucker Hoffberg out so cold he won't get confirmation of the time of day. And when we get through with the assholes that let this out they'll think meter-maiding would be a promotion—and one they couldn't get! Damned fuck-ups!"

Fry had to agree with Grantham.

Apparently a couple of the uniforms who had been at NOIDS that morning had stopped on the way back to the station for coffee at a doughnut shop that was a well-known hangout for off- and, if you believed the papers, on-duty cops. They were in the washroom standing side-by-side at the urinals relieving themselves, unburdening themselves of the horror they had just seen, assuming they were alone, never dreaming that anyone could overhear their conversation.

They were wrong.

Hoffberg, the *Bulletin*'s fat, boorish police reporter, had been sitting in a stall, just about to flush, when he heard them. He waited, silently listening, furiously scribbling in the notebook he had quickly, quietly spread open on his bare white thighs, peeking through the crack in the door to see who the officers were.

They had barely sat down at a booth outside and taken a sip of coffee and a bite of cruller when he waddled over to them and asked them to confirm what he had just overheard. They refused. One of them, Stanton, choked on his doughnut and almost threw up. The other, Wilson, cursed, then started to threaten Hoffberg, then thought better of it when he saw that it only made the reporter smile. They asked him not to print the story, as much because of the trouble they feared it would cause the city as because of the trouble they knew it would cause them. Hoffberg refused, mumbling something about the public's right to know, and ran to phone in his scoop, hoping, as he impatiently waited for somebody in the newsroom to pick up the phone, that he was in time to make the early edition.

He had made it. And he had made Fry's job even more difficult. The story getting out now was potentially a disaster. Fry had to agree with Grantham. And Fry hated to agree with Grantham.

As he sat seething, listening to Grantham's repetitive tirade, he was not sure what made him angrier: the stupidity of the two young, and maybe never-to-be-veteran officers, the slavering irresponsibility of the reporter, or simply finding himself onside with the insufferable inspector. Or perhaps it was the killings and not knowing the killer—not knowing the woman he had found shattered in the shattered window, not knowing the link between the beautiful woman he did not know and the beautiful boy he had found in the dumpster, knowing there was a link, knowing he had to find it, knowing he had to find it before there were other (other beautiful?) victims, knowing it would be harder now.

No matter.

The anger was there now. Over the years, by dint of constant, conscious effort and, ultimately, some professional help, Fry had managed to raise his once dangerously low boiling point. He was a violent man who had learned control. But control was no cure. Just as an alcoholic is simply a drunk who is not drinking, Fry was a violent man who was not giving in to his violence. He would always be a violent man. He had felt the old rage returning, had felt a sudden powerful need to move, an almost irresistible urge to lunge across the desk at Grantham, snatch the newspaper from his hand, and beat him with it—grab his expensive silk tie, and strangle him with it.

But then the telephone had rung.

Even as he was on his way to follow up the call, Fry did not regard it so much as a live lead as an excuse to leave. He needed an excuse. He needed to leave, to get away—from the office, from Grantham, from himself. He could not sit. He could not wait. He did not have the patience. He did not know why. Usually he had infinite patience as an investigator. As an investigator he could usually sit and wait, and wait, and wait.

Not this time.

Something told him that he did not have time. He felt as if the investigation were in another's hands, and that he had to conduct it at the other's pace, which was fast, too fast—out of control.

1:45 PM

The Riverhill Centre was aptly named. The multi-level concrete and masonry structure stood on a slope in northwest Calgary. The windows on the east overlooked the Bow River as it wound through its cottonwooded valley toward the stark towers of the city centre. The windows on the west looked out on the foothills as they began their ascent toward the mountains ranged across the distant horizon like a broken saw blade. Natural light poured through the high, vaulted glass ceiling and flooded the central courtyard, glinting off the reflecting pool. Low murmuring tabletalk, the polite tinkling of dishware, and occasional quiet laughter came from the tearoom beside the pool. In a corner almost hidden behind thick plantings, a television screen was glowing, the volume turned down. Music was being piped in from somewhere—not Muzak, but Mozart.

The Riverhill Centre hardly looked like what it was: a place to die.

The sprawling palliative care facility made Fry think of the tiny northern Saskatchewan hospital where he had watched his father die, even though it looked nothing like it, smelled nothing like it, sounded nothing like it, felt nothing like it.

Riverhill nurses wore no crisp clinical whites, only soft pastels—pinks, greens, and blues. The smell of disinfectant did not hang in the conditioned air like exhaust fumes over the city on summer days when the winds did not come. The big room did not echo with the sound of rattling pipes, rattling carts, rattling coughs.

What gave the place away was not the place, but the people who were the reason for the place. Shuffling, or wheeling, being wheeled about, they had the pallor, the look of frailty and failing of those waiting for an end that now was almost visible. It was the same pallid expression Fry had seen on his father's face in that small room in that small hospital in that small prairie town.

He had sat by the bed listening to his father's shallow, ragged breathing and looking into his once hard, blue, now hardly seeing, eyes all that morning and through the afternoon. He was still looking into those eyes when, at five o'clock, the breathing finally stopped. Fry remembered the doctor's hand, firm and comforting on his shoulder. He remembered reaching across the bed with his hand and closing his father's eyes, lingering for just a moment on his rough white-stubbled cheek. He remembered emerging from the room into the corridor, which, freshly mopped, glistened under weak fluorescent lights.

Standing today in the entryway of the Riverhill Centre, new tile floor gleaming in the strong light from the overhead glass, Fry remembered.

It's the same, he thought.

And he wondered what somebody living in this place for the dying could possibly know about the life of the woman he knew only dead.

At a sleek, light-oak reception desk stationed strategically, yet with seeming informality, in the centre of a clump of plants near the entrance to the central courtyard, Fry presented his gold shield to the duty nurse, whose own shield, with black capital letters engraved on a white plastic rectangle—D. SMITH-VAUGHAN, RN—was pinned over her left breast on a soft white sweater she wore over a pink uniform. She was probably younger than her world-weary expression and the tiny lines around her eyes made her seem. She studied Fry's identification, then Fry himself. He could see that she was not particularly impressed, and certainly not intimidated, by either. She called over her shoulder to a nurse in robin's egg blue standing at a coffee pot on a stand behind the desk.

"Cover for me, will ya, Deb. Back in a sec."

D. Smith-Vaughan, RN, swivelled out of her chair and came round to the front of the desk. "This way, please. Mr. Waldo's expecting you," she said to Fry as she brushed past him.

She looked back at Fry as if she had a question to ask. But then she turned her eyes straight ahead and did not ask. She walked across the courtyard to an elevator hidden behind two beams thick with climbing foliage. Fry followed.

Inside the elevator, he was surprised to see that the building had eight levels. He would not have believed it was so large. *The hillside. That's how they did it*, he thought to himself. D. Smith-Vaughan, RN punched six. The elevator door closed with a solid thunk. The machine whisked them almost silently to the sixth level, where Fry followed the nurse again, down a wide, soothingly lit corridor, listening to the slip-slip-slip of her panty hose and the soft rustling of her skirt as they walked. He noticed that she was wearing white sneakers instead of standard-issue nurse's shoes.

She stopped at an oak doorway about halfway down the hall, knocked once softly, and opened it.

"Mr. Waldo," she said. "Detective ..." Fry was about to help her with his name when she shot him a glance that told him he need not bother. "Fry is here to see you."

"Thanks, Nurse Smith-Vaughan," Fry said.

"Certainly," she replied, showing him into the room, showing herself out, quietly closing the door after her.

The room was spacious, with a double bed and a bedside table, a four-drawer dresser and, in the far corner, a comfortable-looking padded armchair. It might have been as brightly, soothingly painted as the rest of the Riverhill Centre. Fry could not tell. The room was dim, the only light coming through a rectangle of window on the side opposite the door. Sheer curtains were drawn in folds across the glass. The room had the grey, indistinct, washed-out look of early morning even though it was mid-afternoon and the spring sun was slanting on this side of the building.

Fry could not help thinking again of his father's small, dingy hospital room. He had to force himself to step farther inside.

"Mr. Waldo?" he called to the figure sitting with his back to the door in a wheelchair at the window.

He seemed not to hear. His left hand was holding back a corner of curtain and he was staring intently through that small opening in the gloom. Then his hand dropped. The curtain closed. Fry heard the whir of a small motor. The chair spun slowly toward him. The left hand reached toward the bedside table and switched on a lamp with a parchment-like shade.

Soft white light bathed the corner of the room, accentuating the pallor of the man's parchment-like skin, deepening his sunken cheeks and hollow eyes. Fry moved toward him and was about to extend his right hand when he saw the useless right claw of a hand positioned on the arm of the wheelchair. The man nodded pathetically, knowingly, at Fry, and then, struggling to hold his head erect, motioned Fry into the armchair with his still-good left hand.

"Detective Fry," he said, haltingly, carefully, as if he had to fight himself to speak. "I'm sure you are busy. Thank you for coming."

"Mr. Waldo. I won't say it's a pleasure, considering. Thanks for calling."

"Yes … considering …" Again he jerked his drooping head, slurping back into his mouth the drool that had started to drip down at the corner. "Sorry—I apologize for my condition."

"There's no need to."

"It's that ballplayer's fault."

"Ballplayer?"

"Yes. The Yankee. From the twenties and thirties. The famous slugger that played with Babe Ruth."

"Lou Gehrig?"

"Why, yes. Are you a sports fan?" Fry did not answer. He did not know how he knew the name. "Anyway, yes, he's the culprit. Lou Gehrig. I've got his sickness."

"Lou Gehrig's disease."

"Yes. Amyotrophic lateral sclerosis, in the medical textbooks. But I'd rather blame old Lou. Or not-so-old Lou. He wasn't forty when he died—when it killed him. Some 'Iron Horse.'"

"I'm sorry."

"Yes— of course—though not nearly so sorry as I am." He forced a hoarse laugh. "How old are you, Detective Fry?"

"How old? Well, forty-four—forty-five later this year."

The man laughed softly, as if he had just heard the punch line to a good, wry joke. Fry did not understand, until the man, his mouth half-open in a kind of cadaverous smile, said:

"That's territory I'm not likely to explore. I'm just barely forty-three."

Fry knew he was failing to keep the shocked surprise out of his eyes. He would have said the man was twenty, maybe thirty, years older. He felt embarrassed, then ashamed. The man absolved him with a gentle wave of his left hand, which was followed by another violent shake of his head.

"I know," he said. "I know. I know."

He reached falteringly for the bedside table with his good hand, picked up a newspaper and, with some effort, tossed it onto the foot of the bed. The paper was folded to Alf Mathews' sketch of the woman in the window.

"I think ..." the man said, again struggling for coherence, "I think she's my wife."

"Your wife," Fry said, although he knew he made it sound more like a question.

"Yes."

Once more, with more difficulty, the man reached over to the table with his left hand. The sheer physical effort showed on his face. He picked up a colour snapshot in an acrylic frame: two cross-country skiers, a man and a woman with flushed, healthy, smiling faces and bright, fashionable ski outfits, leaning on their poles under a brilliant winter-blue sky. He held the photograph out to Fry, who leaned forward in the chair to accept it.

"This is," the man said, "this *was* us. A little over three years ago." He saw the surprise Fry was unable to suppress. "Yes—it acts quickly, Lou's disease—in some ways."

The woman in the man's photograph could have been the woman in Fry's photograph, the woman in Alf Mathews' drawing, the woman in the window. Fry could not be sure. He wondered how the man could be sure. He asked him.

"I ... I thought something was wrong when she didn't come," he said.

"Didn't come?"

"Yes—to visit. She comes, came, every day—except the weekend, of course. We had an understanding about the weekend. I insisted on it."

"Insisted on what?"

"That she not come, weekends. That she go out. That she live, a little. That she have a life. I didn't want to know about it—just wanted her to have it. We had a life—money, good jobs, a home, even a ski chalet in Canmore, health. We were waiting to have children. Figured we had lots of time. I wanted her to have some life."

"And you say she didn't come."

"No, she didn't. Not yesterday. Not today. And she never missed. Not once. Never. She didn't call. I knew something was wrong. Then I saw the sketch in the newspaper. A good likeness—not perfect. Over-made-up, I'd say. But it could be—I think it's Jane."

Fry placed the snapshot on the foot of the bed beside the folded newspaper. He reached into his inside coat pocket for a copy of the coroner's photograph. He leaned forward and handed it to the man, who studied it briefly, then returned it, nodding his head, unable to speak. Fry would have sworn he could see life leave him.

1:50 PM

Constable Ken Oliver of the Calgary Police Service morality squad had been in and out of the sleazy taverns and up and down the dingy hotel stairs of half the east end's twelve-square-block prostitute row with Alf Mathews' sketch of the woman in the window. And all he had for his trouble were sore feet, an earful of slurred abuse from sleeping-in hookers and a notebookful of "never saw her before." If she had been a working girl, either none of the other girls knew about it, which, knowing them, he could not believe, or they were lying to him about it, which, knowing what had happened to her, he could not understand. For all he had been able to learn in more than a half-day of walking the streets looking for street walkers, she might just as well have been a space walker—a hooker from Mars.

Or maybe from Edmonton, Oliver thought as he pushed through the old-fashioned but still smoothly swinging, brass and glass revolving door of the Warwickshire, another east-end hotel with an elegant past and shabby present. If the revolving door had not already been in place, they would have had to install one to accommodate the clientele the hotel attracted these days.

Oliver kicked himself for not thinking of the Edmonton angle before. Police in the capital were fed up with the frustrations of trying to deal with prostitution. Of course, police in Calgary were fed up too. Oliver had heard Jack Roberts, the staff-sergeant who ran morality, complain about it so often that he knew the lament almost by heart:

"Thanks to the fuckin' judges, we can't bust their sour-smelling little asses for soliciting unless they actually grab an unwilling customer—preferably a seminary student—by the nuts. *And* squeeze—grabbing alone wouldn't be sufficient grounds. Hell, we can't even nail 'em for loitering unless they actually park themselves bare-bottoms-up on a park bench; and considering how fast they can shake their tits and grind their hips, we probably couldn't even make that charge stick. And all the good people want us to clean out the hookers. Chriiist! Tell it to the fuckin' judges."

Edmonton police had decided that if they could not hassle the hookers, they could hassle their customers (not, of course, for *being* customers; the courts made that next to impossible too). They simply waited until a streetwalker climbed into the car of a drive-by trick and then stopped the car for a vehicle spot check. If they found an infraction—and they *always* found an infraction—they charged the driver. Now business was drying up in Edmonton. And the hookers were heading south.

Maybe she had been one of them, Oliver thought. Maybe she had not been on the street here long enough to be noticed. Or maybe she had been noticed, and what had happened to her had been a signal to other interlopers from the north.

Oliver stopped on a soiled, unevenly scissored piece

of beige carpet just inside the door on the unpolished black and white marble-tiled floor. He took out his notebook and jotted down his theory, making a mental note to pursue it. He wanted a transfer to homicide, figuring it was the quickest route to a detective's gold shield and then, well, who could tell? He had hoped that working on this case would do it. After today's dry hole, he had almost given up.

Until now.

His little black notebook still in his right hand and a ballpoint pen in his left, Oliver continued across the marble to the ornately carved walnut reception desk. A paunchy man in an open-necked grey silk shirt and black slacks lounged behind the desk in an oak swivel chair while watching a small wall-mounted black-and-white television, the heels of his fancy, two-tone-grey cowboy boots propped on the edge of the counter.

Oliver stood tapping the edge of his notebook on the counter for several moments, failing to get the man's attention. He reached over and smacked the top of a tiny brass bell bolted to the counter top. The small bell had a loud ring. The chime had almost stopped reverberating when the man shifted his gaze from the afternoon *Adam-12* rerun on the small screen to the real uniform on the big man looking down at him.

"Officer Kenny," he said. "What can I do you for today? A little afternoon delight?"

"In here, Bryce? Don't think so. 'Fraid I'd have to get deloused afterwards."

"Don't know what you're missin'."

"I've seen what you've got. I'm not missin' much. Don't imagine you miss much, either."

"Meaning?"

Oliver pulled a copy of Alf Mathews' sketch from his uniform jacket pocket. He put it on the counter, turned it to face Bryce and slid it toward him.

"Know her?" he asked.

Bryce stretched his arms and yawned widely, showing a mouth full of fillings. Without getting out of the chair, he reached over to the counter and picked up the sketch. He looked at it for a few seconds, and put it back on the counter.

"Nope," he said.

"Ever seen her?"

"Nope."

"You're as helpful as ever."

"Well, I always try to support my neighbourhood policeman. Who is she, anyway?"

"Who *was* she, you mean. What, you don't read the paper, watch the news?"

"Not much. You know, too much crime and violence."

"You know, I could station myself at the foot of the stairs there. Ask everybody who comes down if they knew her. Get their names, addresses, home phone numbers, tell them to expect to be called in as potential witnesses. What'd that do to your business, you think?"

"Look, Oliver. You asked. I answered. I don't know her. I never seen her. Maybe she's new."

"Was."

"All right, was. But whatever she was, she wasn't here."

"Well, keep the picture anyway. Maybe ask your ladies if they knew her. You never know, they might."

"Come on, I told you I don't know her. They don't know her. They got—I got other things to do than—"

"Oh, well, don't bother then. I'll do it. Now. I'll just head on upstairs...."

Bryce was weighing whether Oliver was serious, which would have dictated one kind of response, or whether he was bluffing, which would have permitted another, when their shadow boxing was ended by a sudden scream and a string of curses from upstairs.

"Ow! You bastard, you cut me! You red motherfucking asshole, I'm bleeding! You stay the fuck away! Away! Stay away! Bryce! *Bryce!* He hurt me! Goddamn you! Ouch! Jesusouch! You bastard!"

Bryce dropped his boots from the counter, spun out of his chair, ran round the front of the desk and headed for the stairs. "What the Christ...!?"

Oliver was ahead of him, already halfway up the stairs, his right hand on the walnut grip of his service revolver. He followed the woman's screams, which continued in a foul, uninterrupted torrent:

"Bryce! Goddamn you, you son-of-a-bitch! You red stinking mother...! *Bryce!* He hurt me! He hurt me!"

Oliver ran down a narrow corridor with worn, faded, floral-patterned carpet and dim art-deco wall-lights until he came to the door he thought was the right one. He pounded hard on it, once, shouted, "Police!" and kicked it open. Inside he saw the bare hairy buttocks of a fat man bent over and fumbling frantically with his pants and, sitting upright in the bed, a wide-eyed, almost-breastless girl who, in an almost comical show of modesty, pulled the sheets over her small chest when she saw Oliver.

Oliver ran out of the room to the next door down the hall, pounded, shouted, and kicked, drawing his weapon, flinging himself inside, half-crouching at the doorway, clear blue eyes rapidly surveying the room, the blued-steel revolver at the end of his extended arms swivelling threateningly as if it were on a turret.

They were across the room. A big bed, with the bedclothes stripped to its soiled mattress cover and scattered as if by a frenzy of love making, stood between them and the door. From the doorway, Oliver could see it was not love they had been making.

The still-screaming woman had backed into the far corner of the room near the head of the bed, stomping her feet like a petulant child. She was nude. Her pendulous breasts jiggled to her frightened dance. Blood streamed down the side of her thin face from her bottle-blonde hair and trickled from cuts on her arms and hands, which held a shredded pillow, the stuffing oozing out from it like entrails, in front of her like a shield.

The Indian man—a boy, really, not yet out of his teens—stood at the foot of the bed, fully dressed in a T-shirt, embroidered jean jacket, and tight, faded jeans. He was five-seven or five-eight, maybe a hundred-fifty pounds, with sleek black hair, and a child's smooth-skinned face, except for a long scar on his right cheek. In his right hand was a short, shiny, double-edged knife, which he held low, swinging it in a small arc in front of him with the practiced efficiency of someone who knew how to use it—who *had* used it.

Seeing Oliver, the woman stopped stomping, stopped screaming, and, still holding her pitiful pillow shield in front of her, started to whimper.

The man/boy did not move. He did not stop moving the knife.

"Put it down!" Oliver thought he said. He could not tell that he was shouting. "Drop the knife! Drop it, asshole! Drop the fucking knife!" His revolver was no longer on a swivel, but was trained on a spot about halfway between the Native's Adam's apple and his belly button. "Now, motherfucker! You hear me? Now!"

The youth did not respond, but simply stared at Oliver, wide-eyed and wild like an animal backed into a corner. Like a cornered, frightened animal, he seemed to draw into himself, to make himself smaller. Oliver could not tell whether he was cowering in submission, or poising to strike. Oliver kept talking to him, or rather, kept shouting at him.

"Come on, young man, put it down! You got nowhere to go except through me. And you ain't going through me. So don't be an—"

The Indian sprang forward, leaping onto the bed, lunging with his knife toward the door and Constable Ken Oliver. To Oliver it all seemed to happen in slow motion. He saw it all so clearly, heard it all so clearly.

He saw the Native make his move. He heard himself shout, "No. *Freeze!* Don't!" He saw the scuffed tan cowboy/work boot land on the bed. He saw the knife coming toward him. He heard an explosion.

No.

Three explosions. One after another.

Did he fire? Did he mean to? Was it instinct? An accident?

He saw the Indian snap back as if he had run into an invisible clothesline, saw him fall back onto the bed, one leg bent back under him, the other extended straight out in front of him, saw his empty left hand fly helplessly over his head. He saw the knife hand fall onto the bed, the blade stabbing the other pillow. He saw the smoke rising from the end of his own hands. He saw the thick, dark fluid bubbling from the young man's chest like oil from a shallow well. He saw the body twitching, the glazed-over eyes not seeing. He heard a siren in the distance, and a radio playing down the hall. He heard his own heart beating, his own hoarse breathing. He saw Bryce, almost brotherly, going to the nude, bleeding girl and wrapping her, weeping, in a blanket, wrapping his arms around her. He heard voices in the doorway behind him, women's voices:

"Oh, my God, he shot him!"

"Is he dead?"

"Where's Sheila? It's not Sheila, is it...? Oh, thank God."

"Omigod, look at her!"

"Wasn't it an Indian guy nearly ripped Joan last week, remember?"

"Yeah ... think so."

"Jesus! The blood ..."

3:30 PM

Jane Waldo had lived within an easy stroll of the Stampede Corral in one of those four-storey stucco walkup apartments with frilly, old-fashioned little-girl names—the Priscilla, the Souellen, the Charlotte, the Adelaide. Hers was the Maryanne. The colour of the stucco was rose. Except for a corner of her closet, one drawer of her dressing table, and a photograph on her bedroom mirror, the colour of the building where she had lived appeared to have been the only colour in her life.

Fry had learned from her husband that she had worked not far from her apartment, as a bookkeeper for a small oil-drilling equipment company in a three-floor sandstone building across from the CPR tracks, near the VIA Rail terminal, just beyond the shadows of the oil-patch towers.

He had learned from her employer that, because she worked Saturday mornings, she had Mondays off. When she did not report for work Tuesday morning, he was at first mildly surprised because she never missed a day, never called in sick, even ate lunch at her desk. And then he was concerned, though not as much for her as for her husband. He knew about the illness and feared that the inevitable had finally happened.

It had never occurred to him that what had happened had happened to her. And even if he had seen the police artist's sketch in the papers or on television, he said, he would not have recognized it as Jane Waldo. It looked nothing like the Jane Waldo he knew.

Alf Mathews' "tarted-up" drawing looked nothing like the Jane Waldo the Maryanne's superintendent knew either. Standing in a bathrobe, fuzzy slippers, and tight curlers at the locked, plate-glass security door, she had at first refused to believe that Jane Waldo *was* the woman in the drawing Fry pressed against the pane. Only after he took out his shield and identification and held them against the glass for her inspection did she even believe that he was who he said he was. She let him in, reluctantly. But she had not been about to let him into Jane Waldo's apartment.

"I run a quiet, respectable building here," she said. "Never any need for police here. Surely not for Mrs. Waldo. One of my best tenants. Courteous, always says hello, never makes a peep. Pays her rent a day early. I just can't let you go traipsing around her apartment, rooting through her things. Why, when she gets back, she'll—"

"She won't be coming back, ma'am," Fry said quietly, but coldly, matter-of-factly, producing the police photograph of the scrubbed-clean face of the corpse, producing on the super's face a look of genuine shock and a different kind of disbelief. "I'm sorry," he said to her.

Meekly, the woman led him up the stairs to the

third floor. Jane Waldo's apartment was at the front of the building. The superintendent's age-spotted hands shook as she fitted her key into the lock. She opened the door, stepped aside, and let Fry in. Then she stood at the doorway, trembling, on the verge of tears, unsure what to do with herself.

Fry gently dismissed her.

"I'll lock the door when I leave, ma'am. Thanks for your trouble. If I need you for anything more, I'll let you know. I am sorry about this."

She looked at him and nodded her head. Then she put her hand to her mouth and fled down the corridor. Fry closed the door.

Jane Waldo's apartment reminded him of the foothills in winter after a light dusting of snow—browns, beiges, and greys against the white backdrop of the empty walls. Jane Waldo had hung no pictures—no family photographs, no shopping-mall prints, no art-gallery paintings, nothing. She had displayed no personal mementoes, no idiosyncratic knickknacks or bric-a-brac. She seemed to have gone out of her way not to mark the place as her own.

Even the furniture was generic, the kind of cheap stuff sold by the room in full-page ads in the Saturday papers or in annoying thirty-second clips on late-night TV—a hard, nubbly-surfaced sofa and matching chair, coffee and lamp tables with laminated "walnut" tops, a "colonial maple" dining table, and four "colonial maple" chairs.

If she bought a newspaper, she did not keep it. She apparently subscribed to no magazines. The superintendent had said Jane Waldo received hardly any mail. She had a few books—paperback bestsellers—but no television set, no stereo, not even a radio.

It was as if she had been living without living, occupying the apartment without taking up any space. Fry thought of the twisted, drooly shell of a man trapped in his washed-out room at Riverhill Centre. He thought of Jane Waldo trapped in her washed-out rooms here at the Maryanne. The disease had crippled them both. They had been living the same slow death. For the second time today, Fry had the feeling of walking into the husk of a life.

Walking into Jane Waldo's bedroom was like walking into a black-and-white photograph.

The walls were white, empty. The steel headboard of the bed was enamelled black. The bed was made with only a sheet and blanket, both white. The three-drawer, semi-antique wooden dresser and dressing table had been hastily hand-painted black to match the bed. The bifold closet doors were the same flat white as the bedroom walls.

The colours stood out; they seemed out of place, seemed not to belong in this picture.

Fry noticed the photograph first, a colour snapshot tucked into a corner of the three-piece dressing-table mirror. It was a print of the same snapshot he had seen earlier in the day, in an acrylic frame in the gloomy room at the Riverhill Centre: two healthy skiers smiling at the camera on a brilliant winter's day.

The few tubes and jars and compacts of the "hardly any" makeup Jane Waldo had worn at work—subtle, delicate, almost non-colours—sat on the dressing table in front of the mirror. The real colour was hidden in the top right-hand drawer. There, Fry found the heavy makeup she had used on weekends: lipsticks in vivid coral, hot pink, and deep blood-red; a rainbow of eye shadows and blush; long, glistening-red fake fingernails.

He discovered her weekend costumes—sleek short skirts, multi-coloured fake-fur wraps, high shiny leather boots—in a far corner of her closet, separate from the no-nonsense dresses and suits and sensible shoes of her drab, workaday world.

Fry wondered where she had gone on her make-believe weekends. Whether they *were* make-believe. Or whether she had become what she pretended to be. He wondered how far she had gone. Whether she had gone too far. Whether someone had caught her in her charade, had demanded that she go farther than she was willing to go. He wondered how her tawdry fantasy—if it *was* a fantasy—had turned so deadly real.

In the morning, he had known her as Jane Doe, an unreal corpse without a name. Now, this afternoon, he knew her as Jane Waldo, a real woman with a real identity. Jane Doe. Jane Waldo. What a difference a single syllable had made, Fry thought as he closed the door on her austere and empty rooms—the difference between knowing nothing about her and knowing everything. But by the time the Maryanne's front glass door had electronically locked itself behind him, Fry was having second thoughts, wondering if it really made any difference at all. It told him everything about her he wanted to know, except the things he most needed to know: Why she had died—and what the beautiful, long-haired woman in the rubble had to do with the beautiful, long-haired boy in the trash.

5:45 PM

The onion in the Bob's Bigger Better Alberta Beefburger that Fry had gulped down for supper while standing up at a counter in a downtown fast-food mall was already beginning to repeat on him when he returned to the office. By the time he got to the third floor, the question was repeating in his brain: "D'ya hear about the shooting?" He had heard about it, in detail, from the first uniform he encountered in the parking lot, and again from the second just inside the rear door, and then again and again.

Calgary was a violent city, and its violence was as mean and personal and coloured with rage as the violence in any North American city. But it was a *north* American city. Its violence seldom ended in death, not for want of a will, but for want of a weapon. Handguns were not easily available here. Knives and fists were the weapons of choice. To kill required either the savage intent or plain bad luck that was usually lacking.

Violent death was simply not yet commonplace in Calgary. Violent death at the hands of a police officer was almost unheard of. When it happened, the shock waves echoed through the small city like thunder in the mountains, reverberating even louder through the corridors of the red brick and glass police headquarters building on Seventh Avenue SE.

When Fry finally had run the gauntlet of bad-news bearers and reached his desk, his stomach was churning and his head pounding with the news and with memory. He almost forgot what he had come looking for, until he saw it on his desk blotter: the typed medical examiner's report on the death of Jane Waldo. He had barely flipped over the manila cover when he heard chuckling voices and looked up to see what he had not come looking for: Sergeant Paul Strahan and Inspector Phil Grantham approaching.

Jesus Christ! he thought. *Aren't the onions punishment enough?*

Strahan had his thumbs hooked under his thick, black

uniform belt and his mouth curled into a malicious smirk. He was swaggering even more obviously than usual. Grantham was still smacking a rolled-up newspaper into the palm of his hand. But he was smiling now.

"I'd've thought you'd have that baby throttled by now, Inspector," Fry said.

"What? Throttled? Oh, this," Grantham replied, looking at the newspaper. "Throttled. That's good. And you damn bet'cha we did." He whacked the paper once more into his palm, then tossed it onto Fry's desk. "Throttled the buggers this time, eh, Strahan, didn't we?"

"You got that right, Inspector. Of course," he said pointedly to Fry, "it took a uniform to get the job done right."

"You gentlemen have me at a disadvantage, I'm afraid. You seem to know what you're talking about. I don't," Fry said, running his steady gaze from Grantham to Strahan and back. While he was saying it, he was thinking: *Games. More goddamned games.* He asked: "It took a uniform to get what done right?"

"Why, don't you know, Ghost? To catch your bad guy, of course," Strahan gloated.

"*My* bad guy?"

"Oh, come on, Ghost, don't play fuckin' games with me. You know what I'm talkin' about."

"And you know I don't play fuckin' games," Fry said coldly, his anger rising.

"Whoa, J.J., settle down," Grantham intervened. "It's the killer, the woman who was scalped. We think we got him. We did get him."

"You got him? Where? How? Who?" Fry did not realize it, but his hands were pressing hard on his desktop and he was more standing than sitting at his chair.

"It was Oliver, Kenny Oliver," Strahan said. "You know, the eager kid in morality who keeps applying for a transfer into homicide?"

"Yeah," Fry said. "I know him. Too eager. I heard about the shooting—" He instantly realized that what he had said could be taken the wrong way, or at least in a way he was not sure he had meant it. "Don't mean he was too eager today. Probably not. Don't know. But what's the connection?"

"Well, let's just say he might get that transfer now," Strahan said.

"Let's just say you quit shovelling the oral horseshit and get to the goddamned point," Fry snapped. "If you've got a goddamned point. Or is this just another of your half-assed redneck theories?"

Again Grantham verbally separated the two.

"You guys are makin' me feel like a G-D referee. You want to get at each other on the mat downstairs, that's fine. I'd pay to watch. But not here. So cool it, all right? I'll tell him, Paul. Why don't you pull a copy of Oliver's report and give it to J.J.?"

Strahan opened his mouth to argue, but then thought better of it. With a snide, sidelong glance at Fry, he executed a sloppy salute and a clumsy about-face and strode out of the room, heels sounding noisily on the bare tile floor.

"Okay, J.J., it's like this, fact not theory," Grantham said when Strahan had left. "Actually, more fluke than anything. But what the hell. They do say it's better to be lucky than good anyway."

Crisply, almost in point form, without a wasted word, Grantham described for Fry Constable Ken Oliver's fateful afternoon at the Warwickshire: his getting-nowhere-slowly conversation with the pimp

Bryce, Bryce's inability or unwillingness to identify Alf Mathews' sketch, the screams of the woman from the bedroom upstairs, the blood streaming from her head wound, the little Indian waving the knife, Oliver's repeated warnings, the Native's refusal to comply, the lunge, the shooting.

While Grantham was speaking, Fry was trying to listen hard, although—in bits and pieces and with differing emphases and varying degrees of accuracy—he had heard it all before, and before. But his concentration waned and he found himself observing Grantham more than listening to him, thinking how good the Inspector must be at meetings, armed with flow charts and diagrams and an opaque projector. Realizing for the first time that Grantham really would be police chief one day, Fry wondered what kind of cop shop he would run, and doubted that there would be room in it for a cop like himself.

"By the book, it looks to me. Even the three shots. Bang-bang-bang. Centre mass. Just the way we teach it," Grantham concluded. "By the book, letter for letter."

"You don't think that, ah, there's maybe a couple of pages missing?"

"Missing? How?"

"Oh, I'm not saying it was anything but a righteous shooting—no way. But, well, what makes you so absolutely sure, you know, about the connection between this guy and my guy?"

"Well, let's strip it down and look at it. Girl here was a hooker. Yours probably." Fry did not interrupt nor try to correct him. "Guy cut her with a nasty knife. Didn't get to finish but … and apparently he'd been hassling other hookers with a knife."

"What about the boy?"

"What boy?"

"The boy. The kid in the dumpster. He was scalped too, remember? Story getting out got you all pissed off at the press?"

"Oh, yeah. Fuckin' Hoffberg. Closed him out this time."

"The boy?"

"You, ah, say he was a druggie. Well, this character had drug connections too. Maybe that—besides, he just had a bad attitude about whites in general."

"That should apply to about ninety-nine percent of the Native population."

"It adds up," Grantham continued, ignoring Fry's last remark.

"May-be."

"Anyway, you can do the addition for yourself. It's all in the report."

"And here, Ghost, is the report, hot off the photocopier," Strahan said, sliding the three pages of the document one page at a time onto Fry's desk. "Read it and weep."

"Cut it out, Paul," Grantham said, sighing. "Just cut it."

"Where's Oliver now?" Fry asked.

"Home," Grantham said. "Sent him home. He was pretty shaken."

"Yeah, why don't you give him some space, Ghost?" Strahan said sharply. "This is something you of all people should be able to understand. Shit. You and your damned Native lee-ya-zon committee. Sometimes seems like you forget what side you're on. Who you for? The force or one fuckin' little Indian?"

"Oh, for Chris' sake! Sit down, Jake!" Grantham

ordered Fry, who was now standing behind his desk and leaning across the top toward Strahan. "And Strahan, you get out of here. Get out now. That's not a request. Get. The. Fuck. Out."

Strahan spun on his heels and stormed out of the office, cursing as he walked. Grantham leaned over Fry's desk, put his hand on Fry's shoulder, and pushed him back down into his chair.

"So Strahan's an asshole, J.J.," he said. "So what else is new? You don't have to encourage him."

"That's right, you don't. He's a natural."

"Come on, let it go. He's right about Oliver, though. He *is* upset. Naturally. And you should understand that. Now, don't get your back up, I'm not suggesting you don't understand. He's got desk duty until the shooting team finishes anyway. He'll be available. Look, I know this isn't the way you wanted it—"

"What do you mean, the way *I* wanted it?"

"Well, I know you didn't want it to be a—you know what I mean."

"I do, do I?"

"But no matter how you feel personally, the idea's to catch the bad guy, right?"

"I always thought the idea was to catch the *right* bad guy."

"And it doesn't matter who does it s'long as it gets done," Grantham continued his lecture, not listening. "And this one was better done quickly, no matter who or what it turned out to be. It's just not a perfect world, my friend. But there it is."

Grantham removed his hand from Fry's shoulder, made a fist, and gave Fry a light patronizing tap on the jaw. He stood erect, put his hands on the small of his back, and groaned deeply and contentedly.

"I know I'm already starting to feel better," he said. "And you will too."

He winked, clicked his tongue, and walked away, whistling again, this time something from *The Sound of Music*.

6:35 PM

No matter how often he witnessed it, Fry was always amazed and at the same time appalled by the alchemy the police worked, turning blood into paper.

It was part of the job. It was necessary. It was procedure.

Doing justice was every bit as much a manufacturing process as making cars, or furniture, or widgets. The raw materials had to be processed and refined before they could be put to use. The raw materials of crime—the hatred and greed, the rage, bigotry, jealousy, and indifference—had to be flattened into facts that could be joined, literally *pieced* together, to build strong cases that reproduced a veneer of order, created the appearance of justice.

A crime scene pulsating with anger and fear and smeared with once-pulsing blood was reduced to a few scrawled lines in a police officer's notebook and a few black-and-white glossies and maybe some colour polaroids from the police camera—paper. A crime victim was reduced to vital statistics in a medical examiner's report and a few forensic photographs—more paper. A frustratingly long and painstaking crime investigation was reduced to another report, perhaps several reports, labouriously two-finger-typed on an old machine and filed in triplicate—still more paper. When, months after the truth of the crime (whatever that may have been), the facts of the crime were finally brought to court, paper was about all that remained of the crime, except for a few bagged and boxed objects. The notes, the reports, the photographs, the files—paper.

Blood into paper. Fry understood the process. He was a part of it. He believed in it. He valued the arm's-length distance it created, distance that allowed him to take everything in without being taken in, to consume everything without being consumed. He was an alchemist himself, a master of the art, if it *was* an art. Yet he was still amazed by it, and still appalled.

The alchemist was more than usually appalled as he sat at his corner desk in the homicide section reading medical examiner Dr. Clifton Shields' official report on the death of Jane Waldo. Fry was having trouble keeping his distance. He had gotten too close. In only a couple of days, he had gotten too close. It was unlike him. But he had worked too hard to put the flesh back on Jane Waldo to see it stripped so quickly and clinically away. He had resurrected her from a flat black-and-white paper creature, and he resisted seeing her being reduced to one again.

His resistance was vain. Once the alchemy was at work, not even the alchemist could stop it, even if he wanted to. Fry knew it. The medical examiner's report merely reminded him of it, reminded him that Jane Waldo's corpse was not Jane Waldo, but only a piece of evidence in the murder of Jane Waldo.

The report told Fry that her last meal had been the same as *his* last meal, a hamburger and french fries, probably at a fast-food restaurant, no telling which one. He tried to visualize her, perhaps sitting on a plastic stool at a plastic table eating plastic food from a plastic tray, or maybe standing at a stall, standing exactly where he had stood only an hour or so ago, feeding at a downtown mall. *Was she alone then?* he wondered.

Sexually, she had been alone. Shields had found no evidence of relations, forced or consensual, no fluid, no semen, no bruising, nothing. She did not seem to have had sex for a long time.

When dealing with Fry, Shields frequently included with his official reports unofficial comments scribbled on yellow self-adhesive memo pads with the heading "From the desk of God." On one of these pads he had written, in his wry, self-defensive deadpan:

"If she was a hooker, she was having trouble making ends meet."

Fry peeled off the memo and kept reading.

Jane Waldo had been drinking, although, with a blood-alcohol level of point-zero-four, she was hardly drunk. And, according to Shields, she had been no more promiscuous with the bottle than she had been with her body, exhibiting none of the signs—nothing in the liver, nothing in the brain—of alcoholism.

The medical examiner had found no obvious trace of drugs in her body.

He did find—under one of the false fingernails on one of the hands the uniforms at the scene had plastic-bagged and sealed at the wrists with elastics—traces of leather. Just enough to know that it was leather, but not enough to tell where it came from—a jacket, a coat, or a bag of some sort. Shields wrote that he would only be guessing. He was not a guessing man.

He did not have to guess at the cause of death. The autopsy had confirmed the preliminary report: one crushing blow with a blunt instrument to the back of the head, fracturing, actually penetrating, the skull.

The blunt instrument was some kind of wooden club. Shields had found a fine splinter in the wound that did not match any of the wood fragments from the ruined Beltline house.

The weapon that had scalped Jane Waldo—and, in another aside "From the desk of God," Shields wrote that that was exactly what had been done, in, he said he would have guessed if he had been a guessing man, "the old-fashioned Indian way"—was a knife, a very sharp knife, probably a hunting knife, with a medium-long blade. It had been wielded quickly, in a roughly circular motion.

From the counter-clockwise nature of the knife wound, Shields concluded ("inconclusively," he scribbled) that the killer was probably left-handed. From the downward angle of the fatal blow, he concluded that the killer was tall—six feet or more. From the force of the blow, he concluded that the killer was big, at least two hundred pounds, and probably a man.

On a final memo from God, in the fine clear hand that Fry had always thought was too legible for a physician, Shields wrote that, while he had not yet completed the forensic work on Lesley Connor, his preliminary conclusion was that the person who had killed Jane Waldo had also killed Connor and, Shields said he would have guessed, for the same reason, about which he did not have a clue.

"But I don't deal in clues and guesswork, Jake," he wrote. "That's for you direct and impatient types—*cops*, I think, is the word for you."

Fry peeled off the note, crumpled it with the others in his hand and threw them into the trash. He closed the folder. He closed his eyes, trying to remember something first Grantham and then Strahan had said when he was hardly listening to them, something about... the little Indian. *The little Indian waving a knife,* Grantham had paraphrased Oliver's report. *One little fuckin' Indian,* Strahan had cursed.

One little Indian.

Fry gathered up the three photocopied pages of Constable Ken Oliver's report on the shooting. Grantham and Strahan were right about Oliver. He was shaken. It showed in his writing, which alternated between the too pompously official: "After securing entry to the subject hotel room, this officer observed an individual of apparently Native Indian background in possession of a large hunting-type knife, which he was wielding in a threatening manner" to the too unprofessionally personal: "Then the guy made a break for it and come running right at me."

But however he had managed to get it into the report, and however he had spelled it, Oliver seemed to have left nothing out of the report. Despite the stress of the moment, Oliver had observed the scene in detail. And despite his even greater stress after the fact, he had recorded it in detail, including the details Fry was looking for.

Fry slipped the police officer's report into the folder containing the medical examiner's, and went looking for Grantham. He found him in his office, primping at his reflection in the undraped window looking out on the downtown. The streets were lighted, and already almost deserted. Fry knocked once on the open door. Grantham turned to face him, patting the perfect knot of his silk tie.

"J.J. I was on my way out," he said. "What've you got there?"

"Oh, reports," Fry said. "You, ah, you were right

about Oliver—easy to see he's pretty shaken. But it *was* a by-the-book shooting, I'd say."

"Told you. Knew it was righteous."

"And it does look like the same guy who killed the woman also killed the boy at the club."

"There you go." Grantham was beaming. "And, on that high note, I've gotta go."

"There's only one thing."

"Oh? And what's that?"

"The same guy is not your guy."

"What?"

"Your guy is not my guy."

"What do you mean, J.J.? What the hell are you talking about?"

"I'm talking about the reports. Like you said, it's all in the reports. But there's more than one report. There's Oliver's. And there's the M.E.'s. You didn't read it?" Fry asked, already knowing the answer.

"Why, uh, no, not yet. Was pressed for time and I figured—"

"You figured wrong. You should read it." Fry tossed the folder onto Grantham's immaculate desktop. "You should've read it. You'd know the M.E. says the killer's a big fella, six feet, maybe two hundred pounds. Your 'little' Indian is, was, what? Five-six or so, hundred and a half with his boots on? M.E. also says the killer is likely left-handed. Your 'little' Indian was right-handed, right? Right. Like you say, a righteous shooting—but the wrong guy."

"But that's impos—" Grantham was holding tight to the back of his oversized executive chair. "I mean, that can't be."

"What do you mean, it *can't* be? It is."

"The news ... the news is already out."

"Out? How'd it get out? And *what* got out? Who the fuck authorized any statement?"

"Well, I, ah—you know, I wanted to stick it to that fat bastard at the *Bulletin*. Put him in his place. I called the TV. Didn't give any names—just leaked it out."

"Well, Inspector," Fry said in a voice shaking despite his effort to control it, "I'd suggest you make like a little Dutch boy."

"What?"

"And try to plug the fuckin' leak."

7:40 PM

Geographically, the *Bulletin* was on the wrong side of the CPR tracks. Journalistically, it was stalled at a crossroads.

The wide swath of Canadian Pacific right-of-way that choked off north-south access to the downtown also cut the *Bulletin* off from the downtown, stranding it in a semi-seedy, light-industrial no-man's land. Next door to the sprawling, nondescript single-storey newspaper building was a vast, overgrown vacant lot littered with shattered brick, the stone outline of the foundation of the razed tannery still showing. Across Eighth Street to the west was an outdoor outfitting business—a Quonset hut with an art-deco front. The *Bulletin* building's setting was fitting for what the *Bulletin* had become— the second newspaper in a two-newspaper town.

The *Herald*, nestled smugly comfortable in an imposing brick-and-marble building in the city's fine old-business district, had won the competition to be first so long ago that *competitive* no longer usefully or accurately described the relationship between the two newspapers. The question was not whether the *Bulletin* would succeed, but whether it would survive. It was an open question.

In recent years, in fits and feeble starts, the eastern chain that owned the *Bulletin* had made changes in and at the newspaper. Whether or not they were improvements was another open question. About half the *Bulletin*'s operations had been half-heartedly computerized. And, on the recommendation of a Toronto market researcher, the newspaper had undergone a complete redesign, being transformed over a weekend from a conservative broadsheet that looked like the *Bulletin* into a racy tabloid that did not.

Fry had not noticed the makeover. He did not subscribe to the *Bulletin.* He did not subscribe to anything. He did not read newspapers. He did not watch the news on television. He did not tune into the news on radio. He did not pay attention to the news.

Once he had. Once he had followed every story that involved him. And the distortion, the sensationalism, the plain inaccuracy of too much of the reporting only infuriated him. He forced himself to stop paying attention to the news. He learned—and for him it was a difficult lesson—not to pay attention.

He talked to journalists now when he had to because he had to. But he gave them as little as he could, and what they did with what he gave them he tried not to notice. He did not hate the press. He simply did not trust it. He knew how wrong the police could be when they tried to turn the truth into facts. That, he did have to worry about. But he did not have to worry about how wrong reporters could be when they tried to turn facts into stories. And he did not want to know.

Fry was unaware of the *Bulletin*'s perilous condition as he came up the front walk to the *Bulletin* building, his overcoat buttoned and collar upturned against the chill. He was wondering about the strange, soft snapping sound he heard overhead. He stopped, looked up, and saw, silhouetted against the evening sky, a large flag flapping in the stiffening westerly breeze. Over the top of the low-rise building, across the tracks, he saw the empty office towers, glittering.

The front door was unlocked. Nobody was sitting at the front desk. The front offices, ADVERTISING and CIRCULATION, were deserted. Fry followed an arrow on the wall, with the word EDITORIAL painted above it, left down a corridor lined with framed front pages of past *Bulletins*: provincehood for Alberta, the ends of both world wars, the Leduc oil strike, the death of the King, coronation of the Queen, John Kennedy's assassination, the October Crisis, the Arab oil embargo.

The historic *Bulletins* came to an end, and the corridor opened into the *Bulletin* newsroom, a kind of historical artifact itself, with its vintage office desks, vintage filing cabinets, and vintage typewriters. This was not the computerized half of the operation.

About half of the twenty-odd typewriters were clattering. Wire-service teletypes nattered in a far corner of the room. Every few seconds a telephone rang. Then, from a desk near the front of the newsroom, Fry heard Hoffberg's shrill voice ring out.

"What's the friggin' idea?"

The fat police reporter struggled out of his chair and squeezed between his desk and a filing cabinet to get to Fry, stopping only when his pink, round face was literally within inches of Fry's. Fry could not tell whether it was because of Hoffberg's journalistic tactics, his utter tactlessness, or a case of cataracts. He did not care. He did not like it. But he did not back away.

"The idea about what, Hoffberg?"

"What do you think? About leaking the goddamned story on the scalping suspect to Binkley there at CF'ingCN, of course."

"You know I'd never take a leak on TV."

"C'mon, don't bullshit me."

"Christ, Hoffberg. You don't know number one from number two?"

"What?"

"First you said it was a leak. Now it's bullshit. Make up your mind."

"Ha-friggin'-ha. It's not friggin' fair. You guys are gonna have my ass in a sling down here."

"Interesting concept, that. Probably worth the price of admission. But don't *you* start shovelling bullshit about *fair.* Thanks to you, a couple of fine, young, semi-competent constables are probably going to end up a couple of fat, old, complete fuck-up constables—if they get to stay cops at all."

"What? Oh, them. Well, nobody forced them to open their mouths. I was just doing my job."

"Oh yeah, I forgot—you're one of those *urinal*-ists. That is about your speed. Got the right kind of paper for your kind of stories too. Good luck doing your *job* from now on."

"Now what's that mean? Oh, I get it. I'm gonna get it now. Police harassment, eh?"

"Why, whatever are you talking about, Hoffberg? You know the police are only here to serve and protect."

"Yeah, right—serve themselves maybe, and protect their asses."

"All right, listen, shithead: if I ever do decide to harass you, it'll be personal not professional. And you will know your fat ass is being harried. So let it go, all right, let it go. Besides, you ought'a know you can't believe everything you hear on TV."

"What? You mean the Indian the cop blew away isn't—"

"I don't mean a damn thing. Right now I just want to know one damn thing."

"And that is?"

"And that is whether the reporter that wrote this story is here."

From a large manila envelope, Fry removed a folded-once full-page tear sheet of the morning *Bulletin*, the same *Bulletin* Grantham had been alternately strangling and pumelling all day. When the Inspector had tossed the rolled-up newspaper onto Fry's desk, it had curled open to this page. Fry had not meant to read the story. He had not even noticed it. And he would not even have recognized it from the headline:

'Flip side' of boom
Sunshines shine on sunshine city

Fry was about to toss the paper into the trash when he did notice the photograph that accompanied the story: Benny and Bonnie, John and Gina, the Sunshines Family minus one, posing in the sunroom of their rented, condemned Mount Royal mansion.

Fry unfolded the page and showed it to Hoffberg, who squinted at it and then at Fry, puzzled.

"What you want Melton for?"

"That's police business."

"The police *are* my business," Hoffberg sniffed.

"Oh, that's right, I forgot. Well, you want an official statement, call public affairs. Yeah, do that. Ask for Grantham, Inspector Phil Grantham."

"And what'll I get from him?"

"About this? Probably nothing. But count on it, Hoffberg, he'll have something for you. I'm sure he'll be tickled to death to talk to you. Me, I'm tired of talking to you. I'm tired of you. I'm just plain tired. This guy here or not?"

Hoffberg squinted at Fry again through his thick lenses, tilting his head back as if trying to focus. His thick lips were moving, but they were making no sound. He seemed to be debating with himself about what to say. He looked over his shoulder then, and shouted toward one of the desks clustered in the centre of the newsroom.

"Hey, Foley—Foley!"

"Yeah, yeah, yeah. What?" A florid man with thinning red hair and a thick red beard looked up from a page dummy, a fat editing pencil in one hand, a thin sheaf of typewritten copy in the other.

"Melton here?"

"Ah, yeah—least he was. Said he had to step out and 'have a think.' I'm 'fraid he's *creating* on us again. Ought to be back soon, owes me the story."

"What about the photographer?" Fry asked Hoffberg.

"'What about the photographer?' What am I, your friggin' messenger boy?"

"Thought that's what you reporters got paid to be."

"Ha-again-friggin'-ha. What about Miloche, Foley? Where's he?"

"Where's Miloche? Where's Miloche? That's the question. Been askin' myself that question ever since he started workin' here. What am I saying? He hasn't started *workin'* here yet. Who knows? Down at city hall plannin' our future. Up at the university pontificating. He owes me a pic, too, an hour ago. Maybe I'll get it. If I do, I'll tell you where he is. Otherwise, I don't have a clue."

"Any other messages you want delivered, detective?"

"Yeah."

"Shit! What?"

"Where's he sit?"

"Who?"

"The reporter, Melton."

"Uh, over there, far side of the room."

"And you sit just over here, up front?"

"Yeah."

"Good. I'll wait. At his desk."

8:05 PM

About twenty minutes later, across the room, Fry saw Hoffberg waddle from his desk to flag down a gangly, dark-haired man who had bounded grinning into the newsroom. The two conferred conspiratorially, Hoffberg nodding over his right shoulder in Fry's direction, the tall man looking at Fry over his left. Then the tall man left Hoffberg and negotiated his way through the desks toward Fry, his grinning face turning grim.

"I believe you're in my chair," he said when he reached his desk, crossing his arms across his chest, glaring at Fry through his black-rimmed glasses.

"I believe you're right, Mr., ah, Melton, isn't it? Sorry," Fry said, rising from the chair, reaching into his coat pocket with his left hand for his identification, extending his right toward Melton. "I'm—"

"I know who you are."

"Yes. I suppose you do. Well, good. That saves time." Fry left his shield in his coat pocket. He let his right hand drop to his side. "I'll get right to the point."

"Before you do, I'll have to tell you I'm not revealing any sources."

"Oh? Sources of what?"

"Sources of anything."

"Well, now, that does cover a lot of territory, doesn't it?"

"Is this an interrogation?"

"Can be if you want it to be, Mr. Melton. I've even got a special little room for it down on Seventh Avenue. Shitty little room, though. Full of bad memories—of *bad* memories. Be better, and a whole lot nicer, if we could just have a little chat right here. You got a room where we could do that, Mr. Melton?"

Melton uncrossed his arms. He stroked his moustache thoughtfully with his misshapen right thumb. He glanced across the newsroom toward Hoffberg, who was squinting intently, almost jealously, at Melton and Fry. Then Melton asked, working hard to maintain his cockiness and his cool, "A little 'chat' about what?"

"Didn't Hoffberg tell you that, too?"

Melton said nothing. But when he grabbed a notebook from his desk and held it protectively against his chest, Fry knew that Hoffberg had tipped him.

"Those the notes for your story here?" Fry asked, showing Melton the clipping. The reporter did not answer. The brown eyes, suddenly looking everywhere in the room but at Fry, betrayed his nerves. "About that room," Fry said. "Is there a place a little more private?"

"Ah, snack room, upstairs, I suppose."

"Suppose we head on up there then? And maybe you'd bring those notes along."

"I'm not giving them to you."

"I haven't asked you to—yet. Which way?"

Fry followed Melton through a doorway at the back of the newsroom into a corridor parallel with the one to the framed *Bulletins.* On their right was a machine shop and a small cubicle where a proofreader sat reading a paperback. On the left was the composing room, where several elderly men in new white shirts and old work pants sat uncertainly at computer terminals. Other men stood at slanted, brightly lit tables pasting up pages.

Just before the corridor ended at the doors to the press room, Melton turned right and climbed a short, narrow flight of stairs to the snack room. The room was darker, but only slightly grungier, than the lunchroom at police headquarters—worn linoleum, an old Formica-topped kitchen table, and chrome chairs with torn leatherette seats.

Melton sat at the table across from Fry, his elbows on the tabletop, notebook clutched in his two hands, his clubby thumb rubbing along the metal spiral. Fry dumped the contents of the envelope onto the table in front of him: Melton's story on the Sunshines and the glossy black-and-white photograph of Lesley Connor, Lee Boy's last pretty picture. He slid the photo across the table toward Melton.

"Know him?" Fry asked.

Melton looked at the photo, then at Fry, then at the grimy window behind Fry.

"Yeah, er, I mean no, not exactly," he said. "Well, yes and no."

"That pretty well covers all the bases."

"I mean I know of him. I don't know him. He didn't show up for the interview. They showed us his picture—this picture, looks like. Wanted us to use it. Miloche, though—he's the photographer—only uses his own stuff. I can't tell you anything about the guy. He's not in here," Melton said, tapping the notebook. "I can't help you. Can't say I'm all that sorry, either."

"You're pretty cool—cold, even. You can't help me—you can't help him, either."

"What do you mean?"

"What do you mean, 'what do you mean?'? You know, don't you?"

"Know what?"

"This is the boy who was murdered at the club downtown last night."

Melton's jaw fell. The notebook fell from his hands onto the table. Fry realized that the reporter did not know.

"Jesus! You people are as bad as cops," he said. "Don't you talk to each other? What the hell'd you think this was about anyway?"

"Um, the, ah, story" Melton stammered. "I ... I figured probably the drugs. You were gonna hassle them—try to use me to get at them."

"Oh, for Chris'ake! Now, those kids may get themselves hassled, maybe even by the police, and they may even deserve it. But like I told them, it's not going to be by me. It's that dead boy I'm interested in—and who made him dead. Now, you got anything in that fucking notebook that might help or not? And spare me any high horseshit about freedom of the press. I know all about your so-called freedom—and you do treat it like it's *your* freedom. Public's right to know and all that. Unless it's something *you* don't want to tell. Well, what I'm talking about is the po-*lice's* right to know. It's enforceable, and I'll damn well enforce it. You gonna make me?"

Melton put his hands on the edge of the table, lowered his head and took a deep, shaky breath. He raised his head then and looked directly at Fry, his pale face seeming even paler in the weak fluorescent light, some of the passionate intensity gone from his brown eyes.

"No," he said.

Melton slid his notebook across the table. Fry opened it, saw the virtually indecipherable makeshift reporter's shorthand, and slid the notebook back to Melton.

"I don't want your damned notes," he said, "even assuming I could make 'em out. I want to know if you heard anything, if any of them said anything, if you noticed anything, something that might help."

Melton could not help. And he was trying to now. But he could not remember hearing, or seeing, or noticing anything in particular, particularly anything that would help explain Lesley Connor's murder.

"Unless it is the drugs," he said. "They did mention the drugs and him. Maybe it's the drugs."

"May-be," Fry said, not believing it. "What about the photographer?"

"Donnie? Donnie Miloche?"

"Yeah—Miloche. You think he might've picked up on anything?"

"I don't know. He didn't mention anything. You could ask him—if he's around."

"I take it that's something he's not a lot."

"He's got a lot of outside interests—I think he wants to be mayor."

"Politician, eh? What we all need more of. Well, show me where he might be anyway, in case he is here."

Melton led Fry back into the newsroom, to a door in the corner behind the bank of nattering, chugging teletypes. Over the door, a red light was flickering. Inside, someone was singing:

"Oh, I've got some good ones, some good ones, some good ones. Oh, I've got some good ones todaaaay."

"Well, somebody's in the darkroom," Melton said.

"And from the noise, I'd say it's Miloche." He rapped on the door. He hollered: "Donnie? Donnie, it's Grant. Can you come out? It's the police."

"Oh, yeah?" said the voice in the darkroom. "Sure, I'll be right out. Don't come in, though. You'll ruin my beauties."

In about a minute, the red light went out, the door opened, and the big photographer emerged. His string tie was loosened at the unbuttoned collar of his western shirt, the sleeves rolled about halfway up his big, hairless forearms, his stomach rolling over the big-buckled belt that held up his stiff new blue jeans. The denims, rolled once at the cuff, ended at the shiniest, pointiest-toed cowboy boots Fry had ever seen.

"Donnie, this is, ah, Detective Fry," Melton said. "Detective, this is Don—"

"G. Donald Miloche, sir," the photographer interrupted, grabbing Fry's hand in his own strong, yet soft, right hand. "What can I do to help?"

"Well," Fry said, almost wincing at the photographer's unexpectedly firm grip, studying his pleasant, expectant moon face, thinking of a big, clumsy dog eager to please, "for starters you could let go there."

"Oh, sorry. Excuse me."

"Not to worry," Fry assured him. "No harm done. I think."

Fry smiled. Miloche smiled.

"It's about that feature we did—the Sunshines Family." Melton said.

"Yeah, the ones lived in that neat house in Mount Royal."

"Right. The one who didn't show up, actually—the one they had the pic of, you know, they wanted us to use it, remember?"

"Yeah, sure, I remember. A pretty good pic, too, but just not mine. What about him?"

"He got killed."

"He got what?"

"Murdered, Mr. Miloche, murdered," Fry said. "Last night at a club downtown."

"You mean *he's* the one in Hoffberg's story? Hoffberg know?"

"Yes, Mr. Miloche. He's the one. From what I can gather, Hoffberg doesn't," Fry said. "What I want to know, what I was asking Mr. Melton, and what I'll ask you, is whether you remember anything, anything unusual about the interview, something somebody might have said, anything you might have noticed."

"Oh, jeez, I don't know...." Miloche said, thinking for a moment. "No, I don't think ... only the smell. Gawd, the smell. Don't know how anybody could live like that."

"But nothing else?"

"No—guess not. All I remember about him is the photo. That was all I saw of him. I'm sorry. Wish I could help. I'll look at the contact sheet of that shoot. Believe me, sir, if I do find anything, I'll be in touch."

"I'd appreciate it."

Fry shook Melton's misshapen hand and, then at the risk of having his own hand misshaped, shook Miloche's. As he passed by Hoffberg's desk on his way out of the newsroom, he said nothing to the curious, furiously squinting reporter, just saluted him with the index finger of his right hand, and smiled.

10:50 PM

Fry was too tired to see straight, much less to saw straight. Typically, he had chosen to ignore the signs of fatigue and, instead of heading upstairs to bed when he got home, headed downstairs to his low-ceilinged basement workshop. He was still working on the scrap-wood bookcase for Andy Stimwych's son. He had found a piece of backing for it leaning in a corner of the cellar: a weathered four-by-eight sheet of quarter-inch plywood splintering at the edges. Fry had salvaged it himself one afternoon after it nearly knee-capped him.

He had been walking back from a hot-dog lunch downtown when he saw a stake truck turning too fast onto Fourth Avenue from Fourth Street. The truck, unevenly loaded with stacks of plywood boarding that had surrounded an excavation site, came round the corner on two wheels. With a *whumph*, the truck righted itself, bouncing its load, tossing several boards onto the street, sending one of them right at Fry like a huge skipping Frisbee. Fry jumped. The plywood skimmed under his legs and skipped to a stop on the sidewalk behind him.

The truck did not stop. Fry had run after it, cursing, stopping after a block and a half, his eyes burning from the wind, his chest burning. He got a plate number and a company name. Later, he would send a uniform to lay a charge. Now, he was going back for the plywood. He could use the boards in the street as evidence. The board that almost took his legs off he was taking home. Even if he never found a use for it, he was not going to leave it. It owed him. Fry took the fairly light, but awkwardly flopping boards back to the office with him, struggling with them against the wind.

Now Fry had found a use for the plywood. The boarding would make a perfect back for the bookcase, strengthening and tightening it without adding much weight to it. Fry had only to cut it to fit.

But tonight was not the time to cut it. Even so, Fry tried, flopping the board onto three sawhorses, snapping a couple of chalk lines, trying to follow them with his father's big rip saw, nearly splintering one end of the piece into uselessness. He cursed, first the wood, then the saw, then himself. He gave it up, yanked on the overhead-outlet chain and lumbered up the steps.

Lips was waiting on the landing, where he had been lying with one paw draped over the top step, watching with amused detachment as Fry tried to work. Lips was a cat, a strapping male cat with a white head like a heavyweight's fist and a ring of bright red-orange fur around his mouth. Fry called him Lips, among other things. He had no idea what the cat had been called before he found him—or rather, before the cat found Fry.

Lips had been living in the four-storey red and yellow brick apartment building at the end of the street. Fry had often encountered him on his walks, lounging on the front steps to the building, sunning himself in the postage stamp of a front lawn, or taking shade under one of the cars in the parking lot.

From his front porch early one morning, Fry saw Lips again, emerging from the rubble and shattered glass of the now half-demolished apartment building. Fry watched as the big white and orange cat padded silently down the centre of the street. Behind him the building looked as if it had been bombed. Rooms where people had recently lived—had fought and made love, had eaten, bathed, defecated, and possibly died—stood ruined and empty, indecently exposed by the wrecking ball. Lips stopped in the middle of the street in front of Fry's house. He strode purposefully up the walk, came up the porch steps and, without ceremony—no rubbing or purring, no chirping or whining—settled himself down on the porch next to Fry.

Fry was intrigued, but he ignored the cat. He had never liked cats. He had had to tolerate them when he was married. Carol and their son Tony loved them. There were never fewer than two around the house. He did not have to tolerate them now. There were none in his house. And the last thing he wanted to do was encourage this one.

In a few moments, without stroking or speaking to the animal, Fry picked up his coffee cup, got up, and went inside. When he came out for work, the cat was still there. And he was there when Fry came home, and again the next morning. That night, though, he was gone—for good, Fry figured, and good riddance, he thought.

But when he emerged from the house in the morning he looked for the cat, and when he did not find him, he found that he missed him. Late that night, as he walked, Fry looked for him, but again did not find him. The next morning, though, he did—lying on the porch, exactly where he had lain down that first time.

"So, you're back, are you, shit-bird?"

The cat looked at him as if that were the most stupid question he had ever been asked. Thinking about it, Fry had to agree.

He put out milk for the cat. Later that day, he bought cat food for the first time in his life—the cheapest kind he could find, in case the cat did not stay. Lips loved it. And he stayed. The two had been together ever since, except when Lips, for a few days at a time, would mysteriously disappear.

Fry admired his independence and what seemed to be his inner strength, his quiet persistence, his intelligence and composure, his ability to get on without fuss or display. What the cat admired in Fry, there was no telling. Perhaps the same qualities.

Fry pulled a beer from the refrigerator, took a short gulp, and carried the bottle by the neck into the living room. For a few moments he stood in the centre of the street-lighted room, as if he could not decide what to do next, where to go, whether to pace or to sit, to sleep. He ran the cold bottle across his forehead and closed his eyes. He put the bottle down on the oak mantelpiece of the bricked-up hearth.

He knelt down at the stereo—one of the few things he had taken with him out of the house in Canyon Meadows. The turntable was old, the speakers older. Carol had wanted a new machine. Fry tilted his head to the side and leaned forward, trying to read the blur of titles on the worn record-jacket spines on the shelf below the stereo. He snapped on a lamp clamped to the top shelf. He slipped an album from the stack, a new one, flipped up the scratched plastic turntable cover and placed the record on the spindle. He flicked a switch on the turntable. The stylus dropped onto the album, skating past the beginning of the first song. Fry turned up the volume on the tuner.

He picked up the beer and collapsed in the stuffed easy chair beside the hearth, one other thing he had salvaged from the rancher in the city's southwest. Like the stereo, it was old and worn. Carol had wanted new. He closed his eyes and let his head fall back onto the chair. His arms dangled over the wide, worn arms, and the beer dangled, by the neck, between the index and middle fingers of his right hand. He listened.

Short-grass music—assorted strings, guitars mostly, some bass and percussion, a squeezebox, piano and plaintive vocals, even a country-riffing sax. More western than country music, though. Songs about drifting and drinking, about cowboys and cocaine, about cigarette smoke and the street, about love lost or never quite found. It was simple music, simple and clean and direct. Fry thought it captured the essence of the northwest he loved, the prairie and the city, the city on the prairie, the prairie in the city. It was strong and honest, a little raw, unsophisticated, unpretentious, unpolished. Yet he heard in it something pure. There was not much purity in his life these days.

The stylus skidded past the end of the record and then back again, back and forth, back and forth. The old tone arm did not have the strength to return to its rest. Fry put down his beer. He pushed himself out of the chair. Carefully, without stopping the turntable, he lifted the tone arm, removed the record, flipped it over, and centred it on the spindle. He gently lowered the tone arm onto the spinning album.

Another song about loneliness and pain, longing, leaving. Another song about life.

Fry sat on the floor between the speakers, his legs drawn up and crossed at the ankles, his arms wrapped around his knees, hands clasped in front of him, his head down, eyes closed. He was listening. But he had also started thinking again.

There was loneliness and pain in what he was thinking, but no music, no life. He was thinking of a dead woman's loneliness, of a dead boy's pain. He was thinking of the sickness that had taken them, another's sickness, or evil. No one would write a song about their leaving. Only one could. And Fry could not imagine that there was any music in *his* thoughts either, only the sickness, and no life, only the sickness, only the evil.

Fry felt soft fur and solid warmth under his right hand. He opened his eyes. He saw Lips nuzzling his hand, heard him purring. It was unlike the usually cool and self-contained, undemonstrative cat. Fry reached out and patted the big white head as he might have a faithful old dog's.

11:55 PM

He looked like one of the sandstone lions that guarded the bridge, only fiercer. A mane of wild, greying hair swept back from his florid face. Over his eyes, his thick brows were growing out of control. The deep fissures around his eyes ended in a gaze that was dark and furtive and tinged with red. His grey-stubbled skin was weathered and leathery. Only his nose marred the impression of ferocity. It was bulbous, blistered, redder than the rest of his face, almost a snout. It had earned him the accurate, if unimaginative nickname, "Big Nose." He was only in his late thirties. He looked like he could have been anywhere from forty-five to sixty.

He was hunched like a shadow beneath the lions, below the bridge, his one-size-too-big grey Salvation Army overcoat scraping the ground. Almost exactly where he was squatting, the river, sixty years before, had flooded and ripped out the last of the pilings of the old bridge and washed it away. Tonight, the drought-lowered Bow trickled under the arched sandstone structure. Above him, straggling Centre Street traffic rumbled across it. Over his shoulder, like a giant torch in the night sky, was the lighted Calgary Tower.

If Big Nose had looked up, across the river to the east, he might have been able to make out the north hill, from where, just over a hundred years before, the Mounties of F-Troop sighted the river valley where first the wooden, then the sandstone, and finally the steel concrete and glass city would grow. The Mountie in charge had given the city its name, from what he thought was Gaelic for "clear running water."

He had got it wrong, appropriately. From the beginning, Calgary had been a place where impressions were more important than facts.

But Big Nose was not looking north and east, across the river, toward the lights in the tall, old buildings beyond the tall, old trees along Memorial Drive in the neighbourhood now called Crescent Heights. He was not thinking of history, factual or fanciful. He could not see the lights of the tower behind him, nor, below it, the lights of the quiet Wednesday night streets of Chinatown. He was not thinking of the enduring strangeness around him. He could not see the lights playing on the water. He was not thinking of the winding river that flowed like an arched eyebrow around the city centre.

He *was* thinking though. And he was seeing. His mind and his one good eye were focused on one thing, on *the* one thing, on the *only* thing.

With the pointed end of a dime-store bottle opener, he punctured a small hole in one side of the bottom of the aerosol can and then another, slightly larger hole in the opposite side. Holding the can between his knees, he reached into his coat pocket and pulled out a big, empty aftershave bottle. He had drunk the last of the Aqua Velva that morning. He unscrewed the cap. Like the mad scientist in a forties horror melodrama preparing to mix some weird and deadly potion, he brought the bottom of the can to the top of the bottle and tipped it. Carefully, running his dry tongue over his chapped upper lip, trying to keep his hands from shaking, he poured the contents of the can into the bottle, filling it about three-quarters full with fleeting oblivion: about six ounces of liquid Lysol, nearly seventy percent alcohol, as potent as ten or eleven shots of whiskey, or a couple of bottles of wine.

He took a sip, only a sip. He had promised himself to make it last. He felt the burning in his throat, which passed, and the burning in his stomach, which never passed. He screwed the cap on the bottle and buried it deep in an inside coat pocket.

He started, as if at a sudden sound, although there had been none. He jerked his head violently to the left, then to the right and back, trying to compensate for the cloud over his left eye, squinting into the night, trying to make out the intruder in the shadows, although there was none.

He was alone.

Did he remember when he was not alone? Did he remember Gloria and the three kids and the bungalow he had built and the auto-body shop he had owned and operated in Red Deer? Did he remember what happened? What happened to them? What happened to him? Did he remember? Did he remember why?

Sometimes he thought he remembered. Sometimes the thoughts would come to him, not thoughts so much as images, fragments of pictures, like torn photographs. And he could see, almost see, almost remember. But then the fragments would disintegrate, the images would fade. And the thoughts would leave him, as she had. The thoughts would go missing, as he had.

Only the burning would remain.

He grabbed the bottle from his coat and took another drink, a deep, long, bitter gulp, shaking his head as he swallowed, trying to remember to be careful, reminding himself that it would have to last. The bottle would have to last the night.

The thought of the night and the thought of the bottle brought the thought of another night, another bottle, another fragment of memory, another indistinct picture fading, receding even as he saw it. That was the night he was promised the bottle. When was that night? The bottle of rye was the promise, a bottle of rye, good rye whiskey, twelve years old. When was that night? What happened that night? The bottle. The bottle of good rye whiskey, good Canadian rye. What happened to the bottle? Did he get the bottle? He could not remember his bottle. What happened to his bottle? It was a promise.

And all he had to do ... What did he have to do...? Where was the bottle...?

The light. He remembered the light. The flash of light in the darkness. Outside. Inside. The explosion of light. The flash of light. In his eyes. In his head. The flash of white.

And then the black. All black. In his head, all around, all black.

And then … what? What...?

Weight. The weight. Weight on his shoulders pushing him down, holding him down. And the pulling, something pulling on his head, pulling at his hair, cutting, cutting his hair, cutting … into his head, cutting away the top of his head … and the blood. The blood. Whose blood...?

No! No! *Nooo!*

Big Nose reached for the back of his head and felt frantically for the scar, the ridge of flesh under his mane. He found it.

"The sumbitch!" he hissed. "The sumbitch! The dirty sumbitch!"

He flung the empty spray can into the water. He put the bottle to his lips and drank—one gulp, two, three.

Inside, he burned.

may 4 8:10 AM

When Fry saw the small mountain of telephone messages from Thomas Red Crow on his desk—the first call came in at seven-fifteen, the second at seven-twenty-three, the rest at roughly five-minute intervals for about the past forty-five minutes—he knew what they were about and he did not return the calls.

He had already seen last night's reports. Phil Grantham's correction, Fry assumed, had come too late to make the late local news. Or if it had made it, they had ignored it, or downplayed it (in fact, CFCN had run it, in the first ten minutes, as the fifth story, forty-five seconds between a minute-thirty piece on the province's concerns about drug offenders and another minute-thirty on the drilling of new water wells to provide drought assistance). Or maybe nobody was watching. Or if they were watching, they were not paying attention.

None of the above would have surprised Fry. One of the reasons he had forced himself to stop paying attention to the news was to stop getting angry when he saw how much less prominence a correction received than a mistake, assuming that the correction received any ink or air time at all. Reporters liked being wrong—no, they liked being *found out* to be wrong—about as much as the police did. They liked a good story, right or wrong. Mistakes were better stories than corrections, just as charges were always better stories than acquittals. A good thing, Fry thought, that what the public believed was usually true: that the people the police charged were usually guilty. No mistakes, no corrections. No harm, no foul.

Not last night, though. The people harmed by Grantham's mistake—the ones his correction *was* too little, too late to help—had been guilty of nothing more than being in the wrong place at the wrong time, or of having the wrong genetic makeup.

They've been in the wrong place at the wrong time ever since we got here, Fry thought as he disgustedly read the overnight reports. *And it was their damn place to begin with.*

A couple of Natives had been bloodied in a scuffle at the Queen's Hotel in the east end—broken noses, split lips, torn eyebrows, loosened teeth—"nothing serious," according to the investigating officer's report. Another Native, just in town from Gleichen, a boy scarcely old enough to drink, had been stabbed in the throat in the washroom of another east-end tavern. He had lost a lot of blood but would live.

Miraculously, so would the white john who had been punched and kicked senseless by a Native pimp after the john started slapping around one of the little Native girls who worked the strip on Eighth Avenue SE. All three had been arrested—the pimp and the girl were in the cells, the john in stable condition at the General.

Around midnight, somebody ran up onto the porch of the Indian Friendship Centre in Chinatown, kicked over the wooden planters, and tossed a brick through the front window.

Another Indian, this one from New Delhi—an engineering student at the University of Calgary—had been accosted at a bus stop in the northwest, sucker-punched in the stomach, and kicked in the face while he was gasping for breath on the ground. All he could remember the three teenage white toughs who attacked him saying was "Goddamfuckin' Indian! Goddamfuckin' Indian!"

The telephone on Fry's desk was ringing again. It had been about five minutes. He did not answer it. He did not want to talk to Tom Red Crow on the phone, not about this. He would have to see him in person.

Thomas Red Crow was a Sarcee and a lawyer, which made him, as far as Fry was concerned, half-worth dealing with and doubly difficult. He had an extra measure of the fierce independence that had always marked the tribe. He was at least as bullheaded as Bull Head, the stubborn old chief who, late in the last century, had secured for the Sarcee the hundred square miles of land they still occupied west of the city limits. Thomas Red Crow had made it his life's work (it could not have been much of a living) to see to it that the Sarcee—*all* Natives for that matter, treaty Indians or not—were as secure off the land as they were on it.

He operated out of a storefront law office in the southeast, just beyond the shadow of the downtown towers, on one of those one-way speedways the signposts called a street that zipped Calgary's white-collared, mostly white, elite into and out of the shining city centre without their having to pay much attention to the shabbiness they had to go through to get to it. Affluence in the city was inversely related to traffic flow. If cars were moving freely, the boom either had not arrived or was not coming.

The boom was not coming for Red Crow's clients. What was coming for them, too often, was the law.

Red Crow used the law to keep the law at bay, to keep his people—whom he defined broadly—out of jail, or, if not out, then in for as short a time and as close to home as possible. He was good at it. He was as fluent in the mind-twisting language of the white man's law as he was in the tongue-twisting language of the Sarcee. He could think in both worlds. He had acquired a reputation as "the Indian lawyer." Among cops and Crown attorneys, he was "the fuckin' Indian lawyer."

But he was not good enough. Or there was not enough of him. The law was coming for too many Natives. Too many Natives were going to jail, more than should have, given their percentage of the population, far more than Red Crow could save. More than was necessary, more than was healthy, more than was right.

The chiefs—Red Crow's, the other bands', and Fry's—had decided that something had to be done. What they did was form a committee—Chiefs' Liaison between Indians and Police, or CLIP. According to the press releases, the purpose of CLIP was simple, and breathtakingly ambitious: to break down and break through a century of mistrust between Natives and the enforcers of white law. The need for something like CLIP was statistically and painfully obvious: contacts between Natives and police were all too frequent and almost always negative. CLIP's goal was to lessen the frequency and the intensity of those contacts through the appointment of a full-time Calgary police Native liaison officer, who would explain the police to the Indians, and the Indians to the police.

Ultimately, the chiefs hoped, the Native liaison officer really would be a *Native* liaison officer. But at the moment, the only Indian on the force was a Mohawk from Ontario. It was hard to attract local Natives to police work, even harder to keep them. As one Alberta Indian police officer told a CBC reporter after quitting: "I don't mind being called a pig. But I don't want to be called a pig by my own people—a roast pig sucking on an apple—you know, red on the outside, white on the inside."

As far as the band chiefs were concerned, Thomas Red Crow was an obvious choice to sit on CLIP. As far as the police chief was concerned, so was Fry. Fry himself was not so sure.

It *was* true that, growing up, Fry had played with Indians as much as he had played with anybody—the dark children of the occasional family of demoralized Cree passing quickly through the Cypress Hills, where his father had been posted early in his career, and Blackfoot boys in summer, sons of the threshing crews his grandfather hired to work his farm southwest of Gleichen and allowed to camp in the front yard. But, playing with them, he had never thought of them as Indians.

That came only later, when he was past playing, when he overheard others, ignorant white men, talking about them, *as* Indians, as thieving, treacherous, unreliable, drunken, useless Indians. Briefly, he had even adopted their second-hand prejudices and thoughtless racism as his own, until he found it impossible to reconcile them with his own few, clear memories. He soon cast them aside, as he did most things he could not square with reality.

Fry was not a prejudiced man. Still, he was not sure that he was the right man for this committee. He was not sure that he knew or felt enough.

Nor was Thomas Red Crow.

"So they not only send us a white cop," Red Crow had said as the members of CLIP sat down for their founding meeting at the crime prevention office on Sixteenth Avenue NE, "but about the whitest-looking white cop I've ever seen."

Eyes turned to Fry. There was a collective holding of breath. Fry said:

"And I'd say you're about the mouthiest mouthpiece I've ever heard—and I have heard some large-mouthed shysters."

Eyes turned again, toward Red Crow, whose blazing eyes were fixed on Fry, and were met by Fry's hollow, penetrating gaze. Still no one was breathing. Finally Red Crow nodded his head as if satisfied, opened the folder on the conference table in front of him, and said:

"Maybe we can work."

They did work. The Native liaison officer still existed only on paper, but he would soon exist in fact. By fall, he would be working out of an office here at crime prevention, patrolling the streets where he had jurisdiction, visiting the reserves where he did not, trying to bring the law closer to the Natives, trying to keep the Natives from getting too close to the law.

Fry and Red Crow themselves had grown close, despite the fact that Red Crow had no use for the police and Fry did not like lawyers. They had, in fact, become friends of a sort, a kind of red and white odd couple—the tall, barrel-chested Sarcee with the booming voice and the beaded headband around his jet-black hair, and the wiry, reserved, gunmetal-greying cop with the smoker's cough and dark circles around his eyes.

They found they had some of the same likes: smell of woodsmoke, thunder in the mountains, second-hand bookstores, the twisting rivers, Ry Cooder, forties black-and-white mystery movies on late-night television, women who laughed out loud. They shared some dislikes: politicians, cottage cheese, the press, drivers who cut in, snowmobiles, women who didn't know how to laugh. They shared a quickness to anger and the determination not to give in to it, to always remain in control.

The two actually seemed to be bridging the distances between them and, without saying it to each other, they had begun to hope CLIP could begin to build a bridge between their cultures.

Until now.

Until these killings. Until this shooting. Until this mistake.

Until this … evil.

Fry knew it would be different between them now. During the twenty-odd minutes it took him to drive the two blocks from the police building to Red Crow's office through downtown construction, he had thought about little else. He knew it would be different. He knew it would set them back. He did not know how far.

As he pulled to a stop in the no-stopping zone outside the storefront and stuck the POLICE sign on the dash, Fry wondered if the distance now would be too great for them to bridge.

8:15 AM

"You folks in the north tryin' to get south might just as well crank up the volume, stick 'er in neutral, save the gas, sit back and relax, 'cause there's no shortcuts today," the voice of CFCN's traffic reporter crackled thinly from his helicopter hovering north and east of the Bow River. "It's a three-to-five-light delay no matter *where* you are on Sixteenth Avenue this morning. And you, ah, 'uh-oh-slept-in late-starters' in the Properties can go ahead and have another cup of coffee and blame it all on the traffic when you get to work *some*time today. Cars are backed up for-*ever*, just tryin' to get onto Thirty-sixth Street. We're headin' south now, Rick—easy pickin' from up here—see if things are any better at the Elbow-Sifton circle. Don't hold your breath, though. Hey, isn't this why they call it the rush *hour*?"

"You're a funny man, this morning, Hap," the station's happy-talk, top-forty morning DJ chimed in, "one seriously funny, genuinely sick individual—and lucky to be where the folks down below can't get their hands on you. Well, I got my hands on this old one by the Drifters. Like the little fella said—sorry, Hap, I know I promised no short jokes, but, hey, I lied—sit back, relax, turn it up, and try to enjoy. Looks like you're gonna be here—wherever you are—for a while."

From the traffic helicopter, as it banked and, nose lowered, headed southwest, the big, weather-washed-blue sixty-two Imperial looked like just another one of the hundreds of multi-coloured steel beads trying to string themselves onto the asphalt necklace throttling the city's northern quadrants. From the "beads" themselves, jammed bumper-to-bumper, wheel-well-to-wheel-well behind, beside, and in front of it on Sixteenth Avenue North—which is what the Trans-Canada Highway becomes when it gets to Calgary—the long chromed schooner of a car did not seem unusual either. V-eight "boats" fifteen, twenty, even twenty-five years old were not uncommon in the rush-hour traffic lined up "forever" in Calgary.

The Alberta Transportation Department did not use road salt during the province's bitter winters. Salt would only melt the snow, which the cold would promptly turn to ice, which would promptly turn the roads into even more horrendous traffic nightmares than they already were. Instead they used sand for winter traction on Alberta roads. Cars lasted.

Nothing made the blue sixty-two Imperial stand out in the rush-hour traffic so congested that it seemed to have congealed—except for its Nova Scotia licence plate, and the Nova Scotia road-salt- and Nova Scotia salt-air-induced rust eating it away.

"Holy lifting!" Jimmy Maclean barked in his high-pitched voice, smacking the palm of his hand on the Imperial's heavy steering wheel. "Takes us just two and a half days to get across the friggin' country. Now looks like it's gonna take us at least another two and a half to get into the friggin' city."

Maclean did not need CFCN's traffic reporter to tell him what he already knew. He was not listening to CFCN's traffic reporter anyway. The Imperial's radio was not tuned to CFCN, but, like a plurality of radios in Calgary, to the top-ranked country sound of CFAC.

"Never seen nothin' like this at home, eh?" Ben Surette said from the passenger's side of the broad bench of a front seat, tapping the palm of his right hand lightly on the dash in time with the music. "Must be true then."

"What's that?" Maclean asked.

"About all the gold on the streets—can't imagine anybody'd do this otherwise."

"You got that shit right," Maclean laughed. Then he said, seriously, "Hope this baby doesn't decide to give up the ghost here."

"Yeah, wouldn't that be a kick in the nuts, just when we get down to the fine strokes." Surette caressed the dash. "That's a good girl. You just keep on hummin', darlin'. We're almost there."

The long, steel-heavy, high-riding car *was* a boat of

sorts, for Maclean and Surette the modern equivalent of the prairie schooners in which the last century's westward-bound immigrants had rattled across an endless sea of grass toward the promise of land. Like those settlers, Maclean and Surette had packed everything they owned into their schooner. They did not own much, even less than the possession-poor pioneers who had preceded them.

Maclean had a sleeping bag and a duffelbag stuffed with socks and shorts and a couple of changes of clothes, a box of chipped and mismatched dishes and kitchenware, a box of country records, and a cheap Zellers record player with a broken changer and tinny speakers. The leather jacket he was wearing was the only jacket he owned. He was wearing out his only pair of shoes.

Ben Surette had a garbagebagful of shoes—he loved shoes. And he had real suitcases—his one-time travelling salesman father's hard-siders—crammed and bulging with bedding and freshly mother-laundered clothes. Surette was the younger of the two, twenty to Maclean's twenty-seven, and away from home for the first time, while Maclean had not really *been* home for a long time. Surette also had dishes, but a fine set, real bone china pieces packed carefully in newspapers in a box from his Aunt Dot's basement in Bridgewater. On the dash in front of him, to the right of Maclean's fuzzy purple dice dangling from the mirror, was a planter with a cutting from the ivy in his mother's kitchen that he had promised to keep alive.

The car—it was Maclean's—was littered with empty chip bags, cracker boxes, candy wrappers, and pop cans. On the front seat between them were the remains of the case of beer they had bought in Kenora.

They had been hours out of Kenora, where northern

Ontario becomes Manitoba, where the east begins to become the west, before they had really begun to feel that they were headed for another place, a different kind of place—someplace new.

They had travelled nearly two thousand miles by then, yet not through a mile of country they did not know, at least not through country they could not associate with memory. The winding highway through New Brunswick could have been the Trail in Cape Breton, the colourful Quebec countryside the French shore in southwest Nova Scotia. Gently rolling rural Ontario might have been land around Truro. They missed the real rush in Montreal and Toronto, and for all they could see traffic was no worse there than at eight o'clock Wednesday morning heading out of Dartmouth for Halifax via the Rotary and the bridges. Northern Ontario looked not unlike the Eastern Shore minus the shore.

But here, where the road tunnelling endlessly through trees and rock opened suddenly, unexpectedly, breathtakingly, into this awesome perfect flatness, here was something new, something memory could not help them with, something they had never seen.

It took them half an hour to be able to see it. Their eyes had to adjust. Their pupils had to dilate to take in the expanded, seemingly limitless view. It was as if they had to learn to see again.

The expansive moment did not last. The expanse of land did.

Maclean quickly became bored with it. He began to curse it, to wonder when it would ever end, to wonder how anyone could live without a tree. He joked about how this land must have driven the pioneers' dogs crazy.

Surette, who was a reader—he had a box of paperbacks in the trunk—had read about the harsh prairie winters, the cold, the snow, the madness. He looked toward the horizon, where sky disappeared into earth, earth vanished into sky, and he thought about the winter, white on white, nothing into nothing, and he thought he understood, and he shivered.

He did not tell Maclean what he was thinking. He knew Maclean would not have understood, only laughed.

Maclean had tried to make it "away" before, in Ontario at the beginning of the seventies. He had hitchhiked to Oshawa, where he had a cousin working for GM. He had hoped his cousin could find him a job. But by the time he showed up at the door, his cousin had lost his own job, laid off, he said, "thanks to that G-D auto pact—fuckin' Yanks did us again."

His cousin was eligible for unemployment insurance. Maclean was not. He could not qualify for welfare. And he could not find a job, not even a dead-end, menial job that would have allowed him to hang on to his little dream a little longer.

He hitchhiked home.

Before he left, his cousin treated him to a movie, *Goin' Down the Road*. It was no treat. Maclean hated it more than any movie he had ever seen. He saw himself in the two losers. He hated what he saw. He heard the audience laugh at them. He heard the audience laugh at him. He hated what he heard.

No one would laugh at him this time, he had vowed to himself when he made the decision to head west. This time, *he* would do the laughing.

8:35 AM

"Aren't you ever in your office, John Jacob?" Thomas Red Crow asked, looking up from his oak-veneered, government-surplus desk stationed near the centre of the convenience-store-turned-law-office.

Red Crow had not removed the TONY'S VARIETY painted on the plate-glass front window. He had merely hung a hand-painted, red-on-white plywood sign—EAST END LAW CLINIC/Thomas Red Crow, BA, LLB—over it on the outside and drawn heavy curtains over it on the inside. It was as if he was not sure how long he would be staying. Calgary landlords being what they were, and Red Crow being Red Crow, it was only prudent.

The rest of the office had the same makeshift/make-do quality. Used filing cabinets, about the same vintage and probably from the same source as the desk, filled the lower half of the wall on Red Crow's right; above them, in black frames, hung Red Crow's bachelor's and law degrees and a small photograph of the great Blackfoot chief Crowfoot surrounded by his children. On the wall behind him, law books groaned on the crudely made, unfinished pine shelving that Fry had kidded him about mercilessly. In a corner in front of the shelves sat a small, round, Formica-topped table and two sagging Scandinavian chairs, where Fry and Red Crow had often sat talking late into the night over the lawyer's bad coffee and the leavings of the morning's box of doughnuts, where Red Crow tried to teach Fry to play chess. On the otherwise empty wall on Red Crow's left, the Sarcee chief Bullhead surveyed the room from an unframed, poster-sized photograph.

"About as often as you are, Tom-Tom," Fry said from just inside the door, tossing his black overcoat over the big manual typewriter on the oak secretarial desk at the front of the office where Tony's cash register used to be. The desk was reserved for the woman who came in on Tuesdays and Thursdays in a vain attempt to keep Red Crow's life and work in order. "Got your message."

"My mes*sage?*"

"All right, then, messages. But then, who's counting? I mean, they were all about the same thing, weren't they, Tom?"

"They were."

"Figured. Figured may-be I ought to talk to you face to face, not phone to phone."

"As you say—may-be."

"It was a mistake, you know."

"What, not slicing off your curly scalps and kicking your skinny white butts back across the water before you had a chance to make first landfall?"

"That too, maybe—probably. But I'm thinking a little more recent. You know what I mean, leaking the bogus story to the TV about the Indian kid being the one—you know, the killer. It was a stupid mistake."

"Just the leak? Not the shooting?"

"No, Tom, not the shooting. Sorry, but the shooting was traumatic for everybody concerned. But it wasn't a mistake. It was a good shooting."

"'A good shooting.' Now there's a really interesting concept."

"You know what I mean."

"You keep telling me I know what you mean—you mean you're sorry? Come to apologize on behalf of the whole force and all the fine citizens of Calgary? 'It's all a mistake. Ooops! Sorry about that. S'cuse us.'"

"Easy, Tom," Fry said, beginning to feel some resentment of his own, beginning to feel the old anger rising. He gestured toward the photograph of Crowfoot above the filing cabinets. "The kid who bought it—and he *did* buy it, went out of his way to purchase it—was not exactly a direct descendant of that great old bugger and you know it."

"I do, do I? Do *you* know that those descendants, those *direct* descendants, the ones in the photograph, Crowfoot's *real* children, were all dead of TB in about five years? White man's disease. And it was white man's disease as much as your bullets that killed the boy. So don't *tell* me he wasn't Crowfoot's child."

"Whoever's kid he was, Tom, he was a mean piece of work."

"No doubt. And how do you think he got that way?" Red Crow's eyes flashed. He slapped his palms hard on the desktop.

"I wouldn't have a clue."

"No? You want me to tell you?"

"No—I don't."

"What do you want, then?"

"Not sure, now. What'd you want anyway? They *were* your dimes."

"Never mind."

"'Never mind?' Dammit, Tom, we've come too far for 'Never mind.'"

"Oh, yeah? Have we? Just how far have we come? Ask the little red tart who got herself slapped silly and, to add insult, slapped in the cooler just because she is a little *red* tart. And how about the brothers who got themselves sliced up? Ask them. And ask that Commanche from Calcutta how far *he* thinks we've come."

"I said *we've* come too far—you and me. *We've* come too far. And *we* haven't come nearly far enough—but *we've* been workin' on it. Them? I'm not talking about them. Fuck them! We're gonna have to drag them along, probably kicking, probably screaming. And some of them won't come along, no matter what. But what else is new? We always knew that. We—"

"We? You keep talking about *we*. You know what *we* are?"

"What do you mean, 'what *we* are?'"

"Characters, that's what."

"Characters?"

"That's right. A couple of characters. In a goddamn western movie."

"What movie? I don't—"

"From the fifties. Cavalry and Indians flick. *Broken Arrow,* I think, was the title. It's on the late show once in a while. Technicolor and all that. About a noble savage, Cochise, and a noble Indian agent. They fight the wicked whites, fight the renegade reds, become blood brothers, all in a couple of hours, commercials included. That's us, except for the commercials and the casting—I'm prettier than the white guy they got to play Cochise, Jeff Chandler, good Indian name. And you're uglier than Jimmy Stewart. But it's us—except for one more thing."

"And that is?"

"It doesn't happen in two hours."

"We knew that."

"It doesn't happen."

"We knew it wouldn't be easy. We knew it would take time, probably more time than either one of us has."

"It doesn't happen."

"But we don't quit."

"We don't?"

"I hope not, Tom. I hope not."

"I know you do, John Jacob. I know you do. And I know I'm tired—Jesus! It's funny."

"What's funny?"

"This place—this great, throbbing, modern, *civilized* city." Red Crow flung his arms wide, toward the window, embracing the streets beyond the heavy curtain, beyond the TONY'S VARIETY painted backward on the glass, beyond the EAST END LAW CLINIC sign hanging outside. "You ever really look at this place? I mean, *really*? The steel. The concrete. All this fucking reflecting glass—this frenzy. You ever wonder, 'Jesus Christ! Who thought this up? What do they see in that glass? What the fuck *are* they trying to do?' You ask them and they'd probably tell you they're buildin' 'the city of tomorrow,' a model city for the twenty-first century. You ask me, and I'd tell you they're building a hell. I look at it and it scares me—scares the shit out of me. Every bit as much as 'the wilderness' must have scared the first of you white folks. Maybe that's how you turned white—just sheer bloody terror. Why, the damned wilderness scared you so much you killed it. And you keep on killing it. You can't seem to ever get anything quite right. So you knock it all down, start all over, forget where you started, or why. And yet you think where we live out there—"

"Out there?"

"The reserve. In the foothills and the valleys. What's left of our natural places. You think *that's* the wilderness, the dangerous place, and *we're* the savages. And you're wrong. This city is the wilderness. This is the true wild, savage, dangerous place—this place *you're* building. *You're* building a wilderness. *You're* the savages. And you're killing us. Not much wonder when one of us tries to kill one of you. Wonder is that not more of us do."

"But isn't ..." Fry was struggling for words, for wisdom he could not find. With every "us" and every "you," he felt the distance between them increasing. "...isn't that what we're about?"

"There's that *we* again."

"You and I—the committee. This business about the police liaison officer. Isn't it all about keeping that, the killing, from happening, literally and figuratively? Maybe getting it right, for once, finally?"

"Yes, yes, John Jacob," Red Crow laughed, a hollow, heavy laugh. "That's what it's about—what we're about. That's what we've always been about, cops and Indians, working hand in hand, trying to make it right, since the beginning."

"Beginning of what?"

"Hell, John Jacob, didn't they teach you the history? What am I asking? Of course they didn't. Well, my friend, here's today's lesson about police and Indian liaisons. Ever since you cops first got here—and cops were the first whites to get here—you've been supposedly 'protecting' us, knowing 'what was best' for us—"

"Sorry, Tom, but I don't—"

"You will, if you shut up and listen."

"I'm listening."

"Right. One time, when we, Bullhead and two, three hundred others, laid siege to Calgary—that's right, we actually did that once, over winter rations—Mounties knew better. Shook their heads at us, waved their index fingers at us as if we'd been naughty, and stepped in and tore down our teepees. And then persuaded Bullhead to move along. Rode with him ten days in the cold to the winter camp. Red coats 'protecting' redskins right onto the reserve. Some 'protection,' eh? And you cops are still 'protecting' us onto the reserve. Hell, you *still* think we're gonna lay siege to Calgary. But you and I, the big red lawyer and the little white cop, we're finally going to get it right. Yessir! *We're* finally gonna get it right."

Fry was silently cursing himself for the emptiness, the total uselessness of what he was saying even as he was saying it. He berated himself even more harshly as he listened to Red Crow. His friend had shown him an open, gaping, unhealing wound, and he had offered him a Band-Aid. That was always the offer. The words were always empty, always useless. Strike a committee. Hold a meeting. Appoint a task force. Issue a report. Do something. But do nothing.

"We—*I*—am learning," Fry said, lamely, he knew, even as he heard himself saying it.

"I know. I know you are."

The exhaustion and utter despair on Red Crow's face told Fry that his friend no longer believed that it made any difference.

8:40 AM

"There!" Ben Surette shouted, pointing out the window toward a thicket of road signs: words and arrows in green and white, yellow and black—EAST, NEXT LEFT, RIGHT-TURN ONLY, ROAD CLOSED, DETOUR, LOCAL TRAFFIC ONLY, DO NOT PASS.

"There where? Where? What?" Jimmy Maclean asked, flustered.

"There. Our turn. Right there—left right there—"

"Left, right, left, right. Whaddaya think, I'm in the fuckin' Forces? Left, right, fuckin' left—Jesus, Bennie!"

The Imperial was in the right lane. Without even glancing into the wide-angle truckers' side-view mirrors he had had installed for safety's sake, Maclean swerved suddenly to the left, across two lanes, cutting off a seventy-two Camaro, nearly clipping the front bumper of a seventy-seven Buick, just making the sharp left turn south at the intersection on two screaming tires, nearly sliding off the road onto the soft shoulder. He left behind him screeching brakes and angry-sounding horns, which he could hear, and furious, contorted faces and obscene hand signals, which he could have seen if he had looked into the rear-view mirror and if the view through the back window had not been completely obscured by pillows and blankets and Surette's bag of shoes.

"Jesus! That was some close," Maclean said, righting the car, easing his foot off the gas pedal, exhaling the deep breath he had taken at the beginning of the turn. "But we made it, eh, buddy? We're really down to the short strokes now. Wouldn't've wanted to miss that turn. Not there. Not with this damned traffic. By the time I got us goin' in the right direction again I might'a got us into the friggin' mountains."

"Oh holy oh jesus!" Surette sighed dejectedly.

"Oh holy oh jesus what now?" Maclean asked, glancing at his seatmate.

Surette was straining to look into the trucker's mirror on his side of the car. Maclean looked into the mirror on the driver's side, saw the flashing red and blue light on top of the white and blue Calgary Police cruiser, and groaned.

"Oh, fuck me, fuck me, fuck me … why me, why me, why me?"

He braked, pulled the big car onto the gravel shoulder, and came to a lurching stop. He put the Imperial in park, set the brake, and turned off the ignition, slapping his hands hard on the steering wheel, then dropping them into his lap. As he did, his elbow brushed the edge of the three-quarters-empty case of beer, sending a jolt of panic surging through him.

"Oh, Christ! The fuckin' beer—that's all we need. Cover it, Bennie—cover it!"

"Cover it? Cover it? And with what the fuck am I supposed to cover it? My ass?"

"No, asshole, not your ass—here. Use this."

Maclean was ripping off his leather jacket and handing it to Surette even as he was speaking.

"Hurry up, Bennie. Just put it over the top, tuck it under there ... ah ..." He grabbed the newspaper folded open to the classifieds on the dash. "... here, toss the paper on top there too."

Surette had just flapped the newspaper onto the box and was still unfolding it flat when he heard the sharp tapping on the glass and turned to see blue uniform pants and a big, black gunbelt filling the driver's-side window. Maclean quickly rolled the window down and peered up at the black-billed uniform cap and opaque sunglasses glaring impassively down at him.

Maclean and Surette could not have had worse luck in their first encounter with the Calgary Police Service. The Calgary police officer standing at the car window was Constable Chris Stanton, who was a *Calgary* police officer, city-born, city-raised, city-educated, and city-proud. He did not like the boom. He did not like what he thought it was doing to *his* city. He did not like the two thousand people a month the boom was bringing to *his* city. He did not like what he thought they were doing to *his* city. He seldom missed a chance to do something to them.

And today he was also smarting from the fierce, unofficial dressing-down he had had to endure from Inspector Phil Grantham for "pissing away" details of the scalp-murder story to fat-ass Hoffberg in the doughnut shop john, and he was sweating what the official reprimand Grantham had promised would do to his chances for promotion, to his career—the only career he wanted. Today of all days was no day to be on the wrong side of Chris Stanton.

"What's the trouble, officer?" Maclean asked lamely and far too politely.

"Are you shittin' me?" Stanton asked.

"Beg pardon?"

"I assume you're aware of the asshole trick you pulled back there."

"Back there? Well, yes, yessir, I know what I did—and I know I shouldn't've. I am sorry, but we're new to the city and—"

"What, where you come from, they *allow* people to drive like that? Let's see—failure to yield, improper left turn, failure to signal, maybe reckless, maybe even dangerous driving. You tellin' me those are the rules of the road where you come from?"

"Well ... no sir ... not ..."

"Well, thank God for that. You've restored my faith in the laws and police of Nova Scotia. May I see your licence and registration, please?"

Maclean reached into his back pocket for his wallet with his right hand and with his left motioned anxiously to Surette, who fished the registration from the glove compartment. Maclean handed the documents to Stanton.

"So being new is just a bullshit excuse," Stanton said as he studied the papers.

"Well, we were afraid of missing the turn—you know, getting lost—I guess I panicked a bit."

"A bit?"

"Okay—a lot. I am sorry."

"You are that."

"What?"

Maclean felt his bad temper getting the best of his good judgment. He was about to say something he, and Surette, inevitably would have regretted—more than they possibly could have known—when Stanton turned on his heel and walked back to his cruiser, flapping the documents into the palm of his left hand.

"Motherfuckin' son of a bitch," Maclean cursed, but quietly. "And catch those fuckin' sunglasses. You see any sun?"

"Jesus, Jimmy! Shut up!" Surette hissed at him. "I don't think this is a cop you mess with."

"No? Well, he's messin' with us," Maclean said, watching Stanton at his radio in the side mirror, "and for no better reason than where we're from. I'm fed up to here with that bullshit."

"Maybe, Jimmy. But today I think you better eat just a little bit more."

Stanton, having learned, with genuine regret, that there were no outstanding wants or warrants on the big Nova Scotia car or its driver, was about to head back to the Imperial, ticket book in hand, multiple charges in mind, when the dispatcher came back on the radio: a three-car pileup at Crowchild and Sixteenth Avenue near Motel Village, personal injuries, possible fatalities, massive traffic jam. He looked at the Imperial, looked at his ticket book, looked at the radio, cursed, and acknowledged the call.

"It's your luckiest of lucky days, fellas," Stanton said to Maclean and Surette, tossing the licence and registration through the window into Maclean's lap. "I've got a *real* call to answer and don't have time to write you up, as I'd dearly love to do. Somebody may be dead—probably because of some assholes like you—so consider this a warning. From now on, watch out for yourselves. *I'll* be watching out for *you*."

"Y-yes, officer, yessir," Maclean stammered, his heart pounding, but a laugh rising in his throat, which he was trying to choke down.

"And another thing," Stanton said, leaning on his forearms through the car window.

"What?" Maclean and Surette asked in unison.

"I'd, ah, keep the top *on* your 'arm rest' there," Stanton said, pointing with his ticket book toward the beer case. "Could be real damned unsafe otherwise."

"Oh, right, officer. We'll do that. We'll surely do that—for sure," Maclean replied.

By then, Stanton was striding back to his cruiser. He did not hear Maclean's reply, nor what he muttered at the end of it:

"Fuckin' pig."

And Maclean and Surette did not hear what Stanton mumbled as he walked away:

"Fuckin' Coasters."

9:45 AM

As far as Fry was concerned, old Aesop had it wrong. Familiarity bred not contempt, but indifference, which, in truth, was far more destructive. That certainly had been the truth, the intimate and trivial truth, of John Jacob Fry's life.

Not contempt, not hate, not jealousy, not bad faith, not an explosion of feeling, but an absence of it—indifference—had cost him his marriage. He knew that now. He had not known it at the time. At the time, he had been bewildered by it. He had not seen it coming. He had no inkling of it. He had no idea. That was, of course, the point. He who had made a career out of paying attention to other people's lives had not been paying attention to his own.

The day she gave him the news, Carol had reached across the salvaged-pine kitchen table in the rancher in Canyon Meadows and handed him a poem she had scribbled in pencil beneath a short grocery list—milk, bread, juice, marg—on the back of an envelope:

We live in the same house you and I
but in different spaces.
Sometimes we come together
and it's great.
But mostly we don't.
And it's not.

He sat at the table reading and rereading the poem, his mind racing, stumbling over itself, a stupid half-grin on his flushed face. He felt like an embarrassed seventh-grader who had not done his homework. He could not give the meaning. He did not have the meaning. He did not get the meaning. He looked across the table at Carol and he asked:

"Is there somebody else?"

She looked at him, sighing, slowly shaking her head from side to side, a sad quarter-smile on her lips, merely sadness in her eyes. "Yes.... But that's not why," she said, like a patient teacher to her exasperating student.

"Then *why?*"

She never told him. She left him to figure it out for himself. She left him.

Rather, she asked him (it was not really a request) to leave, to make legal and official the separation that was already emotional fact. He did not argue with her. He did not even try—to spare Tony, he told himself at the time. Possibly that was the truth. It was also true that he could not think of an argument. Like the student in the hotseat, he had not done his *home*work.

He left, quietly, civilly, amicably, which only helped make her case.

Making cases was the one thing he was not indifferent about. He had never been indifferent about that. He threw himself into it, especially after Carol threw him out. He threw himself into his work with such intensity that sometimes he almost forgot why he was working and where and sometimes he looked up, startled to see the sky.

Fry had learned over the years to see only the city he needed to see to be able to do his job. The rest of it he did not notice. He did not have to pay attention to it. He was indifferent to it. It was not important, he thought, when he thought about it at all.

Only long after the separation, after he had worked through the bitterness that quickly replaced the civility, after he had reconciled himself to lingering, ineradicable feelings of betrayal, after he had stopped drinking and started walking, only then did he begin to think that he was wrong. Only then did he, for the first time, actually begin to see the city whole, to take it all in, to pay attention to it all. It was a gradual thing. He had to learn to see it all, literally teach his eyes to see the city on the ground as clearly as they saw its underside.

He loved some of what he learned to see: the rivers and the few tall trees, the fewer old stone buildings, the high, blue sky that never ceased to amaze.

Some of what he saw he hated: the dirt, the traffic, the sprawling anonymous subdivisions (he found it increasingly hard to believe that he had actually lived in one of them), the featureless, self-reflecting towers, the almost visibly flexing muscles of growth.

To some of the city he remained indifferent. He did not like the Calgary Tower, but only from a distance, vaguely. He had never been in it, had never climbed the six storeys to the top, never looked out from the revolving restaurant to see the city spreading north-south across the prairie, the jagged outline of the mountains in the west. He did not believe he would care for the view; he was not going out of his way to take it in. He did not go out of his way to see the cramped and mediocre new developments with grand, space-promising names—the Properties, the Estates, the Downs—being burrowed into the short grass like gopher towns. The new developments were out of everybody's way. He did not appreciate the incongruity of world-class ocean sailors learning to tack against the tricky winds of tiny, man-made Glenmore Reservoir. He did not dress for Stampede Week. He did not root for the Stampeders. He still had never seen them play.

Memory kept him from returning to other places.

Fry avoided Canyon Meadows and its dipping, twisting streets, all beginning with "Can," where he and Carol had walked with the toddling Tony. The now nearly teenaged Tony preferred the adventure of visiting Dad on his own, on the bus. Fry had not been back to the zoo in years, since the unusually summery spring Sunday when Tony, then about ten, ran along the paths through drifting, snowy cottonwood fuzz. They stopped that day to stare at the gorilla in the Great Ape House—yellow-painted concrete blocks and weathered iron bars—staring back at them despairingly. Fry knew he could never see that Tony again. He did not want to see that gorilla again. He had no reason to go back to Heritage Park, where the slow, chugging, black train had enchanted and the garish, unblinking carousel horses had frightened Tony. Tony was outgrowing his childish fears and delights.

Fry feared at times that the boy was outgrowing him, feared that Tony's once-great trusting need for him would, like the boy's parents' once-great trusting need for each other, fade ... fade ... into indifference.

Fry was glad Tony was with him today, if only for a few hours, even though he was working, and despite what he was working on. He had not expected to see Tony today. After he had finished his dispiriting talk with Thomas Red Crow, he had called into the office to see if there were any messages. There was one.

The call he had left ringing at his desk when he left to see Red Crow, assuming that it *was* Red Crow, in fact had been Carol: something about Tony was all the message said. Fry called her, dialling quickly, impatiently waiting for her to answer, thinking, *Come on, come on,* worrying, as he always did now when he thought of his son out of his sight, out of his control—out of his life.

"Took you long enough," he said, when Carol picked up the phone.

"Look who's talking," she replied. "You're a hard man to get hold of—I'd almost given up on you."

"I'm just a man with a crowded dance card," he said, thinking: *You did give up on me.*

"Spare me the details. All I need to know is whether you can make some room on your card for your kid."

"Why? What's wrong? What's wrong with Tony?"

"Oh, nothing's wrong with him. It's one of those in-services."

"One of those whats?"

"In-services. You know, the days when the teachers don't teach."

"Why don't they call them 'out-of-services' then?"

"Good question—you're the detective. You answer it. But answer this one first: Can you look after—" Fry heard a groaning, "Oh, Mom!" in the background. He could almost feel the boy's wounded pride, see him raising his eyes in disgust. "I know, Tony, I know. You hate it when I say that. I forgot, okay? Forgive me, forgive me, forgive me." Fry smiled as he listened. "Anyway, Dad, can you have a meeting with man-child here this morning, maybe buy him lunch downtown? He can meet me at work after."

"Well ... I'm on this thing."

"I know, I know—and I don't want to know. I don't want to hear about it." *What else is new. You never did,* Fry thought. "What I want to know is whether you can. If you can't, I understand. He of course thinks he could stay alone, I guess he could, but—"

"I can," Fry said, silently marvelling at her ability to make demands of him without demanding, to pluck at his fatherly guilt as if it were the strings of a bass. "For real. Actually turns out that this 'thing's' taking me to an okay place this morning. Okay for Tony too."

The "okay place" was the Glenbow Museum, housed in eight storeys of cold concrete at the dark wind-tunnelling end of the Eighth Avenue Mall, where downtown began its speedy, seedy decline into the east end. The simple MUSEUM sign on its drab CALGARY MODERN facade gave no clue to the institutional San Simeon inside. Dubbed "Harvie's attic," after the eccentric, acquisitive, Hearst-like oil millionaire whose passion for the west created it and whose passionate collecting almost overwhelmed it, the Glenbow possessed not only the greatest collection of western Canadiana in the world, but also thousands of paintings, tens of thousands of books, coins, statues, weapons, and objets d'art from Chinese wares to Haida totems, even "true to life" replicas of the Crown jewels. The new Glenbow—formally the Glenbow Alberta Institute—had only been open since the fall. Until then, Harvie's passions had been scattered around the city: in the old sandstone courthouse, in a converted branch library, in an improvised gallery in an auto-parts warehouse, tons of them still in boxes in the dark.

Fry felt that he was also in a box, in the dark. That was why he was here. He had never been inside the new Glenbow. It was another part of the city he had not yet learned to see. Usually when he was this close to the east end he was on more urgent police business, and coming into the Glenbow never crossed his mind. Coming into the Glenbow today had crossed his mind because he *was* on police business, the most urgent police business of his career. He had come to the Glenbow at the dark end of the mall hoping to come out of the dark.

He stood in the foyer, just inside the Ninth Avenue entrance, his right hand resting gently on Tony's left shoulder.

"Wow! Neat!" the boy whispered excitedly, running coltishly toward the mirrored base of a shimmering explosion of brushed aluminum and acrylic that rose three storeys from the lobby.

Fry smiled, following him, watching him, taking pleasure in his enthusiasm. He glanced toward the information desk to see whether the boy's outburst, quiet by Tony's standards, had been too loud for the Glenbow's. The woman behind the desk was smiling.

The security guard rocking on his heels outside the museum shop was yawning.

The boy was right, Fry thought when he caught up with him at the base of the sculpture and looked up with him to see the piece soar through the spiral of stairs that led to the Glenbow's exhibition rooms. The creation—"Aurora Borealis," by Canadian glass artist and writer of the north James Houston—really was "neat." Fry was no art critic, but he liked the sculpture's strength and confidence, its eloquent play on a primordial theme.

Outside, just steps away, Fry would have found the mirrors, the plastic, the cold, gleaming metal and hard, glittering light of the soaring new west city offensive and unreal, a kind of betrayal. Yet here, in this new-west homage to old-west heritage, they seemed fitting, genuine, and true.

Perhaps he was seduced by the workmanship, which he could see was impeccable. He would have been even more impressed by the handiwork if he had seen it: workmen in white jewellers' gloves painstakingly fitting the thousand-plus acrylic prisms to the sculpture's metal core. It was enough to see the result, today, with his son, to see the light with his son, to see the light in his son. The moment was enough.

But the moment vanished almost as soon as Fry recognized it, before he truly could savour it. He remembered what had brought him here: the handiwork of another—crude, cruel, pains-giving play on another primordial theme.

10:20 AM

Two tightly woven, jet-black braids dangled from the side of the warrior's head to halfway down his chest.

His headdress was a cap made from the skin of a wolf's head, with beads sewn into the eye sockets. A single eagle feather protruded from just behind the wolf's left ear. Around the warrior's neck, in concentric circles all the way down his chest, hung necklaces of strung beads. His pants and the vest open at his chest were made of tanned animal skin. His left knee was still between the shoulder blades of his victim, who lay face down in the dirt, the top of his head covered in blood. The warrior's arms were upraised. In his right hand was the stone knife, crude yet sharp, stained with red. In his left was the reeking scalp. His mouth was frozen in an exultant scream.

Crouched on his right knee, his right hand pressing against his right thigh, his left forearm resting on his bent left knee, Fry had been studying him for some minutes, unmoving, wondering: *Is that how?* Suddenly he stiffened. A flash of movement. Not the Indian. It could not have been. In the brush to his right. But that was not possible either.

Was it?

No.

Fry sensed her before he saw her: her strong presence, her delicate perfume, his watcher's feeling of being watched. Still crouching, he looked up into the glass that covered the Glenbow Museum's diorama of the "Indians of Alberta, Before the White Man." He saw the distorted reflection of her standing behind him, her arms folded across her chest, carrying a stack of books the way he remembered schoolgirls doing. She was studying him, as he had been studying the scene of the scalping.

Fry was on the third floor of the Glenbow.

He and Tony had walked quickly through the white-walled maze of paintings and sculpture on the second. Tony was not interested. Fry felt out of his element. He had liked a striking black and white fabric sculpture by Harold Town, although he was not sure, and certainly could not have explained, why.

The two had strolled more slowly through the western Canadiana exhibited permanently on the third floor, stopping at the story, told partially in uniforms, of the North West Mounted Police, which eventually became the Royal Canadian Mounted Police.

"Hey, Dad, that guy looks just like Grandpa did, doesn't he?"

Fry had leaned toward the glass and examined the mannequin in the constable's dress uniform, circa 1905: the red coat with black epaulets, the black leggings with the gold stripe, the wide, round-brimmed felt hat, the gleaming Sam Browne belt, leather gloves, polished boots, and spurs. It could have been his father in full riding regalia. His father would have been comfortable in the uniform, probably comfortable in the times, maybe more comfortable than he had been in his own.

"Yeah. Yeah, Tony, it does, although your Grandpa was a bit heftier, don't you think? This guy looks like Sergeant Preston."

"Who?"

"Never mind." Fry pointed toward the very British-looking, white-pith-helmeted Mountie of 1877: "But I can't see Grandpa in that getup, can you? Or how about that one?" He gestured toward the little black pillbox strapped to the top of the daintily moustached 1873 Mountie's head. "Can you picture your Grandpa in that?"

"No way, Jose," the boy had laughed, shaking his

head. "I think he'd've felt pretty silly. And Grandpa wouldn't've liked that, would he?"

"No."

They had continued their tour, quickly through the ten thousand years or so that the Indians had occupied the west alone. The physical record was sparse. They had depended on stone, wood, bone, and leather for their survival. Only the stone and the bone had survived them. Fry wondered at their ability to live so lightly on the land. Tony was merely bored.

But the boy's interest was piqued when they came to the scene of the battle between the Plains Cree and the Peigan, to the scalping. So was Fry's. He had wanted to look at it more closely. He had not wanted the boy to look at it more closely. He sent him, complaining, ahead, upstairs, to the fourth-floor exhibits of militaria, minerals and "jewels," promising that he would be along in a few minutes. When Tony, reluctantly, had left, Fry had crouched a few feet from the triumphant Plains Cree brave, studying the grisly denouement of his killing.

Fry rose from his crouch now, painfully, his knees protesting, his thigh muscles resisting. He turned to face her.

She was small, tiny in fact, a walking definition of what the women's-wear catalogues meant by petite. She was wearing a soft, jade-green sweater over a black skirt over what Fry imagined were well-shaped, slender legs. Her flawless complexion was lightly made-up: hint of blush, subtle red lipstick, the suggestion of green shadow around almond-shaped eyes only a slightly less vivid green than her sweater. Her eyelashes seemed to be her own. Her brows had not been pencilled in with a brush. She was a perfect China doll—except for her amazing green eyes, the wave in the silken black hair falling below her shoulders, and the unmistakably European line of her nose and set of her jaw.

"Yes?" Fry asked her.

"Yes?" she replied.

"You seem interested in what I'm doing here."

"I get paid to be interested."

"And you are?"

"I am what?"

"What is it that you get paid to do that makes my business yours? Are you security?"

"No. Assistant curator. Particularly of the Native exhibits—in which you seem to be taking a particular interest. Particularly of this particularly grisly scene—at this particularly grisly time in the city."

"Good speech."

"And you are?"

"I am what?" Fry mimicked her, almost immediately regretting it. "I am sorry." He pulled his identification from his coat pocket. "I'm Jake Fry."

She took the shield with her right hand, holding the books against her with her left arm. She looked at the identification, then at him. Her eyes flickered with recognition.

"Oh, you're the one who's investigating the killings."

"Yes."

"I saw you on the news. You look older in person."

"Thanks. I feel older in person."

"Now I'm sorry. I'm afraid I'm not only, well, nosy, to put not too fine a point on it, but I also have a bad habit of saying what comes to mind. You can't imagine the trouble it gets me in."

"Oh, yes I can. Don't apologize. I'm nosy myself—occupational hazard. And I've also been known to speak first, think later, Miss ..."

"Ms."

"Sorry—I'm also a little slow to keep up with changing times. Ms....?"

"Fitzgerald."

She caught the momentary bewilderment in his eyes. It was as if she were looking for it. She almost smiled.

"Miyoko Fitzgerald," she said. "My father's in the import-export business in Vancouver. He 'imported' my mother from Japan."

"Am I that obvious or did you set me up?"

"Yes. And yes."

"Hmmm. Guess I'll have to work on my poker face. It's not a good idea for somebody in my line of work to be so obvious."

"It's not so obvious what somebody in your line of work is doing here, uh, oh, there I go again, nosy Parker. But I mean," she said nodding toward the savage diorama, "I'm sure you don't believe we've got your killer under glass there. He does have a pretty good alibi."

"I'm sure. No, he's not a suspect."

"Then this means you're still thinking it was a Native?" It was more an accusation than a question. Her voice took on an edge, a hint of indignation. "I thought the TV said you were wrong about that boy."

"'Still thinking it was a Native' suggests that I ever thought it was a Native. And I didn't. I didn't think it wasn't, either. I don't know what I think. I'm here trying to find out. And you're right, it *was* a mistake about that boy, although *I* wouldn't shed too many tears over him. And it wasn't *my* mistake."

"Oops. Guess I struck a nerve. I have a nasty habit of doing that too."

"You certainly have nerve."

"Thanks."

"Don't jump to conclusions. I'm not sure it was a compliment."

"Thanks anyway. How are you going to find out what you think here anyway?"

"Oh, I don't know," he answered, nodding over his shoulder toward the glass, "technique maybe. How it's done—was done. Seems likely that whoever's doing it, for whatever reason, is copying old ways, so I need to know the ways. You have any other material—besides Chief Slasher here—books, old drawings, that sort of thing?"

"Yes. Upstairs, sixth floor, in the library and archives, we've got a few—"

"Can I have a look?"

"—a few thousand."

"That many, eh?"

"Mr. Harvie was a serious collector. This place reminds me sometimes of a remark a professor of mine made once, quoting, probably misquoting, some German writer: 'Only the exhaustive is truly interesting.' We have a 'truly interesting' collection."

"Sounds to me like it'd be truly exhausting, *and* time-consuming."

"Well, of course, it's not all about Natives, let alone scalping technique. There's material about the tribes and their histories, customs, some eyewitness accounts of battles, oral histories, diaries, journals ... but you would have to do a lot of looking."

"And I don't have a lot of time."

"No, I don't suppose." She gnawed thoughtfully at her lower lip. "There *is* Russell."

"There's who?"

"Russell, Ted Russell—Dr. Theodore Patrick Russell, PhD. Teaches at U of C, Native studies. I took a course from him last year, after I got the job. My specialty's the northwest Indians, not Plains. I needed a quick fix—like you, I guess. Anyway, he's full of stories. Thinks he's something of a mountain man himself. You could talk to him."

Fry was writing Theodore Russell's name in his notebook when Tony came running up to him.

"Come on, Dad. There's some really cool stuff up there. There's armour. And you ought'a see the—"

"Whoa! Slow down, partner. Be right with you," Fry said, catching the boy's head in a gentle armlock.

"Yours?" she asked, already knowing the answer, something like disappointment in her eyes.

"Mine."

"Where's Mum?"

"'Mum's' at work. Junior here has a day off school. Thought I'd mix business and pleasure."

"Strange mix."

"Yes."

"Well, I have work," she said, hugging the books more tightly to her chest, seeming suddenly anxious to get away, "and you do too, I imagine."

"Yeah. Me too."

"Well, good luck. Goodbye."

She started to walk away, briskly. He called after her, without quite knowing why.

"Hey—*Ms.* Fitzgerald."

"Yes?"

She stopped, turning at the waist toward him.

"When 'Mum' gets off work, she'll go home to her house. When I get off work, I'll go home to mine."

She looked at him, furrowing her perfect brow, still nibbling at her lower lip. Then, slowly, she nodded her head, as if she almost understood.

1:30 PM

Jimmy Maclean was restless. For the third time in ten minutes, he glanced down at his wristwatch and then up at the clock tower of the city's sandstone old city hall. Either his new Timex was five minutes fast or the four old faces of the tower were five minutes slow. Not that it mattered. He was neither early nor late, just here. *Just* here? *Getting here* had cost him so much—not just his last little bit of money, but his last big dream. He was annoyed that *being here* did not seem to be ... well ... more. Yes. It should have been more. It had to be more. It had to be.

Maclean and Ben Surette were dangling their legs over the edge of a huge, as yet unplanted, concrete planter in one of the mini-parks around the imposing-old-sandstone/impassive-new-concrete city-hall complex. The few benches had already been taken. Maclean was slapping a thick, rolled-up newspaper against his open right palm. Surette was poring over a newspaper folded open in his lap and pinned against his thighs with his forearms to protect it against the gusting breeze.

The afternoon was sunny and spring-like, though hardly warm. That hardly bothered the downtown shop and office workers who, at noon, as if a whistle had blown, poured out of their downtown shops and offices onto the street, into the sun. Men left their overcoats in their offices. A few shivered in crisp white shirt sleeves, striped ties blowing over their shoulders. Women sat in groups on ledges, steps, and planters, balancing lunches on their knees, coats open to the air, lifting hems to expose their winter-pale legs to the sun.

Maclean and Surette had seen them on the Eighth Avenue Mall, where the two had walked after somehow finding their way south from the Trans-Canada into the city centre, winding around and around and around the one-way streets, finally deciding to park in the first space that looked big enough to accommodate the Imperial. They followed the downtown crowd as it spilled off the mall, into any spot it could find where the sun had found its way between the towers. Even the drunks who had got to the city hall mini-park ahead of Maclean and Surette had come out from under the benches to sleep on top, in the sun.

It was as if the long, cold, sun-stingy winter had left these westerners all slightly insane.

Just like Maritimers, thought Maclean, who had unbuttoned his own faded jean jacket and rolled up its sleeves, and who had toyed with the idea of putting down the old Chrysler's cloth top and driving around downtown waving at the girls in their wind-blown dresses—until he remembered how half the time the top got stuck either halfway down or halfway up. Remembering that made him think of home, which made him think of the newspaper Surette was reading—a week-old *Halifax Herald* he had picked up at a newsstand at the mall, where Maclean had bought today's *Calgary Herald* for the want ads—which only made him feel even more restless and annoyed.

With his thick, rolled-up *Herald*, he knocked Surette's thin, unfolded *Herald* from his lap onto the sidewalk, where the swirling breeze picked it up and sent it wafting across the mini-park.

"Fuckin' A...!" Surette cursed, darting an angry, befuddled look at Maclean, shoving him in the chest, knocking him backward into the planter, onto the hard-packed, winter-littered soil. "What the fuck'd you do that for? What the fuck's wrong with you anyway?"

"S'wrong with *me?*" Maclean asked, regaining his balance, leaning back in the planter on his arms. "You're the fuckin' one. Readin' that goddamned paper. For Chris'ake! That paper was out before we left home! And you never read the fuckin' papers when we *were* home."

"Well, we're not home now," Surette replied, defensively.

"That's right, Bennie, we're not. We're *here*—where we been talkin' about comin' for months, eh? So whyn't you fuckin' forget about *there*? Don't you be gettin' goddamned homesick on me now. You want to read a paper, you ought'a read *this* paper." Maclean speared Surette with the rolled-up *Herald*, over the heart, on the gold crest of his black-cloth, gold-leather-sleeved minor hockey jacket. "Wasn't no jobs in the one you was reading."

"No? Well, there was no fuckin' jobs in *this* one either," Surette said, grabbing the rolled-up paper from Maclean's hand and flinging it into a trash can next to the planter. "Not for fuckin' guys like us anyways."

"S-sure there's jobs—plenty of jobs." Maclean countered, sounding unconvinced even to himself.

"Yeah, right, buddy—and they're ours for the askin'. And we'll get one of them first thing in the morning. All we gotta do between now and then is get three, four years of university under our belts or a trade-school diploma or a heavy-equipment certificate in our hot little hands. You got any bright ideas how we might go about that, Jimmy? Eh? *Eh?*"

"Come on, Bennie, come on. We just got here—don't you be goin' south on me, not now that we just made it to the west."

"Oh, don't get your balls in an uproar. I'm not gonna

fuckin' let you down," Surette said, putting his hands onto the edge of the concrete and slowly raising himself back onto the planter. "I just thought ..."

"Just thought what?"

"I dunno—that it'd be easier. Oh, fuck me. Maybe I sort'a thought the streets really were ... well, you know."

"What? Gold?"

"Yeah. Gold."

"They are, Bennie, they are. We just gotta figure out where to go mining for it. What we gotta figure out now is where to crash."

Maclean jumped down from the planter, bent down, reached into the trash can and retrieved the newspaper. "*I'll* read the want ads for jobs," he said. "You can take the furnished rooms. But first we better find old Bertha before some cop comes along and tickets her or some tow truck comes along and takes her *and* all our worldly goods, such as they aren't."

He tapped Surette lightly on top of the head with the newspaper roll. "Come on, Bennie. We're here, buddy. We made it—and we're *gonna* make it. We are," Maclean said, to reassure himself as much as his friend. "You watch. We're gonna make it."

Surette looked at his companion for a long time, trying to decide whether he dared to believe the promise. Then, deciding that he did not dare not to believe it, he sighed, and slowly nodded his head. Maclean put his arm around the younger man's neck, playfully poked him in the belly with the paper, gently wrestled him down from the planter, and marched him east on Seventh, toward where he thought he remembered parking the big blue car.

4:15 PM

Fry sat on the long bench in front of his open metal locker in the locker room in the basement of the headquarters building on Seventh Avenue. He looked like an over-the-hill athlete after a hard practice. The sleeves of his pale-grey sweatshirt were rolled up over his elbows, the underarms and chest stained charcoal-grey with perspiration. The backside of his sweatpants and the backs of his calves were the same dark colour. His elbows rested on his knees; his arms dangled between his legs. His head was lowered, his face still flushed, his breathing laboured.

He had been putting it off. He always put it off now, as long as he could, sometimes longer than he was supposed to, longer than regulations allowed. This was one of those times. He was out of time. And still he had been putting it off.

He had tried to convince himself that he *could* use a workout first. Maybe, he told himself, Phil Grantham was right, and he *did* need to sweat off a few pounds in the police gym. He had not fooled himself. Fry hardly ever worked out in the gym, and when he did it was not to lose weight, and certainly not because of something Phil Grantham might have said.

The workout was a copout, to use the current phrase. He had been stalling. The workout was over now. He could not put it off any longer.

He reached into the locker where he had left it, wrapped in a white towel, when he headed for the gym: his holstered service revolver, the standard police issue double-action Smith and Wesson .38-Calibre Military and Police Special Model 10.

He was obliged to carry it all the time, even home.

And he did. But increasingly he felt the burden of the obligation. Every day, the lightweight revolver seemed to him to weigh more, to be weighing him down.

He had to qualify with the weapon at the basement firing range three times a year. Today was one of those times; today was past one of those times.

Fry pulled the towel-wrapped holster from the locker. As he did, he brushed the suit coat he had hung on a metal hook, momentarily revealing the small photograph of two young policemen in full dress uniforms taped inside. One of them was Fry, with his hair cut so short at the sides that it was impossible to tell if it had started to grey. The other was Gary Adams. Fry reached into the locker again, brushed the coat aside, and studied the photograph, remembering.

* * *

The call was routine, the kind of call young constables gagged on and groaned about and tried to beg off whenever they could: a dog barking in the backyard of a house on the southeast fringe of the city. Staff Sergeant Gary Adams was in a car not far from the location, headed back to the station after a "guest appearance" in a Grade-eight classroom, a favour to his daughter, Jeannie. He took the call to prove his point that there *were* no unimportant calls. He radioed in. Dispatch acknowledged.

Adams was northbound on Blackfoot Trail. Instead of jogging west on Glenmore Trail to Macleod as he had planned, he negotiated the Blackfoot-Glenmore cloverleaf and dipped south and east into Ogden, a lower-middle-class island on the flat-floored Bow River valley doubly cut off from the rest of the city—by the Bow, the freeway, and an irrigation canal, and by the low-lying oil-patch industries spreading around it. Ogden was a neighbourhood with nowhere to grow—not up, not out. Southeast of Ogden, the City of Calgary vanished into the sour-gas prairie.

Adams found the house, a tiny nondescript bungalow on a street of tiny nondescript bungalows. The postage stamp of a front lawn had been abandoned to fairy rings and dandelions. Adams shook his head. He knew about lawns. He had a good lawn.

He knocked at the front door. No one answered. From the back he heard the dog, a big dog from the bass-bellowing sound of the bark. He went round the side of the house and knocked at a side door. No answer. He heard the barking again, not from the backyard, though, from the garage. The garage door was open a crack. Adams leaned down and pulled open the door. He heard the barking inside, furious now. He could not see the dog.

He did not see the flash. He did hear the two almost-instantaneous explosions that reverberated in the confined space. He felt a ferocious, one-two sucker punch to his chest that took his breath and bent him double. He did not hear the third explosion, nor feel the round that tore off the top of his head and sent him flying backward onto the driveway, dead before he hit the pavement.

Sirens were sounding in the near distance before Adams' body stopped twitching. Within five minutes, two other officers were lying in the driveway, felled by the sniper, alive but bleeding profusely in a kind of subdivision no-man's land. In twenty minutes, the garage had been surrounded and the immediate neighbourhood evacuated. For thirty minutes more, the gunman kept up a steady barrage of automatic riflefire, wounding a third officer and disabling two squad cars. The police—by now there were a dozen on the scene—ineffectually returned fire, with woefully underpowered .38s and wildly inaccurate shotguns. Finally they called in an armoured personnel carrier from CFB Calgary to dislodge the sniper from his concrete-block pillbox. The killer leaped from his cover just as it started to tumble down on him, bolted through a side door, and ran into the backyard, where seven police slugs spun him to the ground when he stopped at a rusted-metal swing set, turned, and brought up his rifle to fire another burst.

Silence then, except for the barking dog.

The dog was still barking when Fry arrived at the crime scene, too late to help, too late to see Gary Adams' body, in time only to see the blood. "A good thing," they told him. "You wouldn't have wanted to see him, Jake. Sorry. Sorry. Sorry...."

Sorry. Yes.

Gary Adams had been Fry's oldest, closest friend. They had joined the force together. They had worked the street together. They had played and bitched and drank together. If Fry had believed in godfathers, Adams would have been Tony's. Adams had given Fry the nickname Ghost. And now Adams had become one.

Yes. Sorry.

Fry was also sorry. Sorry that he had been testifying in court, that he had not been in the driveway, that he had never told Gary Adams that he loved him and now never could. Sorry that he could not have added an eighth slug to the killer's body, and a ninth, a tenth. He was sorry.

He changed after that, drew into himself. He did not talk about what happened, about his pain. He did not sleep enough. He drank too much—too much coffee, too much scotch. He trained with his weapon too much, depended on it too much, trusted it too much, trusted no one and nothing else. His unnatural weariness gave his natural wariness an edge, turning it into suspicion, almost fear—and then not almost.

The low simmering rage he struggled constantly to control threatened to boil over and take control of him.

It was true even at home. He never struck Tony. It never occurred to him. But the boy, as children always do, sensed the change, the danger, and began to shy away, to stay away from him. He never struck Carol, never raised his hand, although he thought about it, and more than once had to check himself when he felt the anger rising and, with it, his right arm. He never even raised his voice, but actually grew quieter, eerily soft-spoken, maintaining an illusion of composure.

On the street, it was easier to keep up the appearance. On the street, nobody got close. But even on the street, he began to lose his composure. On the street, he almost lost control.

He almost lost it in a blood-spattered kitchen in Victoria one unusually sweltering evening during Stampede Week. A domestic argument had ended when a husband stabbed his wife in the heart after she stabbed him in the ego.

The man's inconsolable, incomprehensible blubbering drowned out the cheers drifting through the open window from the crowd at the chuckwagon races at the Corral a couple of blocks away. Fry was standing at the window, just as he would usually do, smoking, waiting for the man to wind down. But, unusually, he was also thinking of grabbing a handful of sweat-

and-blood-soaked T-shirt, lifting the guilty grieving killer from his kitchen chair and smacking him, hard, on the right cheek with his palm, on the left with the back of his hand, and then dropping him. He shocked himself with the thought. Abruptly, surprising the uniforms who had answered the call, he walked out of the kitchen onto the back porch, where he held the railing tightly until the thought receded, although never entirely went away.

Fry had almost lost it early one Saturday morning in the grim fluorescent glare of the interrogation room.

In an attempted robbery the night before, an Ontario low-life who had been in the city less than twenty hours had taken the life of a Lebanese convenience store operator who had been in Calgary for more than twenty years. The thief ordered the merchant to open the till. The merchant refused. The thief hit him above the right ear with a tire iron, fracturing his skull. Then he calmly opened the cash register, stuffed the few bills—fifty-eight dollars in total—into his pocket, snatched a carton of cigarettes from behind the counter, opened it, opened a pack of smokes, and lit one before strolling out the door—right into the arms of Constable Reg Hunter, who was making his regular Friday night stop at the store for coffee and a chat.

Now the suspect was in front of Fry, leaning smugly back in a chair at the interrogation table, clumsily self-tattooed arms folded across his chest, a smirk on his face, answering none of Fry's questions. It did not matter. His cooperation was unnecessary. But Fry imagined himself rising slowly from his chair at the opposite end of the table, walking around it until he was behind the suspect, and kicking the chair out from under him, sending him to the floor on his back, landing hard on his throat with his knee. Fry did not leave his chair. Quietly, so quietly he had to say it twice, he asked Hunter, who was sitting beside him, to take the suspect back to the lockup. Fry sat at the table for several moments after they had gone, shaking.

Finally, Fry had almost lost it in full public view on Macleod Trail in a matter that was not so much police as personal, and not even genuinely personal at that.

It was a lucky Monday on which, inexplicably, he was either ahead of or behind the usual morning crush. He was travelling ten kilometres above the speed limit, positively speeding for a Monday morning. But not fast enough for the heavily bearded man in the black ballcap and sunglasses who was driving the black pickup behind him. The truck was tailgating; Fry hated tailgaters. He slowed, to the speed limit, then slower. He could count the dots on the fuzzy dice dangling from the truck's rear-view mirror. The truck stayed with him. It could have used another lane, but apparently the driver wanted Fry's. Fry sped up, then slowed, then slowed again. The truck stayed glued to his bumper until, finally, it roared past, its horn blaring. Fry hit his horn and saluted with his middle finger as the trucker went by. The truck cut in ahead of Fry, forcing him to brake, and then suddenly braked, swerving, tires squealing, rubber smoking. In the middle of Macleod, in the middle of the morning rush, the truck stopped, and its infuriated driver jumped out and headed for Fry, who, inflamed himself, tore open the car door and went to meet his tormenter.

"You motherfuckin' asshole. You want to play fuckin' games, do you?!" the truck driver bellowed, clenching and unclenching his fists.

"Yeah, asshole," Fry said with a calm that belied

the blood pounding in his temples. He stopped in the highway about twenty feet from the trucker bearing down on him, spread his legs, squatted slightly, and reached back for his holster, starting to, *wanting* to, snatch his .38 from it and whip it around, take dead aim at the trucker's midsection, freeze him in mid-stride, and say: "Yeah, asshole, let's play."

He caught himself, horrified. He took his hand off the revolver. His face turned the same ghostly ashen colour as his hair. He had just learned something about himself that he did not want to know.

By then traffic on Macleod had come to a standstill in both directions. Motorists laid on their horns, an angry cacophony sounding irregularly up and down the street.

Fry looked at the belligerent brute of a truck driver still headed on a collision course toward him. He had to stop the man. He could not shoot him. He could not even threaten him. With the hand still inside his coat, he grabbed his gold shield, pulled it out and flipped it open, hoping it would stop the man, doubting it, preparing himself for a fist fight he could not win even if he won.

Yet the trucker did stop, dead in his tracks, as if he had struck a wall. Something in the man's eyes told Fry that he had seen a badge before.

Fry took advantage of the opening.

"Unless you want to get both our weeks off to the worst goddamned start you can imagine," he said, "I suggest you get your ass back in the truck and haul it out of here."

Fry did not wait to see if the truck driver would obey. He pocketed his shield, turned quickly on his heels, and walked away, oblivious to the traffic and the horns and the drivers' angry shouts and obscene gestures. He flung himself into his still-idling car, yanked it into drive, wheeled sharply right, gunned the engine, and roared north toward the city.

At the station, without knocking (the first time he had ever done that), Fry marched into Ben Drayton's office. Drayton was the inspector in charge of homicide. Fry took out his shield and holster and dropped both onto Drayton's desk. Drayton looked at them and then, from under his bushy, grey eyebrows and his stiff, grey military-issue crewcut, up at Fry. He asked:

"Why?"

Fry told him what had been happening to him, what had happened this morning, and what had almost happened this morning.

Drayton, who had seen it coming, was prepared for it. He told Fry to sit down. Fry sat. Drayton stood. He left the office. Fry watched him go.

Drayton returned in less than fifteen minutes.

"You're on medical leave," he told Fry, who opened his mouth to protest, closing it when Drayton, easing himself back into his chair, said: "Shut up. You're on leave, thirty days. And it's not just rest you're going to get. You're gonna get help too—professional help. That's the deal, and you're gonna take it." He snatched the badge and gun from the desktop in one of his surprisingly large hands and deposited them in a desk drawer. "These'll be here when you get back. Now go home."

Fry went home.

At home John Jacob Fry had a shelf-full of pistol-shooting trophies. But Marcel Phillipe Laurier, the cop-killer—a crazed, recently paroled thirty-seven-year-old loser with a history of violence and a glue-addled brain—had proved to be the better marksman, putting the same three slugs through two policemen who were miles apart, killing one, mortally wounding the other.

* * *

Is it four years now, Gar? Fry thought, still staring at the young faces in the old photograph taped inside his locker. *Seems like only yesterday.... Seems like forever ago....*

Fry let the folds of his coat drape over the photograph again. He sat upright on the bench, inhaled, and sighed deeply. He widened his eyes, as if trying to adjust to the light. He unwrapped the white towel.

4:30 PM

"Ready on the line? Jake? Ready on the firing line? Jake, you ready to fire or what?"

"...what?" Fry only dimly heard the voice of Sergeant Tim Mihofsky, the firearms training officer, as it sounded metallically on the speaker system of the basement firing range at the Seventh Avenue police headquarters.

"Come on, Jake," Mihofsky barked over the speaker. "Where's your head? You're already three weeks late on this. Qualifying, remember? Even hotshot detectives have to do it. Especially a not-such-a-hot-*shot*-anymore detective like you. Can't cover for you any longer. You ready or not?"

"Yeah. Yeah, I'm ready—shoot."

"Very funny. We'll see if you can shoot your weapon as well as you can shoot off your mouth. Hey, you're not gonna wear headgear?"

"No, I like to hear what I'm doing."

"And how can you hear a fuckup?"

"What was that?"

"Very funny—assume the position."

Fry faced the target, only fifty feet away, a human silhouette diagrammed like a side of beef, but with numbers one to five in place of prime cuts. The higher the number, the higher the score, the deadlier the aim—five for the mid-section, only two for an elbow. Fry was standing in the middle of four other officers standing at similar cubicles. They were wearing uniforms, and stereo-type headphones to protect their hearing. Fry's service revolver lay on a small counter in front of him. Behind him, in a room with three windows, Mihofsky, and anybody else who wanted to, was watching.

Fry unsheathed the piece from its holster. He opened the revolver to ensure there was a round in each chamber. He closed the cylinder. He released the safety. He fixed his eyes on the target.

The blue-steel revolver with the dark walnut grips weighed only a couple of pounds. But as Fry stood at the firing cubicle, his feet spread comfortably, his shoulders squared, the gun at the end of his hands trained on the black human silhouette seemed heavy, so heavy that he could hardly hold it steady.

"Ready on the firing line. Fire at will."

Fry squeezed the trigger, and as he did the four uniforms on either side of him also squeezed. The sharp pop-pop-pop, pop-pop, pop, pop reminded him for an instant of the cheap firecrackers he had once brought back from a family trip to Montana and set off in the backyard just after dark on Dominion Day, to the delight of four-year-old Tony.

Lately Tony had started to delight in the real thing, as his father used to do. Fry often watched as Tony leafed through sporting-goods catalogues, lingering at the gun pages. And it was not the armour that the boy had wanted Fry to see at the Glenbow earlier in the day, but the guns: the Navy Colts and six-shooters and Winchester '94s.

Fry wondered when Tony would ask him to buy him a gun. He wondered what he would say. He wondered whether it was genetic.

Fry fired the first five rounds with his usual indifference. When Ben Drayton had given him his weapon back when he returned from "medical leave," he found that he no longer wanted it. When he had to shoot at the range, he shot just well enough, adding up enough elbows, wrists, and shoulders to qualify. Even that was not exactly according to regulation.

Despite the so-called "high-powered" .38 special round that exited its five-inch barrel at about nine hundred feet a second with a 158-grain load, the Smith and Wesson's stopping power was notoriously poor. The theory was that it was powerful enough to stop a perpetrator, but not powerful enough to continue on through into an innocent bystander. That was the theory. In fact, it took four or five direct hits in what the firearms training manual called "the centre of the visible mass" to knock down and disable an opponent. And that was what officers were trained to do: empty their guns as fast and accurately as they could.

The officers firing with Fry had followed the manual, clustering their shots in the centre of the chest, finishing ahead of him.

As Fry was slowly squeezing off his sixth round, the androgynous human silhouette fifty feet away took on not so much a different shape in his mind as a different substance. He suddenly saw in it what he was looking for, not who, but what—the evil. Once again, as they had been so many times before his physical and emotional near-collapse, his hand, eye, and weapon were one, and he fired, the round exiting from the pistol, but in truth coming directly from him, from inside of him.

The feeling was unnerving. He could feel himself sweating, shaking. He quickly emptied the revolver of its empty shell casings, holstered it, and began to leave just after Mihofsky called, "Cease fire!" and before the target started back to him on its electrical pulley.

"Hey, wait a sec, Jake," Mihofsky, who had emerged from the three-windowed room behind the firing line, called after Fry. "Don't you want to see how badly you did this time?"

"Naw," Fry called without looking back. "I'm sure you'll let me know."

"Spoilsport. Let's have a look anyway," Mihofsky said, standing at the cubicle where Fry had been firing. He unclipped the target, examined it: hits in a wrist, an elbow, two shoulders, and a thigh. "Looks like no teddy bear for you again today, Jake. Wait now—what's this?" He saw the sixth hit: dead-centre in the head, right between the eyes. "Hey, Jake, maybe I'm wrong—maybe there's still a touch of John Wayne in you after all. What do you think I ought'a do with this?"

"Oh, I don't know, Hof," Fry said, looking back from halfway through the door to the locker room. "Maybe take it to the crapper with you next time you go. Might be short on paper in there."

9:45 PM

The swirling wind had picked up and straightened out late in the day, becoming westerly at a steady thirty kilometres an hour, bringing with it thick, low clouds and, after nightfall, the first real rain of the spring. The darkness now was nearly complete, interrupted only by the faint, late-night aurora of city light far north of the ravine and the slivers of lantern light through cracks in the boarded-up windows of the abandoned log cabin on the grassy terrace just south of it.

"Goddammit!" Ben Surette cursed as rain water dripped from the cabin's failing shake-shingle roof into the bag of chocolate-chip cookies he was eating and onto the car magazine he was reading. "Just goddamn you to hell anyway!"

He and Jimmy Maclean were half-zipped into their sleeping bags and propped up on either side of a cold sandstone hearth in the larger of the cabin's two dirt-floored rooms. A pan of water steamed on a propane camp stove sitting on the hearth. The lantern sat on a case of beer tipped on its end between them.

Like a half-man/half-caterpillar, without unzipping his bag, Surette, hugging his cookies and his magazine, squirmed out of the path of the water, which by now was spilling from the roof in a thin, steady stream. His gyrations cast huge, otherworldly shadows in the yellow glow of the lantern. Maclean looked up from the centrefold he had been studying and laughed.

"You was the one wanted home, Bennie," he said, cocking his ear toward the sound of the rain pelting against the roof. "Well, sounds like you got it. No rain for a month or more out here, and we get here in the mornin' and, bang-o, it's rainin' by evening. Must'a brought it with us—just like home. Good old Nova Scotia sunshine—windy, wet, and cold. Looks like *home's* comin' right in to get you, eh, Bennie?"

"You're a real fuckin' funny man, Jimmy, a real fuckin' comedian," Surrette said, saluting Maclean with his middle finger and darting an annoyed look at him from the dry corner where he had reestablished himself. He reached into the cookie bag, reopened the magazine, wiped the beads of water off the pages with his shirt sleeve, then cursed again. "Shit!"

"Now what?"

"Now I'm too goddamned far from the light to read anymore."

"Aw, for Chris'ake, Bennie, why don't you give it a rest? Why don't you *get* some rest, anyway? You don't need to read anymore. And you *can't* be hungry anymore—you gotta be full as a tick by now. Come on, we got a big day ahead of us tomorrow."

"Oh yeah?"

"I imagine so—and, my whiny friend, no matter what you think—we didn't end up doin' so fuckin' bad today, either."

"No?"

"What's this? Everything I say you gotta question? Anyway, the answer's no, we didn't do so bad today. We didn't get busted by that prick of a cop. We got a chance to see some more of the city."

"Big fuckin' deal."

"Wait now. Got to find out about the place. Can't find no work if we can't find our fuckin' way around. And we did find out," he said, fishing in his shirt pocket to make sure he still had the address he had scribbled, finding the folded piece of notebook paper, flourishing it at Surette, "where to go lookin' for *real* jobs—no more want-ad bullshit. We, ah, found out that booze is a lot cheaper than home. And, da-da," spreading his arms, "we even found a roof for free for the night."

"Yeah—some *roof* this is. A regular fuckin' Taj Mahal."

"Jesus H. Christ, Bennie! Thought I had you back on side. We're not exactly flush, you know—Taj Mahal nothing. Crummiest Taj Motel would've put us out more'n we could afford. Free room, even without the board—even without much of a roof—well, it's nothing you ought'a be shittin' on."

"Which is something else it doesn't have."

"What?"

"A place to take a shit."

"Sure it does."

"Where?"

"Why, anywhere outside you want to go."

"Ha. Ha. That's all I need—get caught with my pants down and my ass wet."

"Take a little soap with you, you can shit and shower at the same time."

"Fuck you."

"Hey, Bennie, lighten up, okay? Who's gonna catch you out here? You're more likely to catch cold than to get caught—and don't say it—you're *not* gonna catch cold either. Why don't you just try and relax? I know what—I'll play mother."

"You'll play who?"

"Mother. You know. Like at a tea party. I'll pour the tea."

"Tea?"

"You got it, Bennie. Like I said, what you need is to relax. And a good hot cup of white rose tea is just the thing for it."

Maclean unzipped his sleeping bag and climbed out of it like a clumsy butterfly emerging from its cocoon. He squatted at the hearth, pouring what was left of a litre carton of milk into a large, paper doughnut-shop coffee cup, topping it off with hot water from the pan on the camp stove. He turned off the stove. With a grunt, he got to his feet and, dodging the dripping water, shuffled to the corner of the cabin. He handed the concoction to Surette, playfully mussing his hair as he might have a child's.

"There you go. Not our best china, I'm afraid—should've unpacked that box of yours out in the car."

"Somebody could've seen the car, you know," Surette said, after taking a sip of the hot drink.

"Holy lifting, Bennie, you do worry like an old woman. Somebody *who* out here?"

"Oh, I don't know—there was that big house there, when we came down the old road. Somebody there could have seen—"

"Yeah, there was the house, but nobody there did see us, and even if somebody did, so what? Car's parked off the road. We ain't doin' nothin' wrong anyway. Not to worry. Remember what that fella told us, about nobody comin' down here much, only to go bird watching, walk the dog, for a run maybe. And for sure nobody's gonna be doin' any of that tonight. Come tomorrow we'll be long gone. We're safe enough here for the night—you just drink your tea. Me, I think I'll have another of these special-blend malt teas."

Maclean knelt at the case of beer on his way back to his sleeping bag, opened it as if it were a refrigerator, slid a squat brown bottle out on its side, and squeezed off the top. He raised the beer to Surette, took a long drink, and then said:

"Oh, come on, Bennie, come on—where's your sense of, you know what they say, adventure?"

"Adventure?"

"Yeah, sure," Maclean said, zipping the bag to his waist. "Didn't you ever camp out as a kid, you know, pretend to be out in the wilderness, out on your own, on some dangerous mission?"

"Well, yeah, I imagine. Sure, sure, when I was a kid."

"Me too. There was this old huntin' camp in the hills behind our place—cabin sorta like this one, even more tumbledown, half the roof actually caved in. Built on the side of the hill. By then looked like it was about ready to slide all the way down. Anyway, there was a big pine tree a little higher up the hill, must'a been, oh, four, five feet around, a hundred feet high, tallest thing on the hill—struck by lightning I don't know how many times. Wouldn't die, though. We hung a rope swing from one of the big branches fifteen, twenty feet off the ground. Used to pretend we were commandos, hang on to that rope, swing out over the hole in the roof, and drop right inside. Broke my arm one summer. Made my mum right mad. She'da whacked me good if I wasn't already hurtin' so much. Made me promise not to do it anymore. And of course I promised—and of course, I lied. I was back on that swing before the cast was off. Gawd, that was some fun."

Maclean was smiling as he talked, remembering. Suddenly he brought himself up short, as if he had caught himself doing something wrong. He drained the brown bottle in three huge gulps.

"Whoa, Maclean! That'll do it," he said. "Jesus, Bennie, you're gonna have me feelin' homesick if I'm not careful. And Christ all I really was was sick of home. Nothin' there anymore, nothin' there—not even that shack. Hell, not even that big fuckin' pine tree. Lightning finally hit it a good one and it did burn, and the cabin too and half the hill—burned. Bridges are burned, too, this time. Damn straight. Not goin' back this time. No fuckin' way. Where I'm goin' is to sleep—I don't figure this cabin'll burn if I leave the lantern on so we can duck the leak if we need to take a leak, eh, Bennie? Bennie...?"

Maclean looked over toward Surette, who was still half-sitting, half-leaning in the corner, arms folded across his chest, head drooping, sound asleep. Maclean thought about going over and lying him down, but decided not to take the chance of waking him up. He smiled at the thought of tucking Surette in, made a mental note to tease him about it in the morning.

"You're gonna have one stiff neck in the morning, buddy," he whispered. "Might not matter, though, after today. After today, even you might not care. You might not think so, Bennie, but this just could have been our lucky day. We might just go to the head of the employment line now—hell, we might even get famous."

10:30 PM

A fifty-foot length of three extension cords snaked from the outlet under the kitchen table, along the centre hallway, around the corner and down the narrow cellar steps of Fry's tiny rented house in Eau Claire. The three cords together were just long enough to make it possible for Fry to use his circular saw in the basement without instantly blowing the house into darkness.

Reluctantly, Fry had given up trying to hand-saw the plywood backing for the scrap-wood bookcase he was making for Andy Stimwych's son. It had not been an easy decision. He was a stubborn man and a great believer in ceremony and style. How a thing was done mattered to him almost as much as the thing itself. But only almost as much. His father's ripsaw would not have worked on the splintering, weathered plywood. It would have ruined the job. The plywood was the only backing material Fry had. He left the saw hanging on the pegboard over the workbench.

He unpacked the circular saw from one of the cardboard boxes under the bench. He plugged the cord into the saw. He switched on the machine, wincing at the ear-splitting metallic whine, waiting for a fuse to blow. The lights dimmed, but did not go out. Fry took his finger off the switch and carried the saw to the sawhorses, where he had left the plywood the night he had tried to rip it by hand. He lined up the blade with the chalk lines on the board. He pressed the switch and began to move quickly through the wood.

Too quickly, it seemed to him. He cursed the speed and the lack of control and only hoped he could hold the saw to the line. Then he remembered that the line he was trying to hold was the line he had snapped on the board when he was too tired to see. And then he had to hope that his hand had been true, because it was too late to change his mind, too late to follow another line. He could only hold on and try to follow this line to the end.

The end came quickly. The saw passed through the wood and continued into the air, lifting Fry's hand from the board almost in a flourish. Fry did not even bother to check the edge for straightness. He was stuck with it. And it dictated the other edge, which the saw quickly cut along the other chalk line. He lifted the plywood off the sawhorses and carried it to a large piece of cardboard on the floor, where he had loosely fitted the rest of the bookcase and laid it face down. He lowered the plywood onto the back of the bookcase.

"You son of a bitch," he cursed under his breath. "You dirty son of a bitch."

The backing was out of plumb. Fry stood over the

bookcase, hands on his hips, rolling his tongue around in his left cheek, trying to figure out what to do. He did the only thing he could think to do. He knelt down and, with his two hands, gave the left and right sides of the bookcase a sharp whack, raising a cloud of fine sawdust, fitting the plywood backing perfectly.

It's all in the wrists, he thought, with a thin smile of self-satisfaction, *all in the wrists.*

He tried to lift off the plywood backing, nearly tearing off a fingernail. The fit was too good now. Gently he tapped one of the sides with the heel of his palm, loosening it enough to enable him to lift off the backing easily. He leaned the plywood against the cellar wall beside the workbench. He knocked down the rest of the bookcase, leaning the pieces against the plywood.

He picked up the two pieces he had sawed off the board, tossing the larger into a pile of scrapwood in a corner of the cellar. He was about to throw the smaller piece onto the pile when he noticed the faded blue flyer still glued to the rougher side of the plywood. Fry had not noticed it before. He had had no reason to notice it ... before.

The flyer advertised an "alternative music" concert at the University of Calgary from about a year and a half before. The Sunshines Family were playing—had played. The band's name had been hand-lettered in large, fancy black print. Beneath it were fading cartoon figures of the band members: scruffy Benny, buxom Bonnie, curly-haired John and wide-eyed Gina, the two distracted young lovers. And, in the middle, black-haired, beautiful Lesley Conner, the late Lee Boy. Fry recognized them immediately. He remembered the artist's hand from the graffiti on the chipping plaster walls of the tumbledown mansion on Mount Royal.

Fry grabbed a finishing saw from a hook on the peg-board. He laid the plywood on one of the sawhorses and, holding the board steady with his knee, carefully cut around the flyer, leaving about an inch of plywood on all sides. He switched off the overhead lanterns and headed up the stairs, carrying the crudely framed flyer under his right arm, gathering the extension cords in his left hand.

In the hallway, Lips was pawing and playing with the last of the cords as if it were a mouse with an amazingly long tail.

"Get away, shit-bird," Fry said softly, smiling, pushing the cat gently away with his foot. "You must've spent most of your nine already. Don't blow the rest doing something dumb. I think I'm out of fuses anyway. Go on, get out of here."

Lips arched his back, hissed a little, and took one half-hearted swipe at Fry's foot before scurrying down the hall. The big cat was already crunching away at the last of the cheap dry food in his dish when Fry followed him into the kitchen.

Fry squatted, reached under the table and unplugged the cord. He took a beer from the refrigerator, spun a chair around, and sat down heavily at the table, resting his arms on the chair back, propping the flyer against the salt and pepper shakers, studying it, thinking how somebody had "discarded" the beautiful boy who had drawn the cartoon, turning him into scrap no one could salvage.

may 5 3:45 AM

The rain was falling like polite applause.

He was grateful for the rain. Not because of the drought. He did not care about the drought; he never even thought of it. No, he welcomed the rain because the sound of the rain would mask any sound he might make. Not that he would make a sound, nor any wrong move.

He had been clumsy only once, during his first fumbling, failed attempt. He had lost his nerve then. Never again. Since then, he had learned stealth; he had learned to take care, to move slowly, to observe, and to be sure.

Tonight … this morning—yes, it was morning now —when he parked the car at the end of Twenty-fourth Street SE, he had sat inside in the dark for at least twenty minutes, listening to the rain on the roof and looking to see if the sound of his engine or the gleam of his headlights had aroused anyone on one of the silly "Wood-" streets in the tacky new Woodlands subdivision that his old street map still called, elegantly, "Livingstone."

Only when he was certain that he had not been noticed did he get out of the car, pushing the door closed softly until it quietly clicked, walking quickly away on the unlighted side of the street, collar upturned, head down. Only now, when he was out of sight of the subdivision houses, among the trees, did he take the flashlight out of his coat pocket and turn it on, holding it low, training it on the ground. The old road sloped steeply and the rain had made it slick. He had to be careful.

He made his way slowly into the ravine, taking small, sure steps, his right hand holding the light, his left arm hugging the big leather bag to keep it from clattering. The light picked up another light, a reflection in the trees. He froze. Then he remembered. The big blue car pulled off the road here, to be parked out of sight. He continued, switching off the light when he came to where the road forked into the driveway of the single house in the ravine. The house was dark, also hidden among trees. But no need to take the chance. He was sure he could find the way. It was not far now.

He was at the edge of the old pasture, eyes homing in on the thin slices of lantern light directly across the grassy terrace, when, just behind him, he heard a rustling in the brush. He gasped, turned suddenly, but could see nothing. He heard the noise again. Panicking, he switched on the light and shone it into the darkness, waving it first to the right ... nothing ... then left ... nothing ... a hundred-eighty degrees to the right again and ... two eyes, two eyes straight ahead, gleaming in the dark, two eyes blazing at him in the dark, coming for him out of the dark, then vanishing in a blur of movement, an explosion of sound.

He turned to run. His right foot slipped on the wet grass and his legs went out from under him. As he fell, he saw the deer burst past him in the beam from the flashlight. And as he hit the ground hard on his back, he saw the light fly from his hand into the night. He heard the flashlight skitter onto the old road. He heard the deer trampling through the brush. Then he heard nothing except the sound of the rain, falling harder now, and the sound of his hoarse breathing and of his own heart beating.

For a few moments he lay on the ground in the rain, feeling the rain on his face, feeling his racing pulse, wondering whether anyone had heard the commotion, wondering whether anyone had seen the light, telling himself that no one could have, trying to assure himself that he was safe, not quite succeeding. He found that he actually enjoyed the fear. It added something, a delicious edge. He thought of the deer he had spooked, the deer that had spooked him. He decided that the deer had made it almost perfect, had made it almost what it should have been, what it was... then, before *they* all started to come.

As the fear in him subsided, the exhilaration rose in him. He could feel himself smiling. He had to restrain himself from laughing aloud, shouting his joy.

Then: another thought, another shot of fear.

The bag.

The bag had fallen off his shoulder as he had fallen. He had lost the bag. He sat upright, trying to blink away the rain, feeling the ground around him. He could not find the bag. He saw the flashlight still shining on the road. He scrambled toward it on all fours. He grabbed it, turned, and trained it on the spot where he thought he had fallen ... nothing ... a little left ... nothing ... right ... no ... farther ...

There!

Breathing heavily again, his heart pounding, he lunged for the bag. It was lying on its side, open at the top. The loose clasp had let go again. He picked up the bag and shone the light inside. It was all there. Everything was there. He had lost nothing. It was not even wet. He closed the bag and hugged it tightly to his side. He did not get up but knelt in the small spotlight at the side of the old road in the rain, waiting for his breathing to slow and his heart to quiet, waiting for control, waiting until he was sure again.

* * *

They had made it so easy, leading him to them in the night, allowing him to cross the grassy terrace without using his light, leaving a light on for him while they slept, like children afraid of the dark.

If only they knew, he thought as he stood just outside the cabin door, smiling, almost giggling. *If only they knew ...*

He pushed open the door slowly, carefully. There was no lock, not even a knob to turn. But he remembered that the rusted hinges had creaked loudly earlier in the day. Yet, curiously, not at all tonight. *The rain,* he thought. The rain had lubricated the hinges for him. He was glad again for the rain.

He stepped inside. Quietly, without turning his back, he pushed the door closed behind him. He lowered his bag to the dirt floor. For a long time, he stood watching them sleep, still marvelling at how easy they had made it, still struggling not to laugh.

Finally, composed, ready, no longer smiling, he knelt beside the bag and opened it, removing his "tools," laying them side by side, in order, on the dirt floor, with the precision of a surgeon. He selected the two he needed to begin his "operation," stood, and moved in the yellow lantern light toward the sleeping bag in which Jimmy Maclean was lying on his back, mouth agape, snoring loudly. Gently, he kicked the foot of the bag, and was surprised when Maclean, a light sleeper, sat bolt upright, eyes wide open, instantly alert.

"Wha...? What the fuck—oh, it's you. Why...? What are you...?" Maclean stammered, staring incredulously at the visitor, who almost instantly disappeared in a flash of light and the concentric rings of light that followed it.

Maclean reached up for his momentarily blinded eyes, unintentionally fending off some of the crunching blow aimed at his right temple. He reeled sideways, stunned at the force that did get through. He screamed in agony as the bones in three of the fingers of his right hand were turned to bloody mush, and then roared in anger, the cockfighter in him lashing out at his assailant, clawing at him with his good left hand, snatching a handful of leather jacket, and then reluctantly letting go when a second blow slammed into the upper right side of his head, penetrating the skull, leaving him wide-eyed and flopping in the dirt, like one of the spawning rainbow trout fishermen, since time immemorial, had been taking from the creek winding beyond the cottonwoods and aspen, just below the cabin.

The killer, wide-eyed himself, gasped and staggered backward. Then, feeling another rush of adrenaline and fear, raising his bloodied club, he spun toward the corner of the cabin where, incredibly, obliviously, Ben Surette was still sleeping. The killer could not believe his luck. He would take no chances this time. This time, there would be no surprise. He lumbered, half-running, across the cabin floor toward Surette, whose eyes fluttered open just after the flash of white, just before the flash of red that left them forever closed.

The killer sighed deeply then, letting the hand wielding the club, which was suddenly heavy, dangle at his side. He leaned against the cabin wall, hovering over Ben Surette's propped-up body, watching the dark blood trickle from his ear and drop into a pool in the dirt, waiting for the sound of the rain pounding on the roof to be louder than the sound of the blood pounding in his temples.

Easy. He cursed himself for thinking even for a moment that it would be, that it could be, that it should be. *Easy.* He should have known better. If it were so easy, he would not have been alone in attempting it. If it were so easy, the task would not have fallen to him alone. He would have to remember that. To forget was dangerous. He could not afford to forget. He could not afford to underestimate them, no matter how unworthy they were. He could not afford to forget that they were dangerous. *They* were the threat. He must remember. He must.

Quickly but methodically, he completed his task, working his sharp knife with now practiced efficiency, lifting and carefully plastic-bagging his trophies, wiping the blood from the blade and from the wooden club with the towel he had brought with him, bagging the towel in plastic, sealing it. He did it all as he had taught himself to do. He did it well, he knew.

Yet something was different. He was doing everything right, yet something was different this time. Something did not feel right this time. There was something he did not feel this time—or an emptiness he did feel. Something was missing.

Something *was* missing!

He noticed it only as he was preparing to leave. He was putting the last of his tools back in his leather bag when he thought of it. He felt a sharp splinter of fear—not the warm, delicious fear he had luxuriated in before, but a cold, gnawing fear, fear of discovery, of failure. He emptied the bag, running his hand along every edge, into every corner, through every compartment. It was not there. Where could it be? Where...?

He knew.

His fall. He must have lost it when he fell trying to run from the deer. It must have come off then, and flown out when the bag flew open. It was always coming off. He should have remembered that. He should have noticed it then. He should have looked for it then. He would have to look for it now. How would he ever find it now? Did he have time to look for it now? Could he take the risk? Could he not?

He crammed the things back into the bag, quickly, carelessly, his hands shaking, forcing the leather flap closed. He rushed from the cabin, across the wet grass, up the side of the ravine, toward the trees, behind him a rectangle of yellow light from the still open cabin door, in front of him a tiny cylinder of white light searching frantically in the night.

9:15 AM

Fry had only visited the University of Calgary once before, almost exactly a year ago, when the chief ordered him to enroll in a two-week course in Major Crime Investigation. The chief was a strong proponent of what a heading in his department's annual report called "staff development." He had even put a superintendent in charge of it. Nothing pleased him more than to hear about a patrol constable by day who patrolled the books by night, trying to complete a four-year honours degree in sociology, or psychology, or business administration in six or seven.

He could never convince Fry of the value of becoming a philosopher-cop. With Fry, he had to settle for an enforced two-week crash course in advanced investigative technique.

Fry did not think the course did much to advance his investigative technique. He did not mind the sessions on applied psychology. He thought he might even be able to use what he learned, on himself if nobody else. He was unimpressed by the lectures on organized crime, which seemed to lose something in translation from a hundred miles south of the border and three thousand miles east. He had experience dealing with Calgary's crime "families"—the red and black pimps, the fat white bikers, the Lebanese would-be bosses. Their strong suit was not, to say the least, sophistication.

He had been equally unimpressed by the campus, which made him think of a main-street set for a space-age western, High Noon on the Moon, maybe, or Ray-gunsmoke. The U of C's twenty-odd anonymous concrete ivory towers were scattered on three-hundred-odd acres of featureless prairie in the city's northwest quadrant. Its more than eighteen thousand full- and part-time, evening, spring, and summer students either scurried to and from class like moles, underground and in corridors, or shouldered into the stiff wind tunnelling between the stark buildings. Bald Nose Hill, formed by the gravel detritus of the new mountains that were belched from the earth ten million years before, rose north and east of the campus like a barren volcanic island lapped by a sea of subdivision houses. On the west on a clear day was the jagged silhouette of the mountain pyramids themselves.

This was no clear day. If Fry had followed the university's Gaelic motto, "*Mo Shuile Toram Suas*" ("I will lift up mine eyes"), all he would have seen in the west was grey. The upward-thrusting grey of the mountains met the grey of lowering cloud, forming an impossibly high, seemingly insurmountable wall of grey.

Fry was not looking west. He was looking at the ground. He had parked his car in one of the lots that sprawled across the prairie under the towers, thinking that whatever else they learned here, U of C students would be well schooled in one of the city's dominant values: the primacy of the automobile. Hands thrust deep into his black overcoat pockets, he was running awkwardly across the parking lot, trying vainly to evade the puddles and the cold, wind-blown rain, trying to keep from being soaked to the skin before he got to his appointment on the third floor of the squat tower straight ahead, the same building where he had studied investigative technique a year ago.

He pushed hard on the glass entry door, forgetting that it had to be pulled. He cursed and yanked it open. He took off his overcoat and shook it. He ducked into a ground-floor men's washroom. He dried his face and then his shoes with a paper towel. He ran a black comb through his slick, tarnished-silver hair. He straightened his tie.

He was surprised, even shocked, by the face that stared back at him in the too-bright, unflattering overhead light. His greying hair seemed even greyer, almost white, his skin more pallid and deeply lined, the darkening rings around his eyes wider, the eyes themselves not windows to his soul, as the poets claimed, but tunnels.

"Strahan was right," he said to his reflection, taking a last look, readjusting his tie, tugging on his suit coat. "You *are* living up to your nickname."

The building, the entire campus, seemed strangely quiet. The huge parking lots were virtually empty, the corridors nearly deserted. Classes were over for the year; exams had ended. Most of the students had left. Fry had never seen the campus with students on it. He wondered what it would be like.

He wondered what Dr. Theodore Patrick Russell would be like. He had an idea. After Miyoko Fitzgerald told him about the professor, he had decided to do some research on him before talking to him. He needed to do it quickly. He doubted that he would find anything in the police files. And something kept him from asking Miyoko Fitzgerald. He took the chance that Grant Melton was still feeling chagrined enough to be helpful without being a nuisance, and telephoned the *Bulletin* reporter to see if the paper had any information on Russell.

"Are you kidding?" Melton asked.

"No."

"Well, bring your reading glasses then."

Fry did not know what Melton had meant until the reporter met him at the *Bulletin* library, took him to an upstairs reading room with a wall of unpainted, virtually empty plywood bookshelves, sat him down in an old schoolhouse chair, and dumped two fat manila file folders onto the cigarette-burned oak conference table in front of him.

"Have a nice read," Melton said. "And, ah, what are you looking for anyway?"

"Nothing for publication."

"Is he a suspect or what?"

"Neither, so far as I know."

"I can ask 'til Christmas and you're not going to tell me anything, are you?"

"Well, no, I won't—and no, you can't ask until Christmas—I don't have that much time. And I'd appreciate your not publishing anything about this 'non-conversation,' either."

"Not even that you were here?"

"Nothing."

"Figures. You find something *for* publication, you'll give me a call?"

"You'll be the first."

It seemed to Fry that Dr. Theodore Patrick Russell was the first person the *Bulletin* called for comments on everything that had anything to do with "the west:"

The difference between the settling of the Canadian

and American west: law in a red coat and law from a gun barrel. The impact of Natives on the land: negligible, and too bad we whites didn't learn from it. The impact of white culture on Native: murderous. The loss of the city's old-west sandstone heritage: deplorable, but inevitable. The city's "new west" architecture: deplorable, but inevitable. The province's high divorce, suicide, and alcoholism rates: growth that's too fast, roots that are too shallow. Western separation: not likely, hating Trudeau's not enough of a reason. Western history: a bat of God's eye.

It was not clear whether they called Russell because he was an expert or whether Russell was an expert because they called him. It was clear that he had something quotable to say every time they called him. Fry figured that was probably why they called him. He was "a source."

Now, standing at the professor's half-open office door, in the instant before meeting the man he knew only from his opinions, Fry wondered whether the image of the man he had conjured from the words would be accurate. And he wondered whether Russell would be, for him, a source.

9:20 AM

A pungent smell assaulted Fry's nose as he entered Dr. Theodore Patrick Russell's office. The prickly looking bear of a man rising at the cluttered fake-walnut desk to greet him assaulted Fry's preconceptions.

The big opinions had led Fry to expect a little man. He was wrong. If anything, the man was even bigger than his mouth, better than six feet tall, at least two hundred pounds, with a thick neck, broad shoulders, barrel chest, and massive meaty hands like paddles. He had a ferocious porcupine quill of a beard and long, fine hair the colour of dry prairie grass retreating from his high, lined forehead. The "dry grass" was still matted from the morning rain. Heavy chest hairs peeked out from the open-necked collar of his western shirt, and heavy, hairy forearms extended from its rolled-up sleeves. Laughing eyes behind old-fashioned, round, metal-framed glasses over round cheeks gave him the countenance of a mad Santa Claus.

"Fry," he said in a voice that was also big enough to accommodate his opinions, extending a big right hand across the desk.

"Dr. Russell," Fry said, accepting the hand.

After a handshake that was as much a wrestling match as a greeting, Russell, apparently satisfied, let go of Fry's hand and, pointing to Fry's damp overcoat, said:

"Looks like you were about as successful dodging raindrops as I was—this place does make bad weather worse."

"This place?"

"Sure. The campus. Hollywood Acres here. Pure California. Got nothing to do with the land it's sitting on, nothing about the prairies to it. Could be anywhere. Look at the library there," nodding out the plain window behind his desk. "Those windows, so-called. Vertical. Narrow. Puny and small. Looking out on land that's totally horizontal—a big landscape. And these damned wind-tunnelling towers—never mind."

He nodded toward the coat rack next to an almond-coloured filing cabinet in the far right corner.

"You can hang that wet blanket of yours over there with mine."

Fry hung his coat over a bare hook next to the source of the smell, a rain-darkened fringed rawhide jacket still dripping on the floor from the bottom fringes and sleeves.

On top of the filing cabinet, in a small, simple black frame, he noticed the same photograph of the Sarcee chief Bullhead that hung poster-sized on Thomas Red Crow's office wall. On the wall to the right was a large, framed reproduction of a painting by the nineteenth-century artist-explorer Paul Kane—Stoney Indians chasing wild horses. Shelves filled the end wall and were filled with western books and western bric-a-brac: pioneers' journals propped between bookends fashioned from spurs; a small, framed black-and-white Charles Russell sketch leaning against modern biographies of Mounties, missionaries, and Metis; colourful Indian beadwork draped over colourless sociological tracts, political treatises, economic analyses.

"And you wanted to talk to me about what?" asked the burly academic, gesturing Fry into a steel armchair in front of the desk, answering the question himself. "Plains Indian scalping technique, eh?"

"That's right."

"You think it's got something to do with this, ah, nastiness?"

"Could be."

"You mean the headlines actually got it right—'scalp murders'?"

"That's right, they did, for a change. As usual, not because they knew anything."

"But *you* know something."

"I know some … things. You know some … things, I'm led to believe. I want to know whether what you know goes with what I know."

"So you think maybe it's a local Native that did it, do you?"

"You know, professor, it's amazing how many people seem to know what I think even when I don't myself," Fry said, thinking of Miyoko Fitzgerald as he said it. "I don't know what I think, as a matter of fact. I know I have bits of information that I'm trying to put together. If and when I do, maybe then I'll know what I think, as a matter of fact. For the moment, all I've got are questions. And if you don't mind, I'd appreciate your letting me do the asking. The last time I looked, that *was* my job."

"So it is, Fry, so it is," Russell said with a large laugh, slapping his palm on the desktop, pushing himself back in his chair, plopping a big scarred cowboy boot on the edge of the desk. It was a working boot, not for show or the Stampede. It was like the boots Fry had in his closet at home.

"Forgive me," Russell continued. "But I've been asked lots of questions, about lots of things. But never for a primer on scalping technique."

"Maybe not. But it seems to me you've always got an answer, whatever question you're asked. You got an answer for this one?"

Russell put his right forefinger to his parted lips, scratching his beard with his thumb. He lifted his leg off the desk, pushed himself out of the chair, walked to the wall of books, and stood in front of it, fingering titles, mumbling.

"Well, let's see … do I have an answer, do I have an answer? Of course I have an answer. As you say, I *always* have an answer."

From a section in the middle of the bookshelves, halfway up the wall, Russell tipped half a dozen books into the palm of his big left hand, turned, and came back to the desk, spilling the books across the desktop toward Fry: *Myths of North American Indians; The Indians of Canada, Their Manners & Customs; The Blackfeet, Raiders on the Northwestern Plains; The Horse in Blackfoot Indian Culture; The Plains Cree; Indian Days on the Western Plains.*

"I think you'll find what you're looking for in these, some of it even true," Russell said, looming over the desk, rocking back and forth on his high boot heels, both hands in the back pockets of his faded boot-cut jeans. "Mind you, even what's true won't be much. Scalping was part of the culture, sure, but not the only part, and not the biggest, and certainly not the most significant. Fierce people they were, but not savage. Serious writers about Native culture have tended—rightly, I think; fairly, I know—not to overplay the savage part."

"I'm sure that's true—but thanks anyway. I appreciate this."

"Not at all. Though I still say the notion that a Native did it is a dog that just won't hunt."

"No? Assuming for a minute that that *is* my notion, what's wrong with it?"

"Just doesn't figure, that's all."

"If you'll forgive me, professor, that's not a very scientific answer, now is it?"

"Look, it's true the tribes here used to club and scalp with the best of them, or the worst, depending on your point of view. But the operative phrase is *used to.* They've forgotten how. Anybody who'd even have an inkling is long dead. The only way they'd find out now is to get it out of books, like I did, like you're going to. And the ones angry enough to do it wouldn't read up on technique, they'd just stick somebody with a knife, and more likely a kitchen knife at that. The ones who'd go to the trouble of reading up on it probably aren't angry enough—and even if they are, they're probably as sensitive as they are mad, and they'd be more likely to do themselves in than anybody else, out of sheer bloody furious despair. Hell, Fry, I'd be a more likely suspect."

"You?"

"Sure. As I say, I've already done all the reading—an *ex*-pert, as the media put it. That display at the Glenbow, you may have seen it, the scalping scene in the diorama—"

"I've seen it."

"Well, they consulted me to get it right, none of the local bands, *me*. And you know from my many opinions that I'm mad enough." Laugh lines crinkled around Russell's eyes and his breath caught in his throat, as he seemed to be pondering whether to let Fry in on a secret. "Here, let me show you."

"What?"

"Here. Come on over here."

Russell grabbed a bone-handled serrated letter opener from a stoneware crock on his desk and moved to the rag rug in front of the bookcase.

"Get down on the rug," he instructed. "Lie down. Pretend to be dead, or stunned anyway."

Fry slowly got out of the chair and walked toward Russell, wary of the wildly mischievous look in the professor's eyes.

"I think I'm already stunned, just to consider doing this," he said.

"Not at all, not at all!" Russell laughed, with a kind of idiot glee, as Fry lay stomach-down on the rug. "Just a little show and tell is all. Actually more show than tell, as it should be. That's what I teach my students: don't tell me, *show* me. Well, I'm gonna show you."

"Show me wha—"

Russell's knee and the full weight of his body behind it between Fry's shoulder blades cut Fry off in mid-sentence and drove the breath from him. The professor grabbed a handful of hair on the top of Fry's head, pulled, and, with the smooth edge of the letter opener, pretended to make a swift, circular cut at the base of Fry's scalp. He yanked on Fry's hair once more, hard, and then let go and leaped up from Fry's prone body, raising his arms exultantly, almost like the Plains Cree mannequin in the Glenbow diorama.

Fry struggled to his feet and for a moment stood unsteadily, flushed, breathing rapidly, unsure whether to thank Russell for the demonstration or to punch him in the face.

"Just as I told you," Russell said, smiling triumphantly, "I'd be a more likely suspect."

"May-be," Fry said, not entirely without conviction, combing his hair with his fingers, brushing off the front of his coat and pants, feeling the red leave his face, regaining his composure, but still unsure what to make of the experience or of the mountain man masquerading as an academic. "May-be."

"Ha! That's the stuff!" Russell slapped Fry once, hard, on the shoulder.

As he did, the telephone on his desk rang. He picked it up in the middle of the third ring.

"Ted Russell. Yeah, yeah, he is. Jus' sec." He looked at Fry. "For you."

Fry took the receiver.

"Yeah, Fry. What? Oh, fu—where? When'd it happen? Yeah. Yeah. Who's on it? Okay. Listen, Shields out there? Well, I want him there ASAP—no, sooner. Yeah. Right."

Fry cradled the receiver and gathered up the books from the desktop.

"I can take these?" he asked Russell.

"Sure—long as you need them. A problem?"

"You might say. I'm afraid I'll have to cut our … interview short." He grabbed his coat from the rack and draped it over the arm holding the books. "Thanks for these—and for the, ah, lesson."

"Any time," Russell said, leaning against the bookcase, smiling, big arms folded across his chest. "I enjoyed it."

10:05 AM

The north bank of Fish Creek had not been so crowded in fifty years, when the dance hall was packing them in at Paradise Cove just west of Macleod Trail. Today a grove of spruce was growing on the river flat where the dance hall had stood, ringed by cottonwoods and willow that had taken root where black Model T's and blindered team horses had waited for their exhausted dancers to return.

A mile and a half further west, an exhausted Fry ducked under the yellow and black police cordon that ringed the tumbledown log cabin on the grassy terrace above the creek. The cordon was almost encircled itself, with police blue-and-whites and motorcycles, a couple of ambulances, the medical examiner's car, television trucks, radio-station station wagons, and a variety of unmarked vehicles that Fry assumed also belonged to the media.

Fry had left his car at the foot of Twenty-fourth Street and made his way on foot down the old riding trail into the ravine. He wanted to approach the crime scene slowly, to try to take it in whole.

He was surprised at how much different the western section of the creek valley seemed than the eastern, more steeply sloped, more densely wooded, wilder. The contrast between the new west and the old seemed even more pronounced. It occurred to him that a golfer could slice a ball only slightly on the manicured hybrid grasses of the fairways at Canyon Meadows Country Club, and lose it in another century, another age, in the ancient prairie grasses on the terraces rolling down to the creek.

Fry's surprise at what he saw around him turned to anger when he came into the clearing and saw the reporters sniffing and pawing at the edge of the cordon, and his anger grew when they saw him and ran toward him, barking a frenzied babble of questions. He moved through the pack without speaking, leaving them in the mud behind him, yipping at his heels and growling. Just inside the police-flood-lighted cabin, he saw Patrol Sergeant Paul Strahan, leaning against the cabin wall with his arms folded across his chest, supervising MacElroy's and Adams' crime-scene investigation.

"What the fuck's going on, Strahan?" Fry asked.

"Whaddaya mean, 'What the fuck's goin' on?'" Strahan asked, surprised, stiffening, unfolding his arms, holding them defensively in front of him like a street fighter whose masculinity had just been challenged.

"The zoo, Paul, the goddamned zoo outside. That's what the *fuck* I mean."

"Christ! You're lucky it's not worse. Some of them almost beat our guys here. We got it covered though."

"Bullshit you do! How the fuck can you say that?"

"Well, it's clear as day they were killed in here and—"

"Oh, it's clear, is it? That another one of your theories, Strahan? If it is, save it. I don't have time for it. And neither do you. You gotta get them back. They're too close, too goddamned close. Who knows what they've fouled up already?"

"It's those eff-ing scanners," Strahan said, thinking that perhaps he had fouled up, scrambling for a defence. "Ought'a be outlawed."

"I don't care about that now. I want 'em out of here, now."

"*You* want 'em out of here, *now*." Strahan said mockingly, a mistake.

"You got that right, Strahan. *I* want 'em out of here. I want 'em out of here, *now!*"

Fry pushed Strahan hard against the cabin wall. Before the startled homicide sergeant could react, Fry grabbed him by the shoulder with one hand and hauled him out the cabin door like a drunk being bounced from an east-end pub. Still holding him by the shoulder, Fry turned Strahan to face the reporters watching them from the other side of the cordon.

"I want 'em out of here," he said. "Up the hill, all the way up. And neatly, by the book, no bullshit, no bitching. Anybody argues, bust 'em. Think up a charge if you have to. But get 'em the hell out of here, Strahan, before they stomp this place to shit!"

Fry released Strahan's shoulder and returned to the cabin, leaving the sergeant standing humiliated in the rain, a strange look of bewilderment and frustration and rage on his face. Strahan rubbed his shoulder where Fry had squeezed it. Then, clenching and unclenching both fists, he turned and took one step toward the cabin, stopped, turned again, and marched toward the cordon, shouting: "All right, people, party's over. You gotta move—up the hill—all the way. Man wants you up the hill. Let's go!"

"Hey, fuck that!" came a voice from the pack. "We got a right to be here!"

"Who the fuck said that?" Strahan shrieked, spitting,

charging the cordon like a bull, frightening the uniforms at the scene into action. "What you got, if you don't head out now, is a right to get your ass busted. And you think I won't, just be standing where you are in ten seconds—now, *move!*"

Fry sagged against the cabin wall inside the door, listening to Strahan's ranting, closing his eyes, taking deep breaths, feeling his knees almost buckle, momentarily doubting that he could bear up under all the pressure, the incredible weight of expectation. He took another deep breath and blew it out. He opened his eyes. He saw Dr. Clifton Shields squatting in the far corner, looking up at him disapprovingly.

"You keep that up, and I'll be getting you ready to study on a slab," Shields said, pressing the palms of his hands on his thighs and pushing himself to his feet, groaning in pain, his knees cracking almost as loudly. "This rain keeps up, they'll have to wheel me to the table. Damned arthritis. Goddamned rain. You know, I kinda liked that drought."

"You would," Fry said. "Keep what up?"

"As if you didn't know what," Shields said with one raised eyebrow. He nodded toward the police photographer, who leaned toward the body of Ben Surette, focusing the corpse in the lens, shooting it once, twice, a third time, from different angles, the bouncing flash barely visible in the artificially bright light of the cabin. "Sparring with Strahan there," Shields continued. "I mean, if looks could kill, you'd be stone dead in the dirt here right now. I think I'd take it easier on him—you do have to work with the guy."

"Don't I know it, Cliff, don't I know it. Maybe it's this thing. Maybe? Who'm I kidding? It *is* this thing—it's a horror show already. Out there just now, looked like it was turning into some kind of sicko circus. And Strahan and I, well, we're like oil and water at the best of times—if there are any."

"Oil and water? I'd say gasoline and a match are closer to it."

"That your considered opinion?"

"It is—for free."

"And what's your considered opinion of this—the one the taxpayer pays you for?"

"Don't know yet—paid-for opinions take a little longer."

"You got an unconsidered opinion?"

"Probably the same as yours. You called it, what, a horror show?"

"Yeah."

"Well, same leading man, I'd say. Just a different supporting cast."

"Like the others then."

"Exactly. Oh, that one over there," gesturing toward the already plastic-bagged body of Jimmy Maclean, "a bit different."

"How?"

"Looks like he struggled before he died—couple, three blows to the head, broken right hand, broken finger nails on the left."

"Anything under them?"

"You always want answers before I've had a chance to ask the questions. Maybe. Probably, I'd say. Won't know what, or for sure, until—"

"Until I shut up and let you get out of here and on with your job."

"Couldn't have put it better myself."

"Get out of here then and get on with it."

"Yessir. Be in touch."

"Soon, I hope."

"ASAP."

"No."

"No?"

"Didn't they give you the word when they dragged you out here?"

"What word?"

"Sooner."

Fry followed Shields and the bodies outside, leaving Adams and MacElroy inside trying to dust the cabin for prints, mechanically bagging and boxing its contents, in their eyes the same look of disbelieving horror he had seen at the ruined house in the Beltline.

Was it only three days ago?

Outside, the reporters were gone. No, not gone. They were never gone. Kept at a distance. A safe distance? He was not sure there was any such thing. At least he could not see them. And they could not see this. They did not need to see this.

Fry watched the two bagged and brutalized bodies disappear on collapsible gurneys into the yawning backs of the ambulances. He watched the ambulances back across the terrace and make their way slowly up and out of the ravine on the old trail, lights flashing, sirens off, rear tires spitting mud, spattering Clifton Shields' big, grey Chevrolet as it followed just behind.

10:35 AM

Fry knew he would have to talk to Strahan. He knew he would have to do it now. He knew he would have to apologize. And he hated the thought. He did not respect Strahan. He did not like Strahan. He could barely stand the sight of Strahan. But Shields was right. He did have to work with him. He would have to apologize to him. And he would—not meaning it, swallowing his pride, almost gagging on the words. He would. On this, he needed Strahan's help.

On this especially.

He found Strahan beyond the cordon, standing in the rain at the edge of the creek, staring across it toward the stands of cottonwood, white spruce, and aspen on the steep north-facing slope, still pouting.

"Listen, Strahan," Fry said. "About inside there—I'm sorry. I, ah, lost it."

"You got that right."

"I know. This business, well, it's getting to me, I guess."

"You guess?"

"Okay, I know."

"Yeah—like before."

"Before?"

"Yeah, you know—when it got to you so bad you had to book off sick."

Fry's jaw tensed at the remark, but he let it pass. He put his hand on Strahan's shoulder, gently this time, and tried to lead him back to the cordon. Strahan at first resisted like a pouting child, but then relented and allowed himself to be led.

"So," Fry said as they walked, "what'd we have in there? Who'd we have?"

"Just a couple of Coasters," Strahan said, fishing out his notebook, folding it open, not noticing Fry stiffen at the sound of the word *just*. "Ah ... James J. Maclean and Benjamin R. Surette. Both got current Nova Scotia licences. Nova Scotia plates on the old rust-bucket Imperial up there."

"Imperial? What Imperial?" Fry had not noticed the

car in the bush as he walked down the trail. *So much,* he thought, *for seeing the scene whole.*

"In the trees, up the ravine about halfway."

"Gone over it yet?"

"Nah...."

"Got an officer on it?"

"We'll get to it. It's not goin' anywhere."

"Uh huh. And the house there, anybody there see anything? Or do you know?"

"We do. Fella who owns it was the one who made the call. He was out givin' his dog a run—was the dog found the bodies."

"You got a full statement from him?"

"Who? The dog?"

"Funny. The guy."

"We will. He works for one of those companies that got to work on Ontario time—had to be in early. He's comin' in this afternoon. We'll get to him then."

"Right," Fry said, biting his lower lip, trying not to lose control again, not quite managing it. "You should, ah, 'get to it,' the rest of it anyway, pretty soon, don't you think? Before our friends in the fourth estate up there trample everything to rat shit."

"You still got a problem with my control of the crime scene?"

"No. You got it under control—as far as it goes."

"What's that mean?"

"Only that I'd like you to broaden your definition of 'crime scene.'"

"Wait a minute. It *is* clear that they were killed right there, right in their sleeping bags."

"Maybe so. But it's not clear exactly how they got there. And not how whoever did them got there. And there might be something between up there," Fry nodded toward the top of the ravine, "and down here that gives us something we need. I want the whole section swept."

"Whole section? You mean—"

"I mean Macleod to Thirty-seven Street."

"You know how much fuckin' territory that is?"

"Got a pretty good idea."

"You know how many men your idea will take?"

"No. And I don't give a shit. It'll take what it'll take." Fry took his right hand off Strahan's shoulder and put his left palm on Strahan's mid-section, stopping him in mid-stride, facing him. "Look, Strahan, I'm not trying to be a hard ass—"

"No? You could fool me. You always act like you're the only fuckin' cop on the beat, and the *only* one who gives a shit."

"That's not what I'm about. I just want to get this done. It can't go on—it can't. He can't go on. And there might be something out here that'll help us stop him. And if there is, I want it, and I want it now. There is some urgency to this. I'd like to think you agree."

"Maybe. But I'm not sure we shouldn't give him just a little longer."

"What? What the hell's *that* mean?"

"Jesus Christ, Ghost, he's a wacko, sure, but so far the guy's sorta been doin' the city, you know, a favour."

"A favour?"

"Damned straight—sort of a trash collector, you might say. Couple of no-account Coasters, a puker-druggie, and a make-believe hooker. *Where's* the fuckin' urgency? Maybe we should just let him finish."

The rage rose so quickly in Fry that for an instant he again felt unsteady on his feet, almost faint. For several long moments he stared at Strahan incredulously, as if he could not quite believe that he had just heard what he had just heard, as if the man who had said it was some strange new species he had never encountered. He searched for some sign—a wink, a twinkle in the eyes, the suggestion of a smile—that would tell him Strahan had been joking, which was something he could have understood, a kind of sick-humour defence against the unspeakable. He did not find it.

He said nothing.

His silence and the power of his withering glare unnerved Strahan, who sniffed, took two steps back, started blinking rapidly, then looked down toward the ground. Fry turned on his heels and walked quickly up the slope. Looking up to find himself abandoned, Strahan called after him.

"Hey, Ghost ... so you really want the area, the whole area, cordoned off and swept clean?"

"You got it," Fry said, turning to face Strahan, continuing backward up the slope. "Anything that doesn't grow or flow or otherwise belong here I want to see in bags and boxes, and I don't care how many uniforms it takes to fill those bags and boxes. Just get it done. And get it done fast."

He turned away and strode up the old trail toward his car, amazed that the prospect of fending off the pack at the top of the ravine suddenly seemed, relatively, almost pleasurable.

12:40 PM

Ken Clark was sitting exactly where he had been sitting the first time Fry walked into his office on the sixth floor of the once elegant, still graceful terracotta building on the Eighth Avenue Mall: on the front edge of the massive blonde-oak desk/table below the high four-paned window curving around the corner of Eighth Avenue and Second Street SW. In the nearly three years since, Fry had never seen him sit in the high-backed, leather swivel chair behind the desk. He had never seen him wear anything but a tweed jacket, jeans, wild tie, and scuffed sneakers. And he had never known him to be anything but blunt, casual, and disinterested, in the honourable eighteenth-century sense of the word.

Dr. Kenneth James Clark, PhD, was the clinical psychologist Inspector Ben Drayton had arranged for Fry to see when Fry was on the verge of losing his job, possibly more.

That first morning, Fry—nervous, vulnerable, and, for the first time in his life, deeply afraid—had tried to cover it all with a macho-cop swagger that was as obvious as it was out of character.

"What kind of shrink are you?" he had asked, glancing around the sparsely furnished, white-walled office, undecorated except for a big, brass-framed, pastel-coloured city map of Calgary, circa 1912. "You don't even have a couch."

"And what kind of cop are you?" Clark had asked in reply, smiling. "You don't even have a shield, much less a gun."

He fixed his intensely blue eyes on Fry's deep, impenetrable eyes, thoughtfully stroking his thick, reddish, neatly trimmed beard, which contrasted sharply with his thinning, fly-away, dirty-blonde hair. With his hands gripping the edge of the desk, he swung his legs back and forth under it.

"What say we get a few things out front," he said. "You're here, I think, only because you want to save your job, although God knows why you want to do it. I'm here, I know, only because it *is* my job, although

God knows why *I* want to do it. You don't know me. I don't know you. As a matter of fact, I know diddly-squat about cops. Except what I've read, and that's not much; there *isn't* much, and most of that not much is American. And except what I remember from previous contact, and that's not much either, and *none* of it good. You don't trust me. I don't know if I trust you—never trusted a cop before. You're primed not to like me. Well, I'm primed not to like you. You're a cop; from what I hear, a regular brass-assed, dyed-in-the-wool Matt Dillon. I was a hippie—an honest-to-God, pot-smoking, tie-dyed, make-love-not-war, hair-down-to-my-asshole hippie. At heart, if without the hair, I still am. So, we got nothing in common except maybe our mutual antagonism. Is that the basis for a good working relationship? Probably not. But hell, husbands and wives manage all the time on a lot less. Maybe we can. Let's give it a shot. Maybe we'll amaze ourselves. Maybe an old hippie can help an old cop get his badge back. Maybe an old cop can help an old hippie buy a couch."

He jumped down from the desk and collapsed into one of the two sagging leather club chairs in front of it, gesturing Fry into the other. He pulled a thin cigar with a white plastic tip from his inside coat pocket, lit it with the wild flame of a brushed-steel lighter, sucked hard on it, inhaling the smoke, then saying through the cloud as he slowly exhaled, "You gotta be here. I gotta be here. You can stand at attention if you want. But I'm not gonna. And if you do, I'll get a stiff neck just looking up at you. And you'll get a stiff back, sore legs, and probably constipated. Might as well sit down."

Fry sat down.

He was sitting again this afternoon in the same

leather club chair, the chair he had occupied through six months of weekly sessions and another two and a half years of irregular meetings with Dr. Kenneth Clark. He *had* come reluctantly at first, not because he believed he needed to come, but because he had been given no choice but to come. Later, he came expectantly, no longer under orders, because he wanted to come. He *did* amaze himself. He was learning something—about himself. Ken Clark was teaching him about himself—no, he was making it possible for Fry to teach himself about himself.

Fry had not intended to tell Clark anything about himself. He ended up telling Clark everything about himself—things he knew, and things he did not know until he spoke them.

Clark never asked him about himself. He never pressed. He never seemed to try to come to a point, or to make a point. He was no interrogator. But he was a listener. He *listened,* as closely, as intently, as non-judgmentally as Fry listened when he was on the job. No one had ever listened to Fry in that way. Certainly not Carol. When he and Carol had talked at all, they had not so much listened to each other as waited for the opportunity to translate the other's "I" into their own "I." Ken Clark seemed to have no "I."

Fry knew it was professional technique. He knew Clark was "on the job." But Fry admired skilful technique, or rather, technique that disguised its skill. And from that admiration of craftsmanship grew a grudging respect, and from the respect a willingness to trust, and from that trust openness, and from that openness the beginnings of understanding.

Fry had not got free of himself. He experienced no catharsis on the sixth floor. His meetings with Ken

Clark were not the emotional equivalent of enemas. He entered the sessions a lonely, violent man and he emerged from them still a lonely, violent man. But if he had not resolved the violence within him, he had learned to recognize it, and to understand how great a price in intimacy it had exacted, to see how his fumbling unconscious attempts to restrain it had led him never to let down his emotional guard, always to withdraw at the first signs of vulnerability. He was not sure he could ever do anything about it. He felt like a man who had lost his sense of touch and was trying to regain it, but with his fingers wrapped in layer after layer of gauze. Before, he had never seen the wrapping. Now, he did, and, seeing it, at least had a chance to unravel it.

Fry was sitting in the leather club chair in Ken Clark's office again today, hoping to unravel something else. He had not come to talk about himself, but about another, *the* other—the evil.

"Christ, Jake," Clark said, smacking both palms on the edge of the desk, "I've been tearing out what little hair I've got left trying to figure out the demons in a perfectly sane, if slightly obsessive, old bugger like you—and face to face. Now you want me to draw an emotional portrait of some faceless, possessed creature I've never seen, let alone talked to."

"Even a thumbnail sketch would help."

"A kid's stick-figure drawing is about the best I can do—and not a very talented kid."

"It'd be something—more than I've got."

"Maybe. Why don't you go first? Tell me what *you* think."

"That's a switch."

"What is?"

"Somebody asking me what I think instead of telling me what I think. Problem is, I don't know what I think. I know it wasn't the Native punk everybody wanted it to be—don't think it's a Native at all."

"Why not?"

"Hunch. Experience. From what I know. And maybe I just don't want it to be."

"Not very cop-like of you, is it? Objectivity-wise, I mean."

"Who ever said I was objective—or wise?"

"Good point. Not me for sure."

"For sure. Anyway, so now you know what I don't think—tell me what I should think."

"When did I *ever* do that?"

"Never. Surprise me. What's going on? I've got a depressed lady who walked around tarted up like a hooker, a would-be rock star with a drug problem, a couple of loser-dreamers from the Maritimes—nothing in common except being dead, heads crushed, scalped. What the hell is this all about?"

"A statement, maybe," Clark said, standing now behind the other club chair, leaning on his arms on the back of it.

"A statement," Fry said, looking up at him. "A statement about what?"

"Who knows?"

"That's a help."

"Could be anti-east. Or anti-immigrant. Anti-anti-establishment. Anti-low-life. Anti-Native, in a perverse sort of way. Maybe even anti-hair. Only your killer knows, and maybe not for sure."

"Funny."

"What's funny?"

"One of the antis you said—anti-low-life."

"Yeah?"

"Yeah. One of my colleagues called the guy a 'trash collector.'"

"'Trash collector'?"

"Yeah. How'd he put it? A make-believe hooker, a puker, and a couple of Coasters—trash. Thinks maybe we should let him finish."

"Nice fella."

"Yeah. A prince of the city, as they say."

"But maybe not wrong."

"What?"

"No, no—not about letting him 'finish.' Give me a break. But about what gets him started. Maybe it's not—probably it's not—these people, at least not *as* people, but what they represent to him, some wrong he thinks has been done to him, some threat."

"A threat? But how would they be? And why now? Why here?"

"How they're a threat to him, I couldn't tell you. He probably could; I'm sure it makes perfectly insane sense to him. Why now? I couldn't begin to say. If you could ask him, *he* might not be able to tell you. One of the few things I *have* read about these people ..."

"These people—"

"This kind of killer—serial, spree killers. They tend to be cardboard people, not fully developed—so maybe not fully understandable."

Clark moved to the high, elegantly curving window behind his desk, looking down on the windswept, rain-slicked mall.

"But why here," he continued, "isn't difficult to say at all."

"No?"

"No. You know as well as anyone—better than

anyone—that this is not a terribly nice place to live right now. The pace is too fast. Goals are too superficial. Roots are too shallow. Everybody's from somewhere else, probably going somewhere else. The only community spirit comes out of a bottle. It's a great time for liquor stores and divorce lawyers, and quacks like me. Don't get me wrong, now. It's an exciting place, vibrant, alive. But it's not nice. I'm not sure it's even liveable anymore. Greedy. Grasping. To hell with consequences. To hell with tomorrow. Hell, to hell with yesterday. Like this building here.

"Your building?"

"Yeah, my, the building. Get this: they're either gonna declare it a historic site or demolish it—and they may end up doing both. It's—well, forgive my psychological imprecision—but it's crazy. I don't think I'd call it a boom so much as a binge. It's like living in a muscle that's constantly flexing. Hard enough for people who've got it together. Impossible for those who don't. Some folks just can't take the pressure. And some of them explode. Somebody else I read, a novelist ... he said frontiers encourage extreme behaviour. This city's like that."

"Nice theory. Let's me and him off the hook. We just blame the 'frontier city.' Why don't I think I could make a charge stick? Who the hell would I charge? God made the oil."

"But He didn't make the oil *boom.* Of course, you don't 'charge' the city. But you take it into account, I think. Certain kinds of crime happen in certain kinds of places. From what I've read, this kind of place is a hothouse for this kind of crime, this kind of criminal—a special kind."

"Special. That's an interesting way to put it. Special how?"

"I think you know that, too, Jake. Or you wouldn't be here. He's new to here, to you, and rare anywhere, thank God or whoever. But that makes him difficult to find, right? I mean, he doesn't kill the right people, for the right reasons, the usual reasons, *understandable* reasons. Like I say, only he understands—*if* he understands. He's like a bomb with a self-detonator—only he knows what sets him off."

"So tell me, you think he's likely to go off again?"

"I think he'll *keep* going off," Clark said, turning his back on the window, facing Fry from behind the desk for the first time, "until he's finished."

2:15 PM

Fry was twelve hours too late, or twelve hours too early, for the frenetic three AM change-of-shift racquetball games that rattled the walls of the year-old, twenty-four-hour-a-day physical training facility in the basement of the police headquarters building on Seventh Avenue SE. The walls were silent now, the courts empty. The exercise room was deserted except for Fry and Wendich, a pudgy, eleven-year-veteran E District (downtown) beat constable puffing, red-faced, on an exercise bike, perspiring profusely, adding another salt-stain ring to his apparently never-washed, undersized sweats.

Fry had begun to work up a sweat himself, working hard on the one piece of equipment that he did make use of, not to get fit, but to vent frustration: the heavy punching bag suspended on a chain in the corner. Like an under-card brawler on a weak Saturday night of boxing, he leaned against the big, slow-moving bag with his upper body, shouldering it, nuzzling it with his cheek, butting it with his forehead, pummelling it with blow after body blow, feeling the delicious shiver of resistance as each punch hit home. He danced away from the bag, flicking a left jab at head height, then another, another, following it with a roundhouse right, bulling back into the bag, hitting it with a salvo of body punches—one-two, one-two, one-two—smelling leather, feeling leather against his face, hearing leather against leather as his gloves smashed into the bag, thinking of leather ... leather under fingernails, leather under a phony painted lady's painted phony fingernails, leather under a long-time loser's long-bitten fingernails, leather from a coat, leather from a killer.

Fry moved back again, feinted with a left, then a right, then spun on the ball of his left foot and, with his right, landed a powerful karate kick at the level of the groin.

"Hey, Jake, no fair!" Wendich yelled from the far side of the room.

Breathing heavily, Fry looked over his shoulder, a savage grin on his sweat-glistening face. He said:

"What's matter with you, Wendich? Don't you remember? *All's* fair in love and war."

"Which one's this?" Wendich asked, half smiling, half heaving for breath, still pumping his legs, though slowly, hands holding both ends of the white towel draped over his neck.

"Good question. What're you doing in here anyway, especially on off time?"

"Good question. Blame our skinny motherfucking asshole horseless headman."

"Who?"

"The chief, of course."

"Oh, yeah. Who else?"

Fry had almost forgotten that the chief, a slim former

Mountie—a "horseman," to the unimpressed cop on the beat—had been dubbed "the horseless headman" when he left the federal police force to take over the city's. The other adjectives came when he let it be known that any officer with a waist bigger than a beautiful woman's bust—say, thirty-six, thirty-eight inches at most—had some waist to waste.

"Thought this weight business was just a suggestion," Fry continued, "you know, something he'd like but couldn't order. S'nothing in the contract about it. He can't force you to take it off."

"Yeah, right," Wendich snorted. "I'd just end up being the oldest beat cop in the history of police work—and I'm too tired for it *now*."

"Let me get this straight: you figure the only way to get off the street is to get in good enough shape to stay on the street?"

"You got it. Now I know why they pay you detectives the big bucks."

"What if he decides you've gotten *too fit* to take off the street?"

"I don't want to hear that, Jake."

"Sorry. Have a nice ride."

Fry put his right glove under his left armpit, squeezed his left arm against his side, and slid the glove off his right hand. He reversed the process for his left hand. He started across the room.

"Say, Jake," Wendich called after him, wiping his face with the towel, "I dunno if this means anything or not ..."

"Don't know if what means anything?" Fry asked, still walking.

"Well, I had a call like these scalpings this winter—only the guy didn't die."

"You what?" Fry asked, frozen, freezing his eyes on Wendich, feeling a sudden rush of adrenaline, or anger, or both.

"Yeah, it was just like them."

"Jesusfuckingchrist!" Fry exploded, flinging one of the gloves at Wendich, who ducked, almost falling off the bicycle.

"Hey! Watch it!" Wendich shouted.

"'Watch it?' Haven't you been watching?" Fry screamed, incredulous. "Haven't you been paying any fucking attention at all?"

"Jesus, Jake, I—"

"Why the hell haven't you said something? Anything? Where the fuck have you been? What the fuck've you been thinking? *Have* you been thinking? *Can* you think? I can't fuckin' *believe* you...!"

"Aw, shit, Jake.... How was I supposed to know? Just seemed like a couple of rummies fighting over a bottle of old hermit or a can of spray."

"Goddamned co-fucking-mmunity police bullshit!"

"What?"

"You assholes have got yourselves so busy trying to be social-working *community policemen* you forget to be plain old-fashioned cops. You ever hear of talking to a detective, maybe? Helping out in an investigation from time to time? Being what they pay you to be?"

"Shit, Jake, I'm sorry—I just didn't see any connection."

"Sorry—you got that right. You better get your fat ass off that bike before I make a connection between it and my foot!"

"What do you mean? What's going on?"

"What's going on is you're getting off. Now! Come on, asshole, I'll get you your promotion in spite of your fat self *and* the skinny horseless one. I'll even buy you a case of doughnuts. But *move!*"

* * *

Wendich's notebook pinpointed the day, time, and location of the assault: January 20, 1977, a cold, clear Thursday, 2257 hours, in an alley behind the Queen's Hotel. But it was useless in its description of the victim or the assailant, who could have been one and the same person, who could have been one and the same of a thousand persons: male, white, thirty to forty-five, heavyset, wearing heavy winter clothing, smelling of alcohol. The notebook described the injuries as "an apparent blow to the head, deep scalp wound." It stated that the victim had been "removed to General Hospital emergency by paramedic van." It made a vague promise, never fulfilled, to get a complete statement from the victim at a later date. Wendich remembered nothing that was not in his notes.

And Wendich actually believed—Fry thought but did not say—that it was his weight that was keeping him off the promotion list.

Fry tracked down the paramedic who had attended the victim. His memory was better, even without notes.

"Yeah, yeah, actually I do remember him," he said over the phone. "Major whack to the head. Gruesome knife wound—just about scalped him, actually lifted the hair. Never saw anything like it before. Would've been able to take the hair right off if the guy's head hadn't been so hard, or the blow'd been harder. Damned guy said he came to as the other one was tugging on his hair, trying to rip him off, literally and figuratively. Said he started screaming bloody murder and the fella ran off. He was lucky."

"Yeah. You got a name for him?"

"No—sorry, I don't. Never got it. He wouldn't say. Not your basic social butterfly. Was all I could do to get him into emerg for enough stitches to hold his hair on. And then he took off, too, just up and left there. Can't tell you who he is. Can tell you what he looks, at least looked, like, though."

"Do it."

"Well, big guy, a hundred-eighty, -ninety pounds anyway. Pretty sure a rummie—street person, dirty clothes, dirty body, dirty, dirty, dirty—gawd, he smelled. Didn't envy the nurses trying to clean up just his head. Big nose, I mean a *huge* nose, bulbous, red, more like a snout. The most beautiful head of hair though—almost a mane. Guy looked sorta like a lion. That's probably why I remember him—that and the weird way he got hurt. Yeah, like a lion."

Fry had every available uniform in E District and a few from the fringes of A, B, C, and D hunting for "the lion," figuring that he was still in the downtown area if he was still in the city at all, wondering how they were going to find a man who could be everywhere and nowhere, who likely had no one and nothing and no place, who probably would not want to be found, who did not know they were looking anyway, and who, even if he did, especially if he did, might just crawl into a hole and hide.

5:45 PM

The argument began as whispering in the claustrophobic isolation and utter lack of privacy of what architects who never studied there regarded as the "happy," single-building, educational shopping mall called Mount Royal College. It continued as angrily animated conversation during the equally public and crowded but anonymous and indifferent rush-hour bus ride north on Crowchild Trail. It was still going on, raging now as a full-bodied shouting match in the hardly more private, thin-walled, and uninsulated new apartment in the attic of the narrow frame house jammed between other narrow frame houses in a dense, pre-First-World-War boom-era subdivision of narrow frame houses in west-central Calgary.

"No, I'm sorry, Jim, but no, I really don't understand why you don't want to report it—especially you," June Bonecutter said, wrestling the red Stampeder sweatshirt over her short blonde hair, unzipping her jeans, falling back onto the bed, peeling the pants off her legs.

"Goddammit, Junie, I thought I told you!" Jim Kosuth snapped, flinging his leather-sleeved Mount Royal College jacket onto a ratty stuffed chair piled high with a month's dirty laundry.

He *had* told her, again and again, until he almost believed it, even if she did not. Perhaps she sensed that he was not telling the truth, not the *whole* truth, as they said in television courtroom dramas. He did not want to tell her that truth. She would not understand. She did not understand how it was, the way things worked. She had a too-simple, black-and-white view of the world. He had his reasons for not wanting to report it—good reasons it seemed to him, even if they were also small and cowardly and self-serving. He could not tell her his reasons. But he had them.

If he reported it and was wrong, they would dismiss him as a fool—a too-eager, brown-nosing, ass-kissing fool. They would question his intelligence and his powers of observation. If he reported it now and was right, they would ask him why he had waited so long to come forward, why he had not reported it sooner, immediately, when it might have made a difference. They would question his intelligence and the quality of his judgment. Either way, it would ruin his career before it was a career.

A career. That was something Jim Kosuth had never even thought about, let alone aspired to, growing up on the farm near the Great Slave, dreaming only of getting out, getting away, going south. Then the local Mountie came to a high school careers day when Jim was in eleventh grade, and he saw a way out, and started thinking about a career. He did not have the marks to make it into the Mounties. But he made it into police science at Mount Royal, and he was doing all right in his first year—not top of the class, but all right, well enough. And he liked it, the guys, the camaraderie, the potential for excitement, the prospect of good pay—maybe, if he was lucky and did nothing stupid, right here, in Calgary. He liked the city, the pace, the noise, the size, even the aggravation. He was not going to lose it. He was not going to throw it all away, not now, not on this.

She could not understand that. She would not understand. There was no point in getting into that with her.

"How many times I have to tell you?" he asked, sitting down heavily at the side of the bed, his back to her.

"Until it makes sense," she said from the opposite side of the bed, where she sat unhooking her bra. She tossed it into a corner, onto an often-painted, now mostly white wicker arm chair that was her dirty-clothes hamper. She rubbed her large breasts with her hands, leaned forward, pulled a clean brassiere from the top dresser drawer and strapped in her breasts again. She got up from the bed and padded into the tiny bathroom, saying over her shoulder, without looking at him. "I mean, we saw what we saw."

"Shit, Junie, you don't know that for sure."

"Shit yourself. I know what *I* saw."

"Oh, you do, do you?"

"Yeah, I do," she said, leaning back at the bathroom sink, looking at him through the open door. "And dammit, you saw it, too. I mean, you're the one always talking about training yourself to see, observing what's going on, not missing anything. You didn't miss this. Jeez, Jim, you were gonna punch the one guy, the one who got killed, and you almost ran into the other one, the one who—you *had* to see—"

"I *had* to?"

"Yeah. *Had* to. Couldn't-have-missed-it-if-you-had-tried."

"How'd you get so fucking sure of yourself?"

"How'd you get so effing unsure of yourself? They can't be teaching you to wait for guarantees. For the—what do you call them?—oh, yeah, for the perpetrator to walk up to you, hand you a signed confession, stick out his hands and say, 'Cuff me.' You'd never make *any* arrests. Oh, goddammit anyway!"

"Goddamn what? Me?"

"No! Not you! There's no hot water again. Dammit! Dammit to hell! I know we only pay a hundred seventy-five a month, but does that have to mean we only get hot water three days a week? Will you get after him? I've gotta go. I've got an orientation at the General. Talk to him—unless you don't want to report this either."

"Fuck you! I'll go downstairs and talk to him. I'll get you your hot water. No hot water is no hot water—a fact. This other business'd only get *me* in hot water. And it's just ..."

"Just what?" she asked defiantly, pulling up white pantyhose. "Bullshit? Something I'm making up? Hell it is. And fuck you!"

"No, no, you're not making it up. I know. You just can't be sure that's what, who, you saw. Think now. What'd we *really* see? What could we *really* say? Junie, you gotta be really sure about something like this—really, really sure. This is a murder investigation, you know."

"Yeah. I do know. That's my point. If we saw anything, anything at all, we should report it—we should have reported it already. Maybe it would—"

"Maybe it would what?" Jim asked defensively, jumping up from the bed. "Have saved somebody?"

"Maybe."

"Oh, fuck. So now you think because I didn't run right down to headquarters and make a case of it I got somebody else killed."

"No. No, I don't think that. You, we, didn't know. Had no reason to know. Not then. But then that guy's picture in the paper—"

"The picture you *say* was that guy."

"Oh, come on, Jim, get off it. You really think there was another guy with hair like that who got killed that same night within a block of where we saw the guy we did see? The *movie* plot wasn't that far-fetched. All I'm saying is we've got reason to know, at least suspect, now. And we should say something—*now*."

"And just what the hell good would it do 'now,' do you think?"

"I don't know—I'm not a cop. You tell me. You're gonna be one in another year. Wouldn't it, couldn't it, do *some* good? You might've seen something that'll help. You might remember something you don't even know you remember. Or I might. I don't know. I mean, aren't cops always complaining about the public not wanting to 'get involved?' Jeez, you're a public who's gonna be a cop and you've got a chance to 'get involved' and you don't want to. And I don't get it."

"I know."

"You know what?"

"That you don't get it."

In the old mirror with the crackled silvering around the edges, in which she was examining her white nursing uniform, she saw him over her shoulder looking over his shoulder at her. She returned his gaze. Each of them for the first time was seeing a different person, wondering who that person was, fearful of the answer.

"I have to go," June said, pulling on her coat, pulling away as Jim tried to kiss her goodbye.

"Aw, come on, Junie, don't go, not yet. We haven't, you know, talked this thing out yet."

"I think we've talked it to death."

"Why don't you just call in and tell them you'll be a little late and—"

"I-have-to-go-*now*, Jim!" June said with cold and uncharacteristic fury, thinking of the two utterly exhausting years she was just finishing. Two years of wearing two uniforms: crisp white at the hospitals for nothing, robin's egg blue at the restaurant for enough money to keep body or soul—not both—together. Two years of the merciless teasing she took for having no name for a nurse—for a butcher, maybe, or a surgeon (one and the same, of course—another joke). Two years of wondering how she would ever find the time for everything, for study and work and herself, for her man, this man she suddenly did not know and was not sure she could respect. Two years of wondering whether she would ever again be anything but tired. "I haven't busted my buns to get this job just to piss it away over ... what?"

"You, ah, won't say anything, will you, about, you know?"

"*You* say something."

"Me?"

"To the effing landlord at least, about the water—I know when I come home I'm gonna want a long, hot bath."

"Wait up for you?" Jim asked, hopefully, gently brushing her left breast under her heavy coat.

"Can if you want," she said, turning up her collar, turning to leave. "Don't know if there'll be anything worth waiting up for though."

8:40 PM

It was a good night to play the game.

The cold rain was still falling, flying at the city from every compass direction on the swirling, fickle wind. He could hear the wind, and the pelting rain. He shivered, almost feeling them again. Like last night. No. It was only this morning, early this morning. Today. It seemed somehow longer ago. It had been such a long day.

He was tired. He did not really want to go out tonight, into this miserable night. He did not need to go out tonight, did not yet feel the need to go out again. He would, he knew. Soon. Each time the need returned quickly, more quickly with each time.

But not tonight, he hoped. If he went out tonight, about all he would get for his trouble was soaked to the skin, again—as it was, his leather jacket was still not dry. All he would catch was a cold or, worse, be caught cold himself. He did not want that. Did he? No. Of course, not. He shivered again, at the very thought.

He would not find anyone out tonight, no one safe, no one suitable. But who *was* suitable, now? Who should be next? Should there be a next? Questions. He had not been bothered before by questions. He had not questioned himself before. He had been so clear-headed in his purpose and so committed and sure. And now ...

It was a good night to play the game.

He stood in the middle of the room, facing the window wall, his reflection broken by the vertical lines of the sash, as if by the bars of a cell. Beyond the bars, the leaden light of day had faded to a deathly pallor but had not quite died. The lights had come on on the empty streets and in the empty towers. Four city blocks away, through a high, thin gap in the monolithic concrete mass of downtown, he could see, suspended like a lighthouse in the sky, the beacon of the Calgary Tower. From four storeys down, the mingled reds and greens and blues of blinking neon rose to his cell window and played with the light behind him, yellow light, softly flickering yellow light.

Slowly, ever so slowly, he turned from his imprisoned reflection, from his cell window on the present, turned toward the light, the yellow light, the flickering yellow light, toward another time.

He stood in the middle of the room, now facing the gilded bull's-eye mirror on the wall opposite the window, his reflection distorted but unbroken in the round, bulging glass, his image illuminated by the dozen candles in old tin holders on the antique mahogany drop-leaf table beneath the mirror. The yellow light bouncing softly off the reddish wood gave his skin a reddish-brown cast, almost a sepia tone, as if he were gazing into an old photograph, as if, simply by turning, he had escaped into another time; a better time, he was sure—his time.

That was the game.

He had bought the mirror and the table at a downtown antiques store in an old stage works near the tracks. They had come from the east. The mirror was Federal period, almost two hundred years old, the table also a bona fide, hundred-plus-year-old antique, the dealer had told him, and had given him papers to prove it. The table had come on one of the first trains, and the mirror on a wagon with settlers who had arrived before the rails. He liked that. He liked having them together, bringing them together. They belonged together. They belonged here. As he did. He was a pioneer. They belonged with him. He would have liked to have a better place for them, a more fitting place than here. One day, he would.

The mirror and the table made the game work, the mirror and the table and the candlelight, old light. They made it work. The mirror took in everything, everything but the window. When he turned, when he stood just where he stood, the window behind him and the world beyond it vanished, leaving only a hint of light like a halo around him. The only world was in the mirror.

In the mirror he could see, on the mahogany table between the candles, the carefully folded white, yellow, red, and green Hudson's Bay blanket, the Indian drum, the powder horn, the cartridge belt, the Plains

Indian scalping wand with the Hudson's Bay knife on one end. In the mirror he could see, on the wall over the sofa, the huge buffalo gun; on the back and arms of the sofa, the animal skins, pelts of wolf and deer and bear; on the top shelf of the bookcase, the stuffed owl, its one remaining wide glass eye glowing yellow in the candlelight. In the mirror he could see himself, as he should have been, where he should have been, where he belonged.

Of course, the game worked best when he was dressed for it. When he pulled on the buckskin pants he had found in a vintage clothing shop and the new boots he had bought at the saddlery, when he strapped on the bullet bag and powder horn, when he took the heavy rifle from the wall and held it in the crook of his arm, over his fringed buckskin jacket, when he put on the sweat-stained, wide-brimmed hat and pulled it low just over his eyes—when he turned and looked into the mirror then, he could really see himself as he should have been; he could really disappear into the right time, his time.

He wished he could wear the clothing all the time, outside. But he could not. He would be noticed. He could not be noticed. He could not call attention to himself. He did not think he was finished yet.

But he wished at least he could wear his leather jacket. He wished it were dry. Perhaps by tomorrow. Perhaps tomorrow he could wear it again. Perhaps tomorrow night he could play the game again, play it well, play it as it should be played.

Unless the need were to return.

Then—

He froze at the sudden hollow metallic rattling from outside. *The fire escape!* he thought. Someone was coming up the fire escape. The two fellows from upstairs probably. They always came up the back way, giggling, always loud, usually drunk or on drugs, leaning back like monkeys from the railing where the fourth-floor landing of the stairs landed just beyond his window, tapping on his window, making faces in his window, laughing. Maybe they should be next...?

No!

They were too close. He could do nothing about them. Nothing. He could not take the chance.

He lumbered to the window and drew the drapes, department-store-catalogue drapes, but heavy, not unlike the floral brocade he had seen in a book of Victoriana. They darkened the room from the outside, blackened it. No one could see inside, he knew. He had tried. They could not see. Yet he stood at the edge of the window, holding tight to the cord, hardly breathing, waiting for them to rap on his window, and then, when they did not, waiting for them to climb uncertainly up the reverberating steel stairs, not moving until he was sure they had pushed open the sixth-floor fire door and gone inside.

As he was waiting he glanced at his bag on the wicker chest beside the coat rack where his leather jacket was drying. He thought of the tools in his bag. For an instant, he thought about taking his bag upstairs, up the metal stairs, quietly, stealthily, late, after they had drugged and laughed and whored themselves to sleep. He thought of opening his bag, carefully lining up his tools, all the while watching them sleep, quietly laughing at them in their sleep. He thought of their eyes, opening in surprise to the explosion of white light. He thought of capturing their surprise, their last blinded vision, keeping it forever, as he had the others'...

No! *No!*

That would be a mistake. He could not afford a mistake. He would not make a mistake.

He shook his head, as if physically trying to dislodge the thought. And then he thought of the other two, from last night, today. No mistake there. Well, the one. But he was sure it would not matter. He could not find it. No one would find it. And even if someone did, what would it matter? It would tell them nothing. Still, all the more reason for him to be careful, to do nothing rash, nothing stupid, to wait until the time was right. He would know. The need would tell him.

He went into the kitchen and turned on the light, momentarily blinded by the sudden fluorescent brightness. He opened the freezer compartment door and took out the plastic bag. He peeled it open. He reached inside. Cold. Yet still not frozen.

He wished there was a better way. He wished these trophies were as easy to keep as their surprised looks, there, in the manila file folder in the wicker trunk. There was a better way, the old way. He had read about it in one of his books about those days—better days. But he would need a bigger place, a bigger, more private place.

He withdrew his hand. Blood on his fingertips. He closed the bag and placed it at the back of the freezer. He opened the container of ice cream in the back of the freezer door. He dipped his bloody fingers into it. The ice cream was soft. He licked off his fingers. He put the top back on the ice cream, turned the dial inside the freezer from five to seven, and closed the door.

Fry could not figure it out.

He had done everything right. He had taken his time, had taken care. He had measured every piece to a thirty-second of an inch. He had made every cut as precisely as his hand and eyes would allow. He had planed and chiselled and sanded the pieces carefully. They should have fit perfectly. But they did not fit at all. Rather, they fit, but crazily.

The bookcase was crooked, improbably crooked, every piece crooked, crooked in different ways. The top shelf slanted to the right, the bottom to the left; the middle two shelves dipped to the front and back, respectively. The thick slabs of the sides leaned in opposite directions. The support pieces were buckled. The thing should not even have been standing.

Fry could not figure it out.

He knocked the case apart. He grabbed a block plane from the workbench. Perhaps if he took just a bit off the left side. He clamped the piece in a vice. Carefully, deliberately, delicately, he moved the sharp blade across the wood, almost gently against the grain, trying not to split the end grain, trying to remove only the thinnest of shavings.

With the first pass of the plane, a big chunk of the wood came off, splintered as if it had been torn off. A thin trickle of blood began to seep from the open wound in the wood, and then from swelling sores where Fry had clamped the wood. He tried to wipe away the blood, which only flowed more quickly. Panicking, he loosened the clamps. He tried to fit the splintered pieces of the side together. He could not. He grabbed the bottle of yellow carpenter's glue and squeezed—and blood oozed from the plastic bottle. Blood covered his hands and spattered to the cellar floor. He could not let go of the bottle. He could not stop squeezing the bottle. He could not stop the bleeding.

In the distance he heard sirens wailing. He began to run in tight circles around the pieces of his bookcase, every piece bleeding now from every cut he had made—every bite of the chisel, every slice of the plane, every rasp of the file, every tooth mark of the saw, every sanded abrasion.

Blood.

Everywhere, blood.

And the sirens drew nearer, louder and louder. He ran in circles, faster and faster, running in the blood, splattering himself with blood, soaking himself in blood. He was groaning: "Oh, no, no, no, no, no ..." He might have been weeping. And, closer and closer, the sirens, the sirens, the sirens—

A telephone.

A telephone was ringing.

Somewhere a phone was ringing, louder and louder, drowning out the sirens. But where? He had no telephone here in the cellar. Only upstairs. But it was not ringing upstairs. It was ringing here, in the cellar, louder and louder.

Where...?

There! On the pegboard above the workbench, hanging among his tools, his well-oiled, well-sharpened tools, a red wall telephone, ringing, throbbing. He ran toward the workbench, stumbling over the bleeding wood. He reached for the phone. Too high. It was hanging too high, just out of reach. He reached again, straining—

Fry heard the hissing of a cat. He awoke in a cold

sweat, breathing heavily, his heart racing. He did not see Lips leap from the bed and scurry, ears back, tail puffed, under the dresser. He could hardly see anything. He was sitting in his bed, leaning, straining forward at the waist, his right hand reaching toward the foot of the bed. The telephone on the bedside table was ringing. Fry took a deep breath, held it, then exhaled slowly, trying to get his bearings. He rubbed his eyes hard with the fingertips of his two hands, then opened them wide, trying to accustom them to the fuzzy, grey light. He picked up the receiver.

"Yeah," he rasped. "Yeah, Fry."

"Fry?"

"Think I established that. Who's this?"

"Johnson."

"Who?"

"Johnson—Glenn Johnson."

"Oh, yeah—Johnson."

Johnson was a thin, driven, youngish—early thirties or so—constable in the RCMP. Fry had worked with him on a couple of cases. He was not a bad fellow, for a horseman; maybe a little tight-assed for Fry's taste, but not a bad fellow. Fry figured that the Calgary force's thin, driven "horseless headman" had been not unlike Johnson when he was younger.

What the hell could Johnson be calling for now? Fry sighed deeply and closed his eyes, assuming that he knew the answer, figuring that he already knew what he was about to be told.

"Another one?" he asked.

"Another what?"

"Another body, bodies. That's why you're calling, right?"

"Well, not exactly."

"Well 'exactly' why *are* you calling? I assume that at whatever godforfuckingsaken time this is, it's not social."

"No."

"Look, Johnson. I'm tired. I've just been having a helluva bad dream. I appreciate your interrupting it—if you have, if you're not just another part of it. Am I awake or what? If you pinch me I'll know I'm not—"

"It's that Indian, Fry."

"Indian. What Indian?" The only Indian Fry could think of was the young Indian with the knife Ken Oliver had shot dead. "What? Oliver's punk?"

"Who?"

"You know. The one they tried to gift-wrap as the killer. The one who can't be, because he was gift-wrapped himself, in the morgue, when the last ones—you haven't called to play that old tune?"

"It's not him."

"Okay, Johnson, I give up. Just who are we—you anyway—talking about?"

"It's the guy you work, worked, with ..."

"What guy I work with?"

"On that committee—the one the chiefs set up. The Indian lawyer."

"Red Crow?" Fry felt something cold crawling down his spine. He was listening so hard now that his eyes squinted almost closed. His flesh erupted in goosebumps. He shivered involuntarily. "Tom Red Crow?"

"Yes."

"What about him?"

"He's dead."

John Jacob,

You'll be angry with me, I know, and with yourself. Don't be. At least not with yourself. You'll be asking yourself how you could've let it happen, how you could've failed to see it coming, how you could've done nothing to stop it. I can't keep you from asking. I can tell you, though, there was nothing you could've done.

I didn't decide lightly. You couldn't have changed my mind. I didn't act in a brief dark moment of depression. You couldn't, as the song says, have helped me make it through the night.

Please don't think of this as a defeat. I have not been defeated. You have not been defeated.

I had a point to make. No surprise there. I always had a point to make. Mostly small points though. Question marks. Commas. I wanted to make a big point. But not just a period. An exclamation point!

I meant to be noticed. Remember that. This was a political act, a shout of defiance, I hope. It was not a whimper of defeat. Remember that.

Political acts, I understand, have personal consequences. Mine does, I know. I've caused injury, to my mother, my family, injury to you; if I'm wrong, injury to my people. You'll have to try to see to it that I'm not wrong, John Jacob. You'll get over your hurt. You'll get over being mad with me. But you won't forget. You won't let others forget. In your remembering is my power.

I'm not vain enough or arrogant enough or stupid enough to believe that my death will end the killing, all the thoughtless killing of my people, not just because of this latest business, but all along. But maybe it'll make everybody think twice. You—not you, John Jacob, but what you are, what you're a part of, what you can't help being—you can't not know what you do. (Sorry for the almost biblical reference; I don't mean it that way. I don't have a Christ complex either.)

I'm sorry not to see you again, John Jacob. I'm sorry to leave you. You had some potential as a chess player. Among other things.

Tom

P.S. I know I don't have to tell you, of all people, but don't believe everything you read in the papers.

Fry sat at his desk in the police headquarters building on Seventh Avenue SE, holding the note open in front of him, staring at the note, written in Thomas Red Crow's firm, unshaking hand. He had read and read and reread the note, until his eyes ached from the reading, from trying to comprehend the meaning of the lines, to see between the lines, to get beyond the lines. There were only the lines.

Red Crow had been right. Fry *was* angry, with Red Crow, with himself. He was asking himself everything Red Crow said he would ask: How had he let it happen? How had he not seen it coming? How had he done nothing to stop it?

Red Crow was wrong about one thing, though, at least one thing. Fry *had* been defeated, utterly, totally. If he had done his job more professionally, if he had seen the situation more clearly, if he had fashioned more penetrating questions, if he had put it all together more quickly, if, if, if …

A manicured right hand reached down and flicked the note hard with its middle finger, almost knocking the paper from Fry's hand, startling him, snapping him out of himself. He looked up. Inspector Phil Grantham was hovering over his desk.

"That the note to you?" Grantham asked.

"Yeah."

"You'll have to turn it over."

"Turn it over? To who?"

"Come on. You know as well as I do. It's part of the investigation."

"Investigation? Just what is it that's being investigated? What facts aren't clear?"

The facts were clear enough.

* * *

Thomas Red Crow had appeared in provincial court Thursday morning. He succeeded in having shoplifting charges against a seventeen-year-old boy from the Sarcee reserve dropped when the department store security officer admitted he could not positively identify the youth. A Native prostitute Red Crow failed to keep out of jail on an assault charge he did manage to keep out of federal penitentiary, convincing the judge that a sentence long enough to send her out of the province could be a death sentence. He got continuances on two other assault charges, one break-and-enter.

After court, he met with other clients, jailed and awaiting trial, telling them that he had to be out of town on personal business, giving them the names of lawyers who had agreed to represent them if they agreed to have them. He had told the lawyers the same "personal business" story he told his clients.

Red Crow arrived at his storefront office just as the Native woman who cleaned it was leaving. He thanked her and hugged her clumsily, which flustered and surprised her but did not make her think for a moment that it was his way of telling her goodbye. At his desk after she left, on plain letterhead, in his strong hand, he did say goodbye, writing brief personal notes to his mother and to Fry, and a long, polemical, much more stridently political open letter to the media, of which he made ten copies. He folded the notes, sealed them in envelopes, dropped them into his briefcase, and left the office.

He drove home to the reserve. He visited his mother for over an hour. He changed clothes, putting on his old jeans, well-worn cowboy boots, a soft red western shirt faded light pink from many washings, and a dusty black Stetson with a single eagle feather stuck in the beaded band around its brim. He went to his brother's house. They drank coffee in the kitchen. He asked to borrow his brother's horse, to take a ride. His brother thought it odd, to go riding in the rain. But Thomas had always been different. His brother did not notice their grandfather's thirty-thirty hunting rifle missing from its rack just inside the back door until later.

When he had not returned, his brother and some other men went looking for him just before dusk. They found the horse tethered to a clump of cottonwoods in a narrow stream valley, grazing on the new grass. They found Red Crow above the trees, slumped against an outcrop of pink rock overlooking the foothills as they climbed raggedly toward the monumental grey of mountains and sky. A multi-coloured striped blanket was draped over his shoulders. The front of his shirt was dark red again, darker red than when new. The rifle was in his lap.

They found the notes in the briefcase on the front seat of Red Crow's car. After his mother, stoic, dry-eyed, and profoundly grieving, had read his message to her, she debated on whether to destroy the others. She decided against it. They were his will, his last will. She kept her letter. She gave the Mounties the letter to Fry and one copy of the letter to the press. She sent Red Crow's brother into the city with the others.

Thomas Red Crow's angry last testament was on page one of the morning *Bulletin*. His death was the lead story on the morning radio news, bumping reports on the rain being too little to end the drought and on Pacific Western Airlines trying to take over Transair, bumping the morning update on the killings.

* * *

"Never mind the facts," Grantham said. "What's clear to me is that your note is part of an official police investigation."

"Whose?" Fry asked. "Not ours—no jurisdiction, remember?"

"I know that—I don't need procedural lessons from you. The RCMP want it back, for the record."

"The horsemen want it—fuck the horsemen."

Fry folded the note and slipped it back into the envelope. He pulled a butane lighter from his pants pocket. He held the envelope over his ash tray. He flicked on the lighter. He held the flame at the corner of the envelope until the paper was burning.

"Goddammit, Jake!" Grantham yelled. "What the Christ? You can't—"

Grantham reached for the envelope. Fry flicked the lighter's flame to high and held him at bay with the torch until the envelope had burned almost to his fingertips. He dropped the last flaming piece into the ashtray and watched it shrivel to black.

"You can't ... there'll be hell to pay for this," Grantham said. "You're tampering with evidence."

"Evidence?" Fry asked innocently, lowering the flame, raising his eyes toward Grantham. "What evidence?"

8:30 AM

"You want to burn something, Ghost, why don't you burn this shit," Patrol Sergeant Paul Strahan said disgustedly, lowering a cardboard filing box onto the desk between Fry and Inspector Phil Grantham. "What were you burnin' there, anyway?"

"Evidence," Grantham snorted.

"What?" Strahan asked.

"Bridges," Fry mumbled.

"What?" Strahan asked.

"Never mind," Grantham said, reaching to flip open the top of the box. "What's in here?"

"*You* never mind," Fry snapped, smacking the palm of his right hand onto the box top, holding it closed.

"Whoa!" Strahan said, half laughing. "You two boys having a spat? And only me here to referee? That's trouble."

Strahan looked from Fry to Grantham, who were glaring at each other. He continued, clearing his throat, "Nothin' in there, Inspector. Nothin' you'd wanna see. Damn straight nothin' you'd wanna touch."

"And nothing you're *going* to touch," said Fry. "After all, it's *evidence*. You wouldn't want to tamper with *evidence*. Evidence in an *official* police investigation. And *I'm* the official police investigator."

"For the time being," Grantham said after a few moments of tense silence, straightening his already perfectly straight striped tie.

"For the time being," Fry agreed, smiling coldly, still holding down the top of the box.

Grantham tried to work the corners of his mouth into a hard, cold smile of his own, for him an exercise in control. He managed a slight twitch in the lines around his eyes. But he could not budge the firm straight line of his mouth. He reached down, tapped the box top hard with the index finger of his right hand, and walked away. He was not whistling.

"What *do* you have in there, Strahan?" Fry asked after Grantham had left, opening the box.

"Like I told the man, Ghost. Nothin'—surely to Christ nothin' to fight over. What the hell was that all about anyway?"

"Ah, I suppose you could call it a jurisdictional dispute."

"Eh?"

"Forget it."

"Suit yourself. But I'd watch it with him, though. You can get into it with me 'cause you and me go way back and I got the hide of an elephant without half the memory. Him, though ..."

"Yeah. I know," Fry said, surprised, as he always was, at how wise the redneck homicide sergeant could sometimes be. "The memory of an elephant without the hide."

"Sorry about the buck."

"About what?"

"You know, Red Crow. You worked on the be-nice-to-Indians committee with him, didn't you?"

"Yeah," Fry said, instantly bristling at the Paul Strahan he had come to expect but was never quite prepared for. "I did."

"Too bad. Funny about them."

"Funny?"

"Yeah. You just never can tell what they'll do, what'll set 'em off."

"Just tell me what's in the box, Strahan, before you set *me* off and you and I get into it again."

"You got it. You wanted everything from west of the creek there. Well, you got that. Couple more boxes downstairs. Heavier stuff. Bottles, mostly. Beer, wine, liquor, Ol' Hermit type stuff. What's left of an empty case of two-four. Smaller stuff's in here. And like I told him, like I told you it would be, it's nothin'. Nothin' that's gonna catch anybody. More likely to catch somethin' from it. Really is nothin' you wanna touch. First time I ever heard of *re*packaging rubbers. See for yourself. I'd, ah, wash my hands when I'm done, though. Me, that's just what I'm gonna do."

"Thanks for the hygiene tip. And thank the troops for me."

"I'm sure they'll appreciate it. But they'd appreciate it a whole lot more if you picked up their cleaning bills and kicked in some—what do they call it?—some hazardous duty pay."

"Yeah, sure. Jus' sec. I'll write you a cheque from my Swiss account."

"Sorry, Ghost, but under the table—I deal only in cash."

"That's what I've heard."

"You *do* like to lip dangerously."

Fry watched Strahan swagger down the aisle, surprised again: first wisdom from Strahan, now a witticism.

Strahan was right about what was in the box. For once, Strahan's assessment was correct. Nothing was in the box. The box was packed full, full of neatly tagged, plastic-bagged nothing.

Candy and chewing gum wrappers. Empty cigarette packages. At least a dozen used condoms. Fry took Strahan's advice; he did not open the bag to count them by hand. Again as many lost golf balls, good golf balls, Titleists—the Canyon Meadows Golf and Country Club was just north of the creek. The lens cap of a thirty-five-millimetre camera—dropped, Fry figured, while the media pack were barking at the cordon or when Strahan chased them, growling, out of the ravine. A single running shoe, left foot. His breath caught in his throat when he saw the jackknife. But then he opened it, tried to open it, forced the blade open, nearly breaking a fingernail breaking the grip of the rust.

Nothing.

9:20 AM

Fry had stuffed the plastic bags of nothing back into the filing box, not as neatly as Strahan's uniforms had done. He was trying vainly to re-close the lid when Strahan reappeared at his desk and snickered.

"Nice job, Ghost."

"Thanks."

"Nothin', eh?"

"Looks like it."

"Told you. You wanna see the rest?"

"It any better than this?"

"Nope."

"Nope."

Fry looked at the cardboard box crammed to overflowing with nothing and then at the blackened paper filling the ashtray. He sighed, closing his eyes, pinching the bridge of his nose between his right thumb and index finger.

"Unless you want to get in a few more 'I told you so's,'" he said, "I think you can take your box of goodies there."

"'I told you so' feels good, but I did have a better reason, might even have something to do with the investigation."

"Yeah?"

"Well, maybe, in a minor way." Strahan took a couple of loose sheets from his notebook. "Couple of things I found on my desk—"

"*Your* desk?"

"Well, yeah. I told—I said I wanted to have a look at anything that came over."

"And here I thought I was the one heading the investigation."

"Look, Ghost, I'm here, aren't I? You wanna listen to what I got or you wanna bitch about jurisdiction with me too?"

"Let's hear it. We can talk about jurisdiction later."

"Fine by me. One's a call came in last night, er, actually early this morning. Woman who said she and her boyfriend saw the little puker—the long-hair—the night he was killed. Actually bumped into him coming out of a movie. They, woman and her boyfriend, were comin' out of the movie. Boyfriend almost got into a punch-up with him. Anyway, according to the woman, the kid was with another guy, big guy."

"Yeah?" Fry's eyes were open now, focusing on Strahan. "Any other description?"

"Some. He was wearin' a leather jacket, one of those western things, buckskin, fringes and all, blue jeans, new, she thought—couldn't see his face though. Had his collar pulled up. And they weren't really lookin' that close anyway—no reason to."

"She give her name?"

"Nope. Wouldn't. Said she couldn't. Something about her boyfriend's job."

"Sounds like our kind of citizen. She give any reason why it took her so long to call?"

"Well, only that they didn't know what they saw until later, and then her boyfriend didn't want—oh, yeah. She did say one other thing about the big guy. He was carrying some kind of bag, a big bag over his shoulder, a big leather bag."

"Hmmm ... you said you had a couple of things."

"Yeah. This from Stanton."

"Our boy of doughnut shop fame?"

"One and the same. Says he pulled over the two Coasters in the blue Imperial."

"When was this?"

"Day before yesterday. Just off Sixteenth Avenue NW. Was gonna ticket 'em for improper lane change, improper left turn ..."

"Was 'gonna'?"

"Yeah. Says he got a call to that pileup on Crowchild before he could get the ticket book out. Let 'em off with a warning."

"So somehow they got from all the way north to all the way south."

"Somehow."

"Wonder how they found—not on their own. They'd've needed a guide."

"I'd say."

"The 'big guy'?"

"I'd bet on it."

"That's up near the university."

"What is?"

"Where Stanton pulled them over."

"Ah, well, yeah, I guess. Not far."

"Hmmm ... you got anything else?"

"Nope."

"Nothing yet on our wino witness?"

"Who? Oh, him. Nope."

"Damn, I'd bet he met our 'big guy' too—if he can remember him."

"If he can remember his own name."

"Won't know unless we find him."

"Uniforms are lookin.'"

"Well, maybe you'd leave your notes there—and take your box here—and keep on 'lookin.'"

"Yes*sir*."

"And I think I'll get a couple of detectives after him too."

"They'll love you for it."

"So I lose Mr. Congeniality this year. I'm tired of winning it all the time anyway."

Fry picked up the telephone as Strahan picked up the filing box. He dialled the number he had scribbled in his notebook.

"Russell," the professor's voice boomed.

"Jake Fry."

"Fry! How's your hair?" Russell laughed.

"Still on. I've got a couple more questions."

"I'm sure you do. Shoot."

"You, ah, got any students with an unnatural interest in western history, Native lore, that sort of thing?"

"Define 'unnatural.'"

"Okay. Too keen. Weird. Wants to hear lurid stories about settlers' balls roasting on a spit, or Native balls for that matter. This'd be a big guy, maybe wears blue jeans, leather jacket."

"Can't think of anybody like that. But then I'm not sure I'd recognize a third of my students—I teach big classes."

"Um hmm. Nobody a little too anti-east? Or too pro-west?"

"Define 'too.'"

"You're a big help."

"Sorry—but hell, those 'too's' you're looking for could apply to me. And, as I'm sure you recall, *I* wear a leather jacket and jeans. As I said before, *I* could be your suspect."

He laughed. Fry did not.

"Thanks for your time, professor," he said.

"Not at all."

"If you do think of anything, anyone, let me know, will you? If I think it's you, I'll let you know."

"Ha! That's the stuff!"

With the receiver still pressed against his ear, Fry put his finger on the plunger, got a fresh line and began to dial another number from his notebook. He paused halfway through, pondered for a moment, then hung up.

12:30 PM

"Wha- the f...? Who's it...? Where 'm...?"

His eyes opened wide to the light, the sudden flash of light, the bright, painful, blinding light. He closed his eyes against the light. He remembered the light. Was this that light? Was it again that night? But how could it be? He thought ...

No!

He tried to get up. He could not get up. Something was holding him down, pressing him down, pushing against his chest ...

No. No! No!

He struggled, flailing wildly with his arms, skinning his knuckles, kicking, and kicking, and kicking ... kicking through, putting his foot through ... What...? Showering himself with tiny pieces of ...

Glass?

He opened his eyes, looked up and saw, through his one good eye, the steering wheel that had been pinning him down. He looked higher up, into the light, and saw only sunlight, suddenly slanting down through the shattered windshield from the top of the towers.

He remembered.

He had crawled into the car last night to get out of the rain. The sixty-eight Chev up on blocks was behind the vacant house where he used to crash. It was boarded up now. He could not get in. He had climbed into the car, collapsed onto the front seat, passed out, blacked out, as he did sometimes now.

Big Nose fell back onto the car seat, closing his eyes again, still breathing rapidly, his heart racing, afraid he would black out again. He had not meant to sleep so long. Sleep? Ha! Is that what it was? He would have to get up. He had to get moving. He ran his filmy tongue over his cracked lips. He tried to swallow.

He needed a drink. And some food? When did he eat last? What he needed was a drink. Did he have any left?

He got up, pulling himself up with the steering wheel, too quickly. He saw the blackness, the edge of blackness, creeping in. He shook his shaggy head, trying to clear it, trying to shake the blackness away, shaking away only bits of window glass. He coughed.

He felt in his left coat pocket—nothing. His right—nothing. Wait. He reached deeper, where the pocket lining was ripped inside, deeper. There! He pulled out the tiny bottle of extract, almost empty, only a sip. He tipped it to his lips, holding it there until he was sure he had it all, touching his tongue to the bottle to get the last. Not enough. He flung the bottle into the back seat.

He coughed again. And again. And again. Another of the deep, racking coughing spells he had started to have. He pulled a filthy handkerchief out of his pocket and held it to his mouth as he coughed, his whole body shaking as he coughed. Finally, the coughing stopped. Exhausted, he slumped in the front seat, head down, trying to catch his breath. He inspected the handkerchief. At least no blood this time. He blew his nose into the handkerchief.

He had to go. He had to get moving. He could not stay here. A good place though. He might need it again. Back seat would be good. No broken glass. No steering wheel to contend with. He would have to remember the car, to try to remember it. He remembered just enough now to remember that he did not remember much. He squinted into the light again.

He did remember the light. He did remember that night. He remembered ...

Big Nose slid across the torn front seat cover and pushed open the unlatchable passenger's-side door. He climbed out of the car. For a moment he stood unsteadily in the brief sunlight between the towers, both hands on his aching back. He shook his head, sending more silvery bits of glass flying from his luxuriously silvering hair.

He started to cough again, leaning on both arms against the roof of the car, coughing and coughing and coughing. He leaned against the car for several moments after the coughing had stopped, his head bowed, spitting phlegm, catching his breath.

Then he was on his way. *Which way?* he found himself thinking, and then laughing, almost triggering another coughing spasm. What did it matter which way? It was all one way now.

4:40 PM

The killer had not moved. His left knee still pinned his victim facedown in the dirt, bleeding. His arms were still upraised, the bloodied knife still in his right hand, the bloody scalp still in his left. He was still screaming his triumph.

Fry ignored him.

He was no longer interested in the victorious Plains Cree warrior. He knew now that *his* killer looked nothing like him. He was no longer studying scalping technique. But he was studying, kneeling before the glass that covered the Glenbow Museum's diorama of the Indians of Alberta, Before the White Man, examining the object that lay in the dirt beside the Cree, the war club the warrior would have swung to dispatch his Peigan victim before unsheathing the stone knife to take his scalp. Fry knew now that the club *his* killer used looked nothing like it.

Dr. Clifton Shields had removed a fragment of wood from Jimmy Maclean's shattered skull, just a splinter, but big enough for him to conclude that it was from the same blunt instrument that had smashed the life out of Jane Waldo. Big enough for him to tell that the weapon was made of hardwood, slightly rounded, sanded smooth.

"Like a rolling pin," Shields had said in the unofficial note to Fry attached to the official autopsy report. "Maybe your killer's a crazy baker—or a deranged housewife from Bowness. I know, I know. Not bloody likely. Sorry I can't tell you more, Jake."

Fry saw the movement in the brush, the same movement he had seen before—the movement he had come to see? He smelled the same delicate perfume, sensed the same strong presence. He smiled. With an audible grunt and a cracking of knee joints, he rose and turned toward the reflection.

"*Ms.* Fitzgerald," he said; then, nodding toward the books she cradled in her arms as she had the first time he saw her: "They make you carry those things around all the time?"

"Seems like it sometimes," she said. "They never told us in art school we needed weight training."

She was all in black today—black jumpsuit, black pumps—with jade-green accents: her bracelets, her belt with the silver buckle, the silk scarf around her neck. Her wavy black hair was neatly pulled back into a pony tail, held in place with a jade-green bow.

"'Fraid I've got some bad news to tell you, though," she continued.

"And what's that?"

"His alibi's still solid," she said, gesturing with her eyes toward the diorama. "As far as I know, he hasn't been out since the last time you were here."

"No? Too bad. And I suppose you'd swear to that in court, wouldn't you?"

"On the proverbial stack of Bibles—oh, do they still use Bibles?"

"One, anyway."

"You could've phoned to check up on—Chief Slasher, I think you called him. Didn't even have to phone for that. What *are* you looking for this time anyway?"

"Could've phoned. Yeah. Started to. Not about the chief ... I had a pretty good idea about his whereabouts. Looking for? Nothing in particular, I guess."

Fry thought for a moment, looking at her, wondering how he would have felt if he had not seen her reflection in the brush, what he would have done, wondering whether he would have gone looking for her, wondering exactly what he *had* come looking for. Seeing her now, he knew the answer.

"At least nothing in there," he said, gesturing over his shoulder toward the glass case.

She did not look away.

"You look ... hungry," she said suddenly, blushing a deep lovely pink after she had said it, but still not averting her green eyes.

"Yeah. I guess I am," he lied.

He had not been thinking of food. He had not thought about food in what seemed to be a very long time. He had been eating at odd hours, and only when his grumbling stomach and pounding head reminded him that he had to, grabbing a greasy burger or bucket of chicken on the run or a cheese sandwich and a beer from the refrigerator at home.

"Know a good restaurant?" Fry asked hopefully. "My treat."

Now she was studying him. He felt like the Plains Cree warrior behind the glass, only more vulnerable, disarmed. For just an instant, he was a smitten schoolboy again, tongue-tied, gazing moonily at this wonderful new girl in class, the beginnings of a lopsided sheepish grin on his half-open mouth. He thought he felt himself blush. He did feel flustered and suddenly foolish. The innocence and forgotten power of the feelings unnerved him. He looked away, toward the soaring "northern lights" glittering in plastic and brushed metal just beyond the spiral stairs.

"Well, as a matter of fact, I *do* know a pretty good restaurant," she said. "Not far either, if you like Chinese."

"Yeah, I like Chinese. Can we go now?"

"Wow, you really *must* be hungry," she laughed. "Well, we're still on winter hours. Sure. Sure, I can go. Just have to take these," she said, hugging the books against her chest, "things upstairs. Come on up."

He followed her to the elevator, enjoying the soft swish of her hair and the tight rhythmic sway of her buttocks as she walked. Balancing the books in the crook of her left arm, she punched the elevator button with her right elbow.

"Well, I want you to know that you should consider yourself privileged," she said.

"Privileged? How?"

"You're about to become one of the few mortals who get to catch a glimpse of the reality behind the sophisticated facade of this place."

"And that is?"

"Chaos. Pure chaos."

"Isn't that the reality behind most facades?"

The elevator arrived before she could reply.

"Going up," she said.

On the short trip to the eighth floor, they did not speak. She leaned against one side of the car, holding the books in her arms, examining him, faintly smiling. He leaned against the other side, fumbling for something to do with his hands, finally stuffing them into his overcoat pockets. He felt self-conscious; she was gazing at him so steadily, with such intense interest and curiosity. He lowered his eyes, studying the elevator floor, tracing a circular pattern on the floor with the toe of his right shoe.

The elevator stopped. He looked up. She was still looking at him.

The door opened. He stepped out with her into a clutter of packing crates and bulging cardboard boxes, filing cabinets, groaning metal shelving, and old oak office desks.

"You were right," he said.

"Told you. Welcome to Santa's workshop—ugh, I guess that makes me an elf—something else they didn't mention at art school." She laughed again. "If you wait right here and hold your finger on the button right there this little elf will be right back."

"Yes'm," he said, holding the elevator, catching himself smiling, not remembering until he did just how long it had been since he had really smiled.

She hurried to the right, down the corridor, then left, into a makeshift open office framed by the window wall above Ninth Avenue, two rows of straining metal shelves and a low bank of two-drawer filing cabinets with books, plants, and stuffed manila folders competing for space on top. Smiling, she leaned over one of two cluttered desks in the office to speak to a woman in a blue and white striped dress and with long red hair in a tight frizzy perm that made her look like a clown. They laughed. The clown woman craned her neck to get a look at Fry over the filing cabinets.

Then Miyoko Fitzgerald took a soft, light-green sweater from the back of the oak swivel chair at the other desk, waved to her colleague, and hurried back to the elevator.

"Ready?" she asked.

"I am," he said to her, thinking to himself, with genuine surprise:

Yes. I think I am.

9:45 PM

Fry *was* hungry.

He had already finished the serving of steamed pickerel

with black bean sauce that he never would have ordered on his own. "*Chinese,* remember," Miyoko Fitzgerald had scolded him, flipping past the Western selections he had been perusing on the front page of the menu to the Cantonese dishes inside, pointing out the fish, assuring him that he would love it. He did.

And he had loved the oysters with scallions and ginger that she could not finish, reaching across the table with his fork, eating off her plate, to her satisfied amusement. As he chewed, he looked around the room, the craftsman in him admiring the intricately carved imported Chinese fretwork. His eyes caught her eyes, those jade-green eyes. Looking into them, he was not surprised that she had brought him here, to the Jade Garden.

Fry knew the Jade Garden—at least from the outside.

The Jade Garden was hard not to know from the outside. It was almost impossible to miss. The striking bronze dragon panels and lustrous blue-green ceramic tiles on the facade made the otherwise nondescript Third Avenue building stand out, brought it to life.

The whole of Chinatown was, in a way, about life—exotic, improbable, stubbornly persistent life. From its beginnings during the rail-spurred boom of the last century, as a cluster of workers' cabins near the tracks to its uneasy situation under the towers of the oil-fired boom of this century, Chinatown somehow had maintained its character as a *China* town, a tiny foreign village, the *only* foreign village, in the otherwise unicultural city, a fragment of oriental jade in a massive, WASP-grey setting, as striking in the city as the Jade Garden was on the street.

Fry knew Chinatown, though not as a police officer. If the stereotype of Chinatown as a "sin centre" with hidden gambling joints, opium dens, secret societies, and rampant prostitution had ever been true, it was not now. Murder, Fry's work, was virtually unheard of in Chinatown. Fry did not know Chinatown because he worked its streets, but because he walked them.

Some Sunday mornings, when he was lonelier than usual and actually wanted to be among people, when "street life" in most of the downtown was a contradiction in terms, when the commercial strips were closed tight and the mall abandoned, the streets of Chinatown teemed.

Only about a thousand people actually lived in Chinatown, and not all of them Chinese. But on Sunday mornings, it seemed that the rest of the fifteen thousand Chinese who lived in Calgary swarmed the fifty-acre enclave around Centre Street and the Bow, buying preserved duck eggs or bird's-nest-soup mix from the Chinese grocery, picking up "wife buns"—sweet rolls stuffed with barbecued pork—at the Chinese bakery, attending Chinese church services, seeing their Chinese doctors and accountants, bringing their children to the Cantonese cultural school.

Fry spent hours some Sunday mornings walking up and down the streets of Chinatown, watching, listening, smelling. He could see that Chinatown, like the rest of the city, was changing, being caught up in the pressure to develop, being squeezed by it. Out-of-scale, out-of-character, out-of-control development was encroaching on the neighbourhood like a fast-moving concrete mudslide. He sometimes wondered whether the Chinese street signs and telephone books, whether the pagoda-style phone booths and the ancient, elegant Chinese characters scratched onto the facades of bland new buildings, whether Sunday mornings would be enough to keep the community alive for another hundred years. When Sunday morning ended, Calgary's Sunday Chinese did what all good Calgarians did at the end of the working day—they fled to the suburbs.

Fry told Miyoko Fitzgerald about his flight to the suburbs, and his return. He told her about Carol, and Tony, about the separation, the divorce. He told her about the polished tools in his basement workshop, and about his joy in working with his hands, in taking scrap wood and turning it to use, sometimes even into beauty. He told her about the death of Gary Adams, and about his own unravelling, about the terrible moment in the middle of Macleod Trail when he stopped traffic and actually considered shooting a man for tailgating. He told her about the near-death of his own self, his own inner self, something he had never told anyone about, not even Ken Clark. He told her about his therapy sessions with Dr. Kenneth Jon Clark.

Fry asked Miyoko Fitzgerald about herself, about her self.

She told him.

She told him about growing up in an affluent Vancouver neighbourhood with all the advantages: money, loving parents, good schools, friends, lessons in music, dance, and art—and yet never feeling whole, never feeling ... one. She told him about never being quite sure what she was, nor who, not quite oriental, not quite white, caught in a kind of genetic limbo between East and West. She told him how sometimes as a girl—though not now—she had cursed her loving mother and her loving father, hating them, wishing they never had met. She told him about the guilt she still felt sometimes, and the ambivalence.

She told him that was why she so loved the Aboriginal

cultures, for their utter lack of ambivalence, for their arduous, accepting simplicity, and for their grace.

Fry wanted to know her. He wanted her to know him. Quickly. As if he feared they had no time. As if it might already be too late.

It was late.

It seemed as if it had been only minutes, but they had been talking for hours, not making small talk, but talking, really talking, talking about important things, things that mattered.

They were talking now about Thomas Red Crow.

"You knew him, then," she said.

"As well as somebody like me could know somebody like him."

"Somebody like you?"

"White cop—red lawyer."

"But he was a friend?"

"A friend? Well, I think we were headed in that direction. Wasn't a simple thing. He knew it. Last time we talked, he compared us to the characters in an old western movie—what was it? *Broken Arrow.* You know, the one about the Apache chief and the Indian agent—of course, you don't know. Too young."

"What do you mean, 'too young'? But I thought it was a TV series. Michael Ansara was Cochise, the Apache chief, and John Lupton played Tom Jeffers, the Indian agent."

"I stand corrected. And humbled. It *was* a TV series too, wasn't it? I didn't even remember that."

"Too old."

"No doubt. Anyway, simple for them in the movies—even simpler on TV. Not so simple for him and me for real. Not possible at all now. And even if it was, possible I mean, I don't know if we ever could've ..."

"What?"

"Oh, asked the right questions. Heard the answers. He *was* a red lawyer; I *am* a white cop. Even if we were really listening to each other."

"Do you think he was, well, wrong, to do what he did?"

Fry sighed, weighing his words as carefully as he might have in court; no, *more* carefully.

"I can't judge that— judge him. Don't want to anyway." he said. "I just wish he hadn't done it."

"Was it because of the killings, these murders, that Native boy?"

"Only he knew exactly why. It was partly that, I suppose. That all certainly triggered it. I remember the last time I saw him ... but that wasn't all ... he was a little like you, I think."

"Like me. How?"

"Well, a kind of walking contradiction, like you say you are. You know, stuck between East and West. He was stuck too, between red and white, past and future, reserve and city, wilderness and civilization. He had different ideas on where the *real* wilderness was, who the *real* savages were. He knew white law better than any white lawyer I ever met, knew how to use it, how to make use of it, make it work for him. But I don't think he ever really understood it. I know he didn't respect it. Clashed with too much of what he believed in, instinctively, traditionally. He could make it work, but not fast enough to suit him, not well enough. Silly, pointless complications, words for words' sake, well, they made him crazy sometimes. I could see it. I know, sometimes, they made him want to blow it all away. And, this time, he did."

The waiter caught Miyoko Fitgerald's eye. He had

kept passing by their table like a politely prowling shark, neither interrupting nor intruding, but hoping they would notice, hoping they would take the hint, hoping they would leave, hoping to seat another couple. It was, after all, Friday night, a busy night at the Jade Garden.

"I think he'd like our table," she said. She looked at her watch. "Oh, the time. I had no idea we'd been ..."

"No. Me neither. The time just ..." Fry said, adding, reluctantly, "I suppose we should get going."

"I'm afraid I'll have to. I've got some work to do at the museum this weekend and ..."

"Yeah. I've got work, too."

"I know. Ah, my place—it's just a couple of blocks. Maybe you'd like to come up for coffee? or tea?"

"Chinese, right?"

"Well, actually Irish breakfast."

"I would anyway."

11:25 PM

Frank Bergen was not a subtle man. He failed to appreciate the irony. He did not even recognize it. All he knew was that the kind of duty he had always managed to avoid during years of wearing a constable's polyester was exactly the duty he had now been assigned to perform on his first week in homicide, wearing his newly minted detective's shield and elegantly tailored wool suit.

He was supposed to find a drunk in the east end. That would have been easy enough. There had to be two hundred of them—aimless, homeless wanderers being bounced about in an endless pinball game: street to drunk tank to detox to single men's hostel to seedy tavern to street to drunk tank to ... However, he was not supposed to find a drunk, but *a* drunk, a guy with a big nose and a mane like a lion and probably a scar on his head, but no name, no address, no known hangouts, and no sightings since last winter.

"Christ, Jake, where am I supposed to start looking?" Bergen had asked Fry earlier in the day, half hoping that the request was not really serious, but, knowing Fry, knowing better.

"Well, you could start at the end. You could start at the beginning. Or you could start in the middle," Fry had told him.

"Great. A riddle. What's that mean?"

"You could start downstairs."

"Downstairs?"

"The drunk tank. It's all of the above for characters like this. Maybe the guy's curled up on the floor down there just waiting for you."

"And if he's not?"

"East end's not far from here."

"Thanks. Thanks for the advice."

"Don't mention it. That's why they made me chief investigator. Oh, and Bergen?"

"Yeah?"

"I know this seems like a shitty little job to you. Not at all what you had in mind when you pulled on that suit. And shitty it probably is. But it's not little—don't treat it like it is."

Bergen checked the drunk tank, which even in the late afternoon was already crowded, five or ten men on the cement floor of each of the three cells, grunting, gurgling, passed out, just coming to. None of them was the man with the big nose and the mane like a lion.

He called E zone, and then A, B, C, and D, managing only to annoy the patrol sergeants, who told him they were already spread thin enough without having to waste even more manpower searching for a wino in a haystack. If he was so interested in finding him, they told Bergen in a variety of unsubtle ways, he should get off their backs, get off the phone, get off his ass, and get out and look.

Now he was hitching a ride on a police wagon with McDermott and Stiles, who were obviously enjoying his obvious discomfort.

"Nice suit, Bergy," Stiles said. "You sure you don't want to change into a uniform?"

"Naw, he don't wanna do that," McDermott answered. "Fuckin' guy just got the uniform off. Last thing he'd wanna do now is put it back on."

Bergen sat between them saying nothing. He adjusted his silk tie. With the thumb and index finger of his right hand he slowly stroked his fine blonde moustache. He glanced to his right toward McDermott, then to his left toward Stiles, hoping to douse them into silence with a cold splash of his watery blue eyes, failing.

"S'pose you're right, Mac," Stiles said. "He *is* a detective now." He winked at Bergen, smiling mischievously, cracking his gum. "Hang on, *De*-tective, and hold your nose. Here we go."

Where they went was up and down the streets of the east end, slowly cruising the curbside, stopping here and there to make a pickup.

Like garbagemen, Bergen thought, *like fucking garbagemen.*

The wagon pulled over on Second Street beside a man in a three-piece business suit—*Better suit than mine,* Bergen mumbled to himself, *three hundred bucks anyway*—half standing, half stumbling on the sidewalk, dazed, bleeding from the lip, right eye beginning to swell shut, clutching an empty wallet.

"He's in the twilight zone," McDermott said as he and Stiles, with surprising gentleness, eased the man into the back of the wagon.

"Yeah. Looks like he was rolled, too," Stiles said. "Probably flashed his wallet in front of his new drinking pals."

"Uh huh, and they helped themselves. Bet he'd like to shoot his new friends now."

"He's gonna want to shoot himself in the morning once he sees who he's been sleeping with. Come on buddy, bedtime—in you go."

At the Palliser Square parkade, they took a handful of drunks off the hands of two security guards armed with a slavering German Shepherd. The intoxicated men, terrified of the dog, quickly, gladly, clambered into the wagon. The guards laughed. One of them patted the big animal solidly on the head.

"That's a good fella," he said, "such a good good fella."

The shepherd looked up, panting, tongue lolling, seeming to smile.

"One of these days," McDermott said to the guards as he was climbing into the passenger's seat after Bergen, "I'm gonna shoot that fuckin' dog."

Responding to a call from the Calgary Inn, McDermott and Stiles found a man slouched in a comfortable chair in the lobby, unshaven, his hair mussed and greasy, his clothing wrinkled and torn.

"No, no, no, don't push," the man said, fumbling for his crutches beside the chair.

"Nobody's gonna push you, fella. Just take it easy," Stiles said, taking the bottle of Cherry Jack wine from the man's hand, helping him hobble across the lobby, holding his crutches while the man struggled into the wagon, tossing them in after him.

Behind a ventilator shaft at First Street and Seventh Avenue SE, Bergen had to wait while McDermott and Stiles made their tally for the Lysol lottery, a monthly pool based on the police wagons' totals of spray cans and vanilla-extract caps. Ninety-seven here so far this evening.

They headed back. The man with the big nose and the mane was not in the back.

For all Bergen knew, he was not even alive. The man had not been seen since last winter. He could easily be dead. About a drunk a month died in Calgary. He could have been one of them, one of the bodies found sprawled on the sidewalk, slumped in an alley, curled up in some roach-infested rooming house. No one would have paid much attention. He hardly would have been noticed.

"Had enough, have you, Bergy?" McDermott asked back at the garage.

"Yeah, Bergy. You don't want to stay and watch us hose her down?" Stiles asked, laughing.

"Thanks guys, but I'll, ah, take a rain cheque," Bergen said.

"Suit yourself," McDermott said, which made Bergen think of his suit.

He looked down to check the pant legs, coat sleeves, suit front. He craned his neck over his shoulder to see the back of the legs and the behind. Nothing. At least he had not ruined the suit.

He took another long, breath-holding look into the drunk tank. More than fifty men in the cells now, about par for a Friday night. From what he could see none of them was *the* drunk. He asked Steward, who ran the drunk tank, just to be sure.

"What, you think because you're a fuckin' detective now you're the only one keepin' an eye out?" Steward asked, insulted. "Still cops down here, you know. If he was in there, I'd know. He's not."

Bergen was on his way out when he saw Phillips and Thomolsen dragging another bit of human refuse from their wagon kicking and spitting down the hall. They were big men. Each had a firm grip under an arm. But it was all they could do to control him. He was cursing. They were cursing. Bergen stepped out of the way to let them pass, catching a glimpse of the violently resisting drunk as he passed, a man with a red nose, a *huge* red nose, and long hair, long silvery hair—a mane.

"Hey!" Bergen yelled after them, running down the hall, stopping in front of them, physically blocking their way, facing the man with the big nose and the mane, putting his hands on his shoulders, looking closely at him, getting close to him, then backing away—the smell.

"That's the guy," he said. "This is the guy Ghost's looking for."

"No shit, Sherlock," Thomolsen said sarcastically. "Tell us something we don't already know."

"Well, better get him cleaned up," Bergen said, frustrated that he had found the drunk only after the police-wagon uniforms had found the drunk, furious that they would get credit for finding the drunk. "Ghost'll want to talk to him. Better get on it."

"Oh, we will," said Phillips. "And yes sir, we'll be sure to clean him up spic and span."

"Well, okay," Bergen said dismissively, turning to head for the telephone. At least he could make the report.

"Whoa, Bergen!" Thomolsen called out to him. "Where the fuck d'you think you're going?"

"What? What the F do you mean, 'Where the F do I think *I'm* going?'" Bergen asked indignantly, turning to face Thomolsen in mid-stride, continuing backward down the hallway.

"This guy's lousy," Thomolsen said.

"Yeah, so I noticed. So clean him up."

"We will," the two constables said sweetly, almost in unison.

"Okay, then."

Bergen turned again, eager to get to a phone to make his report.

"Hold it, Bergen. You're not going anywhere, not just yet," Thomolsen said.

"What? Just what the F do you mean, I'm not going anywhere?"

"Told you—"

"Told me what?"

"The guy's lousy."

"Yeah, I heard. So?"

"So, you know what that means?"

"Yeah, means he's got lice, asshole."

"Can see why they made you detective. You're so quick. He's got lice. And that means we gotta burn his clothes. That means we gotta burn *our* clothes. And now that you've got so up close and personal with him, it means, asshole—"

Thomolsen did not finish the sentence. The look of bewildered, disbelieving horror on Bergen's face told him he did not need to finish the sentence. He could not have finished it anyway. He was laughing too hard.

may 7 4:20 AM

Fry woke with a start. He heard a siren, wailing, close by, as if it was just outside the window. Had he been dreaming again? Having the same nightmare about the crooked bookcase and all the pieces that would not fit, all the bleeding pieces, the blood, and the sirens, the sirens...?

A light was on. Where? His left arm was numb. He had begun to lose feeling in his left arm. He started to raise it, then stopped, smelling the perfume, looking down, seeing Miyoko Fitzgerald asleep, her head on his shoulder.

He heard the siren again, and then the growling engine and deep nasal blaring of a fire truck. The siren *was* outside the window—and twenty floors below it.

He remembered.

"It's weird," Miyoko Fitzgerald had told him, sliding the patio door open a crack to let in some air, drawing the sheer curtains. "Especially at night, summer, when it's hot, and I have the door all the way open. I'll be sitting here on the sofa, reading maybe, and all at once I'll hear somebody talking, like they're right here in the room. And I'll jump, and look up, and, of course, there's nobody here. And then I'll know where they are, down there, on the street. But it startles me every time. Weird."

Her apartment was in one of the wind-tunnelling, sun-darkening high-rises that Fry hated from the outside, all concrete and glass and hard edges. On the inside, though, the edges were softer.

The walls were all painted the same pale pearl-grey and hung with Native prints and photographs. In the living room, in simple brass frames, red and black Inuit nature studies and a rich stained-glass work by the Ojibwa Norval Morrisseau. Above the black bookcase in the entryway, in thin, black-metal frames, a small grouping of nineteenth-century photographs of Plains Indian women. A large, subtly coloured Japanese print of geese in flight hung over the small, round dining table.

"Nothing terribly original, I'm afraid," she said, seeing Fry examining the artwork. "Only cheap prints and reprints. One other thing they didn't teach us at art school: how to afford art—appreciate, yes, but afford, no. The only honest-to-God work of art I own is this little fellow." She picked up a tiny carved brownish-black bird from the pine blanket box that served as a coffee table. "It's horn, Chinese. A magpie. A symbol of good luck to them. Not in the West, Christians anyway. They believe a magpie perched on the cross mocked Christ as He died. So, bad luck here, I'm afraid." She looked at Fry. "Or not—two would be better, though; good fortune everywhere. Maybe sometime you'll make me a scrap-wood display case for it—even find me another."

"May-be."

A three-panel bamboo screen stood in the corner of the living room beside the window—in front of the screen, a profusion of healthy plants in a collection of Indian baskets. The window framed a fine, clear view of the city, the kind of view they put on postcards and calendars and tourist brochures, softened tonight by the sheer, filmy curtains, making Fry think of how over-the-hill film goddesses were sometimes photographed through gauze to disguise their deepening age lines and smooth their wrinkles. The curtains disguised the city's sharp new lines and gave a subtle patina to its sleek hard surfaces, making it seem tonight, as the filtered lens did for the fading stars, almost beautiful, even ethereal.

The tea kettle whistled, piercing counterpoint to the mellow Grover Washington saxophone on the stereo. Fry turned toward the sharp sound.

"Nice place," he said. "I even almost like the view.

Need any help?"

"Thanks. No thanks, I think I can manage. I can't take credit for the view. Why only almost?"

"You can take credit for making me almost like it. Why almost? Maybe because I know what it's really like—it looks better from here, though."

"Yes? And how's that?"

"Oh, I guess it's a matter of perspective. The perspective from here is, well, better."

"Hmmm," she said, bringing over a tray with a white china tea set with tiny pink flowers painted on a delicate black border around the rim. She leaned to put the tray on the blanket box. Still leaning, she looked up, smiling: "Tea?"

Fry looked at her without answering. Slowly she straightened and stood, unmoving, returning his gaze. He rose from the sofa and went to her. For a long moment, they stood together near the window, not quite touching. He was half afraid to touch her. She lifted her face. Tentatively, he reached out, hand shaking, fingertips caressing her cheek, then gently running through her hair, her soft, silken hair ...

Abruptly, as if shocked, he yanked his hand away and turned from her.

"Wha? What?" she gasped, bewildered, a little frightened. "What is it?"

What could he tell her? What could he say? That, in her hair, her fragrant, silken black hair, he had suddenly seen another woman's hair, silken hair—lovely ash-blonde hair falling to her shoulders, stopping abruptly on the top of her head in a vicious circle of blood, black, shiny, hard. How could he tell her that? How could he make her understand that?

"I can't," was all he said.

"Why...? What's *wrong?*" she asked insistently, putting her two hands on his cheeks, forcing him to look at her. "I thought ..."

"Oh, you thought right. It was right … is … but …"

"But *what?*"

"It's wrong."

"Wrong? It's right. It's wrong. I don't understand."

"I know, I know."

"*Make* me understand," she said, almost shouting, still holding his face, then putting her hands on his shoulders, shaking him. "*Make* me."

He sighed, looking into her eyes, those searching jade-green eyes, hoping he could find something to say to hold the feeling in those eyes.

"When … when I was touching you, wanting you ... I ... Jesus! This is hard! I … I saw somebody else."

"Oh. Your wife?" she asked, stiffening, the hurt registering in her eyes.

"No. God, no! It's nothing like that. I was touching *you*—wanted *you*."

"Then?"

"These murders. Remember the first victim was a woman...?"

"Yes."

"She was a lovely woman. A sad woman. Already had a deep hurt to deal with. Then—I saw her, after. It's what I do, have to do: see people, after. And I just saw her again. That's why I couldn't … why I said it's wrong. Not because it's *wrong*. It's not. I just can't while … I owe her—owe them all. Ach! Probably sounds like—literally—a *cop*-out."

"No," she said, putting her arms around him and her head on his chest, holding him. "No. I think I understand."

"Yeah?" he asked, pulling away, looking again into her eyes.

"Yeah," she said, smiling, brushing her parted lips against his, taking him by the hand to the sofa, snuggling against him.

They sat together on the sofa, breathing in unison, not speaking, listening to the music and, when the last record had dropped from the changer and stopped playing, to the sounds of the all-but-deserted city centre drifting up from the street through the crack in the patio door: occasional footsteps, snatches of conversation, screeching tires, someone humming, a siren, then silence. Exhausted, she fell asleep on his shoulder. Eventually, he nodded off himself—until the sirens. Now, awake, he listened to the sound of her breathing. He was glad for the feeling of numbness in his shoulder, the life.

8:10 AM

From across the room, Fry at first did not recognize the stocky, red-faced blonde man in the two-sizes-too-large, blue tactical-squad coveralls who was striding purposefully toward him, rolling and rerolling the too-long sleeves, baggy pants flapping like flags in a stiff breeze. Then, as the figure neared, Fry could see that it was Frank Bergen, who seemed to have something on his mind.

"What's this, Bergen?" Fry asked, smirking. "New tailor?"

"Oh, *that's* funny. Let's just say that 'shitty little job' we talked about wasn't shitty at all, just lousy."

"Yeah?"

"Yeah. As in bug's eggs, lots of tiny fuckin' bugs eggs. You owe me a new suit."

"You got 'em from him?"

"I got 'em from him."

"But you got him?"

"I—we—got him. Like I said on the phone. Like I tried to say on the phone since last night. We've *had* him. Don't you ever answer your phone?"

"I was out late."

"Late? Try all night."

"Okay, all night. Give it a rest. You're not my damned mother. Where is he?"

"Interrogation room."

"What are you holding him on?"

"Ah, how about 'public lousiness?'"

"How about getting serious?"

"Well, haven't actually charged him yet. Been preoccupied with other matters. Didn't know I needed to charge him. Thought you just wanted him. I don't know: trespass, drunk and disorderly, resist arrest, assaulting a police officer—take your pick. We can charge him up as high as you want. Probably only the drunk charge would stick, if it would. But the others'd hold up long enough to hold him long enough, I think."

"Okay. Bugsy got a name?"

"Yeah, it's, uh ..." Bergen reached into the unbuttoned left chest pocket of the coveralls. "Boudreau, Leonard Boudreau. Think so anyway."

"Think so?"

"Yeah. Well, pretty sure. Hard to believe—you had to see him to believe him—but the guy had ID on him, Social Insurance card, driver's licence, Alberta, expired about five years, even an out-of-date gas credit card. If they're his, it's him."

"You think?"

"No reason not to. Nobody'd fake dog-eared ID like that, sure as hell not steal it."

"You talk to him?"

"About what?"

"Why we brought him in."

"As much as I know about why we brought him in? I knew you wanted him for questioning about these murders, is all, remember? I didn't know what questions you wanted to ask him."

"So you didn't ask any?"

"So I didn't ask any."

"Good—that's good. And, ah, good job, too. You had any sleep?"

"No. Like I say, I was preoccupied."

"Why don't you catch a couple of hours."

"You don't need me?"

"In a couple of hours. And, ah, Bergen?"

"Yeah?"

"That's a really good look for you."

Bergen tossed a cold blue glance at Fry, opened his mouth in a silent, sarcastic laugh, saluted with the middle finger of his right hand, turned, and flapped out of the room in his too-big coveralls. Fry watched him leave, allowing himself a short, silent chuckle at Bergen's expense, then turned toward Interrogation. He had taken about half a dozen steps when he heard a high-pitched voice calling him from behind.

"Hey, Fry? Fry?"

Fry turned. It was Timchuk, one of Patrol Sergeant Paul Strahan's uniforms.

"Yeah, Timchuk, what is it?"

"You got a call."

"A call? Who?"

"Reporter for the *Bulletin*."

"Come on, Timchuk, you know the drill," Fry said with a combination of disappointment and annoyance.

"I'm not talking to the media. I'm sure as hell not giving any one-on-one interviews. They want a statement, they can wait for the official release."

"Yeahyeahyeah. That's what I told the switchboard; that's what switchboard told him; that's what *I* told him. He says it's nothing like that. Wants to talk to you is all."

"About what?"

"Wants to talk to *you*."

"What's his name?"

"Melton."

"All right, I'll take it. What line?"

"Three."

"I can get it here?" Fry asked, sitting on the edge of the nearest fake-walnut-topped steel office desk.

"Think so."

Fry picked up the telephone and punched the flashing light.

"Yeah, Fry."

"Grant Melton."

"I heard. What's so important?"

"Well, I've got something or think I do, maybe not, maybe just a feeling."

"What you've got is to get to the point. What's this about?"

"Well, the murders, I think, anyway."

"*What* about them, do you *think*?"

"I, uh, I've got a photograph—well, one print—on a contact sheet."

"Contact sheet?"

"Yeah. All the pics from a roll of film contacted, printed on one sheet of paper. You can pick the shots you want, what size."

"So you got a picture, what, of those kids in the big

house? Saw them in the paper."

"No, not them."

"Who?"

"It's th—hold on a sec. Yeah, Bill. I'll get on it. Soon's I'm off the phone. You want what, two takes on it? Okay. Yeah. Yeah. Sorry, Fry. Detective Fry, listen, I can't talk here. I'm in the newsroom. Probably shouldn't be calling you at all, at least not until—"

"Until what?"

"Well, until we use it. They're gonna want to use it for sure. Maybe I should ..."

"You got something you think I should have, maybe you should let me have it."

"Yeah, I know. Just feels funny."

"Funny?"

"Yeah. Sorta like I'm on the wrong side. It's hard to—"

"Spare me the hand-wringing. I don't have time. You know the bumper sticker: Life is hard and then—"

"Yeah, I know—you die. I'll bring it."

Melton hung up. Fry took the receiver from his ear and held it in front of his face, looking at it quizzically. Then, shrugging and shaking his head, he lowered the phone onto its cradle and hopped off the desk.

He paused outside the Interrogation room, peering through the one-way glass. Like a scruffy, underfed, caged animal in some fly-by-night circus, Leonard Boudreau, the man with the snout and the mane like a lion, was restlessly pacing the room, up and down, back and forth, around and around the table, looking, squinting around the room with his one good eye, everywhere in the room, everywhere but into the mirrored side of the glass, turning his bad eye to the mirror. He did not seem to want to look into the mirror.

Fry stood for several moments watching him, trying to remember him, wondering if *he* remembered.

8:20 AM

Fry entered the Interrogation room quietly and closed the door softly. But he came in on Big Nose's nearly blind right side. Startled, the man with the mane of a lion and the heart of its prey jumped back and retreated to the far corner behind the long table, where he cowered, raising his good left eye, though not his head, toward Fry, regarding him suspiciously, like a trapped animal watching his approaching captor. He was wearing faded inmate coveralls that were as small on him as Frank Bergen's borrowed blue tac squad uniform was too large. His stubbled face and neck and the huge hands dangling from the too-short sleeves were even redder than Bergen's, and flaked with white, as if he had been scrubbed with coarse sandpaper and a cake of lye soap. His thick silvery hair, still damp, was pulled back from his face in a ponytail tied with a thick, postal-sized rubber band.

Fry could not see a scar.

"Sorry to startle you, Mr. Boudreau," he said, standing just inside the door.

Big Nose squinted at him impassively, showing no sign that he recognized the name as his own.

"It *is* Boudreau, isn't it? Leonard Boudreau?" Fry continued, again getting no response. "Well, we'll assume it is. It's what your papers say. My name's Fry, Jake Fry. I'm a detective here."

"Where's my fuckin' clothes?"

"They had to burn your clothes, I'm afraid. Not to worry, though, Mr. Boudreau. We'll get you some new clothes."

Boudreau straightened and, still pressing himself into the corner, managed to turn his body until he was half-facing Fry. He modelled the ridiculously fitting coveralls, lifting his arms until the sleeves rose just under his elbows, puffing out his chest until the buttons nearly popped. He looked down at the coveralls, and then, questioningly, at Fry.

"No," Fry answered. "Not those clothes."

Fry did remember Leonard Boudreau now. Not by name, but he did remember him. He was surprised that he could have forgotten him.

He had seen him often enough on his long walks through the city—panhandling spare change at the mall, foraging for scraps through fast-food garbage cans, loping, surprisingly gracefully, down Tenth Avenue hugging a cache of beer bottles against his heavy coat, pissing in a snowbank outside Safeway, marking it like a big shaggy dog, moving around Devonian Gardens on a bitter winter's day, eyes averted, as he tried to stay warm, invisible.

Maybe that was why Fry had forgotten him. He was *trying* to stay invisible, to go unnoticed. Fry had seen, but not noticed, him, not really noticed, and therefore not really seen; he noticed him now only in hindsight. Even Fry, it turned out, was still learning to see.

He wondered what Boudreau had seen, and what he remembered, *if* he remembered.

"Mr. Boudreau," he said, "I've got some questions I'd like to ask you."

Boudreau peered at him through his one good red eye.

"What questions?" he asked.

"Oh, about how you got hurt."

"Hurt?" Boudreau asked, with such complete puzzlement that it seemed to Fry that he had no recollection of ever being hurt or, perhaps, of not being.

"Yes, injured, your head."

"Hurt? Wh ... when?"

"Earlier this year—this winter—I heard you almost lost your hair. Remember?"

Boudreau stared uncomprehendingly at Fry, as if what Fry had said had not registered. But then, through the sheer physical effort visible on Boudreau's face, Fry could see that the big man was struggling mightily with that simple question.

Fry pressed him.

"Yeah, you gotta remember a thing like that, Mr. Boudreau. Guy coldcocked you, cut you, tried to tear the hair right off you. Remember that, Mr. Boudreau? Remember?"

Boudreau hardly moved, only the muscles in his jaw twitching and his fingertips pressing white against the tabletop. Yet Fry could sense that his whole body was tensing, like a giant mainspring being wound tighter, and tighter, and tighter. Finally, a hairy right paw rose over the table, hovered, then came down, hard, onto the Formica top.

"The fucker!" he erupted. "The motherfucker!"

He grabbed a steel stacking chair from under the table and tried to throw it, but got chair legs tangled with table legs and managed only to tip the chair over and send it spinning and sliding across the tile floor, finally crashing into the one-way-window wall.

Wheeler, a uniform who had been standing outside the door, flung it open and, for an instant, stood frozen in the doorway as if it were electrified, his left hand on the doorknob, right on the grip of his holstered revolver. Looking wide-eyed at Boudreau and then at Fry, without thinking, he asked:

"Jesus Christ! What the hell's goin' on, Ghost, you finally lose it altogether this time and go to beating on a suspect?"

"Get out of here, Wheeler!" Fry snapped, pushing the constable out the door, pushing the door closed after him. "Get the fuck out of here—before I decide to interrogate you!"

Boudreau meanwhile had grabbed another chair and was wrestling furiously with it, until he started to cough. Leaning on the back of the chair with both arms, burying his face in his left arm just below the shoulder, he coughed, and coughed, and coughed, beginning to fear that, this time, the coughing would never stop.

But then it did.

Boudreau took his face from his arm. Still holding tight to the back of the chair with his left hand, he wiped his mouth on his right sleeve. He leaned over the chair, heaving for breath, afraid that his gasping would trigger another spasm, but unable to stop himself.

"You gonna be all right, Boudreau?" Fry asked, then, seeing the flecks of blood just below the left shoulder of the faded coveralls, knew the answer, at least in the long term. But he was more coldly concerned with the short term. "Don't hack your brains out, man. Calm down. Just calm down—take it easy, all right? You want a drink of water?"

Boudreau, still rasping for breath, raised his head and looked at Fry through his good eye as if that were the stupidest question he had ever been asked. It was almost the same look Lips had given Fry the day he returned for good.

"How about a coffee, then?" Fry asked, unable to keep from smiling. "I'm afraid that's as good as it'll get here."

Boudreau nodded, once, then hung his head and kept trying to breathe.

Fry opened the door, to see about a dozen uniforms, detectives, and secretaries standing, gawking, at the one-way window.

"What are you, Grantham's spies?" he asked. "Hope you took real good notes. Just be sure to spell my name right, okay? But show's over for now. Move along, as the policeman says. That coffee still hot?" he asked no one in particular, gesturing toward the coffeemaker on top of the filing cabinet opposite Interrogation. No one answered.

Fry poured two Styrofoam cups of tepid coffee. He took them into the Interrogation room. He put one cup on the table in front of Boudreau. "You got two choices: black, or black. Sit down, Mr. Boudreau. Please."

Boudreau looked at him wearily, then pulled out the chair on which he had been leaning and sat down heavily on the steel seat, plunking his elbows onto the tabletop, resting his perspiring forehead in the open palms of his two big hands.

"So you *do* remember," Fry said, picking up the chair Boudreau had flung against the wall, bringing it back to the table and sitting down.

Boudreau took his face from his hands and looked across the table at Fry. He picked up the coffee container and, hands shaking, drained it in two gulps. He put the cup down. He ran the fingers of his right hand through his damp hair and, lightly, gingerly, as if just to touch it brought back the memory and the pain, felt the ridged flesh of the scar. He nodded.

"Why don't you tell me what you remember," Fry said. "It's important."

Leonard Boudreau told him.

But for the stubbornly natural intrusion of the Bow River and the stubborn, anachronistic presence of the Stampede Grounds, Seventeenth Avenue would have sliced Calgary neatly in two, a continuous line of east-west asphalt, almost exactly, and appropriately, seventeen kilometres from city limit to city limit. Seventeenth was Calgary's Yonge Street, its Broadway and Strand, a kind of summing up, a socio-developmental cross-section of the city: what it had been, what it was, what it was becoming.

Seventeenth Avenue. Calgary in cross-section.

That was the idea. Actually, the idea was to take a page from the oil patch and take an "above-ground core sample" of the city. That was what he was supposed to do. That was his assignment.

That was *not* his assignment!

How could *that* be his assignment? Especially now. How could he take the time for that when...? How could *that* be his assignment? What *was* his assignment? He *had* known what his assignment was. He had understood it so clearly. He had been carrying it out so well, flawlessly.

Now ...

Mistakes. He was making mistakes. He had not been making mistakes before, none. Now he was, stupid mistakes, careless mistakes, first losing ... and now this. How could it have happened? How could he have let it happen? He had been so careful. He had been so sure.

Now ...

He was no longer sure. Had he become careless because he had become unsure? Was it even carelessness?

Were they mistakes? Or were they signals? Signals to whom? Them? Himself? Was he finished?

No ...

But ...

What *was* his assignment?

Perhaps he could find his next assignment in this assignment. Perhaps that was why he had been given this assignment—to show him the way, to guide him, to help him make the choice. This *was* a good place. There were good choices here, all along the street.

Especially here, in these few blocks, these few disgusting blocks, which had nothing to do with the city, *his* city, which betrayed his city. Smells of mongrel food and foreigners—dark, yammering foreigners. He hated the smells. He hated the foreigners. He hated the trendy—not his word, *their* word—the phony, fancy new shops and their superior-acting help who would look down on him, ignore him, if he ever went inside.

He never went inside.

He never went inside the galleries either, all these pretentious *eastern* galleries, and their pretentious *eastern*-sounding clerks, and their pretentious *eastern*-approved art. Art? Not art. Not western. Not *his* west—not anything. Splatterings of chimpanzees. He hated it.

Yes. He could make a choice here. So many choices here. But. So crowded here. Maybe later ...

Or ...

He could go back. He could go back where he started, where he tried to start. He could try again. He was not ready that night. He was not prepared. It was too cold. He was surprised by the derelict's strength. He had not known how hard he had to strike. He knew now. He would not be surprised now. Maybe he could find him again. Just cut along the dotted line. Ha ...

No!

No jokes. Not about this, his work.

Too risky anyway. And no need. He could find another. One like his first, the failure, his only failure. There were so many like him. Even easier now that it was warmer. They were everywhere now, around garbage cans like blue bottle flies, under benches like so much litter, on the grass in the parks like dog dirt. He could easily find another. He could end where he began.

Wait ...

Of *course!*

He did not need to go back. He did not need to search out another like the first failed one. And he did not need to keep looking here, to wander up and down the street, hoping to find one, an appropriate one, the right one, a safe one. He had already *found* one. He *had* his next assignment.

Remember? Last night.

He had wondered why he was doing it. A joke, he had thought, the followed following the follower. And it had been a good joke. He had laughed, to himself, watching. He had laughed again this morning, working in the bathroom, remembering.

But it had been more than a good joke, he could see now, much more. It had helped him choose. It had shown him the choice. It had made the choice for him. The next.

No! Not *him*. That would be wrong. *He* belonged. *She* did not. *She* was the one. She was a perfect example of everything that was going wrong with the city, the pseudo-western pretension, the mongrel impurity, the patronizing, mocking betrayal of heritage and character—everything. He was surprised that *he* would have been seen with her. *He* should have known better. He would teach him. He would teach them all, show them all, show the way. She was perfect, a perfect ending.

Was it ending...?

Yes.

He could see the end now. Suddenly he could see. He should have seen it coming. He was tiring, wearing down. It was harder to maintain the edge, to lead. He should have seen it in the mistakes. He should have sensed it. He sensed it now.

Now, when he had found the next one, a perfect next one, now, when the need should have been overwhelming him, he was having to summon the need, create the feeling. But the feeling would come. He would make it come. He would feel the need again, he knew, once more.

But what about this assignment? He had time. He could do both. He could do his job *and* his work. He had time. But not much time. He would have to hurry. He knew he would have to hurry.

10:45 AM

At his desk in the Seventh Avenue headquarters building, Fry was poring over the freshly typed statement of Leonard Boudreau, hoping to read in it something more than he had heard.

Patiently, taking pains not to prod or coach him, Fry had managed to get Boudreau to take himself back to that night in January. Boudreau had gone along, haltingly, obscenely, painfully, taking Fry with him. And then, after convincing him, with some difficulty, that the stenographer would take down only what he said and that nothing he said would be used against him, Fry persuaded Boudreau to go back again, thinking, hoping, that he might notice something on the second trip that he had missed on the first. Boudreau did not.

Fry was amazed at the vividness of Boudreau's memories of that night, and frustrated at the vagueness of those vivid memories:

Fella come up to me downtown, outside the Queen's there. Big fella. Big as me, I'd guess. Didn't see him too good. Had a scarf around his face. Wearin' a leather coat, smelled new. Remember the smell. And he had a bag, some kind of bag with him, over his shoulder. But it was dark. I'd been drinkin'. Ha. That's a good one. That'd be true about twenty hours a day. It's what I do.

Anyway he sidles up to me and tells me he'll buy me a bottle if I do him a favour. Well, mister, I'd do the devil a favour for a bottle of the real. So I go with him, fella says it's not far.

We come to this alley and he says it's here and I go on in but already I'm wonderin' what's what and I turn to ask what the fuck is goin' on and ... and ... there's this flash of light, bright white flash, and then somethin' hits me on the back of the head by Jesus it was hard and I go down on all fours don't even remember fallin' and I'm all groggy, pret' near out, and I can feel this tuggin' on my hair, pullin', and then the damnedest pain and I'm yellin' and he's pullin' on my hair, tryin' to yank it right off and I'm screamin' bloody murder and then ... then the fella hits me again, right on the temple, and this time brother I'm out ...

But he musta got scared or run off 'cause the next thing I see is some other fella, looked like a doctor, lookin' at me and askin' if I can see him can I hear him can I move and tryin' to get me to go to the General and I don't want to go but I do ...

Fry picked up the telephone on the second ring.

"Yeah. Fry."

It was the switchboard.

"There's a reporter here who says you said you'd see him. You say that?"

"Reporter's name Melton?"

"Ah ... yes."

"I said it. Let him come."

* * *

Grant Melton had the intimidated out-of-his-element look of a high school kid moving to a new school in the middle of the term, stumbling into vocational shop class on his way to the music room. Fry watched as he approached the desk, half enjoying his discomfort, half empathizing with him.

"You've never been to the inner sanctum here, eh?" Fry asked.

"No," Melton said, distracted, looking over his left shoulder, his right, around the room, as if he were worried that someone, everyone, was watching. Then, regaining his reporter's mask of composure: "Isn't that the way you guys want it?"

"Yeah," Fry said, almost smiling. "That's the way we want it." He nodded toward the manila envelope pinched between Melton's misshapen right thumb and forefinger. "What've you got there?"

Melton tossed the envelope onto Fry's desk. With his fingernails, Fry pried apart the metal tabs securing the envelope flaps. He pulled out the contents: a single eight-and-half-by-eleven sheet of photographic paper—on it tiny, glossy, black-and-white prints of the frames of an exposed roll of film.

"So this what you called a 'contact sheet?'" Fry asked.

"That's what it is."

"What's on it? Or are you gonna make me look for myself?"

Melton leaned over the desk, but did not answer. Fry looked for himself, holding the paper close to his face, out of the way of the reflecting overhead light.

The prints were confusingly numbered. Beginning after a short tongue of black at 3A/4 was a shot of the outside of the sandstone old city hall. 4A/5 was a photo of city hall park, 5A/6 a picture of a third-storey window in the administrative addition. 6A/7 was a candid photograph of the mayor at his desk—a short, too-dapper, youngish man with a pencil-thin moustache and short, slicked-back, curly black hair hovering over his shoulder. 7A/8 showed the little man standing under the city crest; 8A/9 pictured him in front of a tall base map of the City of Calgary; 9A/10 had him pretending to slave over papers on his cluttered desk. 10A/11 was the view from an office window, probably the same window seen from the outside in 5A/6.

11A/12 was a shot of two men in a big car, apparently studying the want ads in the morning's *Bulletin*. The car was a 1962 Imperial pockmarked with rust. The men were Jimmy Maclean and Ben Surette.

After frame 11A/12, the contact sheet went black, shiny and black. The rest of the film had been processed without being exposed.

Fry looked up from the contact sheet. His eyes asked Melton the question.

"I'm working on a feature on the mayor's executive assistant," Melton replied. "He's the greasy-looking little guy. He's been on the hot seat lately for, you know, acting like he's more elected than the councillors who *were* elected."

"I don't know."

"No? Well, I don't know what that car's doing there. I mean, we *are* doing a feature on guys like that, but—"

"Guys like that?"

"Yeah. You know. Dreamers. Drifters. Guys coming down the road to try to get in on the boom—finding out it's usually a bust. Part of our 'underside of the boom' series. But I already got the pics for the piece, already wrote it—running tomorrow. I mention those guys, of course, but they're not in it, not their pictures anyway. Only pictures we had of them were the crime scene shots—I *thought* they were the only pics we had. Editors wanted to run them, but I ... it *is* them, isn't it?"

"Yeah. It's them. Who took these?"

"Donnie—Donnie Miloche."

"Miloche? He's the big guy I met when I came to the paper?"

"Yeah. Listen, do we have to talk here—in the open like this? I mean, isn't there someplace...?"

"Yeah, sure. Conference room."

Melton followed as Fry negotiated through the desks to a room with a large window. As he entered behind Fry, Melton saw the word INTERROGATION in white on black plastic, outside the door.

"Conference room, my ass," he said once he and Fry were inside.

"Ah, but what's in a name? If I start to beat you with a rubber hose, just scream into the mirror. You say Miloche took the pictures?"

"Yeah," Melton said, sitting in the chair Leonard Boudreau had tried to throw across the room.

"You ask him about them?"

"Sure. Of course I did."

"And?"

"And nothing."

"Nothing?"

"That's right. Nothing. It was weird. I mean, I showed him, and told him it looked like those guys. And he ... he just got this blank look on his face and this idiot grin and said he didn't think ... and then he asked me if the shots of Wilson—he's the mayor's exec—were okay. But before I could say anything, he said he had to go, had work to do. And he hustled out. Weird. Weird guy anyway."

"This was?"

"Yesterday. Yesterday afternoon."

"You see him since?"

"No."

"You talk to anybody else about this?"

"No."

"'Weird guy anyway,' I think you said. What'd you mean by that?"

"Oh ... just that."

"That's not terribly specific, is it? Got any for-instances?"

"Well, he's a pretty good photographer when he wants to be. Just usually doesn't want to be. I think he wants to be a cowboy, or a politician, or maybe both."

"You *can* be both here. What's so weird about a little ambition?"

"Nothing, I suppose. Except ..."

"Except what?"

"Donnie tries *too* hard. He's on a real western kick—cowboy boots, real sharp-pointers too. Brand-new boot-cut jeans. String tie. The works—"

"He, ah, wear a leather coat?"

"Oh, yeah. Real buckskin, fringes and everything. Like I say, he's gotta be more west than the rest. Takes western politics seriously too, even the separatist wackos. Lately he's really gotten into local politics. Even late with assignments sometimes 'cause he's been holed up down at city hall with some councillor or other—a lot of the time with Wilson. Seems to've found a real political soulmate in Wilson."

"Oh?"

"Oh. No, it's not like that, not so far as I know anyway. He's just too buddy-buddy—for a journalist, is all I'm saying—if you think of photographers as journalists. Gets too close. I mean, take that proof sheet there. Donnie was only supposed to get a head shot, maybe a simple desk pose. And he comes back with a bloody spread."

"You say you think he wants to be a politician himself?"

"Yeah. Says he's gonna run, too, as soon as he gets organized and some cash. Even trying to get us all to call him 'G. Donald,' like that would somehow be more fitting." Fry remembered. "Of course," Melton continued, "all that gets him usually is a 'Gee Donnie.' Doesn't shut him up though. He's all the time talking about what he's going to do."

"Do? About what?"

"Oh, you know, all the problems—growth, traffic, crime, the feds, the east, too many people. At least he *was* always talking."

"Was?"

"Well, yeah. He's stopped the last little while. Funny, I had him so tuned out—nobody takes him seriously. I didn't even think about it until just now, but you know, he doesn't talk about what he's gonna do anymore."

Grant Melton had been gone about five minutes.

"That all?" Fry had asked him, after Melton had sat silently across from him for several moments, alternately uncapping and recapping the blue plastic top of a yellow ballpoint pen.

"Yeah," Melton said finally. "I guess. You going to talk to Donnie?"

"Oh, yes—but don't *you*."

"No?"

"No. Or to anybody else."

"No ... And, ah, I'd appreciate it if you didn't ..."

"What?"

"You know, let on. that I was here, that I came in, you know ..."

"Yeah, I know. Don't worry. Nobody'll find out. And even if they did, I'd never let on that you were anything but a first-class reporter—a know-it-all, self-righteous, fuck-the-facts asshole from the fourth estate. How'm I doing so far?"

"Fine. Thanks."

"I won't show you out. Wouldn't look right. Wouldn't want anybody out there to think you co-operated. Or, worse, that *I* did. Put on your best hard-assed reporter's face, why don't you? And slam the door if you can. Tear a verbal strip off me. Nobody'd be surprised. Be surprised if you didn't. They'd expect it of me. See, we both got reputations to uphold."

Back at his desk now, Fry was studying the tiny photograph of the two dead losers, Jimmy Maclean and Ben Surette, the last photograph of them alive, their last photo session—

Wait.

Was it the last?

Suddenly something Leonard Boudreau had said popped into Fry's mind. He grabbed the short typed statement, ran his index finger down the page until he found the words: "...there's this flash of light, bright white flash, and then something hits me on the back of the head ..."

Fry thought: *Then* something hit him.

Boudreau saw the flash *before* he was hit, not when, not in the instant after, but before. The blow did not cause the flash of light. The flash came from *outside* Boudreau's head, not inside.

Fry chased after Melton, catching sight of him on the street a block and a half away from the police building.

"Melton! Melton! Hold up!" Fry yelled.

"What?" Melton stopped, turning to see who was calling him, seeing Fry, waiting.

"You, you, ah, your ..." Fry gasped when he caught up to the reporter. "...your ... what'd you call it? your 'underside of the boom' series ..."

"Yeah, what about it?"

"You run any pieces recently on rummie-dumbs?"

"On who?"

"Rummies. You know—winos. Down-and-outs. Derelicts. Skid-roaders. Boozers. Poor unfortunates. Scum-of-the-earths."

"Ah, no. I don't think ... not that I can remember. I didn't, anyway."

"Shit!"

"Wait."

"What?"

"Well, it wasn't that recent—before Christmas. Spread called 'Homeless for the Holidays,' you know, where people go who don't have anywhere to go."

"Who took the pictures?"

"Ah, Donnie, some of them anyway. Yeah, Donnie Miloche took some of them, actually most of them."

"Your ugly losers—goin'-down-the-roaders piece—one running tomorrow. He take most of those pictures?"

"Why ... yeah."

Fry took another stab, confident now that it was not in the dark.

"How about a photo story on hookers? You working on anything like that?"

"You don't read the paper, do you?"

"Not unless I have to."

"That ran last week. Because of all the flak, you know, about Edmonton 'exporting' its prostitutes south. A week ago Wednesday."

"And the photographer?"

"Donnie."

3:35 PM

"This won't be in the official report, o'course, at least not in so many words, not these words anyway," Fred Skerrett told Fry over the telephone, "but if you were to ask me to sum him up, well, I'd say he's a pushy young man with a lot on his mind and not much on the ball, as full of shit as he is of excuses, if not a whole lot fuller. I'll get the report to you later today, by tomorrow for sure, with whatever else we can dig up. Keep me posted."

Fred Skerrett was the Police Chief in Barrettville, Ontario, a lakeshore town that liked to think of itself as one of the crown jewels of the "golden horseshoe" between Toronto and Hamilton. Fry had contacted him earlier to ask for a background check on George

Donald Miloche, who had lived in Barrettville before moving to Calgary.

George Donald Miloche. This was how it began, turning blood into paper, person into suspect, fact into crime. George Donald Miloche. A name on a birth certificate or a high school diploma—or an arrest warrant, a tombstone. George Donald Miloche. Not the name he used. Not the name anyone who knew him used. George Donald Miloche. Not "Donnie Miloche," as almost everyone called him. Not "G. Donald Miloche," as he wanted everyone to call him. Not even, simply, "Miloche," as his editors called him when they were looking for him, shouting, "Where the hell's Miloche?" George Donald Miloche. Blood into paper. This was how it began.

Skerrett had phoned back in less than two hours. Fry *had* said it was urgent. And Barrettville *was* still almost a small town.

The semi-small-town chief's feigned-folksy, over-the-phone play-by-play and crude colour commentary added shading and detail to Fry's fuzzy recollection of the man who had made him think of a big clumsy dog too eager to please, bringing to mind now a big dog kicked once too often, a mean dog—a rabid dog?

Miloche had come to Barrettville from Fredericton in 1969 to study photography at Phillips College. He had latched onto the town as *home* and stayed, working as a news photographer at the *Standard Express*, a small independent daily with circulation troubles.

Grant Melton had had him pegged about right. Miloche was a pretty good, aggressive, even courageous working photographer when he wanted to be, which was less and less often, especially after his off-the-job interests shifted from skulking around the Phillips

College atrium trying to get women to pose for him to posturing around the town hall as the town councillor he thought by rights he should be and told anyone who would listen that, one day, he would be.

He entered the spot news photography category in the Western Ontario Newspaper Awards in 1975, after clambering down a steep embankment early in June of 1974 to get shots of a VW Beetle crammed with six teenagers who died when the car smashed through a guardrail and plummetted forty feet before landing top-down in a ravine at the end of an after-prom joyride.

"He sure showed some golf-sized balls that night," Skerrett said. "And I remember that night."

Miloche's entry did not win.

He entered the race for a local council seat in the 1975 municipal election. His paper opposed him. He did not win.

"Surprised the hell out of him, I imagine," Skerrett said. "Must've shook every hand in the ward—and then got beat hands-down by a single mum on welfare, a good looker mind you, but in *this* town, where welfare's just another four-letter word, to get beat by somebody like her, well ... must've shrunk those balls of his just about down to pea-size."

After that, Miloche seemed to lose what little interest he still had in his job, becoming a loner, even something of a recluse. He left the paper just before being fired.

"Things were goin' south for the young man," Skerrett said, "so he headed west."

Miloche was, depending on who in Barrettville was talking, an overweight lightweight, a big, lonely little boy, an overambitious underachiever, a crude sexist boor, a crashing bore. No one in Barrettville described him as a potential killer.

No one in Calgary was describing him as a potential killer either.

Overruling Patrol Sergeant Paul Strahan, who wanted to call out the tac squad and dispatch half the police garage, flashers flashing and sirens wailing, Fry had sent detectives to the *Bulletin*, to city hall, and to Miloche's apartment building to inquire, unofficially and unobtrusively, about him.

"*Ask* about him!?" Strahan had yelled, incredulous. "For Chris'ake, we oughta just haul his ass in. Then ask all you want."

"Bring him in," Fry said, "for what? Taking some pictures? Wearing silly clothes? Having funny ideas? No, Strahan, this is by the book—what am I saying? There *isn't* a book, not for this guy. When we get him, I want him to stay got. No mistakes. No fuck-ups. No posses. No horseshit dramatics. What I *do* want you to bring in, or *up* anyway, is your box of goodies from the basement, the Fish Creek stuff."

"What? Your rubbers?"

"No. You can have them—just wash 'em out and reuse 'em. I want the lens cap."

"The what?"

"Lens cap. I want it dusted."

"And what do you expect to find? Remember the rain, the mud?"

"I remember. I don't expect to find anything; I *hope* to find just a smidgen of a print, enough of a print. Maybe we'll get lucky."

"You better hope you get fuckin' lucky. What're you gonna do if he goes on the warpath again while we're playing with rubbers and twenty questions?"

"That's a chance, I know. Looks like he *goes* at night, though. He won't get another night. Look, he might be spooked now. I don't know for sure. I don't know how much. I don't want to drive him to ground. And I sure as hell don't want him to rabbit. And one other thing I don't want, Strahan."

"And that is?"

"I don't want Grantham in on this."

"You don't want—what if *he* wants in on this?"

"I don't give a shit what he wants. It's not his case; it's not his job."

"Could be your job. On whose authority you keeping an *inspector* in the dark?"

"Another inspector's."

"Who?"

"Drayton."

Inspector Ben Drayton was as good a politician as Inspector Phil Grantham, in addition to being, as far as Fry was concerned, three times the cop. He had been instrumental in keeping Fry on the force when Fry was spinning out of control in the wake of the death of Gary Adams. He was being instrumental in keeping Fry on the case despite Grantham's best efforts to take him off.

"You sure you know what you're doing?" Drayton had asked Fry the day before, when Fry, knowing where Grantham was headed after their set-to over the box of evidence, had gone to Drayton.

"No."

"Jesusfuckingchrist, Jake, you just never make things easy, do you," Drayton said, running his right hand over the bristles of his steel-grey crewcut, leaning back in his chair, then clasping his hands around his thick neck. "Don't know how long I'll be able to hold him off."

"Long enough, I'm sure."

"You hope."

Now Fry was hoping that George Donald Miloche would hold off long enough for Fry to be able to put something together that would hold him.

The three detectives were not much help.

Miloche's building superintendent had been so charmed by him that she had only sweet nothings to tell Detective Roy Reynolds about him: a nice young man who always has time for a smile and a hello, quiet as a mouse, no, quieter, never hear even a squeak from him, pays his rent on time, just a perfect tenant.

Frank Bergen got the city hall assignment, to talk to Wilson, the mayor's executive assistant and Miloche's "political soulmate."

"This another one of your lousy little jobs, Jake?" Bergen had asked Fry after coming back to the office exactly two hours after he had left, exactly as he thought Fry had told him to do.

"Little? In a manner of speaking, yes. Lousy? Don't think so. Greasy, maybe."

Wilson had not been happy to see Bergen at the door to his Crescent Heights apartment on a Saturday, even less pleased to have been tracked down at all by a police detective. He snorted something about police harassment and at first refused to say anything until he contacted his lawyer. Bergen gave Fry the rundown.

"So I says, 'Fine, you call your lawyer, and tell him you're facing charges as an accessory after-the-fact to mass murder,' and then he says, 'How can I be of service, officer?'"

"*That's* what you said?" Fry asked, shaking his head and sighing.

"Yeah. Well, actually, Jake, I said *you* said to say it."

Another cop-politician, Fry thought, saying: "Thanks. I'm sure I'll hear about it. You should look up *unofficial* and *unobtrusive*. You hear anything that's gonna be worth my trouble?"

"Not much. He started to say something about Miloche's 'passionate commitment to the city' and his 'penetrating understanding' of the city's problems, but then started to fudge and mumble and deny knowing anything at all about Miloche personally."

Alex Michelmore, the *Bulletin*'s managing editor, did give Detective Andy Patterson one useful fact, one piece of information Fry could use: Miloche had not been assigned to photograph the murder scene in the Fish Creek ravine.

"That's my point about him starting to miss assignments," Michelmore told Patterson. "The desk tried to get him out there, but couldn't get hold of him."

If the lens cap in Strahan's box was Donnie Miloche's, George Donald Miloche was in Fry's box.

Fry spent the next three-quarters of an hour trying to figure out his next move, trying to figure out what to do with the pieces of information he had, these little pieces, pushing the pieces around and around in his mind, trying to fit them together, to make bigger pieces, pieces big enough to make a case, big enough to support Fry's conviction about the case, big enough to support George Donald Miloche's conviction in the case.

Finally Fry decided that the only move he could make now was a subtler version of the move Strahan had advised him to make in the first place. He was on his way to make it when, for what seemed at least the two-hundredth time of the day, the telephone intruded. He was already in his black overcoat, several paces from his desk. He looked back, saw the flashing light on the phone. He thought about letting it flash.

He answered the phone.

"Yeah. Fry."

"Ted Russell."

"Yeah."

"You asked if any of my students took an 'unnatural' interest in things western?"

"Yeah."

"Well, there was one—signed on for my evening class, last fall, 'Western Myths, Legends, and Lies.' I'd almost forgot about him because he didn't stick around long. Withdrew after only a couple of weeks. Told me he didn't like my 'presentation'—the 'lies' part in particular. Knew it all anyway, at least he thought he did. But he was really into it, in a skewed sort of way. Mostly just wanted to argue—there's always one like him."

"This student—he dress like a born-again westerner from Toronto?"

"'Born-again westerner?' Well, yeah, I suppose you could say that. Leather coat, something like mine, only brand new, pointy cowboy boots, also new, stiff new blue jeans. 'Born-again westerner.' That's good. That's him."

"He's a big guy, sort of moon-faced?"

"Yeah."

"Would his name be Miloche, Donald, er, Donnie Miloche?"

"Why ... yeah. You're right again. Miloche was the name. But ... G. Donald, he said. Made a point of it. How'd you know?"

"I'm the po-lice. I know everything."

"Ha! That's the stuff!"

"Oh, and Russell?"

"Yes?"

"You were mistaken."

"Mistaken?"

"There's *not* always one like him."

4:20 PM

Armed with the search warrants he had obtained after only the briefest of wrestling matches with Justice of the Peace Cam Taylor and with the Smith & Wesson he had obtained from his holster after a more strenuous wrestling match with himself, Fry entered George Donald Miloche's drape-darkened apartment.

One of the warrants tucked in his inside jacket pocket—the one to search the apartment—was signed; the others were not. They could be "left handed" later if the search took them in unanticipated directions. Fry knew Cam Taylor would go along.

The diminutive probationary homicide detective Frank Bergen had come along with Fry, as had the beefy young veteran homicide constables MacElroy and Adams.

Patrol Sergeant Paul Strahan, also waving a right-handed warrant with left-handed blanks for backup, had taken two squad cars to the *Bulletin*.

Every available detective and the uniforms in each of the five zones were also on the lookout for George Donald Miloche. Fry had issued a warrant for his arrest, for questioning in connection with the murders of Jimmy Maclean and Benjamin Surette.

The grumbling, uncomprehending tenants in Miloche's building had been quickly, quietly cleared from the six-storey structure. They were milling on the sidewalk at the front, being kept from re-entering by two uniforms from E zone stationed outside the front door.

Fry had stationed himself outside and just to the

left, the knob side, of the door to Miloche's rear apartment. Bergen was just behind him, his back pressed against the corridor wall. MacElroy was kneeling on the right, hinge side, of the door. Adams was posted outside the apartment building, in the back, at the foot of the fire escape. Fry knocked hard on the door, three times, and loudly announced himself. No answer. He pounded on the door again and shouted. Again no answer. Again. Still nothing.

With his left hand he put the key the stunned, shaking building superintendent had given him into the lock, turned it, put his left hand on the doorknob, and turned it. MacElroy pushed the door open with his nightstick. Fry hurled himself inside, into the semi-darkness. He crouched low, turning at the waist, training his weapon first right, then left, then back. His breathing was rapid and shallow, the hair on the back of his neck tingling, his mouth dry, his eyes wide.He felt the air as MacElroy swept past him to the right, toward where the superintendent said the apartment's one bedroom was located. Just behind Fry, Bergen, his weapon also drawn, was feeling the wall for the light switch the superintendent said was just inside the door. He found it on the third downward swipe of his hand, swept his hand back up, found the switch again and flicked it on, turning on the single working bulb in a six-bulb overhead chandelier, a feeble yellow bulb in an amber glass shade, bathing the room in a ghastly, ghostly light.

"Jesus Christ," Bergen said.

"Not bloody likely," Fry said, "not in here."

MacElroy emerged from the bedroom and, still in a crouch, immediately ducked behind his extended revolver into the bathroom, then into the kitchen. In a few moments he walked out of the kitchen erect, taking a deep breath, lowering the weapon.

"Not here," he said.

Fry straightened and sighed, something like the sound of the air escaping from a child's three-day-old party balloon. He holstered his revolver.

"Pull those curtains open, will you, Frank," he said. "Let's get some real light in here—Mac, you want to holler at Adams, get him up here. This could take a while. Oh, and get him to radio Strahan first, see if they got any luckier."

They had not.

"Sorry I took so long, Jake. Wheeler was the only one in the car, had to go inside to get Strahan," Adams told Fry after about five minutes. "Strahan says this: Miloche character didn't show up for work today. Did have an assignment from yesterday, shooting pictures on Seventeenth Avenue, some kind of feature page, I guess. Strahan's concentrating the search there now. Did get the guy's employee file, full description. Got a photo too. He's already sent it to the station—should have copies out pretty quick."

Fry worried that he had not acted quickly enough. The fingers of ice that had tickled his neck reached inside him and grabbed hold. Despite the sweat soaking his armpits and covering his forehead, he felt suddenly cold. The cold would only deepen as their methodical search revealed that this ordinary apartment in this ordinary building had become a killer's lair.

That was the thing about it. That a place so full of threat and so palpably about death could at the same time seem so ... ordinary. Everything that had appeared so netherworldly in the dim amber light leaking from the single overhead bulb looked, in the hard, bright light pouring through the undraped window, mundane and, for that, even more threatening, even more hideous, even more deadly.

The old animal pelts over the back of the cheap, uncomfortable-looking sofa were moth-eaten; the tanned leather beneath the bearskin was dry and cracking. The stuffed owl on the bookcase was missing several feathers and one glass eye. The mahogany dropleaf table was obviously an antique, and definitely not cheap. But candles had dripped onto the once lovely, lustrous, lovingly polished surface, ruining it.

Fry examined the Indian artifacts on the table between the candles—the old blanket, the drum, the knife with the crude device he could not figure out on the opposite end. He had stood in front of the bull's-eye mirror, examining his distorted reflection, wondering what distorted ceremonies had been conducted here. He had already found the leather jacket on the coat rack, fringed buckskin, damp, smelling of leather, with three thin, lightly coloured lines running down the right front from about chest height to just above the waist: evidence of Jimmy Maclean's last desperate dying attempt to fend off his murderer. Fry was kneeling in front of the wicker chest now, opening the leather bag. He looked inside. A thirty-five-millimetre camera, a Pentax Spotmatic, the paint on its black body wearing through at the edges. A flash attachment lay beside it. He recalled the words from Leonard Boudreau's statement:

"...there's this flash of light, bright white flash ..."

Carefully, with his right hand in a plastic bag he had brought for the purpose, Fry removed the camera and the flash from the upper compartment of the bag. He unsnapped the black strap securing two red velvet halves of the compartment and lifted the two sides, revealing the bottom section of the bag.

Clifton Shields would be hard to live with. He had not been far off the mark. "Like a rolling pin," he had said of the killer's bludgeon.

Fry did not remove a rolling pin from the lower section of the camera bag, but something close: a baseball bat, about the top third of a baseball bat, a kid's Little League bat, ash or hickory, cut down into a club, sanded smooth. With traces of blood in the tight hardwood fibres, Fry was sure—human blood, blood of five humans. He figured the lab would also find blood on the heavy, curved blade of the skinning knife that lay in a compartment beside the homemade club, even though the four-and-a-half-inch blade and heavy, finger-grooved, black rubber grip appeared to have been wiped clean.

Fry returned the contents of the bag, closing the clasps and snaps and latches. He took the leather bag from the wicker trunk and put it on the floor beside him. He opened the trunk. He saw the manila folder inside, lying on top of the blankets. He took out the folder and flipped it open. He saw the collection of photographs, eight-by-tens, glossy, black-and-white.

The top two photos were of the faces of Jimmy Maclean and Benjamin Surette, taken, Fry was sure, in the instants before they died. Maclean's eyes were wide open with fear or with anger or, more likely, with both. Surette's had the half-open, half-closed look of the already dead. Beneath the photo of their faces was a candid shot of the two of them sitting, unsuspecting, on a planter outside the old city hall, legs dangling over the edge.

Lesley Connor was in the next photograph, eyes unfocused, his lips contorted into a kind of sneering smile, his stoned smirking face harshly lighted. Not a picture beautiful Lee Boy would have wanted a record producer to see. He probably would not have minded the next, which showed him standing in the middle of the CPR tracks, hands on his hips, an angry pout on his face, the Tower and the towers and the towering overhead cranes of the downtown silhouetted behind him.

When he came to the photograph of Jane Waldo's face, Fry closed his eyes, lowered his head and sighed. She had the helpless look of a white-tail doe mesmerized by the headlights of an oncoming eighteen-wheeler. In the photograph below, she was standing pensively, right index finger touching her lips, outside the Red Bandana, a tough east-end bar where every other word had four letters and began with F. She seemed to be trying to decide whether she dared to go inside.

The last two photographs were torn in half. They were of Leonard Boudreau.

"Oh ... God! Jesusdamnchrist...! Oh, noooo...!"

Fry jumped at the sound of Frank Bergen cursing, and then again at the sound of his gagging. Fry ran into the kitchen, to find Bergen leaning on the counter, over the sink.

"Swallow it down, Frank," Fry ordered. "Just tighten your stomach and keep it down. Enough stuff to go through here without that. What the hell's with you anyway?"

Still leaning on one arm at the sink, Bergen turned at the waist and looked over his shoulder toward Fry, his face an odd, pale grey under his blonde hair. He waved weakly toward the refrigerator.

"The freezer ..." he said, "...in the freezer."

Fry opened the freezer compartment. He saw the

container of ice cream and two cans of orange juice on the door and, inside, about a third of a bag of frozen french fries, two beef pot pies, and, shoved to the back, a stack of freezer bags, the one on top yawning open. He reached into the freezer and, after hesitating for a moment—he had forgotten the plastic bag—took the open freezer bag out and looked inside it.

He saw the scalp. It looked like a tiny frozen animal. Red crystals of frozen blood smeared the inside of the bag. Whose? Maclean's? Surette's? Fry could not remember their hair colour. Fry removed the other freezer bags and, choking down bile of his own, opened them. One contained the scalp that must have belonged to the other of the two hapless Coasters, one Lesley Connor's, the hair still shining black and silken. The hair in the third bag was ash-blonde—Jane Waldo's.

"You oughta see the bedroom, Jake," Adams said, coming into the kitchen as Fry was opening the last of the bags. "More pelts in there. Guy's got a whole bedspread of what looks like rabbit skins. Over the bed—well it's just a mattress on the floor—he's got a big poster-photo of a funny-lookin' old-time mountain man, buckskins and fringes, cannon of a rifle like the one on the wall in there, regular fu manchu moustache, little wee porkpie hat. What's in the bag?"

Fry showed him.

"Fuck me!" Adams exclaimed, turning away. Then, as Bergen fled the kitchen for the bathroom: "What's wrong with him?"

Fry looked at Adams as Leonard Boudreau earlier in the day had looked at Fry: as if the question could hardly have been more stupid.

"You guys find anything else in there?" Fry asked.

"Ah, bookcase in there, mostly books about the west,

history, old diaries, letters, that kind of stuff. Another old stuffed animal, this one in a fancy glass case: fox with mouse in its mouth, pretty realistic too. Clothes thrown all over. Oh, and there's a scrapbook."

"Scrapbook?"

"Yeah. All the stories about the killings. Before that, clippings of all kinds, mostly political stuff, almost all local, some pieces about the federal government being nasty and—"

Adams was interrupted by Bergen's choked urgent shouting from the bathroom.

"Jake! Jake, you better get in here! Jake! *Jake!*"

Fry zipped the bag closed, stuffed it back in the freezer and slammed the door. He ran into the bathroom, Adams hard on his heels. Bergen was half-standing over the toilet, hands on his knees, his face still pasty-grey. He was shaking his head.

"I did choke it down, Jake, I did," he said, looking up at Fry. "Like you said. I tightened my stomach and I'm okay, but ..."

He raised his eyes toward the shower. Fry followed them. He noticed that the tiny window over the tub was covered with a black garbage bag folded twice and secured on all sides with black electrical tape. A thin line was strung from the showerhead to the far corner of the shower rod. A single photograph, another black-and-white eight-by-ten glossy, was hanging over the tub, clothes-pinned to the line.

Fry stepped to the edge of the tub to get a closer look. He recognized the setting. The photograph had been taken on Third Street, in the heart of Chinatown. The photograph was of a couple, walking, hands almost but not quite touching, heads turned toward each other, smiling. Fry recognized them too.

The photograph was of Miyoko Fitzgerald and himself.

5:10 PM

Fry tore though his notebook until he came to the page with the number he had jotted down only that morning, Miyoko Fitzgerald's number. He yanked the receiver from the cradle and stabbed at the dial. He waited, drumming his fingers on the phone table, the receiver pressed hard against the side of his head, the ring ... ring ... ringing throbbing in his temples.

No answer.

"Damn!"

He thumbed the plunger down, and then remembered. Work. She said she had weekend work to do. But he did not have her work number. She had not given him her work number. He dialled the operator.

"Yeah," he said when she came on the line. "Number for the Glenbow, the museum."

"You can dial that number for yourself, sir."

"I could dial it if I knew it but I don't know it so give me the number please."

"That number is in the telephone book, sir."

"Listen, I don't have a phone book handy and I don't have time for this shi—I don't have time."

"I suggest you change your tone, sir. I don't have to take—"

"I suggest you give me the goddamned number before I have you picked up for obstructing justice."

"Obstructing justice? Oh. This is a police matter?"

"This is a police matter."

"Well, why didn't you say?"

She dialled the number herself. The phone rang. And rang. And rang. The operator came back on the line.

"I'm sorry, sir, but there doesn't seem to be—"

Fry slammed the receiver down, and held it, as if his hand was frozen to it, unable to let go. He looked at the bewildered, expectant faces of Adams, MacElroy, and Bergen, as if asking them what to do next. They were looking at him with the same question in their eyes.

The phone rang. The jangling coursed right through him, startling him, making him jerk his hand away as if burned. He looked at the phone. They all looked at the phone. The phone rang. And rang.

Fry picked it up.

"Yeah?"

"Ghost? That you?"

It was Strahan.

"Yeah."

"What the fuck's goin' on? You got nobody on the radio?"

"Ah, no. Never mind that. What?"

"Your boy just called."

"My … When?"

"Just now. Just phoned here at the paper."

"You *talk* to him?"

"Naw. He'd only speak to some reporter."

"Melton?"

"Yeah, that's the one."

"And?"

"Weird. Said he was finished with his first assignment—"

"First?"

"Yeah. Something about Seventeenth Avenue—that's where we thought he might be. Now he says he's gonna finish his last."

"His last? He talk long enough for you to put a trace on?"

"No chance."

"Damn!"

"He did sorta tell where though."

"Sorta told you?"

"Yeah. Funny—some kind of riddle."

"What do you mean?"

"Said something about making history where they keep history."

"Making history where they keep history?"

"Yeah. Can't figure—"

"Strahan, shut up!"

"What'd you say?"

"I said shut up. And listen. Forget Seventeenth. Get to the Glenbow. Now. The Glenbow. Get the tac squad there. Now. *Now!*"

Fry tossed the receiver at the cradle, missing, leaving the phone dangling on its cord over the edge of the table. He bolted from the apartment. He punched the elevator button and waited, listening as the old machine creaked and groaned from four floors below, doing a strange agitated dance as he waited.

"Come on! Come on!"

He could not wait. He flung open the fire door, slamming it against the steel railing of the fourth-floor landing. He raced down the zig-zagging stairs, only his right hand on the railing keeping him from flying off, the steel stairs rattling and reverberating with the rat-a-tat-tat of his steps. He leaped four steps down from the ground-floor landing and hit the alleyway running. He ran, stumbling and sliding, around the side of the building to the front, where the still shut-out tenants were gathered.

Seeing him running toward her, not remembering him, fearing that he was the man the police were searching for, an old woman with blue-grey hair in tight pink rollers under a powder-blue hairnet ran away from him, screaming. Others in the crowd, also frightened, parted to let him pass. Then a man in a sleeveless undershirt, suspendered pants, and stocking feet recognized him and chased after him, shouting.

"That's the cop! Hey! How long you gonna keep us out here anyway?"

"Yeah. How long? What the fuck's goin' on, eh?" somebody else chimed in.

Then another: "You cops think you can just push people around any way you please. Come on, let us back in. It's getting cold out here."

And another: "Come on! Open up. You've had more'n enough time to find whatever you're lookin' for. What're you doing anyway, going through everybody's shit? Hey! I'm *talking* to you!"

Fry ignored them, running past them, around them, through them, from them.

He reached the unmarked car, yanked the door open, slid onto the seat, jammed the key into the ignition, and turned it, pressing his foot on the gas pedal. The big engine growled once and then roared. Fry put the car in reverse, spun the wheel sharply to the right, gunned the engine, and backed up hard over the curb, not checking his rear-view mirror, not seeing the man in suspenders and another man diving for safety onto the median strip. Fry braked, turned the wheel hard right, and put his right foot to the floor. The car screamed away, spraying the two terrified men prone on the narrow strip of brown grass with bits of dirt and small stones.

Fry turned left onto Eighth Street and sped north, plunging under the CPR tracks at Tenth Avenue, sparks showering from the big car's undercarriage as it dove into the underpass and again when it bounced out. Ignoring the red light at the intersection of Eighth Street and Ninth Avenue, Fry executed a hard, spinning, nearly out-of-control right turn and then stood on the gas and headed east, the odometer needle nudging ninety, then one hundred, then one hundred twenty kilometres an hour, shops and offices and parked cars and pedestrians whizzing past him in a blur.

Thank God it's one way, Fry heard himself thinking, weaving in and out of the few cars and trucks travelling the street, hearing their horns blaring and quickly fading behind him. *And thank God it's Saturday.*

Then:

A block ahead, a red and blue figure was crossing the street, slowly. Fry hit the horn, three long, loud blasts. The figure stopped—in the middle of the road. Half a block away. Fry hit the horn again. The figure did not move. Wait—he *did* move. He raised his right arm. He was signalling Fry to stop. A fourth of a block. Fry laid on the horn. The figure ignored him, keeping his right hand upraised, with his left motioning a dump truck groaning under a load of debris from a downtown demolition site onto the street. The truck slowly backed up, backed onto Ninth Avenue, backed into Fry's path. The man held up his hand. Fry slammed on the brakes, tires sliding and smoking, car spinning, coming to a stop straddling two lanes of Ninth, pointing north. Fry jumped out of the car and ran screaming toward the figure with the upraised hand, a construction worker in a red plaid shirt, blue jeans, and yellow hard hat.

"What the fuck's wrong with you?!" he yelled. "You couldn't see me coming? Get that truck the fuck out of the way, now!"

"Aw, go fuck yourself, buddy. Didn't you see me? Fuckin' truck'll move when it's fuckin' ready, asshole!"

"Goddammit, this is police business."

"Yeah, right, and I'm the fuckin' premier—where's your siren and flasher, Dudley Doright? You leave 'em home or what?"

Fry unholstered his police revolver and levelled it at the construction worker, who blanched, raised the other hand and stood shaking.

"Jesus, man, don't ... You don't gotta ... Take anything you want, just ..."

"What I want is for you to *move*!"

The man moved, diving under the truck, rolling to the other side, scrambling to his feet and running down the street. The truck driver, who had been watching all along, tried to drive away, but stalled the truck and then could not get it restarted. He jumped down from the cab and fled after his partner, leaving the truck in the middle of the street, blocking Fry's way.

"Goddamn! God*damn*! *Goddamn*!" Fry cursed, stomping the pavement, glaring into the sky.

He reholstered the weapon, ran back to the car, hand-mounted the red flasher on the roof, turned on the siren, put the car in drive, and spun away in a cloud of street dust and rubber smoke, heading west, the wrong way, on Ninth, dodging a Calgary Transit bus, then a young man in a mini, turning right, the wrong way, onto Third Street, veering past a taxi with its horn sounding, then right again, the wrong way, onto Eighth Avenue, hurtling at highway speed down the Eighth Avenue pedestrian mall.

The stores were closed by now, but the early evening was still mild, with a light breeze. The mall was not yet fully in the shadow of the towers. It was not crowded.

But it was not empty. It became a kind of test track, but with people to dodge instead of pylons.

Swerving to miss a young couple who had turned into his path after wistfully window-shopping at Moss Jewelers, Fry came dangerously close to a late-afternoon chess match nearing completion at one of the red-topped, round tables set out on the mall, sending the players and kibitzers scrambling and the pieces tumbling.

He flew past a dapper old man in a blue blazer, grey slacks, white shirt and tie, and jaunty straw fedora who was sitting, hands folded in his lap, on a wooden-slat seat beside a still-bare tree at one of the concrete planters. The old man never noticed him.

The people lining up early for the early movie noticed him, and took cover under the marquee.

He clipped a *Bulletin* vending machine and tipped it over, breaking it open, sending the last paper of the day, old news now, flying on the breeze.

He did not knock over the lamp post he brushed past, but he did rattle it, and did topple one of the four-round lamps from its pedestal to the cement, where it exploded in a shattering shower of white glass.

He knocked down a rubber trash can and failed to knock down a bearded young man with a ponytail and hand-lettered T-shirt outside the arches to the Bay. He glanced in the mirror to see the garbage can spinning on its side, spewing litter, and the stunned man standing paralyzed, holding his head in both hands.

Fry came to the end of the mall, cut hard right onto First Street and immediately right again, the wrong way again, onto Ninth. He brought the car to a screeching, tire-burning stop and jumped out, siren still wailing, red light still flashing.

The car was still quivering on its springs when, seconds later, pressing himself against the drab concrete outside the glass door, he counted to himself, *one … two … three …* and threw himself, Smith & Wesson Police Special upraised in his two hands, into the ground floor of "Harvie's attic."

5:25 PM

As he crouched in the entry to the cavernous space of the Glenbow Museum, Fry had exactly the same feelings of dread and disorientation as when he had crouched in the entry to the claustrophobic space of George Donald Miloche's apartment.

It was the light, the same dim, eerie light.

The only lights in the Glenbow were the lights on "the lights," the northern lights, James Houston's soaring shimmering chandelier, prisms shimmering antique gold this evening as the recessed lights overhead reflected back and forth from the dark, spiralling stairs. It was as if Miloche had managed to draw dark curtains here, as he had in his apartment, illuminating his crude, crazed handiwork in the same hideous light.

Shuddering at the thought of the work Miloche had come to the Glenbow to do, Fry continued inside, pressing his search with even more urgency, even greater dread, his mouth open, breathing laboured, tip of his dry tongue dragging over his front teeth until they almost cut through.

The information desk was deserted. Fry saw no sign of security. The doors to the museum shop and bookstore, to the lecture theatre and conference rooms, were locked, as the door to the front entry should have been, but was not. The museum should have been closed.

Winter hours, Miyoko Fitzgerald had said.

Fry started up the stairs, keeping his back to "the lights" glinting above and beside him, straining his eyes and training his weapon into the yawning gloom the thousand splinters of light hardly penetrated.

The stairs wound round the lights to the second floor, the sprawling art gallery that housed the Glenbow's constantly changing temporary exhibits. Fry moved into the maze of white walls and half-walls and pedestals, pillars, and banquettes filled with shapes and images he could hardly make sense of in the bright light and now could hardly make out in the dark.

He leaned against a wall ... in the middle of the room? He was not sure. He felt the wall give slightly, soften, as if he had backed into a heavy curtain hung from the wall. He felt something tickle the back of his neck, like soft silken hair. Her hair? Her body...? Hung from the wall like a ...

Gasping, he turned, reached out and touched ... a body...? No. A curtain? No. But it *was* cloth, multi-textured, woven, threads as soft as spider's silk, nubs as hard as cheap carpet. He remembered. He had seen the fabric sculpture hanging earlier in the week.

He swallowed hard and sighed. He closed his eyes. He forced himself to take slow, deep, even breaths, trying to silence the drumming in his temples, to slow his racing heart, only partially succeeding.

Holding his revolver almost prayerfully in his two hands in front of him, he peered around the edge of the wall to the next wall. The gallery was one big hiding place, all dark corners and posts and shadows indistinguishable from substance. He snapped his head back, and the breath caught in his throat.

A head.

He saw a head, a big round head. He remembered Miloche's round, moon-shaped face. He looked again, carefully, stealthily. It was still there, only steps away, between this wall and the next. But where was she? What had Miloche done?

Fry spun round the corner, crouched, trained his weapon at the head's height, opened his mouth to command— when he saw that the head had not moved, not an inch, had not even flinched, not even at his sudden, violent movement. Weapon still aimed at the head, he moved toward it, closer, closer, until he was only a few feet away, and then still closer, until he could reach out and touch it, which, taking his left hand from his revolver, he did.

Cold. Smooth. Polished. Stone. The head was made of marble. It was a sculpture.

Fry sighed again, regained control of himself, resumed his search again, hugging every pillar, peering around every corner, investigating every shadow, finding only his way out of the white-walled maze and back to the spiralling stairs and the eerily shimmering soaring northern lights.

He was more sure of himself and his footing on the third floor, where he had perused the exhibits of western Canadiana with Tony, where he had studied the scalping technique of the Plains Cree warrior behind the glass, where he had first seen Miyoko Fitzgerald in the glass. He could almost remember the layout.

Still, he was careful. He was still alert. Just as many corners here, just as many shadows. Just as many places to hide. Under the wheel of the oxcart there. On the floor of the buckboard. Inside the bread wagon. Behind the old oil rig.

Fry moved from artifact to artifact, dodging, ducking,

as if on the set of some surreal western movie. But this was no set. This was no movie. He was no stolid Hollywood lawman striding purposefully down a precisely dusted main street toward a carefully choreographed showdown with a scripted-to-die desperado—able to do a retake, or two, or three, if the first was not just so. He would get one take, if that. He had no script. He was an out-of-breath, scared-to-death, small-city cop hiding behind antique farm implements and modern fine art, sweating bullets at the idea of firing one, walking, no, tip-toeing on ...

What...?

What was suddenly underfoot, grinding, crunching under his feet?

Fry looked down to see just as his right foot hit something on the floor, something solid and substantial yet soft, and he stumbled over it, staggered, fell. He remembered instinctively how to fall, rolling to cushion the blow, turning at the waist, holding the revolver high, to protect it, to hold it, careful not to fire it. Still he hit the floor hard on his right shoulder, grunting, rolling onto his back onto ...

What the hell *was* it? Gravel? In here? No—not coarse enough anyway. What then?

He lay there for a moment, catching his breath, trying to figure what had happened. The stars disappeared from his mind's sky. He gazed at the high ceiling, which was softly, faintly illuminated by the seemingly faraway northern lights, as if by a hazed-over orange moon. There were no sounds, except the drumming of his heart and the faint hum of the air conditioning and, as he started to move, the grinding and grating beneath him. The smells were of must, and of time, and reconditioned air, and himself and of fear and of ... excrement?

Fry sat up, wiping his right coatsleeve across his face, putting his left hand on the floor beside him to support him, jerking it back, feeling the short, sharp pain at the tip of his middle finger. Glass. He had been walking on glass, broken glass. He had fallen on broken glass.

But how did it...?

He saw the head, lying in front of him, almost at his feet. The light was just good enough. He reached out with his left hand to touch it. Not stone. Not cool. Flesh. Still warm. Not polished. But slick. With ... blood? His blood? No. Too much for the cut on his finger. Not smooth. Matted hair, high forehead—what had been a forehead. Crushed, like an eggshell. Fry felt the neck, felt for a pulse. Nothing. He understood the foul smell. The security guard.

He rose, carefully, to one knee and knelt for a moment in the shattered glass, getting his bearings. Yes. This was almost where he had knelt before, studying the violent scene behind the glass, seeing her sudden movement in the glass. Just over there. He stood. He walked across the crunching glass. Here. He could see well enough.

He understood how.

The Plains Cree warrior's arms were still upraised and he was still screaming, but more in outrage now than in triumph. The Plains Cree warrior had been disarmed.

5:40 PM

Fry did not sense the ripple of movement over his shoulder that he might have picked up in the glass if the case had not been shattered. But he did hear the sharp crunch of a footstep on the broken glass behind him and turned toward it and looked up—just as the war club missing from the dirt beside the Plains Cree warrior began its downward arc. Fry ducked, almost too late, to the right. The primitive club hit him on the side of the head, just above and behind the left ear—a glancing blow, but it drove him to his knees like a shot deer. He knelt in the splintered glass, stunned and reeling, his ears ringing, in his eyes a constellation of stars that had not been overhead.

He felt a tug on the revolver, and then a hard pull. Someone was pulling on the barrel of the revolver, trying to wrench the weapon away. Fry tried to hold on, but could not. The Smith & Wesson flew from his hand and skittered across the glass as he fell forward, forward into the glass.

Again he heard the sound of footsteps on the glass, and then of someone grunting, as if straining, and then footsteps again, slower, heavier, and the sound of something being dragged over the glass and, in the distance, sirens wailing.

Fry was on his hands and knees in the shattered glass, dazed, shaking his head, trying to clear his thoughts, still only dimly aware of where he was and of what had happened.

Then he saw them. At least he thought it was both of them, moving labouriously toward the eerie orange light.

And from somewhere within him, somewhere deep and primordial, a brute force surged. Like an animal he roared, "Noooooooo...!" and bolted, on all fours, across the glass, not feeling the shards as they cut him. He found his revolver, grabbed it in his now-bleeding hands, rolled once on his back, and, still semi-dazed, came up kneeling in firing position, aiming the Smith

& Wesson at the ugly, awkward silhouette retreating toward the light.

"Stop!" he commanded. "Stop *now!*"

George Donald Miloche had reached the third-floor landing and had taken one step down the spiralling stairs. He hesitated momentarily when he heard Fry's voice, but then took another step.

"I said stop *now!*" Fry ordered him again, struggling to his feet, moving toward them, never lowering his eyes, never lowering the weapon.

Miloche stopped, turning toward Fry, leaning against the stairwell, holding Miyoko Fitzgerald in front of him like a broken china doll. She was so light, yet he seemed to be straining under her weight. Dead weight? Fry could not tell. He could not see if she was breathing. He could see that she was bleeding, a thin stream as red as her full lips trickling down from her forehead. Fry was only steps away now, straining his eyes to see her, looking for some flicker of movement, some whisper of breath, some sign of life, seeing nothing.

Outside the sirens grew louder and louder as they came nearer.

Fry came nearer, took one step more. And he saw the knife in Miloche's hand, the Plains Cree warrior's stone knife; he saw it move, tickling her throat. Fry heeded the unspoken, half-smiling warning. He stopped, his revolver still trained on Miloche, his eyes moving from Miloche to Miyoko Fitzgerald and back, studying George Donald Miloche.

And one word came to his mind: "Meat-iss."

"Meat-iss" was Cecil B. De Mille's mispronunciation of *Metis* in his ponderous, biblically intoned voice-over introduction to his 1940s Hollywood Mountie potboiler, *Northwest Mounted Police.* Fry had dozed through a commercial-riddled version of the film on late-night television. "Meat-iss" was about all he remembered of it, a perfectly silly word for a perfectly silly movie.

Now "Meat-iss" had new meaning, still silly, no longer harmless.

"Meat-iss" could have been coined for George Donald Miloche, who had obviously smashed another window and trashed another display. He was wearing the moosehide Metis coat Fry remembered from an exhibit on Metis life on the prairie. The coat was too small for him, tight at the shoulders, extending barely halfway across his broad chest, sleeves stopping three-quarters of the way down his arms. The war club he had used to kill the guard and to stun Fry was stuffed in the wide, western-style belt that held up his stiff new blue jeans. Hanging on a strap from his right shoulder was a black-bodied camera, a flash gun jutting awkwardly from one side. He still had a half-smile on his moon-shaped face. He looked ridiculous—and deadly.

He noticed Fry examining him, shrugged, and smiled sheepishly.

"I couldn't get my equipment," he said. "You were already at my apartment. I had to make do. Jacket was still wet anyway."

"Why?" Fry asked after seconds that seemed like minutes of silence between them. "You don't have to tell me, don't *have* to tell me anything, but I'd—"

"'Why'...?" Miloche asked, perplexed. "I *did* tell you.... Because ..."

"No. *Why?*"

"Oh ... *why* ..." Miloche regarded Fry as if the answer to that question too was obvious, a look Fry was getting used to. But finally, as if he were leading a particularly stupid child through a very easy lesson, Miloche replied.

Outside the sirens were still wailing, almost right upon them.

"All you have to do is look," Miloche said, shaking his head at the sheer obviousness of it. "Just look at the city. How clogged it is, growing too fast. And listen to it." He cocked his head toward the sound of the sirens. "Too much crime. And they keep coming."

"They?"

"Them. The low-lifes, scum. Stupid lazy dreamers. Trash. Trash. Trash. They come from everywhere. They keep coming. And they're not wanted. They don't fit. They don't belong."

"But aren't you—"

"Aren't I what?"

"Well, in a way, aren't you one of them? I mean, didn't you—"

"*Noooo!*"

The word exploded from Miloche's mouth and he caressed Miyoko Fitzgerald's delicate throat with the stone blade.

"Sorry. I'm sorry," Fry said, wincing at the sight of the knife against her skin, silently cursing himself. "I didn't mean to suggest—"

"This is my *home!*" Miloche said, extending the word *home* into a kind of moan, almost a prayer.

And the sirens screamed, echoing in the cavernous space, filling it, as if they were right *here*, inside. And then they were silent, suddenly silent, totally silent, and the silence reverberated, and then was shattered, like the glass in the diorama cases, an explosion of sound, hinge-loosening whack of doors being flung open, pounding of heavy footsteps, men shouting. The tac team. From the sounds, Fry figured, probably both teams, at least a dozen men, a living sight-and-sound diorama of new-west policing, pouring into the museum in their blue coveralls and caps and high, highly polished military boots, twelve-gauges and automatic rifles at high port.

Miloche could see them over his shoulder, spiralling up the stairs. He watched them coming, with their guns; he looked at Fry, with his gun. His eyes grew wide. He pressed against the stairwell, pressing her against him, raising the knife again, holding it tighter against her throat, raising himself toward the top of the railing, raising her with him, until he seemed on the verge of going over the edge, taking her with him.

Fry's mind was racing. He had to do something. He could not shoot. He could not be sure. He had to be sure. But if he did nothing—

He shouted: "Walsh! Walsh, you there? It's Jake, Jake Fry!"

Staff Sergeant Tim Walsh had been head of the support section responsible for the tac team since it was created in response to the death of Gary Adams. Fry was sure he would be here.

"Yeah. Yeah, Jake, I'm here!" Walsh's voice boomed from below, somewhere on the stairs.

"Then *stay* there!" Fry shouted. "*Right* there—everybody. Guy's got a hostage and he's got a knife and he's on the edge, literally. So stay put!"

Walsh shouted the command and, almost instantly, the thundering up the stairs stopped.

Fry looked at Miloche, who was still looking wide-eyed from Fry to the stairs to Fry to the stairs, panic tugging at him, he tugging Miyoko Fitzgerald closer to him, tugging them both closer to the edge. Fry tried to calm him, tried to remember his session on abnormal psychology at the university, tried to remember what he had learned, wishing he had paid more attention, wondering if it would make any difference even if he had.

"There. They've stopped," Fry said, making a show of lowering his revolver. "See? Everything's cool. Take it easy. Just take it easy. We can deal with this. So this is your home and ... and they...?"

"And," Miloche looked at him, and then again over his shoulder, until he was sure they were not coming up the stairs, and then back at Fry. "And they had to die."

"*All* of them had to die? I mean, the woman really wasn't—"

"Not my fault. Her fault. I thought she was a prostitute—she looked, acted like one. Like trash. Not my fault. Hers."

"You, ah, you missed the first one?"

"Missed? Oh—that wino. No, not missed—just didn't finish, couldn't. I didn't know how then. I learned. I didn't have my courage—but I found it."

"Yes, you found it," Fry said. "But why this way?"

"This way?"

"Not just killing, but ..."

"Scalping?"

"Yeah. Why?"

"It told them."

"Told who? Told them what?"

"Everybody. Them especially. It told them that's what happens. It's what used to happen—to interlopers, invaders, intruders. To trash. It's what happened—what happens."

"But this isn't the wild west. Hell, this never *was* the wild west."

Miloche looked at him blankly and did not respond.

"What, you wanted to shift the blame?" Fry continued.

"What?"

"Shift the blame—you know, make it look like it was an Indian."

"Oh, no, not that. No, no. Well, I *was* going to put her," Miloche said, nodding toward Miyoko Fitzgerald, "back in the case there, where the dummy is, put his knee on her back, put the knife back in his hand—until you came in. Only a joke though."

"A … joke."

"Yes—but that's all. I never thought of that other ... what you said. They just needed to know that this is what happens. It's what happens. Then they won't come. The trash. They'll stop. And I can be ..."

"Can be what?"

"I … I can be what I want … I can … belong. I can …"

Miloche looked as if he were beginning to lose touch, to lose contact, making him seem even more unpredictable, even more dangerous. Fry tried to draw him back.

"The photographs," he said. "Why did you take the photographs, just before you ..."

Miloche puzzled over the question for a moment, as if he had never thought about it. Then his face brightened.

"To remember," he said. "You know, souvenirs."

The answer stunned Fry emotionally as much as the club had stunned him physically. Again he was reeling—until he focused again on Miyoko Fitzgerald in Miloche's grisly embrace.

"But the girl. Why pick her?" he asked, pointing

toward her. "She doesn't fit. She's not one of them, not really. Is she?"

A doubt, unwanted, unwelcome, planted itself in Miloche's mind, shadowing his face. He shook his head, trying to dislodge it.

Fry pressed the point. "And me," he said. "You got to me. I saw the picture. And I'd bet it was me, not her, you were after. Am I right?"

"…yes …"

Confusion was pulling at Miloche like a puppeteer, making his eyes twitch and blink, yanking the corners of his mouth up into a brief smile and then abruptly down.

"You think maybe *I* fit?" Fry asked.

"No. You're not one of them."

"That's my point, man. It's done. You got to me. There's nobody else—you said it yourself. You don't have your equipment with you. You know, in your bag. Your special camera. The club you made. Your knife. Your jacket. *This* knife is just a prop, not real, not the real thing. That's over. It's done. You're finished. I mean, you wouldn't want to make a mistake now, to get it wrong."

"No. Wouldn't want to get it wrong," Miloche agreed, disoriented, looking down at Miyoko Fitzgerald in his arms. "Can't be wrong ..."

"Come on then, let it go."

Miloche looked at Fry, nodding his head as if in agreement, sighed, and smiled.

"Maybe we should have talked sooner," he said.

He released his hold on Miyoko Fitzgerald and she slipped away from him, to the stairs, sliding slowly down three steps, then lying still. The hand holding the stone knife dangled at his side. Fry moved toward her, but Miloche brought the knife up again, waving it at Fry, still smiling. Fry raised his weapon.

"Put-it-down—please," Fry said.

Miloche looked at him, still with a wan smile, then looked over the edge of the stairs, toward the lights, then back at Fry. He dropped the stone knife. But before Fry could take a step, Miloche's left hand reached to his side like an old western gunslinger's, brought up the camera and fired, blinding Fry with the light from the flash. Miloche lifted his left leg to the stair railing and, with a grunt, pulled himself over the edge, tumbling, tumbling down, fingers still frozen on the buttons, motordrive whirring, flash firing, bouncing off the northern lights all the way down, a play of light and sound the museum's multimedia programmers could not have imagined and the sculptor in his worst nightmare could not have dreamed, a show that did not end even at the bottom, where Miloche's head hit with the sound of a melon being dropped from a high-rise, where his dead finger continued snapping shots from his bizarre final assignment, capturing the museum from angles never thought to be photographed, illuminating corners where "the lights" had never reached.

Fry had lunged too late to keep Miloche from falling. He leaned now over the edge of the stairs, blinking away the single bright spot in his eyes, looking down, seeing blue uniforms converge on the widening, dark-red pool at the base of the lights ...

Blood.

He remembered. He knelt beside her on the stairs. He felt for a pulse. He pressed his ear to her breast, listening for a heartbeat.

He screamed: "Get an ambulance here! Get it here now! Now! *Now!*"

Below, the flash failed, for one frame, two, as the motordrive whirred. Then, again, the flash fired, once more, for the last frame on the roll.

And the motor stopped.

december 6 2:15 PM

Fry could have been playing the part of Death opposite mad Vincent Price in a campy fifties horror movie. His greying hair, seeming to have been powdered snow-white, flew wildly over his high forehead into his eyes, which seemed themselves more like black, unfathomable holes in his skull. His always pallid skin was absolutely ashen, like a corpse's. His jaw was set. His teeth were clenched. His mouth was frozen in a cold sneer. Extending from the too-white hands emerging from the black folds of his overcoat was no Grim Reaper's scythe, but something just as ominous: another black hole, huge, deadly, seemingly without end—the yawning muzzle of his Smith & Wesson .38-Calibre Military and Police Model 10.

Fry watched himself go by, as the *Beacon* truck rattled past on the Louise Bridge. He had never got used to seeing himself. And he could not seem to get away from himself. The black-and-white photograph was all over the city, fading now, but still everywhere: on billboards promoting the *Beacon*, on yellow *Beacon* delivery trucks, on every yellow *Beacon* vending machine.

The photograph was the shot George Donald Miloche had snapped just before launching himself to his death at the Glenbow Museum. The *Bulletin* had immediately launched suit to obtain the film, contending that since, technically, Miloche was on assignment for the newspaper when he took the pictures, the photographs were *Bulletin* property. The court agreed, rejecting out of hand the Crown's contention that the photographs were evidence in a murder investigation with the pointed comment that, in fact, the investigation had come to an abrupt end when George Donald Miloche had come to his abrupt end.

The newspaper published the photographs. But the newspaper that published the photographs was not the *Bulletin*, which disappeared less than a week before the court made its ruling, sold to the proprietors of a scurrilous, sensationalist, right-wing tabloid in the east, the *Beacon*, which, almost overnight, became the new name and news ethic of the old *Bulletin*. The *Calgary Beacon* launched its inaugural western edition with the murderer's photographs: a centre spread with the headline, **Lens of a Killer,** and a full-page, front-page photograph of Fry, beneath the heading, FREEZE! The edition sold out, something that had never happened to an edition of the *Bulletin*.

Buoyed by that success and by the similar circulation jolt it received with the publication of Miloche's photographs of Seventeenth Avenue—**Slaughterer on 17 Avenue**—and hoping to repeat it, the *Beacon* appealed the court's rejection of the *Bulletin*'s claim on Miloche's other photographs, the ones taken on the old Pentax that Fry had found in the leather bag in Miloche's apartment. The appeals court agreed with the lower court's judgment—that those photographs were the personal, private property of George Donald Miloche, and, as such, no business of the *Bulletin*, even less of the *Beacon*. The newspaper appealed again, and lost again. The *Beacon* never got the chance to publish the photographs.

The *Beacon* did not get the chance to publish one other photograph.

When Fry came into his office one morning in July, he found, on his desk blotter, a plain business envelope addressed to him, with no return address. He tore open the envelope. Inside was a note on new *Beacon* letterhead and, fluttering from the note onto his desktop, a single negative frame scissored from an exposed roll of thirty-five-millimetre film. The note read:

Fry,

This one they don't need to publish.

Melton

Fry picked up the negative. He held it to the overhead light. It was George Donald Miloche's photograph of Miyoko Fitzgerald's surprised, terrified face in the instant before he struck her down. Fry quickly took the negative away from the light, the image away from his eyes. He took out his lighter, flicked the flame to high, and held it to a corner of the frame, then dropped the negative into his ashtray, watching it burn.

Watching the twice-life-size photograph of himself rumble by on the bridge now made him think of that photograph, and made him burn, rekindling the sense of horror and violation he had also never gotten over. But the feeling passed almost as quickly as the truck.

It had not been such a bad day.

He tapped his glove on the piece of wood tucked under his left arm, a piece of crating, two-and-a-half feet long, a quarter-inch thick. Perfect.

Miyoko Fitzgerald had kept after him to build a display case for her good luck/bad luck little magpie. He kept saying yes, but kept putting it off. He wanted it to be special. But he did not know how to do it. He was at a loss until his mother sent him a surprise parcel of childhood mementoes: report cards, a notebook of his drawings, a cap pistol, a friction-powered Model

A police car. The box also contained the miniature hutch he had built from an orange crate—the first piece of scrap-wood furniture he had ever made. One door was missing, a shelf was cracked, and a carefully carved right rear leg was broken. Fry had no replacement pieces in his workshop and had been able to find none this week in his scavenging walks around the city—until today.

Fry had time to explore this week. He had been suspended.

Inspector Phil Grantham had brought him up on internal charges: destroying evidence (for burning Thomas Red Crow's note), making threats (for Frank Bergen's handling of Wilson, the mayor's greasy assistant), improper use of a firearm (for training his revolver on the Ninth Avenue demolition crew), and dangerous driving (for speeding down the Eighth Avenue pedestrian mall). Grantham had pressed to have him put on probation and suspended for a month. He managed to get a week's suspension and an official reprimand placed in Fry's file, alongside the Chief's Commendation that Inspector Ben Drayton had recommended. Fry regarded both with equal seriousness.

On his way home today from the Hillhurst Bookstore, Fry, on a whim, had stopped in at the new fruit and vegetable market, one of the scores of tiny shops and small cafés that were giving the neighbourhood north of the Tenth Street bridge a small-village air.

"You, ah, have any crates?" Fry asked a slim dark man with thick hairs peeking out from his open-to-the-chest white shirt and a beard that looked as if it needed shaving three times a day.

"What?" The man screwed his face at him, uncomprehending.

"You know, crates, wooden crates, for shipping—oranges, lemons, that kind of thing."

"Naw, naw naw," the man shook his head. "No crates … Wait…." He stuck his right index finger in the air and then put it to his lips, thinking. "Yeah, yeah ..."

He motioned Fry to the back of the market, where he had the exotic produce displayed: Turkish, Greek, Chinese, Lebanese, Israeli. He gestured toward some strange fruit from Israel: a crate, exactly what Fry remembered, exactly what he was looking for.

"How much?" Fry asked.

"What? For fruit?"

"No—for crate."

The man, who had been stealing furtive glances at Fry ever since he came into the market, gave up the pretense and studied Fry's face so intently that Fry wondered for a moment if he had lost an eyebrow. The man's face brightened. He smiled, beaming, crouching in the aisle, pointing an imaginary revolver at Fry.

"You the cop, right?" he asked "The one in the picture, right?"

"Right," Fry sighed.

"No charge. How much you want? Whole thing? I can empty."

"Ah … no, just a piece—one would be more than enough."

With two quick whaps of his right hand the man knocked a slat loose, and with a twist and a turn and a turn and a pull and a pull … and … a … pull, he yanked the piece over the complaining nails and offered it to Fry, slapping him hard on the shoulder, smiling. It was the first time Fry had had a chance to get anything he wanted from his unwanted celebrity. He took it.

He could restore the hutch now. He had the wood

he needed. He could do the work. If he was careful and took his time, no one would ever know that the piece had been damaged. Of course, neither would anyone know how much effort it took to put the piece together again. But that did not matter to Fry.

Miyoko Fitzgerald would have a special place to put her special little magpie.

At the Hillhurst Bookstore, Fry had found something to help Tony place his birds, which had become one of the boy's passions.

Constable Andy Stimwych's son, Rick, had been so pleased with the scrap-wood bookcase Fry made for him that he came by in person to say thanks before heading north to university and summer football practice. Tony was at Fry's house that day. He and Rick Stimwych hit it off immediately. Rick was a linebacker. It turned out that he was also a bird watcher. And, as far as Tony was concerned, "a neat guy."

Tony decided he wanted to try out for football in high school. Fry bought him a set of weights. He also said he wanted to be a naturalist. Fry enrolled with him, without telling anyone at Seventh Avenue SE, in a city-sponsored bird-watching course.

At the bookstore today, Fry had picked up a copy of *A Field Guide to Western Birds* to help Tony with his notebook of bird sightings. Tony had never asked him about buying a rifle.

It had not been such a bad day.

It *was* a drab day, with the faded, grainy texture of an early photograph. Pedestrians moved like the herky-jerky figures in a vintage newsreel, hurrying through the blowing snow and brutal, breathtaking cold. The temperature was hovering around minus thirty, the wind around fifteen kilometres an hour, gusting to more than thirty. It was the kind of day when the weather office issued warnings about exposed flesh freezing in less than a minute.

Fry headed south across the bridge, glad the wind was at his back. On the riverbank below, beside one of concrete pilings, a bare stand of cottonwoods huddled, black against the greyish snow. The river was still open, barely, trickling under the arches like liquid lead.

Fry could see him coming from the far side of the crossing, a smudge of black against the grey of swirling snow and sky. He watched as the figure neared, black toque pulled tight over his head, tails of his new black greatcoat streaming in the wind, its too-narrow waist revealing a splash of white sweatshirt, a streak of faded blue jean. He looked to Fry less like a man than a bird, like the bird represented by Miyoko Fitzgerald's tiny old carving, the one she told him was only lucky in pairs, like a bird Fry knew was in Tony's new book, a bird Fry had been allowed, even encouraged, to shoot as a boy because they murdered songbirds—a noisy, resourceful, scavenging Heckyl and Jeckyl of a pest: a magpie. When, just paces away, Fry finally recognized him—the florid stubbled face, even redder in the wind and cold, the big snout of a nose, silvery mane trying to escape from under the toque—he thought: *One's lucky enough.*

Fry had seen Leonard Boudreau only once since the spring, in mid-August, in the east end, in the covered entrance to Jaffee's Bookstore, where they had both taken shelter from a torrential downpour. Leonard Boudreau had not noticed him then.

Face down, chin buried in the collar of the black greatcoat, eyes squinting against the blowing snow, Leonard Boudreau did not notice Fry today, until he was almost upon him. He glanced up, then quickly away, then back, a flicker of recognition in his eyes. As he passed, he doffed the black toque and rubbed the top of his head as if it were a talisman. He winked at Fry and smiled—the widest, fiercest smile.

Eugene Meese was an editorial writer and columnist with *The Albertan* during Calgary's first boom in the 1970s, and a reporter and editor with the *Daily Journal Record* in Oakville, Ontario. His writing has also appeared in *The Globe and Mail*, *The Vancouver Sun*, *The London Free Press*, and *The Ottawa Journal*; and in the magazines *Atlantic Insight*, *The Novascotian*, and *The Owl*. For twenty-five years, he was a professor of journalism at the University of King's College in Halifax, Nova Scotia. He now lives in Truro, Nova Scotia, with his wife, Donna.

The production of the title ***A Magpie's Smile*** on Rolland Enviro 100 Print paper instead of virgin fibres paper reduces your ecological footprint by :

Tree(s) : 8
Solid waste : 494 lb
Water : 4,665 gal
Suspended particles in the water : 3,1 lb
Air emissions : 1,085 lb
Natural gas : 1,13 ft^3

Printed on Rolland Enviro 100, containing 100% post-consumer recycled fibers, Eco-Logo certified, Processed without chlorinate, FSC Recycled and manufactured using biogas energy.